RAZ STEEL

BLOOD BETWEEN LOVERS

THE ETERNAL EROS TRILOGY

MATTERHORN PRESS

Published by MATTERHORN PRESS, LLC
PMB 13-148, 13 Summit Square Center, Langhorne, PA 19047
Copyright 2015 by ©RAZ STEEL
ALL RIGHTS RESERVED

This is a work of fiction. All characters in this book have no existence outside the imagination of the author and have no relation whatsoever to anyone, living or dead, bearing the same name or names. All incidents are pure invention from the author's imagination. All names, characters, places and incidents are products of the author's imagination or are used fictitiously. Any resemblance to actual events or locales or persons, living or dead, is entirely coincidental.

For information, including special discounts for bulk purchases, contact:
MATTERHORN PRESS, LLC
PMB 13-148, 13 Summit Square Center, Langhorne, PA 19047

Book Cover Design ©MoreThanPublicity
Book Cover Artist ©Lora Lee
Interior Illustrated Pages ©MoreThanPublicity
MoreThanPublicity.com

Publishing History
Matterhorn Press/eBook edition/October 2015
Matterhorn Press/Paperback edition/November 2016

ISBN-13:978-1-941508-06-0
ISBN-10:1-941508-06-5

Published & Released in the United States of America
10   9   8   7   6   5   4   3   2   1

PRAISE FOR
RAZ STEEL

"For a genuinely fresh and fantastic new take on vampire romance, Raz Steel is your go-to-guy and the one to watch!"
- SUSAN SIZEMORE
NYT & USA TODAY Bestselling Author

"This debut is a highly entertaining and unique take on the vampire genre. Steel's novel is sure to keep you guessing, especially after you think you have it figured out."
-Romantic Times BOOKreviews

"This is an engaging urban romantic fantasy that starts off with an exciting bite and never looks back as readers will relish entering the reddish Raz realm..."
-Harriet Klausner, #1 Amazon Reviewer

"A unique and fascinating vampire romance...
LOVE WITHOUT BLOOD is exciting from the first page with a unique writing style and fascinating build up... I am very curious to see how the next book takes shape."
-Fresh Fiction

More Books By
RAZ STEEL

In Stores Now

LOVE WITHOUT BLOOD

BLOOD BETWEEN LOVERS

Coming Soon

PASS THE KRYPTONITE

LADIES OF THE PTA

THE BLACK STONE OF CALCUTTA

THE SHADOW STONE OF SOLEBURY

LOVE'S BLOOD LOST

THE LOVE DOCTOR BITES THE BIG ONE

LOVE AND OTHER SIDE EFFECTS

DEDICATION

*This book is dedicated to the readers who offered
encouragement after LOVE WITHOUT BLOOD was
published with such success. I want you to know how
much I appreciate your support.*

Thank you, sincerely.

Acknowledgments

BLOOD BETWEEN LOVERS spilled out of me in a different way than Love Without Blood. LWB surprised me as the characters seized control of their lives and directed the story. But in this book, perhaps because I understood the characters before I began to write, I realized where the story was going before the pages were filled. I have to thank Lara and Bobby for that.

My heartfelt thanks to Shannon Aviles, my marketing director at MoreThanPublicity who has orchestrated my success in every movement, and special thanks to Shannon's team: Stephanie Scofield, Victoria Mattera, Lora Lee, and Stephanie Davi for their hard work on my behalf; thanks to editors Neal Hock, Amanda Sumner, and Eliza Dee; Douglas Michael, MD, who continues to offer medical advice, and Mimi Michael for unrelenting research are invaluable and precious for their technical support and more importantly for their friendship.

Special Thanks to the Pineapple Hill Inn Bed and Breakfast for their indulgence of my vampires.

A very special acknowledgement to the greatest gifts I've ever been given, my children. Kids, you may not want to read sexy scenes that Dad wrote, but I hope you read this: I'm proud of you both, and I love you very much.

BLOOD BETWEEN LOVERS

CHAPTER 1

Starvation drove Dr. Lara West from the comfortable brownstone and flung her into the dank Georgetown night. She shivered. Once she'd been a surgeon who saved lives; now hunger compelled her to think of blood in a different way. Three weeks since the transition—three weeks with no nourishment. She didn't want to be a predator.

Hunger caused her to salivate. Vampire spasms retched from stomach to throat, then roiled around her brain. Repugnance warred with unfathomable craving.

Peripheral movement captured her attention. A boy on a skateboard. Wheels grated on cement and clicked on cracks, then an unexpected tumble and a scraped knee. Lara sniffed. Her thoughts failed to walk a straight line, drunk on the sudden scent of blood. A stiff breeze captured the early autumn chill and wrapped the aroma around her. Inconceivable instinct—and the voice of an inner demon—urged her to attack this child and sate her thirst.

Lara cringed. But if she didn't feed, her blood hunger would incite frenzy. Frenzy, Bobby told her often, overwhelmed all other emotions and would introduce Lara's human persona to the savagery of vampire culture.

Bobby Eyre had turned her because death was the only other option—doomed by another vampire. But Bobby wanted a self-reliant partner. Hell, starvation threatened to end her existence unless she allowed the inner beast to control her consciousness. What if her beast killed? What if she failed to wrest back control, her humanity overwhelmed by a bloodthirsty demon?

A headache tightened its grip. Muscles knotted in her shoulders. Massaging didn't help. Short bristles on the back of her neck dredged up dark memories. Her brother. The Witness Protection Agency–Vampire Unit. The WPA first buzzed her hair six months ago to disguise her as nurse Meridian Jones, then had manipulated Meridian to hunt vampires as repayment for protection. She'd discovered a vampire—Bobby—also masquerading as a nurse, but instead of revealing his true identity, she'd fallen in love, and love propelled her human soul.

She clutched Bobby's note. *Feed, or lose everything.* Only one interpretation.

RAZ STEEL

Lara stalked the boy. She was cloaked in shadows, wrestling with deprivation. Could she . . .? *Blood*, demanded the inner voice. The wind riffled through her hair. Human Lara teetered on the edge of uncertainty. The only path to survival was unfathomable. The boy remounted the skateboard with one foot and pushed off with the other, escaping into the night. Lara sighed.

The demon remounted her soul and crushed the human will beneath its heel. *Feed, or lose everything.*

She chased the child, who was a year or two younger than her brother had been at his unexpected death. Lara had cherished her brother. They had hidden together from basement monsters and rejoiced together in their triumphs as children and young adults. He'd clenched the nape of her neck in the final moments, clinging to an impossible life. Tears welled, and anguish forced her back into this moment. Without sustenance now, her existence was doomed.

Blood dribbled down the boy's leg.

Lara had struggled with emotional demons for ten years as they'd torn at her soul with guilt-ridden nightmares. Her salvation had finally been in her grasp until the WPA ripped away her life—nightmares extended indefinitely. Worse—this vampire demon raged beyond psychological issues: she had substance, a body, only that body already belonged to Lara, and Bobby assured her vampire demons didn't share.

Cramps twisted her stomach. She grabbed her abdomen and gritted her teeth. Every nerve receptor pounded and hammered Lara to her knees. Blood defined survival. Drink blood? An innocent lined up in the crosshairs of hunger, and Lara recoiled.

Lara West—physician—refused to hijack the essence of life, but Lara West, consumed by a demon, Lara West—vampire—ached for blood.

Cell phone vibration intruded, and she laughed at the irony. Dr. Surinder Byra texted her to work an extra shift in the Jefferson Memorial Hospital ER. She refused her boss nothing. Dr. Byra hovered on the edge of retirement from chief of emergency medicine, and for three years Lara had strived for the status of heir apparent, the sole survivor in a fierce competition. In her third year of med school, babysitting, parents out of town, Lara had rushed her brother to the neighborhood ER—Jefferson Memorial—for help. Neither gunshot casualty nor knife victim, he presented only a severe headache, so he was ignored in the lobby for hours, then died of spinal meningitis. Lara hugged her arms.

Guilt pierced perception, like a stake sinking into a vampire. Her brother's

BLOOD BETWEEN LOVERS

death was her fault, her failure. She should have recognized the seriousness of his presentation and insisted on immediate attention. Incessant nightmares fed guilt. Guilt rearranged her life.

Her eyes widened and her nostrils flared. The bouquet of blood guaranteed yet another arrangement: a sanguine soul interlaced hunger into every aspect of being. Her muscles settled into a bizarre relaxed tension, and she pursued the bleeding child. What the hell was she doing? She mopped perspiration from her forehead. Two minds in conflict campaigning for control of consciousness. The wrong mind guided her toward a horrific goal. Whose brother was this little boy?

After her brother's death, Lara had focused with single-minded intention: ascend to top surgeon, then run the ER with the concern the job demanded. *No one will die from carelessness on my watch.* The Jefferson Memorial ER, run with compassion, remained her only chance for life without remorse in perpetuity. Her only chance to erase the self-reproach.

Turning had magnified the problem. At least as a human, if she never achieved her goal, agonizing nightmares resolved with death. Drinking blood amplified emotions. Unresolved day-mares were eternal for a vampire, and incredibly more vivid. She'd endured the results once, the night Bobby had transformed her and squeezed two liters down her throat. She hadn't had any blood since.

She retched with the memory, air only. Consequences rushed at her with inhuman speed. Survival demanded human blood tonight. Blood inflated shame. But she needed to be clearheaded and pain-free to function in the desired role as a physician.

What about the needs of her victims?

Lara licked her lips and fixed on the prepubescent meal. Migraine-level pain combined with emotional anguish, and she snarled, on the verge of attack. But the vision of her lifeless brother in the morgue and the grief-stricken faces of their parents played against reality. She swiped a tear from the corner of her eye.

I will not kill a child.

No blood from young boys. What, then?

A grimace pushed all but one goal aside. Bobby warned her that without blood, agony expanded daily. Without blood, the beast with whom she shared her body would wrest away control and ravage the human landscape. She groaned. Instinct dragged her to the precipice—surrender her dream and yield

~ 3 ~

to the demon within. And live with the guilt, faced with day-mares and amped migraines for eternity?

Lara needed Dr. Byra's job now. The life she wanted and working for the WPA were mutually exclusive. Administration had thought her dead—courtesy of the government—during her six-month absence from the hospital. What if administration had already decided on a different successor? Jefferson always promoted young doctors to chief roles and kept them in place for twenty or thirty years—a successful business strategy, confirmed by their balance sheet.

If another surgeon succeeded Dr. Byra, Lara's goal would be postponed for decades. Doable for a vampire but unbearable for her human conscience. Remorse demanded immediate attention.

The demon whispered in conflict. *Existence commands a single goal.*

Two aspects of being coexisting in one body—Lara shook her head. Such a bizarre concept—battling for control of consciousness—and no way to expunge the demon.

"Civilization defines us by those demons," Bobby told her. "All vampires are judged evil. We're bloodthirsty, but if we control our beasts, we can survive without killing. Once the demons control our personas, hope for our humanity is lost."

Drink blood or a human Lara West won't exist come sunrise.

Her fangs erupted. She needed to find a host for a meal. A victimless human meal.

She stumbled across the blacktop and fell against a car. The alarm blared. Adrenaline rushed through her, and she raced around a corner, two blocks away in seconds. The agony eased, but for how long? Did all vampires suffer so? Bobby said beasts dominated most vampire personas, but Bobby's human side maintained control. Did she have his strength?

Not if she refused the nectar of inevitability. "Immortality is dependent on human blood," Bobby said. "And vampires have the same right to exist as humans, but without killing."

She repeated Bobby's maxims. *Don't allow anyone to see you. Feed—no more than a liter—then wipe your victim's memory.* In this neighborhood of Washington DC, a discreet dinner required a home with a lone occupant. Lara clutched her stomach, gasped, and doubled over until the pain eased.

A car glided into a nearby parking spot. A heavyset man wriggled out and tucked a hoagie under each arm. *Dinner for two.* Onions and oregano laced the air.

He's big enough to down both hoagies.

The man plodded up brick steps, her possible dining partner tonight. A vestibule light flashed on. Lara strummed her thigh with the agile fingers of her profession. Everything human Lara wanted to be was crammed into well-honed hands. She bit her tongue to the edge of piercing skin and pain screamed *Enough.* Finally, a glow in the bay window next to the entrance, and then, what she hoped for: an upstairs light. Opportunity to enter unseen and discover if the man lived alone.

She cut across the pavement. Every stride magnified hunger, urged her to actions she didn't comprehend, certain of one thing: drink human blood or perish. Who'd started the animal blood rumor? She'd insisted on trying, and Bobby had humored her. She'd vomited the first swallow.

I can't believe I'm hunting humans. She gripped the knob. Unlocked.

The transition from mortal to vampire crowded into this moment. Thrust upon her, never a desire, never a consideration, just the sudden realization of inhumanity: could she deal with the overwhelming urge to drink blood until her thirst was sated and her victim drained? A chill slithered around her torso, and Lara shuddered. She had to consume enough blood to survive yet stop before harming her prey.

Lara slipped inside the stranger's home.

Hardwood floors. Her soles would tap. She consigned shoes and socks to the porch. She imagined a restaurant sign in the foyer: *No shoes, no socks…no blood.*

No voices. The man must be alone.

No time to reconsider. A full-frontal assault? *No way.* A direct question? *Excuse me, may I take a Red-Cross-sized blood donation?*

Another wave of cramps contorted her face. Her tongue grazed her teeth. Blood remained the only salvation.

I have to satisfy hunger without killing.

Mail spattered a table. A cell phone bill revealed the man's name, Dennis Bittner, and his number. She wanted to find the house phone to call him. A magazine, *The Infinite Psychiatrist*, addressed to *Dr.* Dennis Bittner provided a motive for calling   pretend she required psychological help.

Pretend?

Lure him downstairs, then what? *One step at a time, Lara.*

She crept toward the kitchen, and sweat from her feet imprinted the hardwood. A handset on the counter became her goal. The hoagies rested nearby, still wrapped. Baking sheets and a mixing bowl crowded the Formica next to the oven. Lara sniffed cinnamon and apple pie. She choked a scream when a shrill, toothless bark preceded a charging miniature dachshund.

Lara raised a finger to her nose. "Shh. Hush, little doggie. Please," she whispered.

The puppy skidded to a stop at Lara's toes. Head tilted back, he yammered, and his tail ticked like a high-speed metronome.

"Krull," a voice called from upstairs, "cut it out. If it's your daddy, let him step inside."

A bow tie dangled from the collar of Krull the Warrior, and he smelled like bubble bath.

"I'm sorry," Lara said to the barking dog. She bowed, bared her fangs, and growled.

Like a cartoon character's, Krull's paws lost traction on the tile. The dog whined and scurried.

Lara removed the handset. She grasped the counter—her torso twisted. Fangs pierced her lip. Accidental blood inflamed desire and urgency. *Doctor, do no harm.* "Immortality is a gift that requires replenishment from a single source," Bobby told her. *Do vampires really suffer the same right to survival as humans?*

She dragged herself to the front room, switched off the main light, and flicked on a reading lamp. Shadows. She angled a chair away from the steps and sunk into the cushions. A deep breath settled her nerves. She dialed the cell number, and the phone rang upstairs. Dr. Bittner's footfalls chased the sound.

"Very funny, Frank. I didn't hear you come in," Dr. Bittner said.

Lara swallowed hard and massaged her throat. "This isn't Frank."

"Is this a joke?"

"I need your help, Dr. Bittner."

"Who are you, and what're you doing in our house?"

"What?"

"Caller ID."

"Please, come downstairs."

"You bet I'm coming downstairs—with my baseball bat."

Hinges squeaked in the hallway behind Lara.

"Denny, I'm home," a deep-pitched male voice called. "I'm slipping off my shoes and socks too. I didn't realize you invited company for dinner. Who's here?"

BLOOD BETWEEN LOVERS

A skinny man hopped around the corner on one shoe and peeled the sock from the other foot. "Here to play?" he asked Lara. His gaze captured her like a stalker.

The sun tattoo burned on the small of her back, a signal Lara interpreted as a threat. She pushed out of the chair, prepared to flee.

Dennis rumbled down the stairs, baseball bat shoulder-high. "Frank, stay away. She's dangerous."

Frank's bare foot stomped the floor. "Who is she?"

Dennis bounced off the bottom step next to Frank, and the two of them blocked the exit. Didn't matter. Lara collapsed, unable to keep her eyes open. Consciousness drifted in and out, and she caught snatches of conversation.

"She's hurt," Frank said. "We'd better call a rescue squad."

"An ambulance will alert the police. Marissa is still locked in the basement cell."

"They didn't collect her this afternoon? I thought—"

"Yeah, I thought she'd be halfway across the ocean by now. Khalim called. Said they'd be here by midnight."

"What're we going to do?"

A shoe toed her ribs.

"Our deal is too sweet to risk over a stranger, even a pretty one."

"You thinkin' what I'm thinkin'?"

"A curvy blonde. We can make this shipment two-for-one. Double profit."

Slavers? Lara flinched and pushed up, but her elbows failed to support her weight.

"She's sick."

"Half-price then. Didn't cost us anything."

Hands invaded her privacy. Frank hefted her over his shoulder and trotted down the hall. Lara squirmed and groaned.

"Nice," Frank said. "I'll have fun with this one."

"Go ahead, if there's time. I won't be jealous," Dennis said.

Frank laughed and almost dropped her. He adjusted her weight and carted her into the basement. Wide wooden steps, no handrails. Cinder block walls lined a large room. Bare bulbs in a high ceiling. No cell in sight. Mold, perspiration, and a whiff of female pheromones of fear. Dennis rumbled behind her. Lara wiggled and hammered Frank's back.

"She seems excited about the idea," Frank said.

"I'll give her a shot. We don't want trouble," Dennis said.

"You can give her a shot when I'm done. I'll enjoy it more if she bucks. Tie her hands and gag her, though. Marissa still unconscious?"

"I injected a double dose this morning. She'll be in a harem before she wakes up."

Another helpless woman in the basement united Lara with humankind. She needed to save herself and Marissa.

Frank dumped Lara facedown on a cement slab. The cold surface stirred memories of childhood monsters. Shuffling feet, indistinct words, the harsh reality of rope and laughter. Lara stabbed and scratched someone's flesh. She devoured blood from her finger, scent and taste a potent elixir. She winced and spit, yet the sanguine tang luxuriated, and threads of orgasmic spasms swept in all directions from her throat. She swallowed compulsively. Incredible. If a few drops caused this reaction, no wonder vampires craved human à la carte. In Lara's weakened state, a pittance of energy flowed, and she snarled.

The men backed up half a step, then charged. They pinned her arms behind her, but Frank planted his sockless foot in front of her face. Lara scrunched her nose, craned her neck, and chomped. Blood squirted into her mouth.

Dennis shoved his knee into Lara's back. He forced the air from her lungs and her mouth to gape open—spit instead of swallow.

Frank howled and limped away, bleeding. "Bitch." He kicked over a toolbox and grabbed pliers. "She needs a lesson."

"Damaged goods. Don't, Frank."

"We'll take a few thousand less if we have to. She won't need all her teeth for what they have in mind."

Lara flailed beneath Dennis's oppressive frame.

"Hold her head," Frank commanded.

A sweaty paw pressed Lara's ear, jammed her face to the cement, locked in a grimace.

Frank advanced, pliers first.

"Jesus. She's got fangs."

"Not for long."

CHAPTER 2

Pliers clamped onto Lara's tooth. Lights winked out. Dennis puffed his cheeks.

"What the—"

Bobby rushed down the steps. His almond-shaped eyes were wide and feral, impossibly vivid in the dark. He wrenched the pliers from Frank, along with Lara's fang. Stars danced in her vision, and Lara shrieked. Frank whirled, slammed against a support pole, and slumped to the floor. Before Dennis attacked, Bobby shoved his chest. The man dwarfed Bobby's lean six-foot frame but landed with a thud and didn't move.

Lara moaned. Bobby raced to her side and cradled her head. "Are you okay?"

"My mouth is killing me." Lara clutched her stomach.

Bobby peered at the missing fang, then glanced at her hands and laughed. "For a doctor, you have a strange sense of anatomy. Drink."

"What?"

Bobby leaned over, pinched Frank's trousers, and dragged him closer. "His ankle is already bleeding. Drink. You have to."

Smell reignited thirst. Bobby supported the leg above her face, and blood dripped into her mouth. Senses heightened, and hunger swelled. She seized Frank's leg and sucked the wound.

An orgasmic wave expanded from her throat, and compulsive swallowing imitated vaginal contractions. An unexpected sexual excitement coincided with feeding. She wanted to f—

"Fight the urge," Bobby said. "Don't allow existence to be defined by frenzy." Bobby kissed her fingers and relaxed her grip. "You need more, but we'll drink from the other guy."

He punctured Dennis's wrist and savored the first morsel to well up, tilting his head back and allowing the blood to drizzle down his throat. His broad shoulders accentuated a self-assured stance. His scent—like salt on a sea breeze—magnified desire, as powerful as any aphrodisiac. Did blood sexually stimulate all vampires or just her? Heat flushed her face, and Lara drank until Bobby stopped her again.

"Ready to travel?" he asked.

Lara nodded and struggled to balance, but Bobby scooped her into his arms. She was pressed against his chest, and supported by hardened muscles. She caressed his neck and snuggled into the embrace. Bobby's irises and pupils blended together in an unfathomable expression of tension and relief. She hugged tighter, and he whisked her outside.

"There's another girl in the basement," Lara said.

"I'll come back for her."

"How'd you find me?"

Bobby's nose crinkled. "Your shoes. You know this isn't our house, right?"

Lara punched his shoulder. "The pain is excruciating. I can't think clearly."

"Frenzy," Bobby said. "The final stage before a vampire either keels over or surrenders to her beast. I didn't anticipate frenzy tonight. It was a mistake for us to leave Pennsylvania so soon after I changed you."

Lara shook her head. "I can learn vampirism anywhere. My career is here."

"Concentrate on feeding instead of your career."

Lara shrank back against his chest. "Violence sickens me."

"You bit that man."

"He attacked me. I didn't bite to feed. I bit to survive."

"When you understand it's the same thing, you'll be able to feed yourself. How will you survive when I'm gone?"

"Are you leaving me?"

A different knot twisted her stomach. She was an incompatible relationship partner for a vampire.

They climbed slate steps and entered the brownstone. Bobby settled her on a marble bench in the two-story foyer and kissed her cheek. Her fingers grazed across his jutting chin.

"You know, I like you a lot," Lara said.

"Doesn't matter. You aren't my type."

"Sexy?"

"Calm."

Is he mocking me? "It's all right, you aren't my type either," Lara said.

"Handsome?"

"Human. You know I'm teasing, right?"

"You're provocative." He massaged her neck. "Beyond your sexy appearance." His lips brushed her cheek. "I'm seduced by your presence, the vibration in your voice . . . your earthiness." He sounded sincere.

His fingers combed through the bristles of her scalp, and he sniffed her hair. "You're intoxicating. But it's your empathy that appeals to me most. I'm

BLOOD BETWEEN LOVERS

thrilled to have you in my world." Butterflies danced across her stomach.

His lips pressed against hers. He sucked her tongue into his mouth, and his fangs raked across her flesh. She knew he wanted to puncture her tongue and drink the blood of a vampire's kiss. She'd acquiesced once, overwhelmed by a new reality moments after Bobby turned her, but she squirmed out of his grasp now. "I won't share my soul." Even when Bobby's existence had been in doubt, she'd refused to donate blood.

She frowned. "This"—she pinched a vein in her arm—"as much as my mind, is what makes me *me*." *Maybe a little less empathetic now than a moment ago.*

"I don't know how true that is for a human, but it's sanctimonious for a vampire. This"—he pinched a vein in his arm—"is not mine."

"I have never donated blood, and I never will."

"A vampire progenitor is sire and mother with the instincts of both parents to teach and protect. Share your blood or not, we're emotionally involved." Bobby pulled back to gaze into her eyes. "And, at least for now, you must deal with a vampire lover." His tone teased again.

"Wait a minute. You never said you were a vampire."

"You never asked. I figured drinking your blood—or attempting to—gave away my identity."

"What if I don't want a vampire boyfriend?" She shrugged her shoulders.

"Too late." He bored into her soul.

Her fingers drifted in hair much longer than hers. "Why can't I read your mind?"

"Give it time. The closer the emotional connection, the more powerful our telepathic link will become. I sense your thoughts—different than reading your mind, but it's how I found you in that basement."

"Do you know what I'm thinking now?"

Bobby grinned. "You like me. A lot."

Lara tugged on the nape of his neck and pulled his mouth close to hers. "What else?"

Bobby's lips foraged along her skin. "You're worried about feeding."

"I've only failed at one thing in my life."

"You won't fail at this. If you do, the woman I know will be gone forever." He leaned away. "And so will I."

The corners of Bobby's iconic tight-lipped smile twisted down for a microsecond. Body language.

"You don't believe I'll succeed." *He is planning to leave.* "Fourteen years of hard work created this persona. I'm prepared to lead the ER. But three weeks in this unimaginable world, with the constant threat of a demon usurping my identity, is overwhelming." *And promotes insecurity. I'm the best damn surgeon in DC.*

Bobby hopped up.

"Don't go," Lara said.

"The other girl. We can't abandon her," Bobby said. "I'll drop her outside a police station. No feds."

"You won't harm those men? They deserve the worst fate the law will allow."

Bobby offered a cynical smirk. "I'll feed, too." His slender hands stopped her complaints. "I'll alter their memories, as usual. They won't remember you, so if the Vampire Unit of the WPA learns of the incident, you won't be connected." His brow wrinkled. "You need more blood. I'll head back to the hospital for that."

He rushed off with vampire speed, preventing further discussion.

Back to the hospital? He wasn't scheduled to work tonight, and there was too much activity early in the evening to risk feeding then.

He's searching for my replacement.

Lara's tongue slid over her gums, the extracted tooth regrown. Fangs served no function if she refused to use them. A tear slid down her cheek. Why didn't she accept life as a vampire?

* * *

"I want to track down Bobby Eyre now," Jake said.

"What's the urgency?" The director sipped Earl Grey.

Agent Jake Plummer of the Witness Protection Agency–Vampire Unit paced across his boss's Georgetown office. Her gaze followed him with an intensity belying her years. The spiral staircase Jake wandered around led to a narrow walkway—reach extended to otherwise inaccessible shelves. Books lined four of the room's five walls, floor to ceiling.

"I stopped at the In-Step Shoe Store this morning to visit my friend Jason Storm in Langhorne, Pennsylvania." Jake shook his head. Two years ago, Jason had saved Jake's life, a detail omitted in the official report, so the director remained unaware. "Another persona glared at me. Characteristic in subverted eyes—he's under the influence of a vampire."

"Someone we know?"

Jake shrugged. "Katie texted Interpol with the MO. We're waiting to hear from their vampire unit."

The woman mimicked his aloofness. "No need to wait. Destroy the fiend. Tonight."

"We have no idea where he is." Jake settled into a high-backed chair angled on the hearth of a stone fireplace. "Besides, mind control needs to be broken before the monster is destroyed, or my friend will be lost forever. I need him uninfluenced. Bobby Eyre is the only vampire we know powerful enough to intervene."

The director flipped her wrist and frowned. "You recruited Dr. West to ferret out a blood thief. You invested six months of agency time and money, but I never agreed with your decision to allow Mr. Eyre to survive."

"We've never been able to manipulate the behavior of a vampire before. He could prove useful to the agency."

"You can't control a wild vampire, and he won't enlist."

"You underestimate my persuasive power."

"He won't go to Bucks County without Dr. West. She won't leave. I read your report. She wants Dr. Byra's job at Jefferson."

"You never know. Dr. Byra may have a change of heart about retirement."

"Even if I grant the remote possibility that Mr. Eyre may prove useful, why is Dr. West walking around? I can read between the lines. I know she was turned. Our job is to destroy vampires, not train them."

Jake rubbed his chin. "It wasn't entirely Lara's idea to join the WPA."

"By association, we owe a vampire the favor of existence? I don't think so."

"Her antidote to our vampire toxin helped us re-engineer a more lethal version."

"Nonsense. Our chemists would've nailed it in three years."

"Six. If we were lucky."

"Okay, she wins vampire of the month. So? Destroy her. Tonight."

"I can only manipulate Mr. Eyre with Lara's assistance."

"You are so full of bullshit, I think you believe you. You're exploiting the resources of this agency to help your friend."

Jake slapped the armrests and jumped up. "Friend be damned. This agency pays my salary. Tonight I'll destroy the two vampires we know haven't killed anyone, and we'll let the unknown vampire ravage Bucks County until he kills enough people we can find him and destroy him ourselves."

The director shook her head. "You are unbelievable. Suppose you sway Dr. Byra. Then what? Mr. Eyre will never volunteer to help you." The woman settled her teacup on the desk.

Jake sniffed lemon and a hint of bitterness. Did the old woman sprinkle garlic in her drink? Maybe she used allium the same way he used cheap cologne—a common odor to mask his scent. "He just needs the proper incentive," Jake said.

"Lara West and Bobby Eyre are infatuated like teenagers."

Jake rubbed the nape of his neck. "Love is a weakness. We can imagine how difficult the transition to become a vampire is. I'm sure Lara hasn't adjusted yet. She'll be easy to manipulate. We need but a seed of distrust. I'll dredge up Bobby's old girlfriend if necessary. Betrayal will break the romance. Dr. West will storm out, and I'll direct her onto the path of danger."

"You may have to push."

"Can't. If the monster senses any stimulus other than true emotions, he won't fall for the trap, but if an inexperienced vampire like Lara stumbles into his little kingdom, he'll exploit the situation. When she's threatened, Mr. Eyre will be motivated. He'll root out the evil, rescue his lover, and coincidentally rescue my friend."

"How can you be sure she'll go to the shoe store?"

"You've always said I'm a cynical bastard. It's Lara West. I'll tell her not to go there."

* * *

Bobby angled toward the blood bank near the emergency room in Jefferson Memorial Hospital. Long past visiting hours, he'd donned his nursing scrubs and strolled down the hall, head up, eyes wide. He wasn't scheduled to work tonight, but no one questioned his presence. No security cameras. He committed to remove a few blood packets and alter the memory of the patient-care assistant on duty. Passion overrode caution.

Emotional involvement. A thread tethered him to society. Blood defined existence as a vampire; love defined existence as a man. Emotions ruled demons, and Bobby had never found an emotion stronger than love. Bobby's inner demon, Roberre, reigned for centuries in their awareness, washing Bobby in guilt-polluted blood. With Sigmund Freud's help, Bobby had finally wrested conscious control and stopped the killing, but the power struggle remained incessant. Falling in love had tipped the balance of power as Freud had predicted.

He'd been in love fifty years ago with the blond bombshell. She'd masqueraded as Norma Jeane, but Marilyn's sudden suicide resulted from

BLOOD BETWEEN LOVERS

Bobby's negligence. Just as if Roberre had killed her. Bobby's scowl solidified. Being in love with Marilyn had helped him keep Roberre submerged. Guilt riddled his consciousness, and for half a century, Bobby avoided emotional intimacy with any woman and wrestled with Roberre for conscious control.

When he met Dr. Lara West, *she* masqueraded as Nurse Meridian Jones, and Bobby fell in love with Meridian. He refused to think of her as Lara.

Additional work with Freud, more than fifty years before Marilyn, remained his only saving grace. Together, Bobby and Freud had developed Vampirical Harmony. Bobby traded a woman mind-blowing sexual pleasure for a pint of her blood, and in so doing, kept Roberre from killing. In love with Meridian, Bobby maintained a firm grip on consciousness—until he turned her.

Vampires rarely created other vampires, and never did so with casual indifference, but if they spawned, parental instinct rivalled the instinct for survival. Vampires never lived together, but the longer the creation survived, the more proud the parent: *I sired a successful vampire. I taught her to survive.*

Bobby refocused. No emergency room activity. Few people roamed the building.

Jefferson operated the same as any other hospital where he'd worked in the past one hundred years: only nurses and patient-care assistants were on duty at this hour. The white-noise hum of machinery, the rattling of gurney wheels, the electric glide of elevator doors, the incessant drip of an IV, and the antiseptic smell of sterility countermanded so magnificently by the constant aroma of blood.

Blood drew attention. Bobby had come across in the thirteenth century, when missing blood from a person, living or dead, was rarely recognized. In the late nineteenth century, Freud prescribed *love without blood.*

Love blinded even a vampire. Immortality outweighed the importance of love. Allowing emotional intimacy to a point still felt good to Bobby's human side, but too much emotional intimacy was too much of a risk to immortality.

Emotional intimacy drew a fine line, dissected into microfibers by technology, the bane of vampire existence. Technology enabled vampire hunters. Computers and GPS systems tracked vampires as easily as they did humans. Missing blood—necessary for eternity—drew twenty-first-century attention, even in small quantities. No vampire covens endured. No groups of vampires coexisting as a family, working as a team. Competition between just two vampires for the limited supply of hassle-free blood in any one community was too great.

Stalkers had culled the vampire population, especially in the last twenty years, and the few remaining vampires undoubtedly shared the same conclusion as Bobby. Fewer vampires meant less attention, less competition for blood, and therefore fewer vampire hunters. The United States government dedicated an entire agency to the worldwide elimination of vampires and upped the bounties to keep mercenaries motivated.

For centuries, vampires worried about starvation, being staked in the heart, and beheadings. Twenty-first century technology had added vampire-specific bullets.

Bobby circled the emergency room again. Security was concentrating on another floor, and no other vampire operated in this hospital.

Vampires weren't stupid. Creating another vampire created competition. Living with another vampire—even one you loved—doubled the amount of blood consumed from the community. Hunters swarmed over the obvious. Siring a vampire in the twenty-first century wasn't simply frowned upon—it was forbidden, without law, without governing body—forbidden by vampire consciousness, by the demands of self-survival.

Falling in love with a human was finite—doable because of the time limitation and no increase in local sanguine demand. But falling in love with another vampire doctored a recipe for destruction. Bobby had never wanted—never expected—to transform Meridian. Yes, he'd fallen in love with the human, who was fated for agonizing death if he didn't turn her. Bobby contradicted Shakespeare and Hamlet's mother. *All that live must die, passing through nature to eternity.* Turning Meridian had damned their relationship. Now, it was his responsibility to instruct. So far, Meridian failed to wrap her head around life as a vampire. How could he explain that as soon as she succeeded, their relationship would end?

The call of eternity taught him this strategy. The love of a woman didn't override existence in perpetuity. Bobby cherished existence. Seven hundred years served as an appetizer. Eternity spread before him like a feast of infinite proportions.

Bobby nodded his head. Shakespeare had written that line before he'd met Bobby.

Bobby sniffed fresh blood and salivated: multiple gunshot wounds, although surprisingly only one victim tonight. The ER doctor-patient relationship ended with the doctor's success—the patient bagged and stabilized and trundled off to the required specialist, with no chance for Bobby to collect the overflow.

For seven hundred years, Bobby never created another vampire. He didn't want the responsibility. Love for a human had dictated his actions when he'd finally turned Meridian. Vampires cherished their creations from afar. Survival, the true depth of eternity, dictated dealings with other vampires. Don't. Ever.

He had sired Meridian. He'd teach her to survive. He'd cut her loose. Instinct overwhelmed personal safety in the moment only.

Will Meridian be the woman she wants to be or the woman I want her to be?

Bobby had learned centuries ago that passion couldn't be forced. As a human, Meridian had enjoyed a choice to fall in love with him or not. No longer a human, no longer a choice. Simple logic.

No, it wasn't. Love hypothesized an unfathomable equation human-to-vampire, and an unsolvable equation vampire-to-vampire. Love distracted. Love blinded. He should've recognized the onset of frenzy. His failure endangered the existence of the woman he lov—turned. His responsibility. He forced himself to stop thinking of passion and lashed out at the nearest hard object. The fire extinguisher dented under the force of his blow.

Bobby expelled a deep breath. Heart palpitations, normal for a vampire, ran away, and he struggled to regain a human rate, just in case he encountered anyone who might notice. Meridian probably hated him for transforming her into a bloodthirsty monster. Either side of the passion equation, Meridian required sustenance tonight to avoid frenzy.

Toting blood concealed in his duffle bag was chancy, but need trumped risk. He'd sired this vampire and the instinct to help her survive—teach her to survive—demanded he jeopardize his safety for hers.

Bobby's skin suddenly itched everywhere, with no good place to scratch. His fangs erupted. Without visible cause, an inner voice cautioned, *Danger.* A peculiar scent wrinkled his nose; the scent intensified as he approached the blood bank, hackles raised.

An assistant lounged behind a desk, back to the door. A small man by any standards, but broad-shouldered, whistling while he read. The stench of cut-rate cologne draped over him.

Bobby directed a telepathic command at the man. *Bring me four units with tomorrow's expiration.* A quiet ER tonight meant there would be expiring blood destined for disposal. Red blood cells presented a forty-two-day hospital shelf life. Bottled, old blood maintained temporary existence for a vampire; it was never a gateway to eternity.

Instead of standing, the employee spun on the swivel chair, tossed his book on the desk, and glanced up as though expecting the interruption. "I'm pleased to see you again, Mr. Eyre."

CHAPTER 3

Bobby restrained a bark of recognition. Agent Jake Plummer.

"Glad you're alone. Easier for us to talk," Jake said. "How's Dr. West? I mean, Nurse Jones? You think of Lara as Meridian, right? I chose the name when I recruited her into the Witness Protection Agency." He tapped his chest like a proud father. In human terms, did Jake's role parallel Bobby's? Jake sired human Meridian; Bobby sired the vampire.

"The way Meridian explained events, it sounded more like you manipulated her life into the WPA."

Jake chuckled. "Life, death—it's all about perception. You perceive Nurse Jones as Meridian. I still perceive her as Dr. Lara West."

Bobby grunted.

"I wonder if she thinks of herself as Lara or Meridian," Jake said, and gestured toward a chair facing him.

Did Jake douse himself in cologne to mask his presence? He expected me? Humans aren't resistant to vampire mind control. How can he ignore my suggestion?

Jake sipped coffee. "Life in DC isn't as dangerous as in Langhorne, Pennsylvania. A month ago, I wounded a man who'd wounded Lara. You killed him."

And I turned Meridian and altered your memory so you'd forget Meridian and I are vampires.

Bobby sat and forced his fangs to retract before Jake noticed. What did the Vampire Unit want with him?

"Did you think I wouldn't remember?" Jake asked.

"Memories are fragile and often inaccurate."

Jake nodded. "How'd you sell your house so fast?"

"I'm keeping the house." Bobby indicated Jake's hospital garb. "You went to all this trouble to discuss real estate, Agent Plummer?"

"Tennis."

"Excuse me?"

"Do you know what a drop shot is?"

"I'm familiar with the term."

"A drop shot is most successful when it's unexpected. It maneuvers your opponent off-balance and takes him out of his game plan." Jake kept his gaze fixed on Bobby. "Life doesn't always unfold the way the United States government demands. To counter an opponent, we occasionally need to make a drop shot. Dr. Surinder Byra is chief of emergency medicine in this hospital. We don't want her to retire."

"Running out of Social Security?"

"We want you to persuade Dr. Byra to keep working, and we need your help right away."

"Or?"

"There is no 'or,' Mr. Eyre. There are no options here."

"You're anticipating voluntary cooperation?"

Jake shrugged. "Is it such a big deal? Dr. Byra is proficient; the hospital and the community will benefit from her continued expertise."

"What makes you think I'd have any particular influence with Dr. Byra?"

Jake waved. "Certain individuals have an affinity for manipulation."

"I don't like the sound of 'manipulation.'"

"I don't like the taste of it, but it doesn't stop me from exercising my options."

"I thought there were no options?"

"For you. I play by a different set of rules."

Jake floated along an undercurrent of conversation, and Bobby failed to steer clear. *Why didn't he respond to my suggestion to retrieve blood?* "Altering Dr. Byra's decision impacts Meridian."

"Dr. West has a multitude of options. What difference will it make to her if she lands the job now or one hundred years from now?"

"I don't understand what you mean."

"Life springs eternal."

"Hope springs eternal." The blood bank refrigerator door sprang open.

"Life, hope—doesn't matter. You and Dr. West know what I mean."

Agents leaked out, weapons trained on Bobby. He sensed backup behind him, blocking escape, undoubtedly armed with the bullets designed to destroy vampires. A vampire had shot Bobby with a government-engineered bullet a month ago. Meridian—surgeon Lara West—had saved Bobby's life.

Jake raised his hands. "No trouble, Mr. Eyre. We know who you are, and we know you've altered Dr. West. She would've died otherwise, right?"

Jake isn't susceptible to mind control. The bastard faked having his memory altered.

"You did the government a service destroying a vampire. We're asking for a small additional favor. Use your . . . unusual talents to persuade Dr. Byra to continue her work. In exchange, we'll ignore your existence."

"No. Promotion to chief of emergency medicine means everything to Meridian. I don't care if you ignore me. I won't betray her trust." Bad enough he abandoned her emotional needs. At least her career goal remained intact.

Jake nodded. "Okay." He plucked his book from the desk and scanned the open page.

Bobby frowned. Jake wasn't trustworthy.

Jake waved without looking up. "We may disagree with your choice, but we'll still ignore your existence. Enjoy eternity, Mr. Eyre."

Bobby hopped out of the chair. Every agent re-aimed his weapon. No reaction from Jake. Bobby headed for the exit. Jake swiveled in his seat.

"It's a shame about Dr. West," Jake said.

Bobby forgot to breathe.

"Bounties are astronomical. Vampire hunters today are relentless. With your help, she may never be caught, but she'll never know peace again. She'll be hunted. Forever."

"Her survival means everything to me." Vampire instinct forced a human lump into his throat.

"I know." Jake smirked.

Bobby's shoulders slumped. Jake left him no choice. Protection from bounty hunters demanded a price. He pivoted to face a master manipulator. Bobby's stomach knotted with the pain of betraying his lover multiplied by the pain of betraying himself–this was the human he had loved and the vampire he sired.

"Dreams, goals . . . doesn't matter, does it?" Jake sipped coffee. "Convince Dr. Byra work is the best option. She's in her office. Do it now." He tossed four packets of AB positive on the desk. "No blood from the bank. This is for Dr. West, from volunteers." Jake gestured toward his agents.

Bobby had encountered human-Meridian six months ago because Jake had assigned her to the Vampire Unit. Meridian had scaled walls Bobby crafted to protect his human persona. Decades of loneliness had evaporated.

Fate suggested Bobby owed Jake the manipulator. Bobby's nose wrinkled. He didn't like Jake.

"Do me a favor," Jake said. "Don't tell Lara I'm impervious to mind control."

* * *

BLOOD BETWEEN LOVERS

Lara tramped around their library. "What does she mean, she's not retiring?"

Bobby shrugged. "The same thing everyone means. She's going to continue to work."

"As chief of emergency medicine?" Lara paced in front of a marble table.

"Hospital scuttlebutt is she announced the decision last night. Must've been while I collected blood for you."

"I donated three and a half years of hard work to Jefferson Memorial. I managed the ER in everything but title." Lara crossed the narrow expanse of their library. Through the corner window, the hospital sign glared, four blocks away.

She pounded the wall. The full force of Dr. Byra's decision jarred her inner being. Dispassion masked Bobby's expression. Lara's fangs ached. If vampires possessed souls, this news rocked hers.

"I helped plan her retirement. I accepted responsibilities. I deserve her job."

"You're a vampire, not a physician."

"I'm not renouncing my Hippocratic oath." She rubbed her hand. She'd never explained to Bobby why she wanted—needed—Dr. Byra's job. "My dream is my life." She cast a hard glance into Bobby's eyes. "What changed her mind?"

Bobby didn't respond. Lara stalked to the far side of the room, facing an original Rembrandt mural.

"I can't believe my life is being ripped away. Again. The staff thought I died in the fire six months ago, but the administration accepted my return. Jake wouldn't allow me to tell them I worked for the WPA. He put on an HSA jacket, flashed a badge, and mumbled something about national security."

"Either way, Dr. West perished last winter, courtesy of Agent Plummer."

Lara shook her head. "I refuse to surrender my identity. I'll always think of myself as Lara West."

She adjusted a row of century-old books. "What if you used mind control to persuade Dr. Byra she does intend to retire? I'd get the job then."

Bobby's gaze followed her around the room. "I know you." His voice softened. "Emotional harm is as irreparable as ripping her flesh."

"I won't be shoved aside now. Meridian's two-month stint hunting vampires is a footnote to my eleven years of medical training. I've resurrected Dr. West."

Lara balked at her reflection in the window. Incomprehensible. Meridian Jones and Lara West forever linked, two personalities trapped in a vampire body.

"You would've died if I didn't bring you across."

"I may as well be dead if I can't chase my dream. I want Dr. Byra's job."

"Learn to feed. The struggle to control consciousness is constant."

Lara experienced a sensory invasion as if a third party joined their conversation. Her fangs throbbed, like an inner voice calling to her, relentless. Without a sound, a message formed in her mind.

Feed. Now.

Lara blinked.

Blood, the inner voice said. "How can my thoughts leap from Dr. Byra to this gruesome reality?"

Bobby's weight shifted as he studied the play of emotions across her face.

"We can't destroy our inner beasts, but we can learn to control them," Bobby said. "Your beast isn't the vampire. You both are. Your human side will be empowered only by a sufficient supply of blood. Without that supply, the vampire will grow so hungry it leads to frenzy. Frenzy will overwhelm your human side, and your demon will forever dominate consciousness, killing without regard. The vampire is immortal either way. For your human side to survive, you must act."

Laughter filtered through the open second-story window and redirected Lara's attention. She edged into the silhouette of the diaphanous curtain. A young couple strolled along the sidewalk.

Blood.

Lara tilted her head back and sniffed. She'd seen Bobby do it a hundred times. More than the woman's perfume exploded on her senses. Neither darkness nor the expanse of the street kept her from noticing the man's tousled hair or the label sticking out of his neckline. A loose thread extended from the sleeve of the woman's blouse, a beer stain smeared her left sandal, and electric-pink nail polish cracked on the middle finger of the hand the man held. The overpowering scent of sex exuded from them. The bulge in the man's trousers suggested their excitement hadn't dwindled, confirmed by his companion's hardened nipples.

"Too much info too fast." Lara shook her head.

Her perceptions reignited with a clanking roofing truck. Gas fumes, burnt oil, and the putrid sweat of two occupants assaulted her. The men laughed, stoned and still smoking. A front tire squealed, and a CD player blared bad rap. The engine knocked, and the driver's door rattled, tied shut with fibrous twine. Another cloud of exhaust stained the city, and the truck rumbled on.

"How do you absorb all this?" Lara asked.

Bobby stirred behind her. His button-down shirt rustled against her blouse.

BLOOD BETWEEN LOVERS

Vampirical senses augmented every sound and smell in a dizzying array. His heart thudded, and the sweet scent from his recent feeding filled her nostrils. Centuries ago, Bobby had adjusted his feeding cycles to coincide with the full moon.

It's a half-moon tonight. Why is Bobby feeding now?

"You'll adjust." Bobby's words floated in the air and idled with soothing intent.

Lara thrust suspicion aside. "I've never known anyone like you."

"A vampire?"

"A man with your compassion." Tentacles of a headache spread. "You turned me a month ago." Frustration edged her voice. Her fingers glided over her neck, the skin now unblemished. "It's as if I have an itch and can't figure out where to scratch."

She kicked the floor. Disgust warred with anger at her inability to fend for herself. Craving overwhelmed consciousness, surrender not optional. No choice remained: the onset of frenzy.

"I need to feed."

With inhuman speed, Bobby raced across the room, flicked off the light switch, then rejoined her near the curtain. He scanned the scene below. "They'll be perfect."

He tugged her toward the window—she resisted, unprepared for the direct route. They arrived at the street in a more conventional manner. Moonlight, starlight, and streetlights combined in a glorious illumination of anticipation, but her stomach rebelled in spasms.

"Align your thoughts in her mind," Bobby said. "Assume control. We'll feed in the alley." He pointed with his chin. "It's a public area, so don't let her scream."

They crossed the macadam and trailed behind the couple.

"The neck is too visible. Take her here," Bobby whispered, brushing Lara's breast, "but don't tear the clothes. No sign she's been assaulted."

"Puncturing flesh is repulsive." Lara's stride faltered. Her knees weakened.

Bobby grabbed her shoulder. "You're out of options." His voice emerged low and hoarse. She'd heard his inner beast, Roberre, before, and understood; Bobby restrained the beast to prevent unnecessary violence. "When you're close enough to smell her blood, to sense the perspiration on her skin, to hear her heartbeat, instinct for survival will take over, but control the instinct. Feed, then wipe her memory, and you'll both survive."

Hunger consumed all other feelings. Lara imagined the attack from behind.

I'm not a murderer.

You can kill, a voice in her head said. No, the sound didn't resonate in her head; it emanated as an indistinguishable aspect of being. *Drink until you're sated, then fly away,* the voice exhorted.

Fly away? Lara denied the possibility. *No.* Whatever remained of Dr. Lara West refused to kill, and refused to accept—what? Life as a bat?

Lara's subconscious coaxed her into the world of darkness, the reality of a vampire— hunger gnawed, as subtle as a hundred rats in a cage with a single slice of raw meat.

Frenzy.

Lara and Bobby lurked behind the unsuspecting couple. The woman's carotid artery pulsated like a drum calling the vampires to action. The scent of peach schnapps wafted in the air.

Bobby's hand niggled on the small of Lara's back, pushed her forward, like a parent thrusting a shy child onstage. She fought the physical pressure, but every sensation tingled and all perceptions converged on a single thought: *blood.*

She imagined her fangs piercing the woman's skin, the warmth, the moisture, the pleasure of—no, the horror of—no, the overwhelming satisfaction of drinking human blood. Her body craved it, demanded it; her human conscience screamed in revolt.

"Excuse me," Bobby said. "Could you help us?" The words wove a delicate pattern around their victims. "We're lost."

Bobby's telepathy, or Lara's imagination, helped her understand what he wanted her to do: *Take control of the female.* He'd taught her how to integrate thoughts into a human's mind.

An evening of sex and alcohol produced a pliable target. Like an extended hand that grasped a fistful of the woman's hair, the fingers of Lara's thoughts grasped synapses that controlled higher brain function. Lara sucked in a superfluous breath. She sensed no anxiety in the lady. Why should the woman be afraid?

Bobby angled the man toward the alley as they talked. The man clasped his companion's hand and pulled her along. Lara trailed behind.

A wave of energy washed over Lara. Desire boiled beneath her skin and compelled her to quicken the pace. She tilted her head back and reacquired a scent. Her nostrils flared, filled with the pheromones of her intended victim.

The woman's heartbeat thudded against Lara's existence. Lara's fangs erupted, and an unsummoned moan escaped.

BLOOD BETWEEN LOVERS

The man tried to explain directions to Bobby, and the woman laughed at something the man said, her voice an uncomfortable vibration. Lara's perception was flooded with sensations.

Her memory dredged up the taste of blood, and her stomach heaved. Bobby had ministered fresh blood yesterday in Dr. Bittner's basement, insisting she drink to sustain existence. He had held Frank's bleeding wound above her nose, and the scent had incited primal desire. Blood had dripped into her mouth, and yearnings swept through her psyche. She'd drunk, and her mind had shrunk in horror. What possessed her?

Lara had moaned in pleasure last night when Bobby sunk his fangs into her thigh, but she'd pulled away before he could drink her blood. Afterward, he'd guided her mouth across his flesh and encouraged her to bite him. She wanted to please her lover, to share the joy of bonding in blood and orgasm, but the human inside her refused the violent act.

The second real feeding had come from a bottle. He said he'd gone to the hospital the previous night. She didn't ask, and he didn't volunteer information. She'd drunk, surprised by her desire. But cold blood from a bottle satisfied no urge, nor did it slake any desire; it merely sustained temporary existence. Bobby taught her that eternity demanded blood from a human container.

The scrape of a shoe and tinkling laughter brought Lara back into the moment. The man stumbled, the woman swayed; Bobby steadied them as they entered the alley. The human vessel of a meal floated in front of Lara, and Lara's resolve shrank.

Vampire hunger was magnified, but the thirst for blood was vapid to the human. Lara refused to be defined by a vampire's existence. The voice within vowed, *No choice*. Bobby claimed, *No choice*.

Shrinking humanity screamed, *Choose*, and Lara clung to humanity.

She fled the alley with incomprehensible speed.

CHAPTER 4

Lara wanted to cry, but tears didn't form. She flung herself onto their four-poster bed, facedown in the dark bedroom. She didn't hear Bobby enter the house or climb the marble stairs, but she recognized his scent, like salt on a sea breeze.

He crossed the space between them faster than she'd imagined possible. He stroked the nape of her neck, and his lips brushed against her ear. His breath induced a shiver. She twisted her head to glance at his face. A grin curled the corners of his mouth. His eyes flashed crimson, a sign of the nocturnal hunter.

"I can't bite anyone," Lara said.

"Hunger hasn't seized your soul. When it does, either you'll be able to feed yourself from a human without killing, or the frenzy will allow your beast to overwhelm you." His expression of tenderness disintegrated. "There's something else. We're fast approaching a deadline."

"For us?"

"Most vampires don't learn to deal with frenzy early enough. The psychological effects are devastating."

"You've supplied blood—"

"Suppose I'm out of the picture. If you don't learn faster, then when frenzy strikes, the *you* I know will be lost forever."

Her stomach cramped, and her throat tightened. "Twice in two nights you've mentioned leaving. If I can't feed myself, are we finished?" She struggled to speak. "Attacking a person is so . . . ruthless."

"Despite centuries of existing as a vampire, I cling to civilization. You never have to let go of humanity, Meridian. You're entitled to exist just as any other creature is." Bobby's voice soothed. He caressed her back and avoided answering the question. "You can acquire blood without harm when necessity demands."

Lara shook her head. "I'm a vampire, but an aspect of me is human, and my human persona can't stand the blood."

Bobby pushed her shoulder and grinned. "What kind of doctor are you? You can't stand blood?"

BLOOD BETWEEN LOVERS

"Doctors don't drink it. The idea makes one side of my brain nauseated and another part wild with desire. I don't understand."

Bobby pulled her close. His tongue traced a narrow line around her lips. "I want the wild part." His voice demanded attention, low and guttural. "I love having you here in my bed." He lay on his back with Lara on top of him. His hands slid down the thin cotton fabric of her trousers. "I want to make love, and I want to show you how to feed." He stroked her legs.

Bobby enthralled her night after night with the two stages of Vampirical Harmony sexual pleasure: sex for her, sex and blood for him—just not her blood. "Is bottled blood as satisfying as fresh blood?" she had asked.

His expression had answered that question.

"How'd you learn VH?" Lara asked now.

"Freud."

"*Sigmund* Freud?"

"He suggested I trade a woman's enjoyment for a pint of blood." Bobby flipped their positions and teased her flesh. "Movie vampires bite the carotid artery because the neck is most obvious. Real vampires would never do that." Bobby laughed. "We don't want to be discovered. Blood can be taken from less obvious sites: the underside of the breast or the sole of the foot."

Bobby massaged her ear. "Freud taught me how to control my beast by incorporating Vampirical Harmony while I feed, satisfying two lusts simultaneously. I take blood from the femoral artery—hidden from view, but easily combined with sexual foreplay."

Lara's eyes danced for the first time that night. "You admit you love the sex."

Bobby pushed up, creating a gap between their faces, his expression somber. He shook his head. "Nah, I hate the sex."

Her punch bounced off his chest. "Creep."

"But I love your cooking."

"You don't eat." She punched harder.

Bobby struggled to keep from laughing. "But I lie awake next to you during the day."

"Because you can't let me out of your sight?"

"Nah. Because you snore."

This time he caught her punch, rolled, and pinned her beneath him.

"What do you think you're doing?"

"Whatever I want," Bobby said.

"I don't think so."

He stretched her arms above her head. "Nothing you can do to stop me."

She blinked slowly. "Why on earth would I stop you? I want to be ravaged in body and mind." VH focused on emotions first. Bobby had told her he wanted to understand what she was feeling as they made love. *Intimacy on a new level.*

"Freud taught me the emotional exchange is as important to the buildup of an orgasm as is rubbing your clitoris or licking your nipples or massaging the toe linked to your sexual core. It's the caressing of a woman's mind that endears the man. Your sexual excitement enhances mine."

"As much as the ability to feed myself does?"

"Next time we hunt blood, you'll succeed." Bobby's tone soothed, the voice of a concerned partner.

Lara had never had time for a relationship, as she'd focused instead on her career, her goals. The men she'd met in med school and working in the hospital had never seemed interested in her feelings, just their own enjoyment—sexual pleasure in the moment.

"We stalked that couple," Bobby said. "You seized control of the woman's thoughts and kept her calm. You were poised for satisfaction—revel in the sensation." He released her wrist and tickled her palm.

"How can I justify a craving that nauseates me?"

"The world of a vampire is not about blood—it's about eternity." Bobby massaged her middle toe. "Life immortal, Meridian. Allow yourself to believe it's possible. Immortality trumps all emotion. Allow yourself the time to adjust to a new mindset. You're a brilliant surgeon, and you can have a career spanning generations. Let me show you what it means to be a vampire."

His fangs grazed along her neck, and the sharp points prickled. "I'll teach you the essence of a vampire's existence," Bobby said. He unfastened the top button of her blouse.

"When you were a human, your sexual aura outshone the women around you. You have no idea how sensual you are as a vampire." Bobby unhooked her trousers and eased down the zipper.

"Human blood is our vehicle to immortality. You'll learn to puncture skin. You'll accept drinking blood as a natural right of existence." He massaged her ego as gracefully as he massaged her flesh.

Bobby bowed lower to kiss her, but she sensed his care to keep Roberre restrained. Dangerous, but Lara had engaged his beast before in a search for fulfillment, a desire to please her lover as she sensed he wanted to please her.

BLOOD BETWEEN LOVERS

She was a vampire, capable of his sexual gratification, apart from refusing to bite him.

She twisted her head to the side.

Bobby's lips chased hers.

"Can't kiss what you want?" Lara covered her mouth.

Bobby pulled her wrist away from her lips, and growled.

"What's the matter?" Lara's voice filled with little-girl innocence.

Bobby traced his tongue down her neck, then tickled the side of her breast.

Lara sighed. "You don't play fair."

Bobby wedged his knee between her legs and pressed. His hand slipped lower. "I'm sorry, I didn't hear you. What did you say?"

She opened her mouth, and Bobby glided his other hand under her head and kissed her in one fluid motion. Her lips yielded to his, and the kiss brimmed with passion. Her fingers drifted through his hair, her nails clawed his back, and her hand slid between Bobby's legs.

Bobby chuckled. "You don't play fair either."

Lara pushed hard, catching Bobby by surprise. She squeezed. "I'm sorry, I didn't hear you." Her voice vibrated, low and husky. "What did you say?"

She kissed him before he answered, her tongue deep in his mouth.

She broke the embrace before he was tempted to bite her tongue and suck her blood. "Unsheath Roberre. I have something tantalizing in mind." Lara slithered to the side and unbuckled his belt.

"What do you think you're doing?"

"Anything I want," she said.

* * *

Dysfunction for a vampire was not the same as human impotence.

Bobby raced down the brownstone's marble staircase and glanced once over his shoulder. Meridian remained too unsettled in her vampire persona to wake early. The sun dangled over the horizon and bathed the city in an eerie twilight. Bobby's fangs had erupted in anticipation of sex, though he knew they'd remain unused in bed, and now, his fangs didn't retract. Wouldn't retract. The dysfunctional vampire, his nature displayed like a red flag. A field day for Freud.

"Your dysfunction is either physiological or psychological," Freud would say. "Simple test to discover. Try having sex with someone else."

Bobby frowned. His dick had hardened with Meridian's touch. His orgasm had exploded as excitement crescendoed beyond control. Meridian still refused to allow him to puncture thigh or breast or tongue to drink. Drinking from one's partner was a vampire's extension of his climax, the natural orgasmic coupling of blood and sex. Instead, play had ended with the greatest embarrassment a vampire could suffer: the inability to retract his fangs.

Bobby had spent enough time in psychoanalysis with Freud to know the reason. Guilt—powerful enough to waylay sexual desire in a human or manipulate a solitary physiological reaction in a vampire: lost control of his fangs. And the only resolution was to overcome self-reproach.

The sliver of a waning moon stabbed a rooftop. The moon held no particular meaning for vampires, but over centuries, Bobby had adjusted his feeding rhythms to coincide with the full moon, the day before, and the day after. He maintained existence comfortably for twenty-six days without feeding. He didn't need blood tonight, only the assistance of one of Jake's female agents.

Vampirical Harmony lined the path to blood and cooperation and proof of Freud's dysfunction theories. Whatever Jake planned for Dr. Byra impacted Meridian. Bobby needed to discover Jake's strategy.

His tongue grazed his teeth. Garnering information from a WPA agent required mind control. Extreme sexual pleasure opened the door to influence, and V-Harmony with another woman would prove him dysfunctional with all women or only with Meridian. Would his fangs retract upon command with a stranger? He knew the answer, but if Freud were alive, he'd demand empirical evidence.

Bobby stole along DC streets near the hospital. He passed the slavers' house, and the foul scent of an unbathed dog struck him. Bobby stopped.

Yellow police tape sealed the entrance. He ducked the tape and squeezed the door handle. Locked. He forced the door and stepped into the foyer. His nose wrinkled, and he followed the odor into the kitchen. The rapid heartbeat of a small animal directed him under the table.

Bobby stooped and held out his hands. "Come here, little dog."

A scrawny miniature dachshund peered out from behind a table leg.

"I won't harm you," Bobby said.

The animal's ears lay back, its tail dangled, but the dog didn't move.

Chalky film lined a dry water dish. Bobby ran faucet water until it cooled, then filled the bowl and placed it on the floor. He stepped back and beckoned.

"I'm sorry," he said. "I didn't realize you lived here. You've survived for more than two days on your own. Quite an accomplishment for a puppy. I'm proud of you."

The dog's nose peeked out. It sniffed and glanced up. Bobby gestured, and the dog lapped water.

"You must be hungry, too." He poured dried food from a bag and waited while the animal scarfed it up. Bobby knelt. "Come on. You can't live here alone."

The dog jumped into his arms. Bobby carried it outside and hopped the steps to the adjoining home.

A middle-aged woman answered the bell, bleary-eyed, dressed in a housecoat and fuzzy slippers. Her breasts sagged against a bulging stomach. She pushed open the screen door.

"Ain't interested in buyin' nothin'."

"I want you to take care of this dog," Bobby said.

The woman squinted, her brow wrinkled in recognition. "I ain't takin' their dog. Those boys have connections. Don't think they ain't been arrested before. They always get off. They'll come back and sell me as a high-class sex slave."

Bobby forced himself to keep a straight face. "Take care of their dog. It's the only escape from such a tragic fate." His voice, low and guttural, jolted the woman. He thrust the animal into her pudgy arms. "The dog is your responsibility."

Bobby entered Jefferson Memorial Hospital through the emergency doors. He hoped to find one of Jake's agents alone, stationed strategically around the hospital. He'd probe her mind and plant a posthypnotic suggestion. Jake probably tested his agents daily on the chance any of them had been subverted.

Bobby sensed his quarry long before he arrived at the blood bank. Agent Plummer wouldn't be pleased his plans were undermined, but necessity urged Bobby to risk discovery. He treaded a fine line between Jake's orders and a wisp of humanness. Bad enough Bobby planned to destroy his relationship with Meridian. If Agent Plummer carried out his threat and unleashed vampire hunters, a hellish future awaited her. Bobby could protect her from destruction, and Meridian would survive even if she wasn't a self-reliant vampire, though she'd forfeit her career, and her dreams, and any chance for a sublime existence.

He'd loved Marilyn fifty years ago, but Marilyn committed suicide because Bobby left her. More guilt piled on his conscience. She must've thought she couldn't live without him. He planned to leave Meridian soon, but not before she believed she could survive on her own. Convincing one of Jake's agents to keep Meridian supplied with blood after Bobby abandoned her was a prudent backup plan.

* * *

Lara paced the townhouse library. She peered beyond the curtains. A sliver moon glared, reflecting off the Capitol dome. Bobby had left before she woke. No note. She rubbed her cheek, then dragged her fingers through her hair. She read the first twenty pages of a vampire romance in less than a minute. She rolled her eyes, flipped the book on the floor, and grabbed another. What if Bobby never returned? Tears formed.

"We'll hunt again tonight," Bobby had promised before they'd slept.

But sleep was postponed by questions. "This hunger is overwhelming. Why? You fed me. Why isn't cold blood satisfying?" His answers weren't satisfying, either, before or after sleep. Frustration fed impatience. Did she require professional help? Bobby had engaged Freud. Did she need a psychiatrist?

Her cell phone vibrated.

Probably the Jefferson ER calling. She glanced at the LCD display but didn't recognize the number. She unlocked the phone and accepted the call without speaking. A familiar voice grabbed her attention.

"What's the matter, Dr. West, mouthful of blood? Swallow it, dear, and talk."

Joking. Special Agent Jake Plummer knew how to push her buttons. *He has no idea I'm a vampire.*

Does he?

"What a pleasure to hear you," Lara said.

"Ding-dong."

"Excuse me?"

"Ding-dong," Jake repeated.

"I'm sorry?"

"Answer the door."

"There's no one—"

The doorbell rang.

Lara raced with the speed she didn't understand and opened the door before the chimes ended.

Jake nodded and arched an eyebrow. "Maybe you were expecting me." He ogled the dress that clung to her hips and exaggerated the curves of her breasts, a dress Bobby liked.

"What big eyes you have," Lara said.

"The better to see you with, my dear."

Lara opened the door wider. "Come in, Agent Plummer."

Jake angled across the two-story foyer and aimed for a painting on the far wall.

"Probably wants dinner," Lara mumbled.

"Monet? Original?" Jake pointed. "I'll take coffee, since you asked."

"What big ears you have."

"This conversation reminds me of something."

"Or someone. Sorry, no coffee. The faucets work, though. Would you like water?"

"DC tap water? Turning must've addled your mind."

"Excuse me?"

"There's no excuse for being a vampire, sweetheart."

Adrenaline rushed through her system. Jake's expression said he wasn't joking. How would Bobby react? No sense denying the truth to Jake. This was his business. If he meant her harm, he wouldn't be chatting.

"How'd you know?"

Jake thrust his chin. "Your eyes . . . and your boyfriend's."

He knows about Bobby.

She escorted him into the library. "I haven't talked with you since we moved to Washington. I'm sure this isn't a social call. How'd you find the address?"

"Sweetheart, we're the government. Did you think Bobby Eyre and Dr. Lara West, known vampires, could purchase a home without us noticing?" He tilted his head and studied her. "How do you like it?"

"The house suits our purposes."

Jake grimaced. "Not the house. Your new life. Sleep all day? No dental checkups? No coffee?"

Lara plopped onto an ottoman. Jake might not be her favorite person, but he grasped both issues: survival and chasing dreams.

"The nocturnal lifestyle isn't working for me yet."

Jake straddled a Louis Quinze chair and peered around the high back. "Relax. You thought you knew yourself. Well, okay, you don't, but so what?

You'll figure it out. Most vampires don't have a personal trainer, either. You've got one versed and willing to share, and you've got me—a virgin's Nirvana."

"How do you know I haven't bitten anyone?"

"Lara West, physician, would find puncturing flesh to drink blood in conflict with her oath." Jake's gaze reaffirmed his perspicuity.

Lara leaned forward and acquired Jake's scent. A thought flashed, and she recognized thought was related to scent.

"Until five minutes ago, you weren't in the equation. I'm worried now. What do you want, Jake?"

"Honey, I'm just the welcoming committee."

Lara's nostrils flared, and a voice inside said, *Liar.* This set her on guard, as though someone else commanded her defense system. Muscles loosened, senses heightened, poised to strike. She had no idea at what she'd strike.

Not Jake. He'd saved her life, or at least tried. Her stint with the WPA had been fulfilled. What else did she owe him?

Sights, sounds, smells rushed at her. A piece of lint on the shoulder of Jake's jacket, the low drone of an idling car engine parked three doors down the street; Jake didn't come alone.

He didn't need coffee, either. The Columbian aroma on his breath filtered across the room. Jake had lied and brought backup, so he wasn't totally innocuous.

"Dr. Byra isn't retiring," Lara said.

Jake shrugged. "Dr. Byra is your therapist?"

"Dr. Byra is chief of emergency medicine at Jefferson Memorial."

"She's not as old as she thought?"

"She was old enough to retire when we spoke seventy-two hours ago. When you snatched me from the hospital last winter, you ripped away my dream. I've reimagined it. I want Dr. Byra's job."

"Tough break."

"Thanks for the sympathy."

Jake laughed. "You're immortal, and you're looking for sympathy? Sorry, kid."

Lara's nose wrinkled. Did Jake present a threat? He carried a gun; the bulge beneath his jacket confirmed he strapped the weapon into a shoulder harness.

Jake followed her gaze and patted the firearm. "New bullets. Similar to the one you removed from Robert Helstrom a few months ago. You remember the night we inducted you into the WPA? These babies'll destroy a vampire faster.

BLOOD BETWEEN LOVERS

Quite a contrast to immortality."

Jake stirred anxiety. Immortality defied comprehension.

Lara's new senses failed to resolve the conflict Jake's disclosure suggested. He wouldn't shoot her. She could escape before he unholstered his weapon. Jake wanted something else.

She wanted to confide in a friend. But Jake failed the acid test of trust. "Do you understand what life means to a vampire?" she asked.

"No need to floss?"

"I'm lonely," she said.

Jake shrugged and glanced up. "Bobby's not home?"

This time Lara appreciated the scent of a lie: Jake knew Bobby wasn't home. He'd come to see her.

"Big house. You're isolated. Go to work. Lots of people there," Jake said.

Jake is here with an agenda.

"I don't mean I'm lonely tonight. I mean, I'm lonely. I have Bobby, and that's great, but I thought I'd be chief by now. I need to plan my future." If Jake didn't recognize her guilt for her brother's death, she wasn't about to explain. Too much info empowered Jake.

"Calm down. Don't you get it, Dr. West? You've discovered the fountain of youth." He cocked his head. "Or in your case, the fountain of midlife."

The chair deflected the pillow Lara threw at his head.

Jake laughed. "The point is, Lara, you've got all the time in the world to figure out things. Relax."

"Bobby and I should go away for a while."

"Bermuda, Bahamas, come on, pretty mama . . ." Jake trilled a Beach Boys line.

"I'm serious."

"So am I. How does an all-expenses-paid vacation for two in sunny Bucks County sound?"

"You are serious." Lara hesitated. "Thanks for the suggestion. We just returned from Pennsylvania. I think we'll try someplace else."

Jake's smile expanded. "It's not a suggestion."

Lara leaned forward. "What do you call it?"

Jake pursed his lips, and his head swayed. "Think of it as a command from Dog."

Jake always claimed dyslexia. Lara had met his boss at Witness Protection headquarters.

"In case you haven't noticed, I've severed ties with the Witness Protection Agency. We destroyed the vampire who wanted me dead. Mutual services were executed, so the relationship was no longer necessary. I stopped taking orders from Dog, omnipotent or otherwise."

Jake had talked a human Lara into Witness Protection six months ago, but vampire insight processed his histrionics differently.

Jake inhaled an exaggerated breath. He glanced away, as if summoning courage, then gazed into Lara's eyes. "Dog guessed your reaction. She said what a shame it would be if the world discovered Bobby Eyre is a vampire." Jake paused.

"Bounty hunters will pour from the woodwork. No place in the world will be safe for the daytime sleep so necessary for your existence. Bobby won't be able to work or feed in a hospital. And your boyfriend can't kill, not even to survive. Too much of a moralist."

Jake understood vampires. The discussion wasn't about her future, it was about Bobby's: denying human blood—the essence of Jake's threat—denied immortality. Existence ended.

"Witness Protection ripped away my life once before."

Dr. Byra had just squelched her career at Jefferson Memorial and any chance to relieve her guilt. Lara's dream no longer conflicted with Jake's goal for Lara to deliver Bobby to Bucks County. Jake left no options: *protect Bobby*.

The stench of manipulation draped over Agent Plummer. Lara growled deep in her throat. The sound scared her more than it did Jake.

"What're they wearing in Bucks County this time of year?"

"One more thing. Dog said for you to arrange the trip with Bobby immediately."

CHAPTER 5

Meridian unzipped his pants, and Bobby groaned. He wanted to make love, but unworthiness infiltrated every thought. Meridian's fingers wrapped around him. He distinguished every pressure point of her body against his. Nocturnal vision revealed pleasure in her steel-blue eyes. An imperfection in the skin behind her left ear was a frozen reminder of her transformation.

Meridian stroked him. Eyes closed, mouths met, and his tongue traced across her fangs.

His fangs erupted without command; his attempts to retract them were in vain.

Waylaid by guilt. Distractions assailed him. The grandfather clock ticking in the foyer downstairs exploded against his senses. He forced the sound into the background. Eyes open, he ignored Meridian's embrace. He tried again, but his fangs remained immune to conscious control while he made love with Meridian. They had erupted and retracted instantly upon command in the hospital when he'd subverted Jake's agent with Vampirical Harmony.

Bobby fell back on the pillow. Meridian leaned closer, her breath a caress against his cheek and the faint scent of lavender a tickle in his nostrils. An ebony spider no bigger than the nail of his little finger spun a web in the corner.

Existence without Meridian seemed inconceivable, but immortality for both vampires demanded he teach her self-reliance, then cut her loose. And in the moment? He deemed himself unworthy. A vampire who couldn't retract. Bobby grunted.

Guilt over Marilyn's death had caused months of incisor dysfunction, and guilt had kept the emotional animal in abeyance until the human Meridian resurrected him.

Bobby thought about two women simultaneously—another field day for Freud. What was Bobby hiding from himself?

The relationships had exposed both women to similar circumstances: a vampire exercising appetites of the flesh and no memory wipe with either woman. But he always protected Meridian from Roberre, and from the

V-Harmony withdrawal that had led to Marilyn's suicide. He never shared the additional three stages of V-Harmony with Meridian, never acknowledged their existence to her.

Bobby ground his teeth. Meridian needed protection from Jake's threats.

"You must learn to seize human blood."

Meridian played tricks with his flesh. Jake Plummer played tricks with his mind. Meridian encouraged him to manipulate emotions. Jake forced him to manipulate Dr. Byra's decision.

I shattered Meridian's dream.

Bobby flooded into the present riding a flaccid wave of guilt—fangs out and nothing to suck.

"You know how important you are to me, right?" Meridian asked.

Bobby nodded.

"As your doctor"—Meridian kept her voice soft, but her tone teased—"I say don't worry about it." She twirled the hair behind his ear with her index finger. She leaned closer. "As your lover, I say don't worry about it." Her cheek nestled in her palm. "But as a dispassionate observer of vampires, I have to ask, how could this possibly happen? And what does a vampire do about—what did you call it?—incisor dysfunction?" She smothered a laugh.

"I know this isn't funny," Meridian continued with a wide grin.

Bobby groaned. He assumed she joked—only because she didn't understand the underlying issue. Meridian had refused to share her blood from the start, and Bobby didn't want her to feel remorseful about her decision, so he'd never explained to her the orgasmic coupling of blood and sex he relished in. And he certainly wasn't going to confess his betrayal. Guilt lodged in his soul, and apparently his soul lodged in his fangs.

"I mean, it could be worse. Suppose your fangs never erupted? You'd seduce a woman, edge close to her neck, and what? You'd have to use a syringe to suck blood, like a pretend vampire."

Bobby glared in pretend anger. He struggled not to laugh. "You know, as your patient, I can't say much for your bedside manner. As your lover, I can't say much for your in-bed manner. As a dispassionate observer of recently turned vampires, I have to ask, why can't you feed yourself?"

Bobby didn't mean to make Meridian feel inferior, and he grimaced, too late to retract the words. Freud would say he transposed his shortcomings onto her. His failure to instruct prevented her successful feedings. Another vain attempt to retract his fangs ignited a further outburst.

"Most vampires feed and kill," Bobby said. Was Roberre manipulating his responses? "They never learn to control themselves before they're overwhelmed by frenzy. I don't associate with monsters." Though it was painful to them both, he laid the foundation for the end of their relationship, whatever the reason.

Meridian shrank from him, the spark in her eyes extinguished. "I know you're disappointed." She swallowed, and the corners of her mouth curved down. "Would you leave me because I can't feed myself?"

"My inability to coax you to feed endangers your existence. You deserve a companion who's faithful, and a better teacher."

Meridian slid off the bed and knelt on the floor, her face pressed against the blanket. "I don't understand how I can race across the room so fast no one can see me, and how I can hear a whisper across the street. I'm a vampire, but I can't understand why I crave blood."

"You'll settle into your senses," Bobby said. His memories surfaced. "Vampirical self-discovery requires months of introspection. Give it time."

"Time doesn't pass for us. I don't understand that either." Bobby's thirty-something appearance belied a seven-hundred-year-old body. A tear rolled down Meridian's cheek.

"You'd be dead if I hadn't turned you."

"I am dead."

"You know what I mean."

"No, I don't. Can't you see? I don't understand being a vampire. The human we knew as Lara West is dead, but the consciousness of Lara West is still alive in Lara West's vampire body? I can't feed myself, and you're frustrated teaching me. Look what I've done." She pointed at his mouth.

"This has nothing to do with you."

"I'm the woman in your bed."

Did she guess the orgasmic connection or that he'd fed from Dr. Byra and manipulated her boss's decisions? Dysfunction rode on guilt. He hadn't made love to Meridian's boss, but he'd shared V-Harmony in exchange for blood and more effective mind control. He acted to protect Meridian.

Rationalization. Disloyalty pressed down on Bobby, keeping his fangs exposed; not infidelity with Dr. Byra but emotional betrayal with Agent Jake Plummer. Guilt resided in manipulation.

"We should plan a trip," Meridian said. "Escape from the hospital for a while." She spoke, but Bobby drifted with his thoughts. "What?"

* * *

Sunset over the nation's capital ushered in a mid-autumn night. A deep breath expanded Lara's lungs, and her eyes popped open. Urgency fed hunger—*consummate the vampire.* Increased stomach pain attested the frenzy deadline loomed. Violating the psychological time limit heralded the end of their relationship. Bobby's silence said so.

She sensed Bobby sneak out of the brownstone. To feed? Suspicion delivered a headache. She stopped counting how many times Bobby struggled with retraction.

I've emasculated his vampiric control. Geesh. Does Bobby need a psychiatrist, or do I?

Bobby refused to talk about incisor dysfunction, as if problems dissolved if ignored. Or his fangs would. His breath quickened when she touched him. His mouth ravaged hers, hungry for her surrender. Her body yielded to hands and mouth, though she continued to refuse to share her blood. And he remained unable to control his teeth. What was the connection between sex and blood?

If he no longer finds me appealing, will he leave sooner?

Doubt fed the insecure vampire, so unlike Lara West—human, the top-ranked surgeon in DC. Bobby visited the hospital last night and again tonight, and he'd used VH to feed.

Sleeping patients arouse him, but I don't? Will his fangs retract after he feeds from a stranger?

Distrust gnawed much like the hunger for blood. Why did Bobby feed twelve days before a full moon? He never fed early.

Uprooting Bobby had never interfered with his feeding cycle until two nights ago. His willingness to follow her to DC, then his enthusiasm to return to Bucks County, surprised her.

Maybe he thinks I'll be more relaxed there and accept what I've become.

Maybe he thinks he'll be more relaxed there and he won't suffer incisor dysfunction.

Either way, the idea of time for the two of them pleased her. Yesterday,

Jake neglected to share why he'd ordered them to Bucks County. Last time he wanted her to hunt vampires. Why expect anything different?

Her cell vibrated, as though on cue with the sunset. Lara unlocked the phone without answering.

"Twenty-four hours is enough time. Everything ready?" Jake asked.

"We're going tonight. I've taken another leave from the hospital," Lara said. "Told them I returned too soon after the fire, still emotionally drained." Robert Helstrom's flunky, Tony, had burnt down her house around her, and Jake's people never caught him. The new nightmares suggested recovery resided in self-denial. Maybe she really did return too soon. "Sounded hokey to me, but Dr. Byra accepted it."

"With Bobby's, umm, influence, of course she accepted it," Jake said.

"What do you mean?"

"The whole mind-control thing. Your boyfriend is quite accomplished. Why do you think Dr. Byra didn't retire after three years of planning? Do you believe continued employment is her idea?"

Lara's legs weakened, her thoughts swirled, and she plunked onto the edge of the bed.

"Bobby wouldn't use mind control on my boss."

Jake clucked. "Why do you imagine your boss has been meeting with your lover? To play doctor?"

"They haven't been meeting," Lara said. "There's no proof—"

"They have been meeting."

Nausea rode over her. She grappled with Jake's suggestion, but she believed in her lover. "They—"

"Have you checked her inner thigh?"

"What?"

"Her inner thigh. Isn't that where Bobby usually . . ."

"Meridian. What're you doing here?" Bobby's eyes widened, and his gaze drifted down and away. To stare at a wheelchair?

Guilt? Did I surprise him? Bobby's micro-expression exposed true feelings.

"I want a book from my locker, and there're a couple of people I want to say good-bye to," Lara said.

Under no circumstances would Bobby interfere with her greatest desire.

Jake played her. Why? She already agreed to go to Bucks County. Did Bobby meet with Dr. Byra? Tonight?

Bobby shrugged. "I'll be at the house. Don't forget, we need to leave by two a.m. to reach Langhorne before sunrise. I have another idea too. I'll teach you to use V-Harmony to feed from sleeping patients in the St. Mary Medical Center."

He disappeared like a wisp of cloud, a night creature enveloped by the dark. Lara clamped her teeth.

I have to rely on Bobby for survival training as a vampire.

She slipped along hospital corridors unseen. Doubt lingered, and she argued with herself as she roamed.

I trust Bobby.

The other voice in her head rejected self-deception. *Why is Dr. Byra working so many nights?*

Lara bit her lip. "Ouch."

Her fangs erupted without notice. Sweet sanguine fluid trickled into her mouth. She savored the taste but scowled at the familiar corridor. Wandering proved purposeful.

Lara froze outside her boss's office. No way did Bobby meet with Dr. Byra or influence her decisions. A glance at Dr. Byra unclothed would prove Bobby's innocence.

Lara couldn't charge in and demand to see her boss's naked leg. She needed a plan.

She tilted her head back; nostrils flared. The drops of blood she'd ingested heightened perception. A recognizable scent overrode all other senses, a scent uncharacteristically attached to this office, a subtle odor, like salt on a sea breeze.

Pins and needles ravaged her foot. Her gaze narrowed, and a low rumble escaped her throat. Lara fought the urge to kick in the door. She trembled. Violence played a role in vampirism, a role she didn't want to condone.

She tottered backward two steps and slumped against the tile wall. Her fingertips traced the cold surface. Restraint resided with the *Lara* she knew.

She gawked at the door handle, then sniffed again and formulated a plan. Penetrate the office, uncover Dr. Byra's thigh, and, if necessary, reveal Bobby's secret. An alternate explanation for his presence must exist.

Lara directed her thoughts, reaching forward. Bobby taught her this ability too. She sensed the woman's presence behind the façade. If Lara knew what to expect, it might help. Or not.

Awareness assaulted her. The elevator dinged in the distance, gurney wheels, footsteps, the antiseptic hospital odor; she read the fine print on the fire extinguisher thirty feet away.

The woman behind this door may've schemed with my lover. Why?

Her stomach knotted, different than frenzy pain. A lump rose in her throat.

Bobby wouldn't want another woman. He wouldn't influence Dr. Byra to keep me from achieving my goal.

Beyond the door, the woman's heart beat, blood pumped through arteries, and her skin exuded a hint of perfume Lara didn't like. The scent belonged to the enemy.

Lara glanced down the corridor at nurses working. No one saw her. With unfathomable speed she crossed the hall, opened the door, then closed it without a click.

Hunched over her workspace, reading, Dr. Byra didn't notice Lara. A dim desk lamp reflected off a laptop, leaving the office periphery in shadow. Lara stalked around the desk, within arm's reach.

Dr. Byra was a small woman, attractive at fifty-plus years. Raven hair caught in a barrette swept down her back. Tiny ears captured the thin arms of eyeglasses. Mint-green hospital scrubs accentuated olive skin. Her carotid artery pulsated.

Bobby had taught Lara to align breathing and heart rate with the victim. Beads of perspiration rose and fell on Dr. Byra's flesh, movement imperceptible to a human.

Hidden in shadows, Lara adjusted the thermostat. The room warmed, and she imagined a lover's kiss, a tongue tickling her neck, the sensual shiver delivered in his touch. She transferred the image into the psyche of the woman seated before her. A whimper escaped Dr. Byra, biofeedback in a bizarre experiment.

The doctor pushed back in her chair, eyes veiled, her hands massaging her chest as Lara imagined a lover's hands doing.

The next step grew more delicate . . . convince Dr. Byra to remove her scrub pants.

Lara recalled the first time Bobby made love to her. He'd stolen into her townhouse at dawn and surprised her after their night shift at the St. Mary Medical Center. The encounter proved the most erotic in her experience. The memory stirred her core.

Lara projected these feelings. Dr. Byra fondled herself and writhed; she wanted more, needed more, like Lara.

Lara slipped half a step closer.

Dr. Byra's eyes closed. She slid her hand inside the band of the scrub pants.

Lara didn't plan for the woman to achieve satisfaction. Lara needed the truth. Jake couldn't be right.

Breath matched breath, and the rhythm of their bodies entwined. Lara imagined the clothing slid down her hips.

Dr. Byra slipped out of the scrubs. Lara leaned in for a better view.

Her heart pounded with anticipation; no longer the anticipation of a lover's touch, but the fear embedded in discovery of an unwanted truth. Jake couldn't be right.

Bobby wouldn't betray her.

Dizziness invaded Lara. Senses rushed at her, unpredictable and uncontrollable.

The low hum of the laptop, a tiny imperfection on Dr. Byra's naked hip, the musky smell of sex, and the bitter taste as Lara's fangs raked across her tongue and blood coursed into her throat. The self-inflicted wound healed. The taste lingered.

Lara's hands trembled. A vein pulsed behind her ear. She forced the air from her lungs.

Dr. Byra's pants graced her ankles. She gurgled with pleasure, legs spread, the dark flesh of her inner thigh exposed.

CHAPTER 6

B obby completed preparations as best he could, uncertain how long they'd stay in Bucks County. Lying to Meridian remained impossible, as did telling the truth. Didn't leave many options. He anticipated Meridian's response.

Don't let the government intimidate you, especially not to protect me. She'd never sired a vampire, so the overwhelming urge to protect progeny was incomprehensible to her.

Time in Pennsylvania meant time to heal trust. He couldn't lose Meridian before he taught her to be self-sufficient. His fangs ached beyond endurance. Guilt fed hunger. He yearned for blood tonight, despite the mid-moon cycle. A quickie at the hospital would suffice. He'd be home before two a.m., and Meridian need never know.

The doorbell chimed an unwelcome intrusion.

Bobby tilted his head back and sniffed a scent he recognized. He grunted, hurtled out the bedroom window, and landed silently behind the interloper.

Bobby roared. "What do you want now?"

An unexpected appearance drew the desired effect.

Agent Jake Plummer jumped and twisted around, one hand over his heart. "I wish you wouldn't surprise me."

Bobby forced his fangs to erupt. "Wish all you want. Do I look like your fairy godmother?"

Gazes locked for a moment before the corners of Jake's mouth curled up. He glanced past Bobby, then reengaged. "Now that you mention it, I wish you'd invite me inside."

Bobby reacted too fast for Jake to counter. He seized Jake's throat, and hauled him off the ground, pinned against the front door.

Bobby glared into Jake's face. "You're not a nice man."

Jake struggled to speak through the neck vise. "Do you want . . . to do this . . . in view . . . of your neighbors?"

"It's midnight. My neighbors morph into mice. Too short to see out their windows."

Bobby sensed someone approach along the sidewalk. He glared at a solid woman, mid-fifties, with a man's military haircut, weapon drawn.

"I can rip out your throat faster than she can pull the trigger," Bobby said. An idle threat, but Jake didn't have to know that.

Jake signaled and halted his agent.

Bobby grumbled. He tried to probe Jake's mind without success. Whatever protected Agent Jake Plummer from Bobby's memory wipe a month ago must also protect him from a simple mind probe. Jake remained unreadable, but Bobby understood this wasn't a social visit.

Bobby dropped him. The front door kept Jake from falling. Jake massaged his throat but offered no complaints. He pointed over his shoulder with his thumb.

Bobby's awareness expanded. Jake arose a dangerous human opponent, but until this moment Bobby didn't realize how dangerous. Faced with death, Jake neither struggled nor objected. He observed Bobby, secure in his power. Jake coerced him by threatening Meridian, and now Jake wanted more.

Bobby struggled with Jake's manipulations, and for all his strength and all his speed and centuries of knowledge, he saw no way out. Jake's reason for Dr. Byra's un-retirement didn't matter. Dr. Byra's change of mind devastated Meridian, but Bobby acquiesced to protect his progeny's existence. He'd been naïve to think Jake would release him after one favor.

Jake crossed the foyer and studied the Monet hanging on the wall. He spoke without twisting his head. "You know, I'm not an expert, but I have a degree in art history. Monet happens to be my favorite artist. This sure looks like an original, but I've checked. It isn't in any of my textbooks. How'd you come by it?"

"He gave it to me."

"'He,' a collector?"

"The artist."

Jake glanced at Bobby. "Monet gave you this painting?"

"Tours of my art collection are by appointment only. Since Dr. Byra announced her un-retirement, Meridian has been overwhelmed. We're taking a vacation."

Bobby hesitated as though reading Jake's thoughts. Impossible for Jake to have checked his textbooks for a painting he's seeing for the first time.

He's been here. He's seen Meridian.

What role did Jake play in Meridian's decisions?

"Meridian wants to go to Bucks County. We're leaving tonight."

"I know. We'll finish our talk before Lara returns from the hospital."

"You know where she is?"

BLOOD BETWEEN LOVERS

Jake kept from smiling. "Since you'll be in Bucks County, I'd appreciate your help. My friend Jason Storm, owner of the In-Step Shoe Store, is under the influence of a vampire. Mind control. Something you know about.

"I want you to discover what's going on, free Jason, and stop the vampire doing this."

"I don't work for the government. Do it yourself."

Jake scrutinized Bobby for a moment, then aimed at the painting and pointed.

"Interesting manipulation of color and brush. Classic Monet."

Jake rode on the edge of intimidation.

Bobby rushed behind Jake and howled in his ear. Jake jumped at Bobby's sudden proximity.

"There's only one threat-to-Meridian card, and you've already played it."

Jake pivoted and backed up half a step. "I thought we agreed—no surprises?"

Bobby snarled. Fangs exposed. He backhanded Jake across the mouth and sent him sprawling. Jake grasped the marble bench and struggled to his knees. Bobby tossed him against the wall. Jake's hand twisted awkwardly behind him, and he winced before he crumbled under the Monet.

Bobby seized him by his throat again and planted Agent Jake Plummer as though he too were a painting on the wall. Bobby grumbled, low and guttural.

"No neighbors and no backup agents to see us."

Jake opened his mouth, but Bobby tightened his grip to prevent speech. Jake gurgled, gasping for breath.

Bobby bared his fangs in Jake's face. "I diverted Dr. Byra. Nothing else. Understand?"

Jake surveyed him, unable to speak, or unwilling.

Bobby squeezed and elevated Jake higher off the floor. "Understand?"

Jake managed to raise his eyebrows. Bobby accepted the concession and released him. Jake slid down the wall, chugging air.

"Leave," Bobby said.

Jake's legs steadied beneath him. He inspected his pinky, bowed in an unnatural direction.

He inhaled, then glided across the foyer with an air of assurance, riveting Bobby's attention. Jake opened the door and dropped a business card in one motion.

"What's that?" Bobby asked.

Jake glanced up, smiling. "The address of the shoe store. You're going to need it. Did I mention? I have other cards to play."

CHAPTER 7

Bobby spit out the London air. Not the first uterus Roberre had ripped from a victim in Whitechapel. Roberre's thoughts were not shared by Bobby. Why was his beast focused on a woman's womb? He used a knife instead of fangs to tear their throats, to cast suspicion onto a human. No talk of a vampire. Bobby couldn't abide the viciousness of killing. Prostitutes or not didn't matter. Two decades since the American Civil War—since Roberre had killed with such savagery. Bobby never found conscious control of the beast.

Nightmares, as eternal as existence, plagued his soul—Roberre's brutality was Bobby's failure. Decades. Centuries. His first true victim—their first victim—was unthinkable.

Bad enough British newspapers demonized Roberre. Death at least was fast, but desecration of bodies sickened Bobby.

He needed help. A new science and rumor of the best psychiatrist in Europe delivered Bobby—Roberre—to Vienna after his fifth London slashing in November of 1888.

The Vienna darkness wrapped a cold shroud around Bobby's shoulders. The breeze licked his skin and carried the faint strains of an orchestra. For the second evening, Bobby followed the same man out of a tavern. He strolled away with an acquaintance both nights—sounded like a colleague, just visiting. Josef Breuer. They discussed hypnosis and the interpretation of dreams. The man escorted Breuer to a hotel, then traveled away, still on foot, half a mile last night down cobblestone streets, home.

A woman and children in the house. Bobby didn't want to risk exposure—or harm.

This stretch of boulevard was empty, businesses closed, no pedestrians. Bobby stole behind the man, close enough for the man to hear a whisper. "I dreamed last night of drinking blood."

The man stopped, but hesitated before turning around. "Describe the container from which you drank," the man said, then pivoted.

The man's thick moustache and goatee hid his mouth. Shorter than Bobby, stout, his carotid artery pulsing above the collar of his starched shirt. "She was thirtyish, naked, and lacking most of her skin."

The man—much to his credit—blinked twice but didn't flinch. "You're suggesting you drank human blood? You mistake my inquiry. I didn't mean to question the source of blood, though that is very interesting. I meant in what container did you collect the blood and then drink from?"

"Mary Kelly was the name of the container. I drank first from her neck. You're a doctor. You don't need me to describe a neck, do you?"

The man tugged on his goatee and studied Bobby's eyes. In the dim streetlight, he'd never distinguish pupils and irises blended together. "Tell me, did you carry away her womb?"

"Why do you ask?"

"You're playing with me, sir. Even in Vienna we've heard this name, Mary Kelly. And Catherine Eddowes, Elizabeth Stride, Annie Chapman. Victims all of a horrific murderer, someone obsessed with his mother. How would you describe the relationship with your mother? No need to answer, sir. You have other issues."

"I require your services, Dr. Freud."

"Ah, so you do. Pretending to be a killer is a strange way to ask for help."

"A fair description of me: *strange*. I am stranger than you can possibly realize in this moment, though there is no way for you to help me unless you understand my nature."

Freud nodded his head. "What do you believe is the single strangest aspect of your life?"

"As a child, I experienced a child's understanding of who I was. I spoke to myself. Often. A practice that continued as I grew into a young man. I knew myself. I knew it was me speaking to me. After I turned, much to my horror, I discovered someone else talking to me."

"You mean inside your head? You turned into a different person?"

"What I turned into is a different discussion. The strangest aspect of my life is that there are two of me inside me."

"You are describing schizophrenia, a disturbance in the unconscious caused by unresolved feelings of homosexuality. My practice is based on psychoanalysis. Won't help schizophrenia. Schizophrenics don't listen to their analysts. You'd be better served talking with my colleague, Dr. Breuer. I can arrange—"

"I need your help, Dr. Freud."

Freud regarded Bobby with an air of indifference. "Tell me then about the relationship with your mother."

"I killed my mother."

"You're speaking metaphorically, or in riddles. If you have a sincere desire for well-being you must describe your true feelings."

"What I did to my mother was abominable," Bobby said. "You want the essence of my nature. Step under the street lamp so you may see my true strangeness, Herr Doctor."

Freud crossed his arms, steadfast.

Bobby edged into the light. "Come closer." His voice emerged deeper and hoarser. The words vibrated with the night music, and Sigmund Freud danced across the sidewalk.

"I will show you one thing," Bobby said, "and then if you insist you cannot help me, I will walk away, and you will never see me again. I'll only become your patient by request."

Freud waltzed closer, drawn by curiosity or Bobby's will. Didn't matter. Bobby sneered, displaying but a small section of his teeth.

"I commend your dentist," Freud said, "but I analyze minds, not mouths."

"Who do you commend for this?" Bobby curled back his upper lip, and revealed his fangs.

Freud rubbed his eyes, grabbed Bobby's arm, and twisted him into the light. "Remarkable." Perspiration suddenly beaded on Freud's forehead.

"Not attributable to my dentist. I am who I say, two personalities trapped in one body, and fortunately for us both, you're having this discussion with my human side. Still, you must experience firsthand my true nature." Bobby lunged at Freud's throat, and his fangs pierced Freud's throbbing artery.

Instead of struggling, Freud grasped Bobby's biceps and leaned into the embrace. Bobby did not puncture deep or suck hard, but blood poured into his mouth, and an orgasmic wheel of satisfaction and pleasure shot stars in his mind. He fought with urgency and overwhelming desire to push the man away before true harm. He pulled a handkerchief from a pocket and pressed it to Freud's neck, as much to hide the inciting sight as to staunch bleeding.

"The wound will heal quickly. Come." He dragged the startled man to a nearby bench. "I am a creature of two minds, two wills," Bobby said. "I—we—survive from one source alone. Unlike a human who requires food and water, I require only this." He licked blood from his lips.

"Immortality." Bobby answered the unspoken question. "What I've turned into is an immortal being." Bobby's knuckles blanched, latched on to the bench to constrain further sudden movement. His thoughts raged: drain the man, and the gush of blood would fill Bobby with vibrant existence—pieces of the man tossed into the Danube, carried away by the fierce current. No one would know.

"Immortality exists only in our children," Freud whispered, perhaps sensing imminent danger.

"I live on by the continued ingestion of human blood and nothing else." Bobby's voice changed again, deeper. "Immortality exists in this body, doctor. This mind." Bobby tapped the side of his head. "Not too great a price, I think. Though there is one additional fee."

Freud mopped, pulled the handkerchief from his neck, and examined the pittance of crimson. His fingers grazed the skin, nearly unblemished. "Just enough blood to convince me that wasn't hypnosis." Freud shook his head. "May I?" He gestured toward Bobby's mouth.

His fangs had not retracted—in fact, hadn't retracted since the night two months ago in London when he murdered three women. A vampire didn't require that much blood. Bobby snarled, baring the now constantly erupted incisors he used to puncture flesh. Freud cocked his head and studied, and for the first time tonight, flinched.

"My life," he said. "I don't wish to—"

Bobby fought for conscious control. He had enough blood for tonight and enough violence for—what? Ten lifetimes? For whatever reason, curiosity, contentment, or the strength of Bobby's will, Roberre acquiesced. "Your life is sacred, Herr Doctor. I swear an oath to protect you. I will never again take your blood."

Freud seemed little relieved. "I-I have a family. My wife . . . my children . . . *my* immortality. I have to know . . ."

"They are safe. All of them. I swear it again, as I swore to protect you, so I will protect your family."

"So when you said you dreamed of drinking blood . . ." His Adam's apple bobbed.

"I dream of that often, but I spoke those words with the hope of catching your attention."

"Those women in London . . ."

Bobby nodded his head. "Me and my beast. The inner demon I cannot control."

Freud's eyes crinkled, and he sneered. "How then do you claim to protect my life, my family?"

"It is a risk, granted, but small, I think. My demon is sated. We've taken more blood in the past two months than the previous two years. He needs no more in the moment, and I can certainly sense when the need arises again. I know what I can control and what I cannot. We—I—will leave Vienna, Dr. Freud, before the urge overpowers me. You have my promise. My hope, though, is that you can teach me to control my demon, to never allow him to kill again."

"And your mother?"

"Unspeakable what I allowed my demon to do, but yes, it is as I said."

"You must come to my home, my office first thing tomorrow morning." Freud fumbled a small card from a fob pocket. Instead of handing it to Bobby, the card fluttered to the sidewalk.

"What's that?" Bobby asked.

"My address. You're going to need it."

Bobby picked it up and handed it to Freud. "Keep your card. I know where you live. But I can't see you in the morning. There is an additional fee for life immortal. I am a creature of the night, and night only. I have to hide from the sunlight and sleep until the sun sets again."

"Where will you go?"

"I spent daylight today in the basement of an abandoned factory. Safe enough."

Freud regarded him with the same consternation as before. "You're worried about safety while you sleep? While the sun is up?"

"Yes."

"You're vulnerable then? Your immortality is in doubt?"

"Yes. Human blood is the only gateway to immortality; however, our bodies are not invulnerable. My neck can be severed. My heart can be pierced by a stake. People do hunt my beast. I want to think, at least, they do not hunt me."

"Come." Freud hooked his arm. "I have a basement, and as long as you'll allow me to lock you in, so that I may experience a measure of security for my children, you will not be disturbed nor need you worry while you sleep. I will protect you."

Freud fumbled the card in an attempt to return it to his pocket. The card fluttered again, but fell through a grate, and disappeared in the dark. Bobby stooped, but Freud pulled him up. "No matter. I have other cards to play."

CHAPTER 8

"Clear on your role?" Jake lowered his chin and peered at her.

Lara rubbed the nape of her neck, secure with Bobby until tonight, their last in DC. He'd violated her trust. Bobby fed from her boss with VH.

Blood and sex, but not mind control. Lara refused to accept his role in Dr. Byra's un-retirement, despite Jake's suggestion to the contrary. Lara gritted her teeth.

Jake cocked his head.

Lara sucked in her cheeks. "I deliver Bobby to his home in Langhorne, Pennsylvania, or you expose his existence to hundreds of vampire slayers."

He handed her a key. "For your townhouse. You'll find everything as you left it. In case you need time alone."

"In case I can't face Bobby with my guilt?"

"One more thing," Jake added.

"I'm not doing enough betraying my lover?"

"Stay away from the In-Step Shoe Store."

"What?"

"You heard me." Jake grimaced.

"What's wrong?" Lara asked.

Jake raised his crooked pinky. "A minor scrape, but you should see the other guy. Knocked him for a loop."

"I'm more concerned about you."

"Why?"

"I'm still a physician."

Jake craned his neck and examined her fangs.

Lara ignored him. "Dislocated?"

He nodded.

"Must hurt."

Jake exaggerated the head movement.

"Want me to fix it?"

"Nah."

"Don't be such a baby."

"I've already been to the ER. The doc said he was seventy percent sure he could pull it into place. Seventy percent."

"Not good enough odds for you?"

"He said pulling it may hurt more in the moment, but I'd feel better afterwards, if he succeeded. And he said if I didn't like the odds, I should try an orthopedic specialty hospital."

"Why don't you?"

"No time." His face contorted again.

"Didn't they give you something for the pain?"

"I can't be loopy right now. I need my mind clear."

"Souvenirs of the fight?" She indicated his bruised cheek and swollen lip, then rushed away.

"Where're you going?" Jake asked.

Lara returned and thrust a Perrier bottle into Jake's hands.

"Kind of dark for water," Jake said.

"It's the only thing in the refrigerator, and you need something cold to keep the swelling down. Press it against your cheek."

Jake raised the bottle. Lara grasped his injured hand.

"What're you doing?"

"Don't worry, I'm just looking."

Jake inhaled and pressed the blood container against his flesh. Lara probed his pinky, twisted, and jerked hard. Jake howled and dropped the bottle. Lara snatched it out of midair.

Jake shook his hand. "You said you were just looking."

"That was then."

Crease lines on Jake's face smoothed, and his eyes brightened. He flipped his wrist back and forth, staring at his finger. "Looks seventy percent normal. Doesn't hurt, either."

"You're welcome."

Jake's features deadpanned. "Doesn't change anything. Bring Bobby to Bucks County. Stay away from the shoe store."

The palm lock scanned Lara's right hand, and the first front door of Bobby's five-year Langhorne residence ticked open. The second front door opened on a left-palm scan.

Jake had pressured her to deliver Bobby to Pennsylvania now.

BLOOD BETWEEN LOVERS

Why?

The third door opened with a key. Lights flared in the wood-beam foyer. She paused by the handwritten, autographed text of *Romeo and Juliet*. She shook her head; Bobby once spoke with the author. Bobby had lived how many lifetimes? Kept how many secrets?

They'd arrived in Langhorne before sunrise this morning and slept all day. Bobby had woken her when the sun set. He headed for the St. Mary Medical Center to scout for blood. *A lie?*

She flipped a wall-mounted control panel and typed a brief alphanumeric sequence. Metallic shutters slid open, and outside spotlights backlit the stained-glass windows of the converted church.

She paused again, room center. Her senses absorbed the surroundings in a way she never before experienced. Bobby's scent—salt on a sea breeze—attached to everything. A lingering tingle—unexplained. She cocked her head and tried to concentrate. Lara strode from room to room, uncertain what she sought, but testing feral perceptions in familiar territory.

Impressions of this house differed from the DC brownstone. The prickle remained unexplained. Extensive renovations accommodated nocturnal life. Whatever the reason, this house reflected security she didn't sense in DC.

Stairs spiraled close to the four-story ceiling. At the end of a dark hall, she tilted her head back and sniffed. Her lover . . . and someone else.

Beyond the enormous bedroom skylights, the sliver moon frowned, one day past new.

A twinge twisted her stomach. Hunger gnawed. Her fangs erupted, and her cheeks throbbed. Lara scoffed. Fangs appeared of their own accord instead of on command.

She stalked around the bedroom and chased the second familiar scent loitering across her path until recognition struck.

"Philippe."

She unlocked her cell and tapped the number from memory. Philippe answered on the first ring.

"I can't believe it's been a month," Lara said.

"Lara? I've been dying to chat, but I didn't want to bother you guys. Are you settled in DC? Should I call you 'chief'?"

"We're in Langhorne. I—"

"I can't believe you're here," Philippe said. "I'm on the night shift. Let's do lunch tomorrow. You are staying for a day or two, right?" Philippe clucked.

"Silly me. You can't do lunch. Bobby's with you, isn't he? Let's meet for an early dinner." He sighed. "No, no, you guys don't eat. At least not the way I mean, and I don't want to watch you feed. Why don't you guys come here? No, maybe it would be safer for you if I come there? Where is there? Are you at Bobby's? Can I come over?"

Lara grinned at the excitement in his voice, or was it the crystallization of eternal desire in her thoughts?

"Slow down. We're here for a while. At Bobby's. Why don't you stop by before your shift tomorrow? I have plans tonight."

Eternity calls. I have to save my relationship.

Philippe had invigorated her while they'd talked, but now dizziness latched on. She stumbled descending the steps. Her forehead throbbed. She curled her fingers, unable to squeeze tight. Her knees buckled, and she leaned against the wall for support.

"Damn it."

Hunger chewed her innards. Craving for blood constricted her throat and urged action. She longed for human blood, not the bottled stuff Bobby stored in the refrigerator for her. She'd need a swig or two, though, to follow through with her plan.

She staggered toward the kitchen.

I can do this.

Bobby fed at the hospital, a prudent place for a vampire to hunt. Bobby convinced her humans weren't as stupid as they used to be about desanguinated bodies in the community. Mercenaries would swarm over the first sign of excessive unnatural blood loss. Wars and gang violence helped conceal vampires, but their natural feeding ground evolved into hospitals, where excessive blood loss was expected and easy to hide.

Lara guzzled from the Perrier bottle filled with blood. Bobby had crossed off *Natural Springs* and written *Full-bodied*. Vampire humor. Cold blood rejuvenated Lara in a way Philippe's conversation failed to do. Strength returned to her limbs, and an image of Popeye popping a can of spinach flashed in her thoughts. She smirked.

A chill snaked down her spine and hardened her resolve. Hunger infected every organ, every sensation driven by the urge to drink warm human blood direct from the source. She raced with the swiftness of an unearthly hunter, out of the house and across the field, enveloped in darkness.

The night offered comfort within its cloak. Bats flitted around the sky. The sliver moon lingered behind a cloud. Lara approached the St. Mary Medical Center undetected. She tilted her head back and sniffed. What if Bobby still hunted in the hospital tonight? She'd avoid him. Feeding would be a personal accomplishment. Senses integrated into decisions.

She'd avoid anyone who might recognize her. Feeding successfully meant maintaining anonymity. She didn't understand VH enough to use it. Bobby's idea of feeding from a sleeping female patient made her nervous, but feeding from a man—awake or asleep—would be fraught with anxiety.

The glass doors leading from the garage to the main corridor glided open. Construction cones still blocked the new wing. Where did the hospital hide psych patients in the meantime? Bobby always found them on the maternity ward.

No lock protected the administration door, and no security guards roamed this end of the building. Vampire vision led her to the desk of Marty Connor, friend of Nurse Meridian Jones. The vinyl chair radiated warmth as though someone sat in it not long ago. Lara glanced at the wall clock. 12:10 a.m., too late for administrators to work. She refocused.

Hospital computers never shut down. She woke Marty's from hibernation and signed on using his password, an inadvertent disclosure. *ILOVESUE.* His wife.

An information search counted nanoseconds. Psych patient Catherine Cox, admitted yesterday, resided in room 437.

The office light snapped on.

"What're you doing?" a voice demanded.

CHAPTER 9

L ara jerked. *My first night hunting alone, and I'm discovered by a security guard.* No one else patrolled hospital offices this late.

"Who are you?" the voice challenged.

Lara leered and spun around. Her fangs erupted. She recognized the New England accent and the reddened, weathered face of a friend. Balding on top, trousers hiked up high on a potbelly, skin on the back of his hands wrinkled. One more thing: a faint odor tickled her palate. A drop of blood coagulated on Marty Connor's fingertip. Her lips fluttered. Of course. Diabetic, blood-sugar test. Warm seat—Marty's night to work.

Remove all trace of my presence. Her breathing synched with Marty's. Her pulse matched his.

"Meridian." Marty beamed. "I'm so glad to see you. How'd you know I worked late tonight?"

Lara steered her thoughts into Marty's mind.

Marty answered for her. "Of course, someone at the front desk told you. Heard you'd gone to Washington, same time another employee left. Bobby Eyre. Don't know where he went. Sorry I didn't say good-bye to you, seems you left in a bit of a hurry. I remember mentioning it to Sue. She was disappointed we never invited you for dinner."

He stepped closer, grinning from ear to ear. "Say, if you're visiting for a few days, maybe you'll come for dinner now? You know Sue, in bed by eight, so it'll have to be early. How about day after tomorrow, around four?"

Marty glanced at the wall clock. "Oops, it already is tomorrow. Well, you know what I mean, Friday afternoon around four." He hesitated as though he wanted to say something else but lost the thought.

Lara drifted close to him, her gaze locked on his. Her voice emerged as a murmur, but the words danced in the air.

"You won't remember this meeting," she said.

Marty's persona glazed.

"Continue working," Lara added.

Marty meandered away to find his seat. Lara escaped, unconvinced she'd altered his memory. No time to stick around and find out.

At the end of the hall, she ducked into a dark alcove. Her fangs ached.

Be careful.

She glanced left. A nurse pushed the elevator call button, then disappeared into the tiny cabin. If Lara rode the elevator to the fourth floor, someone might see her when the doors opened. Safer to climb stairs, but once she entered the stairwell, the doors locked from the outside, access to hospital main floors denied without the aid of security.

Limited options remained.

Flying. *Really?* She felt strong enough to climb the side of the building, though.

The back driveway was deserted. An open window on the fourth floor grabbed her attention, perhaps the same window Bobby used to enter the hospital tonight.

The brick wall presented no difficulty, and she slipped into the vacant room. She closed the window, and noted the room number.

Hospital aromas struck with familiarity: antiseptic and chlorine overridden by a tantalizing sanguine whiff. Lara poked her head out the door. The empty corridor boosted confidence. She stole toward room 437 and her first unaided taste of blood.

One not-quite-new mother screamed in a birthing room. The soothing voice of a nurse echoed along the hall. Lara angled the long way, past the nursery.

She stopped in a recess, then rushed across the hall and hesitated outside the room of Catherine Cox. Lara's fangs erupted, on command for the first time. She salivated, and a sneer curled her lips.

Her heart pounded. Lara laughed. Palpitations—typical for a vampire—were an enthralling signpost of the human race.

Her prey slept in a drug-induced stupor, courtesy of hospital protocol. Lara edged her breathing into synch with Cathy's slow, uniform respiration. She slipped into the room as their heartbeats aligned. She closed the door silently, and darkness cloaked her in safety.

Lara trained her thoughts into the mind of her first real meal.

Her tongue dragged across her fangs, ripping the flesh and allowing the sweet elixir of existence to trickle down her throat. Senses smoldered. Cathy slept.

Darkness swirled around Lara as she approached the bed. Cathy lay on her back, her wrists strapped to the bedrails, the bleached hospital sheet rising and falling over her breasts with each breath. Petal-pink nail polish glistened in the dim light. Jewelry removed. Fading skin on a narrow band of her unadorned ring finger indicated an ex-husband, somewhere in the night. Cathy's lips parted, dried and cracked, and rapid eye movements behind her eyelids attested to the dream world.

Lara tugged the sheet off her victim. Her thoughts invaded Cathy's mind: *Sleep*.

Cathy's head twisted, and she mumbled unintelligible words. Lara froze.

Faint sounds from a birthing room indicated new life pushed close. Nothing else stirred.

The sheet peeled, Cathy lay exposed. *Feed where the bite marks are least likely to be noticed—the underside of the breast, the sole of the foot, the inner leg.* Blood flowed easiest in the femoral artery. Ankle straps lay limp at the foot of the bed. Attached and tightened, they'd keep Cathy's legs spread.

Lara shook her head. The inner thigh seemed too awkward. Didn't feel right to truss up her victim. And she could only imagine someone biting the sole of her foot—had to be painful. Decision made.

Cathy snuggled in dreamland. The tiny flare of Cathy's nostrils with each breath helped Lara maintain alignment. Cathy's dirty-blond hair smattered the pillow. The hospital gown draped below her knees, and the pale flesh of her legs disappeared beneath its folds.

Lara's fangs throbbed. A bout of dizziness swirled the room. She gripped the bedrail and inhaled deep into her lungs. Pins and needles stung her right foot, and she wiggled her toes.

The flesh around her knuckles whitened. She pinched the cotton gown and eased it toward Cathy's waist.

Anticipation spread this moment over the past month.

The impending deadline—feed or surrender consciousness—compelled action. Bobby said he'd abandon a hapless vampire. Lara had abandoned her brother in the ER, and he'd died. Queasiness eased into her stomach. Abandoned like her brother, how would she survive?

Light reflected off Cathy's pallid knees.

Lara's sight blurred, and she shook her head to clear it. No harm would come to the sleeping patient. Lara would drink blood, no more than a Red Cross donation, and since Cathy remained asleep, no need to wipe memory. Bobby would be proud of Lara's accomplishment.

Myriad arteries stretched down Cathy's legs and spread upwards across her belly. Lara fought a sudden urge to attack. She imagined her fangs buried in the ashen skin, limitless warm blood flowing into the mouth of a suckling, a newborn in the world of darkness. She stirred the prospect of feeding until sated. Her heart rate ticked up.

Lara caressed a stomach vein. *Yours by right of existence.*

Her palm cupped the gentle curve of Cathy's breast and lifted. Cathy's nipple hardened in her sleep, enticed, teased without teasing. Veins throbbed, pale blue in the soft light, and beckoning, tempting Lara to eternity. Resolve to stop with a donation faltered. Her heart beat faster.

She leaned over her victim. The intensity in her mouth, in her throat, in the pit of her stomach, drove her forward, Cathy's flesh but a whisper from Lara's parted lips. Her heart raced.

Compassion infringed.

Doctor, do no harm.

She squeezed her eyes shut and fixed on her identity.

I am Lara West. Dr. Lara West.

A brain-piercing scream rent the room.

Lara jerked her head and gasped, fangs bared.

Eyes open, Cathy screamed louder, her breast a small boundary between a face-to-face encounter.

The walls spun around Lara. Her legs weakened. Cathy inhaled between shrieks, and her breath came ragged. Cathy's heart thumped, long out of synch with her stalker. Lara lost control.

She'd pursued her prey with coldhearted intention. She'd discovered her room, scaled the building, and bared Cathy's breast. What had she become?

Escape, cried an inner voice.

Legs refused to obey. Lara collapsed. The door banged open. She imagined a nurse charged in and flipped on the light, illuminating Lara's fangs. The imaginary nurse yelled for help.

"Come quick. We've caught ourselves a hapless vampire."

The entire fourth-floor nursing staff, along with one newly ordained mother in a wheelchair cradling a baby, and one tall, handsome man with dark hair who answered to the name of "Bobby," poured into the room, the new mother armed with a wooden stake.

"Drive it through her heart," the nurse cried.

"She has no heart. She's not human," the mother answered.

"Give me the damn stake," Bobby said. "I'll rid myself of this impotent curse."

CHAPTER 10

"**M**eridian." Bobby caught her head before she hit the floor.

The woman strapped to the bed screamed. Bobby scooped Meridian into his arms, leaned close to the woman, and hissed her into silence, then dashed from the room with unnatural speed.

"We can't go," Meridian said, "I have to feed . . ."

"No time now," Bobby said. "A raving psych patient will draw attention. We'll come back tomorrow night."

Meridian wriggled in his grasp, strength sapped. "Let me go." Her eyes flashed the lavender-red glow of a feral hunter fighting for immortality.

Bobby had already arrived at the fourth-floor escape room. "You do know feeding is easier if your volunteer stays asleep, right?"

Meridian whacked his shoulder.

"Tomorrow night I'll teach you how to keep a human sleeping while you take what you desire. For now, we need to escape from the hospital before someone comes looking for us."

He settled Meridian on the end of a bed, then slid the window open. He crouched to lift her again, but she stopped him.

"I can manage."

Bobby paused. "We're on the fourth floor. We need to fly."

He didn't mean to be harsh. Scuffling far down the hall warned someone approached. Bobby seized Meridian's hand and pulled her up.

"Either way, we need to leave now."

Her eyes declared she didn't wish to surrender, but she wrapped her arms around his neck. He cradled her, and they disappeared into the night.

She needed blood, and he grasped a tacit understanding she didn't want his help, but necessity demanded action.

The sanctuary home opened to him with palm locks, the third door without the key. He cradled Meridian onto the altar sofa. She scrunched up and hugged her knees.

Bobby found a Perrier bottle in the refrigerator labeled *Not So Natural Springs* and delivered it to her. She yanked the bottle from his hands and gulped.

"How'd you know where to find a psych patient?" he asked.

Meridian didn't answer. Her eyes were half-lidded and she twisted the blood-bottle around and around.

Bobby paced the room, inspecting artifacts. Meridian would talk but wouldn't want to be scrutinized.

"I used to ask Marty Connor. Records of all the new patients crossed his desk, and he always seemed willing to chat."

Meridian recapped the bottle, half-empty. She swiped at her lips with her wrist. "I did the same thing, only I asked his computer. I climbed the back of the hospital and entered through an open window."

Didn't matter she omitted details. He needed Meridian to build confidence.

"You stole into her room without being seen. A noteworthy accomplishment in a hospital this size, even in the middle of the night."

Meridian cried. A single tear at first, then a stream followed.

Bobby swept her into his arms again and held her pressed against his chest. She clung to his shoulders as sobs raked her torso.

He carried her up the spiral staircase and lowered her onto their bed. He rubbed her ankles, pausing to remove her shoes.

Crying slowed, and her gaze found his. Nothing more for him to say until she spoke.

"I wanted to surprise you," she said. "I wanted to prove I was self-sufficient without bottled blood."

He stroked her cheek.

"I'm a burden. I dragged you to Washington; now I've dragged you back to Bucks County.

"You've been trying to teach me, and I haven't been able to learn. I need to run the ER at Jefferson. After that, if learning to feed requires months or years, at least I'd be free of the nightmares and I can finally move on with my life. My eternal existence. My human life has been ripped away again. Please tell me you didn't have anything to do with Dr. Byra changing her mind about retirement."

The question in masquerade was as close as anyone ever came to driving a stake into Bobby's heart. Passion radiated from him such as he'd never experienced. Meridian all but accused him of the betrayal he'd committed. It didn't matter he deceived her to protect her. Betrayal lingered like blood from a corpse. The bitter taste suffused his throat.

His inability to teach Meridian to fend for herself stripped her dignity as a vampire. His inability to retract his fangs when they made love stripped her dignity as a woman. He refused to devastate the dignity she maintained as a human being.

"Hunger overwhelmed me. She was alone in a secluded office—no patients accessible. I fed from her, but I had nothing to do with Dr. Byra changing her mind."

* * *

Liar, said a voice in Lara's head, a voice she refused to believe.

* * *

Relief oozed from Meridian's face. Bobby sighed. She was unable to detect his lie, and now she melted into his arms.

Her mouth found his, and her tongue wedged between his lips. She gasped between clenches, "I want to feel you inside me."

Bobby murmured deep in his throat. Her hands clung to him, her lips pleaded, and her eyes devoured what remained of his soul. Tingling raced across his flesh, his breath quickened, fangs erupted. What had he done to deserve this woman? Didn't matter. Surrendering to her remained the only option in the moment. Teaching her to feed then cutting her loose remained the only option for tomorrow. Demands of eternity.

Chance flung them together, circumstances left no choice but to bring her across, to give her the gift of immortality, thus signaling an end to their romantic relationship, as soon as she proved self-reliant. He'd acted out of love. No premeditation brought them to this path, but he betrayed her by choice. Jake might have been the instigator, but betrayal was nonetheless Bobby's act.

"Take me." Meridian's husky voice wove an erotic dance.

Bobby ripped the clothes from her body, stretched her arms above her head, and ravaged her breast with his mouth. She moaned, and a flush surged across her flesh. Bobby groaned in response, his sexual frustration compressed into this moment, these actions.

BLOOD BETWEEN LOVERS

"Take me now, Bobby."

He jerked his shirt over his head and peeled off his pants. His eyes languished in the beauty of her nakedness, and passion exploded in his brain. Humanity hammered in his chest. His body cramped with excitement.

She has to learn before she's overwhelmed by frenzy. If I can't teach her, she'll find another vampire who can. Either way, I lose her forever. Why did I betray her trust?

The eruption ripped from his loins. His lips parted, his heart swelled, and his extended fangs remained non-part of their sexual experience, his orgasm emasculated mid-explosion.

CHAPTER 11

H unting expedition. Lara read the huge sign on the lower bridge, a quarter mile below the Calhoun Street Bridge they crossed: *Trenton Makes, the World Takes.* Hunger nipped at her throat. Concerned about the psychological consequences, Bobby insisted they try again. Tonight. Unsuccessful in the hospital, unsuccessful in bed—failure bred insecurity.

"Trenton, New Jersey. Bad town," Bobby said. "Not sure what they're making anymore, but we qualify as part of the world."

"What does that mean?"

"Trenton hosts an abundance of homeless people. You can practice feeding."

"I'm not taking advantage of the unfortunate."

"We'll trade a meal for a meal. You drink a pint of blood, I'll shop for a pint of orange juice and a sandwich. A symbiotic relationship. Fortunate, unfortunate, you're an equal-opportunity night creature."

The metal grid of the bridge whined beneath the tires.

"Convenient of Jake to leave you this car."

"SUV," Lara corrected.

"A car isn't even a car with Jake. I don't trust him."

Bobby directed her along the Delaware River, then around the War Memorial Building, Market Street, the courthouse on Broad Street. Traffic lights blinked red or yellow.

"Not many people out at this hour," Lara said.

"Wait another three blocks."

They climbed a hill, and streetlights evaporated.

"Park here." Bobby pointed. "Not the best place to leave a car—excuse me, SUV."

"Why?"

"May not be here when we return."

"The bad town has a bad neighborhood?"

Lara checked to make sure the fob locked all the doors. She peered into the dark as they crossed the pavement and angled onto Academy Street. Glazed eyes gawked from the gloom. A few people escaped the darkness, the lucky ones with homes. Others sprawled on the sidewalk, either in drunken stupors or in starvation stupors.

"Hard to believe this is America," Lara said.

Bobby chuckled.

"That's not funny. These poor people—"

"I know what you mean," Bobby said. "I'm laughing because a vampire said it."

He shoved the small of her back. "On the right, fifty yards, a gap between the buildings—a man, alone, leaning against the stoop. Push him into the shadows and feed there. No one on the street will see."

Lara bit her lip. Feeding this way raised qualms. Bobby hurried her along the uneven sidewalk. The stench of uncollected garbage and un-bathed humans mingled in the still night. Bobby seized Lara's arm and jerked her to a stop. He tilted his head and snorted. His fangs erupted, and his eyes flashed.

"What's wrong?" Lara asked.

"Change of plans," Bobby said. He aimed her towards the steps of the Trenton Public Library.

"I have enough reading material." Lara's nose twitched. "What's that smell? It's not human or trash."

"I'll show you. Remember the odor, though. It's always distinctive."

Lara followed him around the side of the building.

"We have to climb to the roof," Bobby said.

Ledges, protrusions, old bricks provided plenty of handholds. Lara hopped over the metal railing at the top of the century-old building. Bobby froze in the middle of the roof, hands on hips, gaping. She stepped around him to see. A cross.

A head staked on top and one on each end, faces frozen in grotesque pain, mouths open.

"A ritual?" Lara cringed but studied the scene.

"Our ritual."

"A vampire did this?"

"An older, dominant vampire. These are vampires." He pointed at an open mouth. "Notice the missing fangs. This is how an elder marks territory if another vampire invades his feeding ground. The dominant vampire beheaded them, pulled their fangs, and staked them as a warning to any other vampire who trespasses."

"Are older vampires always more powerful?"

"My abilities have expanded with centuries, but there's no vampire school.

How would I know? I can only extrapolate from experience."

"How far back does your experience extend?"

"To the thirteenth century."

"How old is the oldest vampire?"

"Aren't you listening? Vampires don't collect in groups and tell stories."

"There must be a first vampire, right? Vampires didn't evolve like humans. And curses and magic couldn't be the explanation for an entire culture. Vampires had to arise from genetic mutation. Nothing you've heard of?"

"There's one legend. The first vampire was Eve. She sired three vampires, and all vampires since were sired in one of those three lines."

"Whose line are you in?"

"You really aren't paying attention. There's no way to know."

"Do you know who sired you?"

"Temüjin."

"Do you ever see him? Do you talk with him?"

"He was destroyed not long after I was made." Bobby's nostrils flared. "That's odd. There're three heads, but I smell the blood of four vampires."

"The dominant vampire responsible?"

"I don't think so. This territory is claimed. We're not feeding here. Let's go."

Lara scaled down the side of the library after Bobby. Teenagers huddled around their SUV. Bobby bellowed, and the group pivoted in unison, and spread out, like a well-trained platoon.

"Did that man growl at us?" a chunky girl asked.

A short, wiry boy sauntered forward, his baggy pants hanging off his ass, the crotch draped to his knees, but he displayed the mask of a predator. An eight-inch, thin blade glinted in the streetlight as the boy tossed the weapon one hand to the other. The boy's gaze settled on Bobby, Lara summarily dismissed.

"'Scuse me," the boy said. "Janelle thinks you was growlin' at us. That's rude. We was just admirin' your suburban assault vehicle." The boy slipped closer.

Bobby remained poised.

"You owe us an apology," the boy continued. "Tell ya what. Toss me the keys. I'll take your woman for a ride, and we'll call it even."

Voices chuckled behind him.

BLOOD BETWEEN LOVERS

Bobby hid Lara, but she stepped around him and shimmied, tempting.

"Sorry, I'm afraid I'd wear you out," she said.

Laughter swelled, and the boy whipped his head around to silence his gang.

Bobby rushed to within arm's reach of the leader.

The boy wheeled and flipped the knife hand to hand. "A hero?" the boy asked.

Bobby plucked the weapon from midair. He stepped back, twirling the blade over his head. Gasps replaced chuckles.

"No heroes here. I'm the state weapons inspector." He flung the blade high into the sky.

"What the—"

"If the knife is well balanced," Bobby said, "when you toss it in the air it should come down butt-first." He glanced into the murky night and extended his arm, palm up. The knife thudded into his hand.

The group backed up in unison. Their leader didn't flinch.

"Not bad." Bobby shrugged. He hoisted the knife and examined it. He raised his other hand and sliced a line diagonally across the palm, drawing a thin streak of blood, then lapped the tip of the knife and his hand. "There are things in the night badder than you."

Eyes in the crowd widened, and the group backed up another step, creating more of a gap between them and their leader.

Lara grasped Bobby's arm. "You missed a drop." She kissed his wrist and licked.

Bobby winked and edged away. "If it's a good knife"—he flipped the blade end into his palm and gripped it—"it'll pierce a tire from a distance." He flung it across the street. The blade drove cleanly into the rear tire of a beat-up Chevy. "You can't flatten a tire quickly without a sharp knife," Bobby said to Lara.

He guided her elbow and escorted her to the closest SUV door. The crowd parted.

"Climb over the console," Bobby said. He bowed to address the group. "Remember to visit your dentist for regular checkups."

Blank expressions gawked back.

"A sharp weapon will never replace sharp teeth." His fangs erupted, and he jumped forward and roared.

The gang scattered, except for the scrawny leader. Bobby rushed into his space.

"Now I've growled at you. I apologize."

CHAPTER 12

F reud's second-floor office expanded as if a wall separating rooms had been torn down, creating a large space with an arched ceiling, much like a chapel. A king-sized desk commanded the width of the room in front of a window, papers strewn about—a handful fastened in files, others in random display, all headed with names and filled with scratchy handwriting. A high-backed, cushioned chair matched the grandiose desk, and another less formidable chair faced them both. The opposite wall housed a couch with stuffed cushions and a flowered brocade. A wooden bench rested at a close angle, much less ostentatious, though still with a sense of comfort and command.

Freud locked the door behind them. "For privacy," he said. "We will not be disturbed."

Freud's eyes danced with eagerness and the joy of great discovery. "Sit." He gestured Bobby toward the couch. "You may stretch out if you feel more relaxed that way."

Freud snatched a notepad, half-filled with scribbling, and leafed to a blank page. "I have spent the day in research," he said. "I cancelled my other appointments. There is a dearth of authoritative information concerning . . . your kind. You do refer to yourself as a vampire?"

He didn't wait for Bobby to answer. "Myths, half-truths, pure nonsense. There are no experts on night creatures. No one has interviewed a vampire." Freud gestured toward Bobby. "Last night, I confess, I was startled, and my mind agape. Tonight, upon reflection, I recognize the tremendous opportunity with which I'm presented. Schizophrenia of a different nature requires new terminology.

"Either way, you must drink blood, if I understand correctly? Either side of your personality?"

"The urge for survival is defined only by blood," Bobby said.

"Hematophagophrenia. An accurate descriptor. The battle of split wills in a creature, excuse me, person who feeds upon blood." Freud grew silent for several minutes. "Forgive me this, you must understand, I am a scientist first. I believe empirical evidence." He rubbed his unblemished neck. "Incredible.

BLOOD BETWEEN LOVERS

I know now persons of myth–vampires–exist. No proof, however, exists for immortality. While there is no transparent reason for you to lie, the aspect of immortality, according to Darwin, is far less credible than a divergent species of man who subsists on blood instead of food and water. Mutation, Darwin called it."

"I'm sure I don't know enough science to comment. Rumor among my kind, whom I rarely encounter, insists there exists a first vampire, a woman, never of two minds. She sired three vampires, all from humans, and all other vampires descend from one of those three lines. So all vampires after *Eve* have two personalities."

"You can trace your ancestry back to . . .?"

"My sire. Temüjin. He never spoke of his sire, so I know nothing of how he came to exist."

"When was this?"

"In 1227. When I was but a child around the turn of the thirteenth century, my mother and I were taken prisoner by invading Mongols, thrown at the feet of their khan, Temüjin. I broke free of the guard and raced between Temüjin and my mother. 'Don't you hurt her,' I shouted. By the grace of his will, or the guilt of his conscience–his mother had been kidnapped and forced into marriage and serfdom and so bore Temüjin–Temüjin never forced himself upon my mother.

"Concerns of court often transpired in the open, casually, around fires and only at night. Before the sun rose, Temüjin would retire to his tent, enormous in height and breadth. Surpassing our nineteenth-century circus tent. Rumor passed quickly of Temüjin's need to sleep all day. What man slept all day? We lived in his camp one week before curiosity overcame childhood fears.

"My mother stood otherwise occupied, and I stole past Temüjin's guards and crawled beneath the fabric of his tent only to discover a narrow passage lined with torches encircling a second tent inside the first. No guards protected the passage, so I slipped through the slit and discovered yet another narrow passage encircling another tent.

"I entered through the doorway. My eyes adjusted to dark and torchlight, the enormity of the outermost tent explained by the unfathomable ceiling of the innermost.

"Torches burned only in the corners, cast flickering shadows across a narrow bed near the far wall. No other furniture or trappings. Temüjin lay unclothed in repose, breathing more rapidly than I thought any man capable, yet asleep to my childish mind. A beautiful woman curled against his left side, and the air was laced with a pleasing odor I did not then recognize. As much as ogling a naked woman appealed to my boyhood, my attention was captured by a stone tied to a necklace and centered upon Temüjin's chest.

"I circled around the bed, hiding in the shadows. Stronger than the urge to see the woman's sex existed my desire to touch the stone. Black, irregular in shape, the stone called to me, and I crept closer."

Freud pulled his goatee. "Ah, I may be credited with the first documented vampirification."

"Vampirification?"

"Personification, except you're a vampire. You're not suggesting an inanimate object actually spoke?"

"Its shiny surface glinted by the firelight. Crevices, angles, as if by design, yet no pattern. I often gathered stones, but never had I seen one so remarkable. A thousand pinpricks of light reflected back at me, urging me closer, impelling me to possess it.

"Two men entered the tent by stealth, broadswords drawn, crouched as they approached. 'He wears the stone,' the first man whispered. Torchlight danced in his eyes and greed draped across his features. 'The stone will be ours,' the second man said. The men hurried forward, and intent as they were upon their goal, I remained unnoticed.

"Weapons raised, the men charged, and so did I, between Temüjin and the would-be assassins. Startled, one man struck his sword across my back. 'Khan,' I screamed as the blade melted through my tattered shirt and slit my flesh. 'Khan!'

"Temüjin woke with my warning and dodged the second man's blow, though the woman did not. Temüjin leapt from the bed faster than any man. He wrestled the sword from the first and beheaded his enemy at my feet. Temüjin grabbed the second man and dragged him into an impossible embrace. My pain exploded. The tent spun around me. I thought I would die, and I thought I mistook what I saw. Temüjin opened his mouth and with his teeth ripped out the man's throat.

"Blood splattered his face and chest, and the stone. Temüjin lifted me onto the bed, cradling my head. Rather than carrying me to help, he called out, and eventually guards gathered, followed by servants and the chief healer. I did not understand Temüjin's actions. Before the guards, before the healer, he bit his wrist, just a tiny puncture, and dripped a few drops into my mouth. The blood was warm and thick like the papaya juice my mother squeezed, and tasted as sweet.

BLOOD BETWEEN LOVERS

"The healer was credited with saving my life, though somehow I fathomed it happened otherwise. Nothing I spoke about, not even to my mother. Temüjin never questioned why I stole into his chamber. My mother and I were moved immediately from the common tent where we kept but a few square feet to ourselves to a private tent erected next to Temüjin's. I thought this a temporary luxury while the healer tended me, but Temüjin kept us close and treated us with kindness.

"He raised me as he raised sons of his loins. They left him. I stayed, for more than two decades.

"The day he invaded the Chinese kingdom of Xi Xia, I fought at the front of battle. Perhaps sensing his imminent demise, Temüjin came to me that night in our camp with these words: 'You have loved me as a father as I have loved your mother as a wife and you as a son. I have a gift some call a curse. I bestow this gift upon you for eternity.'

"His fangs pierced my neck, and he sucked the blood from my body until I subsisted, all but drained. I did not understand his actions, but I did not struggle, nor could I have broken free if I had desired, his grip was so fierce. He bit his wrist and dripped blood into my mouth until—strange as it seemed—I latched on to his arm and sucked the blood of hunger.

"The transition overwhelmed me, and a voice—not mine—inside my head demanded more blood, and defied comprehension. I sucked harder on Temüjin, and he allowed it. I didn't realize how it weakened him. The world exploded upon my senses, more vivid than imaginable to any man.

"I sensed horses approach from great distance. Swords clashed, and I ran from my tent, our camp attacked in the night. We fought off the skirmish with ease, but the soldiers of Xi Xia found my tent and beheaded Temüjin. My fangs erupted then for the first time, and I ripped the soldiers' throats and drained their blood in anger as much as thirst, too late to save my adopted father. I instructed the healer to reattach his head with skill and thread, and we buried Temüjin in secret in a faraway land with the beautiful black stone he always treasured around his neck.

"In the fifteenth century, the tomb was discovered, the stone taken, henceforth known as the Black Stone of Calcutta. But I digress. With Temüjin dead, I had no rationalization for what I had become. I learned from experience why Temüjin avoided the sun. There occurred no way to defend the single urge that overwhelmed my being, or the double voice inside my head. I have argued with that voice across centuries, fought with that voice for control of our consciousness, and only when our thirst is sated does

Roberre grant control."

"Ah, a name at last. You are Roberre?" Freud asked.

"No." He growled. "Roberre is my demon. In this lifetime I am Bobby. Bobby Eyre, a name I've taken from a novel I so admired of a heroine named Jane."

"May I see inside your mouth?"

Bobby gawked, cockeyed, as if he didn't understand.

"Your teeth," Freud said and gestured. "The incisors you used—use—to rip flesh as you describe."

Bobby snarled, and Freud leaned closer. "Savage," Freud said. "Like those of an animal. Excuse me. I observe only as a scientist, a human scientist. I do not mean to imply—is it not difficult in a public forum to hide such formidable fangs?"

"I retract them in public, so I appear as my human self."

"Ah, may I see?"

Bobby pressed his lips together in a frown. "I am unable. I—we—desecrated three women in one London night. I have been unable to retract my fangs since."

"So I may understand, you're saying your incisor teeth are normally less prominent?"

"These"—Bobby pointed with both index fingers—"look no different than your teeth, unless I am provoked by bloodlust."

"With Mary Kelly?"

"I tell you, my fangs erupted that miserable September eve and have remained erect ever since."

"If this is not your normal condition, we may refer to it as a dysfunction. And it began with the murders beyond your need for hunger, murders you abhor. A direct relationship between your feelings and the dysfunction. Hmm, it is an *erectile dysfunction*. No, that phrase will never catch on." Freud rubbed his goatee as if massaging his chin delivered new thoughts to his brain. "Ah, *incisor dysfunction*. More palatable, more descriptive, and easy to abbreviate in my notes. You suffer from ID, sir. Obviously the vampire version of a common malady that afflicts many human males, the one around which my science has grown up."

"Vampires suffer no human illness."

Freud gestured towards Bobby's mouth. "Empirical evidence suggests otherwise."

"Not true." Bobby rushed to Freud's desk, snatched the letter opener, and gashed his left palm. Blood oozed, and Bobby lapped, leaving only a clearly defined cut. Freud's eyes widened, then bulged as the wound healed, the skin unblemished in a mere moment.

"Truly amazing," Freud said. "Nonetheless, while you may suffer no physical illness, being of two minds—one human—you do suffer psychological affliction. ID. Incisor dysfunction, incited, no doubt, by the same issue that causes such affliction in humans."

"You speak in riddles." Bobby glared, fists clenched, and he ran his tongue across the points of his fangs, which reminded him that the doctor seemed to know what he was talking about, even if Bobby did not. "I do not understand incisor dysfunction," Bobby said.

Freud leaned forward. "Guilt," Freud said. "Amazing how an application of the mind may so control physiology. Please, sit." Freud dropped pencil and pad on his chair and lightly gripped Bobby's wrist and biceps. "Please." He directed him across the room. "This is a significant breakthrough," Freud said. "The human side of your personality has at least as much control over your body as does the vampire in you. We can treat the human, and once we discover the appropriate trigger, we can teach the human to sublimate the demon.

"Can you speak of what happened with your mother?"

Bobby lay on the couch, and Freud resettled in his chair. "I loved my mother, and I hated her. Hers was the gift of life, and hers was the tragedy that put us at the feet of Temüjin, who treated me well, and bestowed his gift and his curse. He could not have realized what immortality meant, or he would not have allowed himself to be so weakened and so vulnerable."

"You are clearly of two minds within one brain. Gift and curse," Freud said.

"Immortality without violence would truly be a gift. But my demon is uncontrollable. He drinks blood as he wishes, often brutalizing our victims."

"Your mother?"

"Brutalized by Roberre."

"How does that make you feel?"

"I suffer, as responsible for her murder as if she died by my will. My dreams of blood are often nightmares of her anguish in death."

"Day-mares."

"Excuse me?"

"You sleep only at day. Nightmares would fill the dreams of a person who sleeps at night. Therefore, what you experience are day-mares." Freud scribbled on his pad, puffed out his chest as if he'd achieved another great discovery.

Freud cleared his throat and regarded Bobby. "You have so vividly described an Oedipus complex, complete with tragic results. Do you fornicate?"

Bobby answered with the slightest head movement and a quizzical expression, as if the question was ridiculous.

"With men only, or are you tempted by women?"

"Men hold neither sexual enticement for me nor blood enticement. I lie with women and I feed only from women." Bobby chuckled, then corrected himself with a flick of his chin toward the analyst. "The occasional male to make a point only."

Freud waved the answer aside. "Another breakthrough. A schizophrenic without homosexual tendencies defies current wisdom. You describe your senses as enhanced beyond human capabilities. You experience the urge to copulate. Is that urge also enhanced?"

"I'm not sure I understand what you're asking."

"As a human, before you were . . . turned, you felt desire to have sex. Is the desire the same now that you are a vampire? Do you still have a sexual desire after all these centuries, at your extreme age?"

"When I grew into a young man, the desire for sex was constant, and my adopted father, being who he was . . . let us say my desires were fulfilled at will by maidens and women alike, a few of whom fulfilled their own desires for sex, while others hoped to fulfill their desire for position in the family of Temüjin.

"Since I turned—and I have not aged a day since—the desire for sex is tenfold, as unexplainable in human terms as my desire to drink blood."

Freud displayed a wry grin. "Let us assume for a moment my understanding extends beyond other humans. Try if you would to explain your vampire urge for sex."

Bobby mirrored Freud's expression. Then he growled and rushed off the couch, straight at Freud. He pinched Freud's nose so no air would pass and pushed up on his chin so his mouth could not open. Freud was so startled by the action that at first he did not struggle. But Bobby maintained the grip. As Freud's air waned, he wriggled to free himself without success.

Bobby lowered his head, face-to-face with his psychoanalyst. "Your urge to breathe will make you do anything in the next moment, will it not?"

Freud's face paled, his eyes bulged, and he shoved Bobby's chest.

"Your desire to breathe is perhaps half my desire to fornicate."

The pressure eased, and Freud's eyes rolled back before Bobby released him, and Freud gasped for breath. "I still can think of no words to express my desire," Bobby said. "My actions were at your insistence."

Freud massaged his chest then mopped his forehead with the back of his wrist. "Yes, I can see you take words literally, and I'll be more explicit in the future to request your answers in words only, as difficult as you may find that for mere human comprehension. If I wish for a physical display, I will be specific in so asking. This is required for my analysis. Are we of one mind on this?"

Bobby chuckled. Freud seemed to have missed his own joke. "I am never of one mind, Doctor. That's why I'm here. I've growled at you, however, and for that, I apologize."

Freud nodded his head and gestured Bobby back to the couch. "Please, no physical demonstrations unless I request them."

"As you wish." Bobby resettled. Freud seemed discombobulated. "You have asked about my mother," Bobby said, "do you wish to know about my natural father?"

"In analysis, your father is of little consequence, though the father of your metamorphosis does hold certain interest as he is as much your mother in vampirism, so to speak, as your birth mother is to the human you. The story you describe has an element of familiarity, yet I am sure I do not know the name Temüjin, your khan."

"Temüjin is more commonly known in history as Genghis Khan."

"I see." Freud struggled to keep the surprise out of his voice and his expression. "Explain as you can, in words only, how your desire for sex sublimates your desire for blood."

"I'm sorry. Again, I do not understand what you are asking."

"Two powerful urges . . . in relative terms, how much stronger is your desire for sex than for blood?"

"My desire for sex is nearly as powerful as the urge to drink blood."

"More powerful."

"You do not understand what I feel. I say the urge to drink blood is the more powerful."

"Trust me," Freud said. "In this, I am an expert. Nothing in human experience—and you are part human—is more powerful than the urge for sex. This is the key for which we search. The key to control your beast."

CHAPTER 13

They drove through deserted Trenton streets. Lara gasped, slammed the brakes, and clutched her stomach.

Unbelted, Bobby lurched forward. "The beast in you hungers for release. She claws at your will, driving you to do her bidding, or she'll force you to relinquish conscious control."

Lara winced and pressed her ribs. Her forehead bowed on the steering wheel, and she sighed. "Thank you for not hurting those kids. I'm familiar with gang violence from the DC ER."

"I restrained myself to protect us, not them. If either of us drew human blood, we'd both end up like those other vampires, our heads staked on a tenement rooftop."

They rode in silence for a moment.

"I sensed we were being watched by the dominant vampire," Bobby said.

"Why didn't I share that perception?"

"Awareness of other vampires will develop after you drink enough blood. You're still a virgin. The vampire claiming this territory isn't someone we want to mess with. We'll stay on our side of the river." Bobby leaned closer. "Every time I talk about consequences of feeding failure, you change the subject."

"No, I don't."

"What will you do if you're alone?"

The tires whined over the Calhoun Street Bridge. Lara's throat constricted. "Why a cross?" she asked.

"Psychological impact on vampires."

"You mean crosses don't affect us?"

"Did you feel anything?"

"A twinge of sorrow."

"You, clinging to civilization. Don't ever let go, but you'd better learn to feed yourself. Now."

BLOOD BETWEEN LOVERS

Sunset. Bobby was gone, no message.

Lara paced the bedroom and paused to study the St. Mary Medical Center through the back windows. Moonlight grazed off the third- and fourth-floor blinds before a cloud shrouded the building in shadows. She bit her lip and continued to march around the room, gripping her elbows and then releasing them, then rubbing the back of her neck. Her gaze darted to the wall of books, then the night table, then out the windows again.

She wiggled her toes and stretched her fingers. Nothing helped. The sensation was like an itch without a pinpoint. Without total comprehension, she understood this feeling meant vampire intuition activated.

Tires cruised over the blacktop, a car engine hummed then died as the ignition clunked, a seat belt mechanism clacked, and a car door opened and closed. She detected the human presence, tilted her head back, and sniffed. Recognition spread.

She raced to the front door and yanked the handle out of the intruder's grasp. Lara's senses rushed at her.

A dust speck on fuchsia leather clogs, a single loose stitch on the side of the belt, a solitary hair follicle protruding from the right ear, and the incessant heartbeat all registered. A Mickey Mouse watch ticked in steady rhythm. It was impossible to distinguish which was louder, the watch gear or the boy's heart. He smelled like buttermilk.

"Meridian, it's so good to see you." Philippe flung his scrawny arms around her. "You're the chief of emergency medicine, right? My bags are packed. Don't forget, you promised me a job."

She embraced him with an awkward grin.

Philippe leaned back and frowned. "Trouble in the night?" he asked.

Lara didn't answer. She directed him into the living room, the former inner sanctuary. Philippe angled to the room's center, grinning like a schoolboy with a package of Oreos in each hand and a glass of cold milk on the table.

Despite the dim light, Lara studied his face, the steady chin, the sympathetic eyes, then pulled him close and sobbed. "I need someone to talk to."

She clung to his shoulders until Philippe leaned back again.

"Isn't Bobby . . . Oh," Philippe said. "This is about Bobby."

"It's about him, and it's about me," Lara said. She disengaged, eyes downcast. "I can't cope with being . . ."

Philippe tried to raise her chin. "Turn me." He winked. "We could cope with night-stalking together."

Lara gritted her teeth and shook her head. "I wouldn't wish this on anyone." She avoided his gaze, wringing her hands, her voice muted. "The thirst for blood eats at you. Bobby can't explain the psychology. I lack the social and cultural compass of a vampire."

Philippe shrugged. "Animal blood . . ."

"Rumor. Movies. Fictional books." Lara flushed. "Makes us nauseous. The urge for human blood is incessant. And hell, it can't be bottled. You know we're immortal, right?"

Philippe shrugged, like, *Duh? Everybody knows that.*

"But we're only immortal if we drink fresh from the tap." She paced around the ottoman, then across the expanse of the room. *Blood*, urged the inner voice. She snarled, and her gaze darted from the windows to the locked basement door, then settled on her visitor. Philippe swayed. His eyes traced every movement, perhaps leery of being stalked.

"I don't know what to do," Lara said.

Philippe inhaled, his hand splayed on his chest. "Start with sitting down." He expelled all the air in his lungs and sucked in another deep breath. "I don't mind telling you, Meridian, you're making me nervous here."

Lara latched on to a chair. Her knuckles paled. "I'm sorry." She forced her fangs to dissolve. "Bobby is frustrated by my inability to feed—"

"You're hungry. Bottled blood isn't satisfying, and you can't assault a human. Here." He unfolded a miniature Swiss Army knife attached to a key ring, cut a surgical slit, then extended his bleeding wrist, palm up.

"You don't have to worry about harming someone. Drink what you need, just stop before I collapse. Hurry, before it drips on Bobby's carpet. If you suck too much I'll be daffy, and Nurse Cron will have my balls in a sling if I'm stargazing during my shift."

Blood scent filled Lara's senses. Instinct drove her forward. Unnecessary now, her fangs erupted an instant before they grazed Philippe's flesh. Warm human blood surged into her throat, and relief flooded consciousness.

Philippe grimaced and stifled a groan. Lara backed away. "Philippe"—she shook her head—"I didn't mean to—"

Philippe shook his head, too. "No, no, sweetheart, it's all right, honest. I just need to sit for a minute." He teetered backward onto the sofa. "I've donated blood before, but you're like a living vacuum cleaner, sucking it out of me." He tried to laugh.

Lara forged a frown. She grabbed bandages and wrapped Philippe's wrist, then sunk onto the sofa next to her friend, leaned her head against his shoulder, and sighed.

"You can't imagine what that felt like," she said.

"Yes, I can, sweetie. I've heard enough moaning in the throes of ecstasy before." Philippe grinned. "That is so cool. You can relax now when Bobby's trying to teach you. I'm sure—"

"Bobby is seeing someone," Lara said. She wiggled sideways, opening a gap between them, fixed on the eyes of her confidant. "Not just someone. My boss. My boss who's been planning her retirement for three years, then meets Bobby and suddenly decides not to retire."

Lara's senses remained leveled on Philippe, but she detected no sign he was aware of any of this, or that Bobby confided in him.

"Bobby knows I'm impassioned to be appointed to her position. What if he influenced Dr. Byra not to retire?" She squeezed her fists. The question had burned since Jake suggested the possibility.

Philippe held her gaze. "You're too important to Bobby. I can't believe he's seeing anyone else for other than professional reasons."

"I saw her, Philippe. Dr. Byra. My boss. I saw her thigh, where Bobby likes to feed. She has bite marks."

Philippe shrugged his shoulders. "He fed from her instead of a patient."

"He said he always feeds from psych patients, and always one day on either side of the full moon. This feeding happened mid-cycle."

"I don't know the setup at Jefferson. What if no patients were accessible, but he found Dr. Byra alone?" Philippe hesitated. "Though I have to admit, that doesn't sound like Bobby. He told me that in his five years at St. Mary's, he never drank blood from anyone other than a patient."

"He told me he fed from Dr. Byra but didn't influence her mind."

"There you go."

"My instincts, these damn instincts I don't understand, insist he's lying. His actions the last two nights were attentive. Another interpretation is he was reacquiring my trust." Guilt also explained his continued incisor issue. "Do you think Bobby made love with Dr. Byra?" Lara's throat constricted. Did Bobby's fangs retract for Lara's boss?

She stomped away, then spun to face Philippe. "What do I do?"

"Eternity is a long time. Talk with Bobby about it."

"About what?" Bobby asked.

Lara flinched. She hadn't sensed his presence.

"Bobby." Philippe squealed and rushed to embrace his friend. "I'm so glad you're here. You can't imagine what it's been like. With the two of you gone, Nurse Cron has no one to persecute except me."

"If you did a better job, she'd leave you alone." Bobby grinned, his voice teasing. He twisted to face his lover. "What'd you want to talk about?"

Lara faked a laugh. "Philippe and I are going shopping. We were wondering if you wanted to join us."

"Shopping?" Bobby lowered his chin, raised his eyebrows, and peered at her. "I'll pass, thanks."

His gaze darted to the bandage on Philippe's wrist, and his nostrils flared. *Does he smell the blood?*

Bobby continued as though his awareness revealed nothing. "It's good to see you, Philippe. We've missed you."

Bobby and Philippe talked, and Lara tried to integrate the enlarged sounds, sights, and smells overwhelming her psyche.

The room swirled around her. She needed to escape.

She and Philippe strolled the sidewalk at Summit Square Center, a strip mall near St. Mary's and close to her townhouse. She just didn't remember leaving Bobby's house.

Commercial lights glittered, but the night air wrapped around them like a protective cloak, and Lara relished its embrace. A gust of wind grazed her arms. Cars sailed along the highway, an ambulance siren headed toward the hospital, squirrels chased each other around a sapling at the far end of the parking lot, and Philippe's heart reverberated in her ears, the vibration like a rocker's drum, calling her to dance. Sights focused sharper, sounds clearer. An assortment of cooking smells assaulted her from the restaurants: the distinctive odor of Japanese food, sizzling steak, and deli meat. She shuddered at the strong scent of garlic from the pizza joint.

Philippe's blood. Life was enriched through all of her senses, human blood the catalyst for heightened awareness. The thick fluid lined her throat and lingered, like a double shot of warm sake.

She didn't recall being in the middle of a conversation with Philippe.

"The best thing you can do is talk with Bobby about it. Be direct." He glanced at her as though studying her reaction to his words. "Meridian, are you okay, honey? You seem to be in another world again. You were disconnected at Bobby's house, too."

Lara allowed the corners of her mouth to curl up. "I forget how we got here."

They stopped in front of the In-Step Shoe Store and studied the display window. Jake had warned her to stay away. Why?

Philippe guided Lara's elbow. "Come on, let's go inside. You can sit for a minute and regain your bearings, and I can try on those clogs. For an old-fashioned store, they have the cutest shoes."

Lara shook her head. Qualms about the shoe store prickled her skin without reason.

They opened the door, and bells jingled. The overpowering scent of leather surrounded them. Indigo carpet, black Formica counter, and hundreds of shoe samples lined parakeet-green walls. The store was long and narrow, with a high ceiling. Two fans, though only one worked; a large clock; a floor-length mirror. Plastic chairs coordinated with stools covered in the same carpet as the floor. The store was an anachronism. The cash register predated electricity.

The man behind the counter failed to glance up, intent on paperwork spread before him. Philippe guided Lara around a center floor display, pointing out the latest fashions.

"I'm surprised they're open this late," Philippe whispered.

"We closed twenty minutes ago," the man behind the counter said.

"Sorry." Philippe blushed crimson. "Your sign says, 'Open.'"

The man's gaze swept over the interlopers. Lean, tall, wire-rim glasses, a touch of silver in his hair belying a young face, he angled around the counter toward the door. He stabbed the display window, flipped the hanging sign, then faced Philippe.

"I'm the owner. We're closed." The man spoke with a venomous voice. Wrinkle lines creased his forehead.

He marched behind the counter again and continued whatever work engrossed him, as if he expected the intruders to leave. Lara tilted her head back, and a strange assortment of scents flew at her, all masked by leather.

"Let's go." Philippe guided her elbow.

Lara touched his shoulder. "Something's wrong."

"What do you mean?"

Lara's nostrils flared. Her fangs erupted, and she twisted away from the counter so the man wouldn't see. Her voice dropped and grew hoarse. "We're being watched."

"I know," Philippe said. "That man wants us out of here."

"No. Someone else," Lara muttered. "Back there." Her eyes widened, and she gazed toward the stockroom. "Something evil."

"Okay, now you're freaking me out," Philippe said. "We have to go." He hooked her arm and dragged her toward the front. He offered half a wave in the direction of the rude man.

The bells jangled against the glass door, and Philippe escorted Lara onto the sidewalk and away from the shopping center.

A brisk pace carried them past Lara's vacant townhouse to a farmer's field before either said anything.

"You know, it's bad enough you eyeing me like I'm your last meal, but when a vampire glares and says something else is evil, I'm pushed over the edge. What's up with that, girl?"

Lara shrugged. "It's one of those things about being a vampire I don't understand. The owner danced like a marionette. I didn't like it in there, but these damn instincts urged me to discover who pulled his strings."

CHAPTER 14

Speed delivered Bobby from one side of the sanctuary to the other, upstairs to the bedroom windows, then back to the sanctuary. The air didn't smell right, tinged with the acrid scent of doubt. Meridian had acted strangely since the night she'd voiced her suspicions.

Betrayal shrouds a relationship like a keyboard cover on a piano. The piano is still there, but no one can play it. He'd been unable to retract his incisors with Meridian ever since she'd asked about Dr. Byra.

She'd lied to him about shopping with Philippe. Mistrust ripped apart any relationship. Salvaging their rapport seemed impossible.

Bobby searched the night through the stained-glass windows. He didn't anticipate Meridian now. Someone else watched the house; he sensed a presence.

Agent Plummer?

An unexpected sound drew him back into the moment. Car tires heading away from his home. Philippe leaving and Meridian returning? The front door didn't open. He'd never shown Meridian either secret entrance.

Distracted. He allowed Jake to manipulate him. Bobby betrayed his lover. Disloyalty exposed what? A slice of humanity? Betrayal didn't define human existence, though.

He pulled the night closer now and rushed through the house. He cocked his head to listen before opening the front door: normal nocturnal sounds.

Philippe's car was parked to the side, but neither Philippe nor Meridian was in sight. He sniffed. They'd headed northwest over an hour ago. He rumbled at another familiar scent, more recent.

Bobby followed the scent, masked by gasoline fumes, a mile into Newtown.

Dark sidewalks and dark windows, except for Starbucks and the Gap, situated on opposing corners in the center of the small town. Bobby landed a block away in the shadows in front of the clock shop. He scanned both sides of the street. Teenagers loitered on benches, sipping Frappuccinos and smoking. A couple crossed the pavement with shopping bags. Jake emerged from the coffee shop, a cup clutched in each hand, and headed toward Bobby as though he flaunted vampire radar.

Bobby wound toward the clock display and waited.

"I've always wondered what time meant to a vampire," Jake said, still outside of normal human hearing range.

Two agents skulked half a block past Jake, and another less than fifty yards behind Bobby.

Bobby waited until Jake was close enough to hear him. "Eternity is meaningless. The trick is to avoid becoming bored with existence."

"Lots of hobbies?"

Bobby glared. Moonlight glinted off his fangs and reflected in the display window. "Just one."

If Jake was fazed, he didn't show it. He extended one of the coffee cups. "Double-shot, no-foam, nonfat, caramelized macchiato." He raised the cup higher. "Decaf. Didn't want to make you hyper. Vampires can drink something besides blood, right?"

Bobby accepted the proffered cup and sniffed. "A doctored drink won't affect me."

Jake extended his coffee. "Take mine if trust is an issue."

Bobby sipped. "I don't trust you either way."

Jake offered a half tilt, half nod of his head. "We have business."

Bobby sipped again. "I owe you for the coffee?"

"You owe me for not ruining Dr. West's existence."

Bobby's smirk evaporated. "You purchased one chit with that threat, and it's been played."

"I told you, my friend owns the shoe store in Summit Square. He's run afoul of a vampire. That's why I need you. I can destroy the vampire myself, but I want my friend back first. I can't wrest away control."

"Your friend is your business. Don't try and make him mine."

"My friend is a human being who needs your assistance."

"I'm not a Boy Scout."

"Boy Scouts are awarded badges for helping old ladies. What you're lacking is the proper motivational reward." Jake relaxed and raised his cup, victory in hand. "Good coffee, huh?"

CHAPTER 15

"We have made much progress in these weeks," Freud said.
"I have no more control over my beast now than the night I first approached you." Bobby snarled, displaying his fangs, not yet retracted.

"But I do. We have delved into your subconscious, and I truly believe I have spoken with Roberre. No one exactly understands the mechanism of schizophrenia, but I am not surprised you have no awareness of his conversations or that he would have no awareness of yours."

"I don't believe that."

"Precisely why psychoanalysis doesn't work for schizophrenics. As I've told you, the schizophrenic mind doesn't listen to its analyst. Regardless"—Freud waved at the air—"I have devised a treatment based upon your inhuman abilities that will accomplish everything necessary for you to sustain your finite immortality without harm to humans and simultaneously sustain conscious control with this persona."

Bobby swallowed hard. Bloodlust engaged in this moment, as powerful as any time past. He gripped the couch as if it were an oversized anchor. Thirst gripped every aspect of being and squeezed until all other feelings and all other thoughts disappeared save one.

He'd sworn an oath to save his doctor and protect his family, but Bobby craved blood tonight. Now. He edged forward on the couch as much as his grip allowed. His tongue grazed across his fangs and hunger pounded his brain and throat, different than the stomach hunger he remembered as a human.

"You need blood," Freud said, "and you need sex. Blood incites Roberre to violence. Sex is the tool by which you may control him, if in fact you can think with your head and not your penis as human males are wont to do.

"I agree with you, Darwin, and John Locke, to a point. You have as much natural right to existence as a human. Your existence is dependent upon blood, however, and while Darwin argued that survival belongs to the strongest—you—you also want to live in our society, not a vampirical society, so you must respect humans have an equal right to survive.

"What Roberre is lacking is the proper motivational reward. For you to procure human blood, you must offer a fair exchange. Here we take our view from Adam Smith. The exchange is not between you and the vessel of your meal, but between Roberre and the meal. You are the business broker."

Bobby snarled. He released the couch, fists flexing. "Roberre wants blood, and more blood. What do I have to trade that a human wants? Money?"

"Much more desirable. Sex. The human female demonstrates as powerful a desire for sex as does the human male. A vampire can offer an orgasm exceeding all other orgasms any woman has ever experienced, then you drink a liter of her blood, and you both live happy lives. In this, you will listen to your analyst.

"I tell you, I have spoken with Roberre. I understand Roberre. Sex is the more powerful motivator. Feed Roberre intensely satisfying sex first; hold him responsible for taking a woman to heights she has never before achieved. In the precise moment before your climax hits, Roberre is at his weakest, and in that moment, you assert your persona, and drink a controlled amount of the woman's blood. Continuously offering this much sexual power coupled with sexual gratification then blood affirms your control of his fulfillment and will keep his persona sublimated."

Freud paced to the front of his desk and leaned against the edge. He stroked his chin. "You attack for survival. You violate that person's right to possess for your greater right to exist. But you take what you want and return nothing. I'm suggesting instead the least you can do is offer a woman an hour of intense pleasure the likes of which she's never experienced before.

"Stimulating a woman to this great extent is a five-stage process. The female experiences two types of orgasm, clitoral and a superior vaginal orgasm. You have the ability to deliver both and to actually transfer the clitoral orgasm to the vagina." Freud unrolled a chart and tacked it to a wall. "Here is the clitoris." He pointed. "And here, deeper, the vaginal walls. By stimulating the clitoris first and—"

"You're suggesting a woman has inside her a miniature male penis?"

"An interesting observation. However, the clitoris is a distinctly female sex organ, though it responds to stimulation much the same as a penis and—"

"What sort of stimulation?"

"You're going to use your fingers, your tongue, and your imagination. Based on the latest papers on the circulatory system and our bare understanding of the female, I suggest a slow, steady rhythm in a counterclockwise circular motion. Your ability to delve into human thoughts without speech will allow you to seek out the sexual fantasies of a woman while she is sleeping. Keep her asleep and incorporate real-world sex into her dreams. I'm sure you'll discover women who do not regularly engage in sex have the most vivid fantasies.

"Now, this is essential. Do not begin with the clitoris. Begin instead with the feet and ankles. A soothing massage, from deep in the arch into the heel. And rub her toes. Especially the middle toe. There is no statistical evidence to be sure, but my observations suggest there may be a direct link between middle toe stimulation and vaginal stimulation."

"I rub her toe and she's going to feel it there?" Bobby pointed between the legs of the diagram.

Freud arched an eyebrow. "Remember, she's your partner, not your prey. Talk with her. Tell her what you find appealing about her physically. We're in her fantasy dream world, so tell her what you find appealing emotionally, too: she's of strong character, she's sympathetic, and she understands her lover. Women have sexual peaks, and a woman may climax at the lowest and then, thinking herself satisfied, stop. Her partner certainly will stop after a woman climaxes."

"You're suggesting I not stop?"

"I'm suggesting, don't allow her to climax so soon. Pay attention to her breathing. As she climbs the first peak and approaches climax, back off–far enough she won't yet achieve orgasm. Then slowly start the process again. This time, since you're starting her at an already heightened level of excitement, the peak will be higher before she reaches climax. Don't let her. Back off again. You can deliver your partner to a peak she has never before attained if you use patience and pay attention to her enthrallment.

"Work your way slowly up her legs, but progress from thighs outward, not inward. Hips, her stomach, toward her breasts, but tease only. Stay away initially from her nipples until you've teased so much she can't wait to be touched there. Touch her face, massage her forehead and especially her ears. By the time you come back to her clitoris, you'll be well beyond the first peak, and perhaps beyond a second.

"As you apply direct sexual stimulation, back off before she climaxes. Again, and again, to peaks beyond her dreams. In a hospital, in the middle of the night, you'll safely have an hour or two. Use all of it.

"After she achieves her first orgasm, do not stop. Begin Stage Two immediately." Freud cleared his throat. "Again, no statistical evidence, but my observations suggest the peak she attains in climax is maintained for a certain time afterward. Take advantage and begin Stage Two at this elevated level of her excitement to raise her to yet another new peak. It may surprise you—it likely will surprise her.

"Stages Three and Four will be accomplished primarily with your tongue. Here, here, and here in Stage Three." Freud pointed to the chart. "Here, and especially here"—he indicated—"in the next stage."

"You've got to be joking."

Freud marched back and forth behind his desk. "You sought me for a reason. Trust me." Freud froze and held Bobby's gaze to accentuate his words. "Now, in Stage Five, this is where you will transfer her orgasm from the clitoris to her vagina. Massage her clitoris with one hand, and enter her vagina with the other, stimulating her here." Freud reengaged the chart. "Then, at the right moment, you will finally mount her."

"How will I know when it's the right moment?"

Freud sighed. "Don't worry, my friend. I'm sure the woman will tell you."

"What woman talks during sex?"

"By the time of her second orgasm in stage two, I suspect many women would lose consciousness, another reason why you'll deliver sexual gratification to sleeping women. You will talk with them in their dream state. Waiting for a woman to regain real-world consciousness risks your discovery."

"A woman awake is more fun."

"Absolutely. But which is the greater gift, your sexual gratification or your immortality?" Freud waved. "We know the answer. You need to take as small a risk as possible to maintain existence. She'll still experience real orgasms—wet dreams, so to speak. You can't deliver a female orgasm in five minutes. Well, maybe you can, but that's not fair trade.

"You're robbing her of blood. You need to give her at least an hour of orgasmic pleasure as payment, and you need to wipe her memory and sneak away from the encounter for your safety. You can read a woman's mind while she's sleeping?"

"Yes, but—"

"You're capable of focusing on a woman's pleasure instead of your own for an hour?"

"Yes, but—"

"You'll keep your temporary partner asleep, you'll only proceed with a woman who has a sexual fantasy you can fulfill, then deliver to her dream world multiple orgasms the likes of which she has never before experienced, and in return, you—Roberre—will orgasm and drink a liter of blood. Ultimate satisfaction on both sides of the market equation. Fair trade. And you control your beast with *Vampirical Harmony*."

Freud offered a peculiar smile Bobby had not seen from him before. "What?" Bobby asked.

"What are you waiting for?"

Bobby shrugged, his brow furrowed.

"The urge for sexual gratification is inflated by our discussion. I'm sure your thirst for blood has been equally stimulated. I've given you a map. Follow directions. Find a sleeping woman. Go. Now.

"I can't wait for your report." Freud giggled like a giddy schoolboy.

CHAPTER 16

Moonlight and uncertainty reflected in Bobby's eyes. Lara sucked in air she didn't need. Was it Bobby's uncertainty or her own? They'd tried to make love again, but Lara had refused to surrender blood, and Bobby's fangs had refused to retract. Bobby remained unable to perform with her, yet fed at the hospital with VH. He didn't say if his fangs retracted there. If she no longer excited him, what would he do?

He acted distant, distracted.

His efforts to teach her to feed lacked enthusiasm. They wandered across the farmer's field and approached St. Mary Medical Center now. Bobby's idea. Her failure with the psycho Catherine Cox two nights ago frustrated them both, yet he encouraged her to return.

Was it her failure to learn that caused Bobby's aberrant vampire behavior—the sexual fiascos and feeding so many days ahead of the full moon? He'd already visited the hospital once tonight, requesting she wait while he fed. He'd drifted home two hours later.

"I have another idea for helping you." He didn't elaborate.

Philippe's encouragement last night enabled trust to reemerge now, and she waited with increased anticipation. She wanted to believe Bobby had played no role in Dr. Byra's decision. When Lara sacrificed herself to save Bobby's life, she understood the consequence: he'd turn her to save her existence. Lara had crossed into a life of darkness anticipating an eternal relationship with Bobby. Eternity alone was unthinkable.

They entered the hospital through the parking garage. The doors slid open, admitting two nonhuman visitors, and no one noticed. Bobby wore scrubs. Lara wore a lab coat over a tight skirt and blouse. Easy enough to disguise themselves as staff.

Bobby had probably recognized an opportunity with another psych patient and had decided to return with Lara and teach her to survive. Lara gnashed her teeth. Fortunately, her fangs retracted.

I'll succeed this time, for myself and for us.

They entered a service lift designated "staff only." Bobby pushed *B*.

"I thought we were going to feed?" Lara said.

"Trust your senses. It's not like being human."

"I don't understand."

"We're in their world. Be prepared."

"For what? The kitchen? You'd never go to the blood bank. With security, we'd never gain access anyhow. The only other thing in the basement is the morgue."

"Suppose Dr. Raymond is working tonight?"

"What difference would it make?"

"Fall dances. More kids driving to movies and football games. More accidents."

A bell dinged, and the door slid open. An empty hallway greeted them. Dim lights, an emergency-exit sign, and a forgotten mop captured Lara's attention. The smell that overwhelmed her wasn't cleaning fluid or blood or decaying flesh.

Popcorn. Wafting on the air escaping from the inner office, butter-tinged.

A microwave snapped shut. Footsteps, then the office door jarred open.

Forensic specialist Dr. Grazella Raymond deadpanned. "Homecoming for two of my favorite people."

She cocked her head and aimed for the morgue inner sanctum. Lara raised her eyebrows, but Bobby shrugged, palms up, and gestured with a jutting chin.

Follow her. Lara didn't understand why. The coroner was young and pretty, with ebony hair and wide hips, confident and mysterious, a woman who would be attractive to Bobby.

Dr. Raymond exchanged the popcorn bowl for a clipboard, scanned the attached document, and performed a cursory inspection of the closest corpse. Cadavers lounged on polished work tables. Dr. Raymond spoke without looking up.

"I was disappointed when you quit the staff and disappeared together. I suspect your reappearance together is not a coincidence."

Bobby nudged Lara. He had taught her how to respond. *Humans are often suspicious. Answer questions with questions and direct the conversation.* What did Dr. Raymond ask?

Lara's thoughts failed to align. "Wh-what brings you to the hospital tonight?"

"I'm sure that's obvious." The morgue doctor scooped a handful of popcorn and spoke while munching, though her attention never swerved from the corpse. "Wouldn't it be more interesting to talk about what you're doing here?"

Lara glanced sideways into Bobby's almond-shaped eyes, but he made no gesture to rescue her. Truth would suffice. "I have no idea," Lara said. "I came with him." She tilted her head.

Bobby remained silent. Dr. Raymond worked and ate. Lara scowled, but Bobby ignored her. Why had Bobby directed them to the morgue? To feed from Dr. Raymond instead of a patient? No way.

Lara stepped closer and took another vein. "How'd she die?"

"Car accident," Dr. Raymond said. "Skirting the issue is too obvious. You'll have to do better." She tossed the clipboard on the corpse, plucked the empty popcorn bowl, and headed for the inner office.

The doors closed behind her, and Lara spun on Bobby.

"What gives?"

Bobby laughed. "Like your skirt, I thought it obvious."

Lara snarled.

"Excellent." Bobby's gaze zeroed in on her mouth. "You've forced your fangs to erupt instead of waiting for it to happen. Do you feel the intensity? The desire?"

"I don't understand."

"Take a bite," Bobby said.

Lara cocked her head in disbelief. "Of Dr. Raymond?"

Bobby gestured toward the stainless-steel tables. "Pick one. None of them will complain."

"You want me to feed from a corpse?"

"Don't feed. Cold blood will churn your stomach. But you can bite the flesh. Puncture the skin. If you seduce the human's mind first, they'll suffer no more than a corpse. Get used to the sensation of your fangs sinking into the malleable vessel of a meal. Familiarity will help you feed from someone breathing."

Lara glanced at the teenage girl on the slab. Innocence masked the child's face, though a faint trace of alcohol exuded from the soft tissue. Lara hesitated. "I'm not going to attack a corpse."

"Bite her arm or her stomach. Doesn't matter," Bobby said. "Think of it as part of the seduction. I promise, the corpse will never know."

Sympathy for a death so young warred with curiosity about biting a human. Bobby was right, this cadaver wouldn't complain. She stepped closer to the dead girl and pulled back the white linen, exposing breasts and stomach.

The door popped open. Lara jumped and dropped the sheet.

"Beautiful, isn't she?" Dr. Raymond said. "Innocence wasted. This child will never know the pleasure of love or the pain of grief." She snatched a handful of popcorn and rested the bowl on the desk.

She paused over the body. "Where'd my clipboard go?"

Lara uncovered it.

"Morbid curiosity draws the majority of visitors to the morgue." Dr. Raymond reinitiated the examination. "I doubt that's why you two are here."

"You're right." Bobby leaned against the desk, a self-assured stance, ankles crossed, hands in pockets. "We're on a field trip of sorts, a scientific investigation—or, more precisely, a philosophical investigation. Meridian and I were having a discussion over dinner—well, more of an argument—and I suggested we resolve the issue in the morgue."

Dr. Raymond peered over her glasses at her visitors, then glanced at the clipboard, then targeted the remains. "Lots of issues resolve in my morgue. I can tell the two of you aren't thrilled with each other at the moment." She paused. "What's the argument?"

Bobby frowned. "It's a question of consciousness. In death, when does consciousness leave the body? When does the soul depart? Is it possible this young woman"—he pointed at the carcass—"feels?"

"Feels what?" Dr. Raymond asked.

"Anything at all," Bobby said. "Pain? Fear? It's not like, as humans, we understand death. There're no documented cases of communication between living and dead. Do we know for certain that the instant medicine claims as death is the same instant as the end of all feeling? Because we measure no brain activity, does that mean there is necessarily no sensitivity?

"If we grant the possibility of the existence of a soul beyond life, then we must grant at least the possibility the soul can be aware as its receptor once was. How do we know this girl's soul has left her body? What if souls linger for twenty-four hours? Does she feel you poking around, cutting into her flesh? What if it hurts?"

Instead of laughing, Dr. Raymond halted her examination. She straightened. "What do you propose as a solution to the issue?"

Bobby's face darkened. Salt on a sea breeze overrode the scent of popcorn, and Bobby's fangs erupted.

"Make more popcorn," he said, voice low and guttural. The words floated on the air and wove a delicate pattern around Dr. Raymond. She cocked her head as though to question her actions, snatched the still-full popcorn bowl, and retreated to her office. A cellophane wrapper tore, the microwave door clacked shut, buttons beeped, and the motor hummed.

Lara glowered at Bobby. Before she managed words, he pointed at the corpse and barked with the same guttural voice.

"Bite her now, while you have the chance. Feel the flesh resist your fangs. Imagine warm human blood squirting into your mouth. Savor the sensation of satisfaction."

"Don't try your vampire mind games on me," Lara said. "I'm not biting a dead person."

"I said, take her now."

Lara scowled. Bobby raced behind her and shoved her toward the uncovered corpse. Lara's thighs pinched against the worktable. Bobby forced her to bend over. She struggled to escape his grasp.

Lara twisted, but he pressed himself against her back, pinning her. She groaned and thrashed. Bobby reached across her face and grabbed her shoulder. With his other hand, he rammed her head forward.

Heat rose in her cheeks. Trapped, her face would be flush against the cadaver in seconds.

Adrenaline coursed through her and energized her actions. No one forced her to do anything. Her jaw clenched. Bobby drove her toward an aberrant act.

I won't bite a corpse.

Lara roared and assailed Bobby's arm instead. Her fangs pierced his skin. Blood squirted into her mouth and cascaded down her throat. She growled and sucked harder. Bobby's muscles relaxed.

The more blood she drew, the more reality swelled. Her senses widened already expanded horizons. Myriad colors charged at her from the darkened periphery. The snap of popping kernels a room away, the odor of hospital laundry detergent on the sheets covering the corpses, the trace wafting from Dr. Raymond indicating a recent sexual experience.

The onrush of Lara's surroundings exploded, as magnificent as any orgasm.

"Enough." Bobby moaned.

The world of darkness stampeded in her direction.

"Enough." Bobby ripped his arm from her mouth.

She spun to face him. Blood splattered her lips, and she mopped it with her tongue.

Anger melted in the same instant realization washed over her: Bobby had tricked her. Never before had she attacked flesh.

CHAPTER 17

"What did you do to Dr. Raymond?" Lara asked.

They'd exchanged no words since leaving the basement. The service elevator had delivered them to the fourth floor, no stops.

"I altered her memory. We were never in the morgue."

They stole along the darkened corridor. Lara accepted the hunt for blood.

The alcove across from room 431 offered shelter. Lara glanced at Bobby's face, reveling in the excitement in his eyes, irises and pupils blended together with no clear distinction, but glowing, the feral hunter. His skin darkened, and the thrill of pursuit unmasked his expression.

"Sense the patient's mind. Mold your thoughts around hers and keep her asleep as you approach. You'll take a small amount of blood. It'll be enough to satisfy your thirst without harming her. I promise." Reassurance was still necessary.

Lara focused on the sleeping woman across the hall. Bobby entered the room behind her. He closed the door, predators and prey sealed in a cage together.

The patient's steady breathing nursed Lara's bravado. She pulled back the sheet, exposing tanned legs. The woman's head curved to the side, her inky curls splayed across the pillow. Lara's fangs throbbed. The urge to feed assembled all her senses in this moment. She hadn't bitten the corpse, but she'd fed from Bobby. She'd sucked his blood as though hers by right of survival. Success loomed now. Drink the blood of existence, alter the woman's memory if she woke, and leave her unharmed. Lara endured the world of darkness.

Bobby would want her again.

Lara's breath tickled the flesh. The victim's skin smelled of vanilla soap. Her fingernails and toenails were French-tipped; the second toe on the right displayed a tiny chip. Hospital sounds blended into the background, behind a beating heart. Lara aligned her breathing with the woman's; she sensed the woman's dreams and fixated on keeping her asleep. Neck, breasts, inner thighs; veins and arteries carried a force strong enough to keep this woman alive for one hundred years. What did life mean to Lara? Five hundred years? One thousand?

Lara's need overwhelmed repugnance; blood was the vehicle to eternity.

Her fangs pierced the skin with delicacy. The elixir of life splashed into her mouth. Blood of nonvoluntary prey satisfied her hunger in a way she'd never before experienced and exploded upon her senses.

The surge of triumph combined with the most exquisite sensation racing through her body. Her toes and her fingers curled. A heat flush raged across her flesh, and she smelled her sex. She caressed her clavicle, hardening her nipples. Blood hunger satisfied, replaced with a different hunger every bit as urgent. Desire welled in her mind and between her legs. Craving extended beyond human requirements as she'd experienced in past life. Lara needed to copulate, and bond with one man to share the most intimate part of her.

For the first time, she valued what it would be like to make love without human foibles, without the walls of protection people always found necessary to maintain a sense of self.

They left the hospital as they'd entered, unseen, through the parking garage, and strolled across the dark field toward Bobby's home. In a couple of hours, the sun would rise.

Lara panted. Her voice emerged husky and visceral, urgency pulsing. "Let's hurry."

"Why?" Bobby asked, a chuckle hidden in the single word.

"I want you," Lara said. "And I want you to unleash Roberre."

Bobby paused. Lara spun on her heel to face him. A smirk spread across his features before lust filled his eyes.

"Why are you stopping?" she asked. "If you want to play, let's hurry."

"I don't want to wait until we're home." His voice resonated. "I want you now."

"In the middle of this farmer's field? What if someone sees us?"

"You mean one of the cows?"

Lara didn't want sex, she wanted to make love. She wanted the intense feelings engendered by the physical union binding two people in the spiritual realm lovers shared. Lara and Bobby had bonded over extreme emotional events. She believed in Bobby's feelings, though the words remained unspoken since Bobby had destroyed Robert. Lara had synthesized the antidote that saved Bobby's life that night. She had been dying, and he'd turned her to save her, cinching the bond.

Her feelings were undeniable, though also unvocalized.

Bobby grasped her hands. "Sex is important, but emotional content is more important. I need to know you, your thoughts, your feelings, not because I sense them but because you share them. It's the exposed soul more than exposed flesh that ignites passion."

He's reading my mind. Another aspect of vampirism she failed to master. She wanted this man, this vampire, this would-be teacher, but she'd emasculated his vampire with her repeated failures. His unretracted fangs glinted in the moonlight. Her triumph feeding tonight might restore his vampire/manhood. The urge to be taken swelled.

She slipped inside his personal space. "More than sex, I'm ravenous for man and vampire. It's the passion of Bobby to connect with my human side and the urgency of Roberre to unleash my beast driving me wild with desire."

From the first time they'd made love, she'd sensed the instinctual animal behavior behind Bobby's actions. Her physicality had always inhibited total abandonment to the moment. No longer.

The unfettered beast in her who'd fed tonight was also a sexual animal. Bobby made love consciously. Vampires were immune to physiological issues, so Bobby's problem lived only between his ears. Maybe guilt kept his fangs from retracting when they made love. Roberre made love with animal abandon. With Roberre's help, she could release Bobby's guilt.

"I'm closer to you tonight than I've ever felt. Whatever we've done to disappoint each other is behind us. Let's live forward," Lara said.

She glided into his embrace. His arms encircled her; her mouth curled up.

He peeled off her lab coat, yanked her blouse over her head, and pushed her skirt down across her hips. She stood naked in the fading moonlight, delighting in the darkness. His mouth traced a line over her shoulder. He cupped her breast and her ass. Her head tilted back, and a moan escaped her lips. He peeled off his clothes and circled her, predatory. She stirred, and he pushed her hand away. In their playful way, he wanted to dominate her. Their gazes locked. His lips curled up, and he fondled her. She shoved his hand away.

She laughed. Control had to be earned.

Bobby was the man she wanted between her legs and between her ears. The power of emotional satisfaction lay in the joy shared by lovers caressing souls, not flesh. Just as she'd maintained the same human body after the transition, so she retained the human soul, whatever that was. And Bobby sought her inner being. She remained convinced he wanted to understand her feelings as much as he wanted to fuck her, because fucking was a conscious coupling of body and soul. Fucking with Bobby was making love, and making love meant embracing her mind every bit as tight as he'd squeezed her hips or her breasts.

"We're not human," Bobby said, "but we maintain a sense of humanity. Humans take a partner for love, security, friendship. Vampires don't need those things, except to stay tied to humanity."

He wrestled her to the ground and forced the breath from her lungs. His body covered hers, his hands possessed her, his mouth burned a path across her flesh. "This is me staying tied."

She wrapped her legs around his waist, and he forced her legs down, pinned beneath his weight. He kissed her mouth before she protested, and abruptly broke the embrace, slid off, and flipped her onto her stomach.

"You learned to puncture human flesh tonight. The next step is to accomplish that alone. Survival demands vampires live in anonymity."

He meant anonymity from humans, of course, not from other vampires.

* * *

Bobby sighed. He'd told her flat out and she refused to accept the inevitable fate of vampire lovers. *Try harder.*

* * *

He straddled her ass, keeping her pinned. Uneven mounds of grass pressed against her belly and thighs. She tried to rotate, but he kneaded her spine. Pleasure outweighed the edge of discomfort. He entwined his fingers in her hair, massaging her scalp, eliciting a moan.

"Don't mistake immortality for a gift," Bobby said. "Immortality is the natural right of a vampire. Bestowing immortality is the gift, greater than all other transactions between beings. Vampires sire so infrequently our progeny are held dearer than human children, their survival almost as precious as our own. Immortality trumps love."

The greatest gift Lara could give remained the one she'd never give—her essence. She would never sire a vampire, never wish this existence upon anyone. Right now, in this moment, she just wanted to make Bobby happy. And whole. "I'm not yours to command." She wiggled, pretending she wanted to escape. "You can't take me like an animal."

He wanted her to protest, as long as they were playing. Roberre enjoyed this game-struggle. He slid backward and spread her legs, kneeling between them. His arm wrapped around her hips and hoisted, his other arm pressed between her shoulder blades, keeping her head to the ground. A clump of grass pinched her cheek. His hand covered her ear and kept her pinned.

"Do you want it now?" he thundered.

Yes!

"No. Get off me." She wiggled her hips.

He tightened his grip and glided into her. His weight leaned against the back of her thighs. Dirt embedded in her knees. Another thrust pushed her shoulders into the earth. A human might've buckled under the pressure. A vampire rejoiced—stripped, forced to the ground, and taken from behind in the moonlight. He twisted her head far enough to kiss her with his tongue, then he sucked her tongue into his mouth. She sensed his grin, and she gasped. Her lover's vampire masculinity restored, his fangs retracted, and her tension rocketed light-years beyond any previous experience. He offered a vampire's kiss.

She'd never share the blood of her essence, but she could take his. Her fangs pulsated with desire, and she buried them in his tongue. Sanguine fluid coursed down her throat, building orgasmic intensity.

He thrust, slow and deliberate, then accelerated to a speed transcending mortals. Heat rose from her neck and burned her cheeks. He crushed her breasts beyond human capacity to enjoy. Her inner vampire squeezed the muscles in her buttocks in return, sucking him farther inside. Orgasmic pressure accelerated exponentially, and his explosion matched hers, transgressions resolved.

CHAPTER 18

Tony Tagliari paced the streets of Trenton with disregard for traffic or pedestrians. Not downtown Trenton so much as the Burg. Chambersburg. The Italian section. Home to Stephanie Plum, bounty hunter, invention of Janet Evanovich. Tony had read four Stephanie Plum novels and begun *High Five*. He read out loud, which would normally disturb passersby, except his size and disposition telegraphed a message easy to translate. No one complained.

Tony's circadian rhythms had aligned with his former boss's, and he slept during the day. He clamped a battery-powered reading light to the binding of the book, and he read as he strolled the Burg, sunlight be damned. He also peed as he walked the Burg, relieving incontinence on telephone poles like a dog marking his territory.

The .38 Special he'd picked up for two large on the corner of Hamilton Avenue and Chambers bulged in his waistband, but his stomach hung so far over his pants, no one saw the gun. Tony patted his belly every once in a while, grinned, and read. Ever since Lara West destroyed his boss—Robert Helstrom—Tony felt more secure with a weapon. He carried legal—permit in another state. Didn't matter. If no one in the Burg stopped him from peeing on poles, it remained certain no one would stop him from carrying.

He saved two bullets Dr. West had reconstructed for Robert, filled with the magic formula the government agents used to destroy vampires, in case he encountered a bloodsucker who wanted to make the fat man a meal. Tony patted his belly over the gun.

The more time passed, the more secure Tony felt. He hadn't seen Dr. West drive the stake through Robert's heart, but he had seen the government agents cart away Robert's body. Lara West was responsible. One day, he'd make her pay. For now, Tony settled into a nice life. Robert had seen to that. Nasty as any vampire, but Tony had served him well, and Robert had rewarded him.

Tony had socked away enough money to live for months. A few years if he stayed careful. But his life was comfortable. Really comfortable. Robert had brought him women to play with before he drank their blood. Robert had treated Tony with respect. That's what life was about: respect. People in the

BLOOD BETWEEN LOVERS

Burg respected Tony. He read aloud as he roamed the streets with his gun and no one questioned him, out of respect.

One day, he'd punish Dr. West for her crime. She'd get what she deserved.

Tony rented a single room over a restaurant. That was all the space he needed. Safe and undisturbed. That's what he wanted. Security and respect. Robert had also exemplified survival skills—until he met Dr. West, anyhow.

Tony was a survivor. You don't work for a vampire for years without learning a few tricks. Your senses heighten. You know when people approach from behind. You become more attuned when a vampire is near. Any vampire.

No alarms sounded when an attractive woman with jet-black hair dangling longer on one side than the other blocked his path in the middle of the sidewalk on Roebling between Columbus and Revere. Attractive women often roamed the Burg at three in the morning.

Tony tried to avoid trouble, so he sidestepped, but the woman was faster and again blocked his path. He had no desire for a streetwalker. Big as he was, Tony never paid for sex. He managed, without Robert's supply of "volunteers." Tony grinned. No need to scare her.

The woman smiled back. Nice teeth.

"Thanks, but I'm not interested," Tony said.

"You haven't heard my proposition yet." The woman spoke with an unrecognizable foreign accent.

"I don't pay," Tony said.

"I do," the woman said. Her thin frame swayed. Narrow hips, skinny legs, not enough there for Tony to grab on to.

He laughed. Perspiration dribbled down his ribs. Attractive women made him sweat, as if he didn't already sweat enough. Some days he showered five times, changed clothes as often.

"I need your help, Tony."

Sirens finally blared in Tony's head. "How do you know my name?"

"How is it you don't know mine?"

Tony closed his book and slid it into his back pocket. His fingers patted the weapon hidden beneath layers of fat.

"You won't need a gun, my dear man. If I wanted harm to befall you, you'd be on the ground writhing in pain."

Suddenly, the woman, graced with speed Tony recognized, positioned herself behind him. He spun around.

"I'm surprised Robert never mentioned me. I am, after all, his mother."

"Robert was born centuries ago. His mother's dead."

"*C'est la vie,*" the woman said.

Tony squinted. He didn't understand foreigners.

"Such is life," the woman repeated. "I was speaking metaphorically, of course. I meant, I'm his maker."

Tony squinted harder. Robert mentioned a sire once. Eve something or other.

"Eyve L'Veigne." She extended her hand.

Tony studied her eyes. Robert had taught him a vampire couldn't disguise his eyes. Pupils and irises blended together in an unfathomable explosion of humanity and night creature. Tony sighed. Eyve's eyes didn't glow scarlet—she wasn't hunting. Eyve didn't lie. *He* wasn't the prey.

CHAPTER 19

Lara's attempts to feed on the next three nights met with varying degrees of success. Together with Bobby, she succeeded in entering St. Mary's unseen and locating potential meals.

On the first night, Lara and Bobby entered room 433. Light from a shaded lamp in the corner reflected off Candy Malloy's silver coiffure; the color couldn't be natural at her age. Lara advanced and peered closer at the roots. Candy woke and screamed. Bobby waited to allow Lara the chance to deal, but she was too flustered. He admonished her later; she should've concentrated on keeping Candy asleep instead of wondering about her hair.

On the second night, Lynn Morrissey also woke, but not before Lara had drawn back the sheet and exposed her body, the beautiful flesh of an athlete. Lynn screamed in Lara's face. Lara shrieked, not clear who was more startled.

The third night represented a microcosm of Lara's fears. She woke from her daylong sleep to find herself alone. The lack of a note fed her insecurities.

Lara paced the house, gazed out windows, and changed her clothes twice. Self-doubt crept into her thoughts. She'd fed herself once, with Bobby standing watch.

Did that qualify her in the realm of vampire culture? Were vampires created by definition or by action?

Did Bobby interfere with the feeding? Was her first victim kept asleep by his will? Was that why she had succeeded then but failed since?

A vampire who required hand-feeding failed the litmus test of a viable partner.

Bobby wanted emotional intimacy. Surely he meant with an emotionally sound woman, which meant a woman capable of taking care of her needs. Female and vampire needs.

Bobby burst into the house and stalked the sanctuary living room, tight-lipped, gaze narrowed in focus. Lara didn't want to ask, *Where were you?* Too accusatory, too possessive.

His demeanor conveyed a single message—*Time to hunt.*

Lara located the room of Linda Hutchinson. Bobby didn't go in with her. The door closed silently, sealing her in the dark with her prey. What if the woman woke? Bobby had protected Lara the previous two nights.

The aroma of baby powder wafted over the bed. No blood for three nights reignited thirst. Lara prioritized her plan—keep Linda asleep. She glanced at the chart dangling at the foot of the bed. Admitted post elective surgery as a precaution. Employer: United States government.

Lara sensed something different. Linda's mind already exhibited signs of being suppressed, drugged for sleep beyond the normal hospital routine. *Why?*

Did Bobby arrange narcotics after the previous two fiascos? Lara glided closer and peeled back the bedclothes, revealing a hospital gown accentuating the rise and fall of Linda's breasts. The gown was already hiked up, exposing porcelain legs. Linda's sable hair splashed across the mattress. Lara reduced her breathing to a rhythmic match with Linda's. Veins bulged. A heart beat, the steady drum of pumping blood. Lara recalled the exquisite taste of satisfaction gushing into her mouth.

Her fangs erupted.

She edged over Linda. The door popped open. Instinct relayed a message: *Not Bobby.* Footsteps and undertones of two men drove her to hide under the bed before detection.

"Lock the door."

Lara failed to place the man's voice. The speaker switched on a corner lamp, creating shadows. A lock clicked.

The logger heels of the speaker's work boots, size tiny, approached the bed. Lara's nostrils flared.

Scent and boots combined into recognition: hospital janitor Davey Blissockiss.

"You picked a winner this time," Blissockiss crooned. "Perfect tits."

Heavier footfalls approached the other side of the bed. Lara recognized a fat patient-care assistant, Timmy Jestkey.

"Yeah, I know how to pick 'em ripe." Jestkey chuckled, then backed away.

Linda moaned.

"She out?" Blissockiss asked.

"Have I ever failed you?" Jestkey replied.

A game they'd played before, and Lara didn't like the rules.

"Gave her enough so you can squeeze and pinch and bite and whatever." Jestkey laughed. "She ain't gonna wake up."

Blissockiss slammed work shirt and T-shirt to the floor, kicked off his boots and socks, dropped his pants—commando exposed—then stepped back into his boots, sockless.

"Never understood why you keep your boots on while you're doing it," Jestkey said.

"You don't need to understand, Porky. You're being paid well enough. Just keep your fat ear to the door."

"Don't worry. I know the routine. This is my patient. Won't be nobody 'round for another two hours, and that'll be me." He chuckled like he was being clever.

Blissockiss climbed onto the bed, and the springs squeaked. "Got the camera?"

Jestkey raised his arm. "Right here."

"Get ready to shoot."

Jestkey angled closer to the bed.

Lara grabbed Jestkey's ankles and yanked. Jestkey's legs went out from under him. He crashed to the floor, banged his head, and groaned. His eyes drifted back into his skull.

Blissockiss bounced up. "What the—"

Lara captured his ankles and dragged him to the end of the bed. Her elbow leaned hard into his back, pinning him facedown across the mattress.

She ripped the laces from his work boots and lashed Blissockiss's wrists to either side of the bed rail. She stripped the clothes off Jestkey, plunked his naked body on top of Blissockiss, then wrapped Jestkey's arms around Blissockiss's chest and bound them together with his belt.

Blissockiss bucked like a bull, but being tied to the bed with the oppressive weight of Jestkey riding his back left no chance to break away.

Lara snatched the camera.

"Who are you?" Blissockiss struggled in vain. "Let me up."

"We need pictures for posterity," Lara said.

"You can't take photos!"

Lara held the camera in his face and snapped several pictures in succession. "Empirical evidence suggests otherwise." She was careful not to include Linda in the photos. Lara flipped on the overhead room light and yanked open the door.

"Where're you going?" Terror squeaked in Blissockiss's voice. "You can't leave me like this."

Lara smirked. "Consequences for your actions, with pictures for the hospital Facebook page. Soon, everyone will know what you and Jestkey are doing to patients, not to mention to each other."

Bobby met her in the hall and peeked into the room.

"You've been busy doing everything but what you're supposed to accomplish." Lara huffed.

"Next time, before you attack, turn out the lights. Darkness is your realm. Use every advantage."

"You didn't stop them from coming in, or warn me."

"I could've done either, but what if we're not together when you need to feed?"

Doubt resurfaced. Did he mean "not together" as in—

Bobby didn't give her time to consider. "Let's find somewhere else to continue the lesson. There's going to be a commotion when the lady wakes up screaming."

The elevator delivered them to the first floor.

"You're important to me," Bobby said. "But I need to know you can take care of yourself, no matter what."

One failure too many. Lara bit the inside of her lip.

Bobby directed her into a dark, empty office at the front of the hospital. He pushed her facedown onto a desk and tugged her scrub pants below her knees, then spun her around and pushed her onto a high-backed swivel desk chair. Thirst for blood, oddly combined with thirst for sex, compelled Lara to struggle. Bobby trapped one arm, then the other, and pinned both behind her back using her body like a vise with the seat back. He slipped his legs through the armrests and tilted the chair to adjust his angle. Lara twisted her head.

"Let me go. I have to feed." Her voice emerged hoarse.

"I know," Bobby said. "You're on the verge. I can't allow frenzy to overwhelm you."

He bit his wrist and extended the bleeding flesh to Lara's chin. Blood slammed into her mouth. Bobby lifted her buttocks, wriggled against her thighs, and thrust between her legs. They rocked in unison, she sucked harder on his wrist, and Bobby groaned and exploded, the pressure of their coupling bursting apart the arms of the chair.

It took a moment for humanity to catch up with vampire bodies. "It feels creepy always feeding in a hospital," Lara said.

"Feed wherever you like. Blood loss in the twenty-first century is least noticed here or on a battlefield. You've never been chased by a paid vampire

BLOOD BETWEEN LOVERS

hunter. You feel insecure in your ability to fend for yourself? Go ahead, feed in the open community and surrender your anonymity. I promise, the mercs will notice. See what insecurity feels like then."

They crossed the hospital foyer, angled for the exit. A stocky nun and a much shorter nun were engaged in conversation near the sliding doors. Bobby stopped and handed the shorter nun a wad of money. "They don't make furniture like they used to," he said.

The nun cocked her head. "I don't understand, but charity is a true gift."

"Understanding isn't necessary in this case." Bobby squeezed Lara's hand. "I'm just fulfilling the third of my goals this evening. The hospital is the benediction of—"

"Humanity," the nun concluded.

"The vampire," Bobby whispered in Lara's ear.

CHAPTER 20

Bobby burst into Freud's office. "I never realized my potential to release such unbridled passion. The power Roberre feels the moment before his orgasm, before I ease my fangs into milky flesh—the magnificent combined scent of sex and blood, the elixir of our existence—and Roberre is held in abeyance to my persona.

"Congratulations, Dr. Freud. Now, if you could save me from the incessant night–day-mares, I'll be eternally grateful."

"How grateful?" Freud waved. "No, no, don't answer that. I would be a poor doctor if I could not help you further. Guilt is what you have often described. You believe you owe a debt to society. So? Adam Smith would advocate to balance the economy. Repay your debt."

"How?"

"You've established the success of Vampirical Harmony. You've cultivated a three-prong goal: blood, anonymity, and charity. You've satisfied the first two. Now, reimburse society for the evils of Roberre. A single beautiful solution presents itself as we approach the end of the nineteenth century. It is the flourishing of hospitals worldwide.

"The hospital locale will disguise the side effects in the women upon whom you feed—dizziness, disorientation, pale lips—all typical of so many patients." Freud leaned closer. "And you can get a job. Humans work. You'll blend into society if you work."

"Businesses aren't open all night."

"Hospitals are. They require night-shift employees, and not many people are interested in working all night. You'll have no problem acquiring a position. Nursing. Just—"

"Doctoring?"

"Doctoring demands too much time and focuses unwanted attention on you. Nursing: sadly more thankless but equally important to patient care. You repay your debt, and in the hospital, find not just any patient but the vessels of meals least likely to ever cast suspicion upon you."

"Unconscious women?"

BLOOD BETWEEN LOVERS

"Most unconscious patients will not be healthy enough to enjoy sex. No, you need healthy patients, so to speak. Sleeping, healthy patients."

"In a hospital?"

"You search for the psychiatric. Nothing wrong with their bodies. Psychiatric patients will be isolated. Good for you. Many will be bound. Good for you. You'll steal into their rooms, enter their dreams, discover their sexual triggers—their fantasies—and deliver to them the most glorious ecstasy.

"Then if a memory wipe fails, no one will believe the female psychiatric patient who claims a male nurse delivered her to the heights of orgasmic rapture, then drank a liter of her blood and kissed her goodnight. You'll be safe, enjoy a constant supply of trouble-free blood, and your persona—this persona—will dominate. The day-mares will dissipate as you repay society with kindness and learn to enjoy existence instead of constantly fighting for it."

Freud's head bobbed. "This is important, so listen to me. From now on your kindness will lead you to success."

"There are no male—"

Freud shushed him with a gesture. "If you truly don't age—sorry, while your history sounds fascinating, I still see no empirical evidence—remember to move on every five years or so. The beauty of this economic plan is there are hundreds, thousands of hospitals worldwide. Eventually, every city will have its own."

"Damn it, there are no male nurses."

"There are a few." Freud tugged on his goatee. "A female revolution is building. When that explodes, a male counter-revolution will follow and culturally female jobs will be invaded by men. For now you can become an assistant to a doctor. When society is ready for a male nurse, you'll shift your path. Either way, the advent of the hospital is the benediction of the vampire."

CHAPTER 21

The sky lightened, and the sun broke the horizon a few minutes later than the Weather Channel had predicted. In the employ of Eyve L'Veigne, Tony hunted for a vampire today. "Spied on" would be a better description. Tony liked accurate descriptions, and he liked Eyve, though he didn't trust her yet. Trust would develop, as it did with any relationship.

Eyve promised him health and well-being, and she shared information new to Tony.

Dr. West was responsible for Robert's demise, but another vampire, Dr. West's friend, Bobby Eyre, actually staked Robert. Bobby Eyre was the vampire Robert had nearly destroyed in Tyler Park. That pointy-toothed bastard.

Tony aimed at two targets for revenge now, and he had one powerful ally. Eyve wanted revenge, too. Her revenge involved pain and suffering, and plenty of it. Destruction ultimately as an afterthought. Pain and suffering satisfied Tony. His assignment today was to find Bobby Eyre. Shouldn't be too difficult. Tony had once delivered a blood message from Robert to the house that resembled a church, near the hospital. It was secluded and secure—there was no reason to expect Bobby to have moved. With luck, Tony would find Dr. West tucked away with the damned bloodsucker.

Eyve supplied transportation, a Toyota with tinted glass. He read the trunk insignia—missing the first two letters—backwards with—what had his mother called it?—dyslexia? *A toy*. Tony had ditched his car the night of Robert's destruction, leaving no trail for the feds or Dr. West, in case she was still pissy at him for torching her house.

Tony stuffed clothes and books into duffle bags, left an envelope with three months' extra rent—a message in the Burg, *I was never here*—and vacated his apartment. He tossed the bags into the back of the Toy, and Eyve tossed him the keys.

She spouted an address in Yardley, Pennsylvania, a neighboring town in which she'd purchased a temporary residence in the Westover section. An old, ranch-style home with a full-length, dark basement. Concrete filled the four turret windows. The lone inlaid basement window, low on the back patio, was removed and cinder-blocked. A heavy metal door, fit snug into the frame, reinforced with locks and bars, replaced the standard basement door.

If anyone tried to enter Eyve's sleeping chamber, she'd have plenty of warning.

Tony left at sunrise. First things first. He needed to confirm Bobby still slept in his church home and that Dr. West was with him. Then he'd have to figure out how to follow Bobby. Eyve wanted any information Tony could ferret out. Did Bobby feed nightly? Where did he feed? What kind of victims did he prefer?

Tracking a vampire without him knowing was no small task, and he had only weeks to learn all Eyve wanted. Didn't matter. Tony chuckled; he wasn't a doctor like Lara West, but he had patience and a health plan.

Tony drove to Bobby's home, careful not to trespass on the property. He drove around the church, then holed up in Core Creek Park and wandered the perimeter, noting the surroundings. St. Mary's, the place where Tony used to steal blood for Robert's experiments, bordered the park, separated from Bobby's home only by a field.

The medical center suggested another strategy. People bled in a hospital. Missing blood was expected. Robert had often fed in hospitals, where it was easier for a vampire to hide his trail.

If Bobby fed at the hospital, Tony could wait there. The vampire would come to him.

He studied the church from a distance. All the windows were covered with metallic shutters. Most likely several doors blocked the entrance to the inner sanctuary. Tony needed to see who came and went in the dark.

He drove into Philadelphia to find a store that sold night-vision goggles with telescopic lenses. He could spy on Bobby Eyre and Lara West from afar.

* * *

Dog squeezed a lemon wedge and dripped juice into her teacup. "We can't have a vampire running such an important shoe store. Destroy him."

"I want my friend back."

"I see no evidence your plan is working. I can't tell if Lara and Bobby are playing house or playing doctor in the hospital, but they're playing."

"Not after tonight."

RAZ STEEL

* * *

Bobby woke an hour before the curve of the earth claimed the sun. He gazed from their bedroom window at the fiery orange ball dangling in the sky. Behind him, sprawled across the bed, lay Meridian, taking her half out of the middle. Bobby's chuckle was smothered by frustration.

Meridian's disappointment added to his guilt. A rift spread between them and threatened to engulf their relationship.

If Lara succumbed to her demon and his creation was taught by another vampire—Unthinkable.

He wandered through the house. Teaching opportunities to puncture flesh and drink blood abounded at the hospital, but it proved impossible for Meridian to focus on feeding and keep her victims asleep simultaneously. She needed a patient who was already sedated. Last night, Linda Hutchinson had been the perfect victim, except for the interruption—though the taste of tainted blood wasn't sweet.

Bobby needed to discover a patient who'd been drugged through normal hospital protocol, not by felonious custodial staff.

He punched the code to open the metallic shutters a fraction. Sunlight angled through the stained-glass windows, and Bobby shielded his eyes.

He unlocked the basement and descended into darkness. A musty smell assaulted his nose. Claws tapped on the cement. Bobby grimaced. Rats.

The heavy metal door swung open on voice command. He stepped over the infrared barrier designed to keep the vermin from invading the vault. Lights winked on, motion-controlled. Beyond the desk, a second, smaller metal door hidden behind a tapestry opened, offering access to the hospital's main sewer line. Bobby's nose wrinkled, and he held his breath.

Moments later, he emerged unsoiled into the boiler room, then climbed the stairs to an empty morgue. A gulp of air filled his nostrils with blood scent, and his lungs sucked it in like an aphrodisiac. Living among humans, Bobby always breathed, always kept his heart beating near human-normal levels instead of the hyper-fast pumping demanded by the metabolic activity in vampire bodies during sleep. He laughed at the fictional vampires without heartbeats. How did humans think blood traveled through a vampire circulatory system?

Most people—including vampires—thought vampires were dead. Or undead. Because a vampire could stop his heartbeat? Hold his breath for hours? He could do neither while he slept. Vampires were alive by definition.

BLOOD BETWEEN LOVERS

A friend and eminent physician and hematologist, Dr. Douglas, had examined Bobby more than once. He postulated that every cell in a vampire's body craved rejuvenation. Rejuvenation resulted from a chemical cascade that ramped up stem cells induced by an as-yet-unidentified human protein absorbed into a vampire's bloodstream after ingesting human blood. Dr. Douglas didn't know what the receptors looked like on vampire stem cells, but the human protein turned them on and churned out differentiated cells of every variety, rejuvenating every organ and every system in the vampire body indefinitely, given a continuous supply of human blood. Once a vampire was created—stem cells turned on—he was in a constant hyper-adrenalized state, causing a racing heart and hyperoxygenation, which promoted wound healing and explained vampire functionality despite severe blood loss. Rejuvenation—eternity—demanded human blood. This metabolic process worked best while a vampire was asleep, without distraction.

To his credit, Dr. Douglas wanted to identify the human protein responsible and apply it to human stem cells—utilizing artificial proteins, ". . . so we don't become a world of hematophagous cannibals. The potential application of this physiology to human disease and suffering makes it a pursuit worthy of the Nobel." Bobby had chuckled. If that many new vampires were created, there'd soon be no humans remaining to vote his friend the Nobel.

Meridian—*Dr.* West—at least understood physiology, and Bobby taught her to slow her heartbeat in the human world to avoid suspicion of an alternate reality. Existence, he taught her, is a natural right; he'd learned that in the seventeenth century from John Locke. *Your existence depends on the blood of others; therefore, you have the right to seize blood, as long as you're careful not to harm anyone.* John had volunteered once to let Bobby feed.

His relationship with Meridian—though soon to end—was unique in his experience. Over the centuries, Bobby had encountered other vampires, but had never encouraged friendship—or love. He'd sired Meridian of necessity. Human Meridian had been the emotional existence denied to him for centuries, jetsam to which he could cling. Love with a human had grounded him in the world he refused to surrender. He'd owed that human the chance to survive.

The vampire instinct to protect his creation surprised him, overwhelming his consciousness and controlling his behavior. Like an eagle who may taunt a fledgling to fly by placing food nearby but out of the nest, Bobby considered a similar strategy to teach Meridian to feed. He headed for the fourth-floor nurses' station to read charts. Hopefully, he'd find a moment the station was unattended, everyone occupied with patients.

Reaching the fourth floor was easy; accessing the records, not so much. Nurses and doctors congregated at the station as if it were a happy hour celebration. Bobby was never in a hospital at this time of day. Activity flourished around the birthing rooms. Bobby sidestepped into an alcove to consider options.

A short man in a lab coat sidestepped from behind the nurses' desk.

Agent Plummer.

It was as though Agent Plummer's vampire radar exposed Bobby's hiding place. Jake headed toward him. Bobby wheeled. He recognized two of the three agents who blocked the hall at the far end. One was a tall man Bobby had seen with Jake in DC, and the other, a muscular woman with a military haircut he'd seen here in Newtown.

No options. Bobby waited for Jake to approach.

"You have a job to do," Jake said, his voice low and gruff. "You're preoccupied with your girlfriend. I've already warned you. I'm playing my next card."

Jake didn't wait for a response. He continued toward his people, who parted and then pivoted to follow in his wake.

Bobby glanced back at the now-deserted nurses' station. Where did everyone go?

Behind him, the WPA agents disappeared. There was nothing in Jake's arsenal to coerce Bobby into action. Bobby had no weaknesses, no other friends for Jake to threaten. The sun danced on the horizon beyond a window—time for Meridian to wake. Meridian—

Meridian was asleep. Unprotected. Jake presented a distraction, his people, decoys.

The corridor exploded with hospital employees and visitors, vampire speed negated. The lingering sun prevented a direct route home. Travel through the morgue tunnel remained the only track.

Meridian.

He had no way to contact her, to warn her. She'd never disclosed a cell number, and he'd never thought it necessary to ask. Bobby hurried as fast as he could without risking exposure in the crowded corridors. Jake kept Bobby's secret to manipulate him. If anyone else recognized a vampire in St. Mary's, a bounty would be issued and Bobby would be forced to flee the community. Did Jake issue a bounty for Meridian?

BLOOD BETWEEN LOVERS

The elevator arrived in slow motion. Someone wanted to get on or off at every floor. The doors finally slid open in the basement, and Dr. Raymond grinned at him. He could modify her memory easily enough, but it wasted precious moments.

He emerged from his vault and flew up the basement stairs and across the sanctuary. He sensed the sun set below the horizon. Bobby didn't doubt professionals could've penetrated the house's defenses. Had Meridian been awake, she might have been able to escape. Her peril was his fault. He should've seen the trap Jake had set.

Bobby froze.

Meridian beamed down at him from the second floor, four stories up.

Safe. And dressed to please. Jeans hugged her hips, and a snug shirt without a bra outlined the excitement in her nipples.

Bobby must've beaten the bounty hunters here.

No. Something else—

Bobby sensed another presence. He spun around. Not inside. Someone approached the house. Speed delivered him to the door just as a knock reverberated in the foyer.

Bobby flung open the door expecting—whom? Jake? Jake wouldn't knock.

Recognition drove a stake into his heart, and Bobby staggered back.

An hourglass blonde glowed with ruby lips. Her dress clung to the delicious hips that swayed with each tantalizing breath.

"Marilyn," Bobby whispered. The word choked in his throat. "I thought you were dead."

Marilyn Monroe's smile expanded. "I am."

CHAPTER 21½

L ara woke with a start. The sun, like an alarm clock, blared below the horizon. Hunger welled up. An overwhelming desire to drink human blood flooded consciousness, then expanded. She wanted blood and sex. Craving stabbed every nerve. She was aware of every sight and sound and smell in the dark bedroom. Her senses extended beyond this room; Bobby wasn't in the house.

The first time she'd woken without Bobby, anxiety had insinuated its way into her mind. Bobby had taught her how to detect intruders in her vicinity, how to guard against the sudden approach of danger or the subtle approach of a foe. Lara no longer woke panicked. Her inner vampire extended, as Bobby had explained. No hidden dangers lurked nearby now.

The moon rose between cycles, not time for Bobby to feed. Where did he go?

Lavender traced the air, a remnant odor from the oil Bobby had rubbed into her skin last night. Along the far wall, an inch above the carpet, a spider the size of a pea dangled in its intricate web. The spider waited without wasting movements. Though it wasn't a chameleon, it blended with the background, a viable harmony with its surroundings, tempting company.

Lara chose clothing—for the first time—to please a lover. Her face warmed. A thong, jeans tight enough she needed to wiggle into them, and no bra— arousal unhidden behind her shirt. She hoped her clothing wove the fabric of enticement.

Outside, dusk darkened into night. Bobby liked the dark and encouraged Lara to wander through the house without turning on lights. Lara left the bedroom barefooted, the pads of her feet gliding over the carpet, coarse bristles tickling her toes. She was grounded here, a sanctuary from the outside world. She carried two keys: one for this house, one for the townhouse Jake had bestowed on her. She hadn't visited the townhouse since their return to Bucks County.

A deep, shuddering thump grabbed her attention, a sound emanating from the basement: the vault to Bobby's private sanctuary. The basement door banged open. She peered over the balcony. Relief smeared across

BLOOD BETWEEN LOVERS

Bobby's face.

Worried about me?

She radiated with his attention. But he flinched, and a mask spread over his features. He streaked away as fast as he'd rushed toward her.

Lara hurried down the steps. The front door opened, and Bobby's announcement held a startled surprise.

Lara sensed a presence. A voice inside her head insisted the intruder wasn't human. How could that be? Lara's fangs erupted, her territory invaded.

A growl escaped Lara's lips and expanded as her gaze narrowed and her fingers curled tight. A voluptuous blonde locked in an intimate embrace with Lara's lover.

CHAPTER 21¾

Dog tapped the porcelain teacup with her silver-inlaid spoon as if to command Jake's attention. His attention had never waned—a trick he'd learned and mastered years ago to appear focused elsewhere when in fact he absorbed every minute detail in his present surroundings—in this case, the Bucks County field office of the WPA–VU. They were videoconferencing on secure computers, Dog from her Georgetown office.

"How are you enforcing Ms. Monroe's cooperation? She's never been in public as a vampire."

Jake shrugged. "She asked to read vampire novels, so we manipulated her reading material. Amazing, really, that so many people in the real world and contemporary fiction still believe vampires are all about blood. We kept those books away from her."

"You fed her eternity."

"We still don't understand the mechanism, but we've studied Marilyn for fifty years. She's the only vampire we've ever captured at her turning, so we can distinguish learned behavior from instinctual behavior. Vampire instinct provides the sense of immortality. Blood is the pathway, but immortality is the goal. What greater gift could there possibly be for anyone? To live forever? What wouldn't any of us do for that opportunity?"

"And you've been able to convince Ms. Monroe we control her fate?"

"She believes it. We've kept her incarcerated from the moment she was turned. She can see her reflection in the window of her cell. She's confirmed her immortality. We've shown her videos and what may appear to be newsreels of vampires being hunted, staked, beheaded, and shot with our magic bullets. Gruesome, but she gets the idea. Refuse to cooperate, and we keep her locked up, literally forever. Cooperate and we allow her to leave jail. Fulfill her role and she gets to stay out of jail. Escape before she fulfills her role, and she'll become the hunted."

"You're asking her to betray the man she loved."

Jake pressed his lips together as if forming a giant kiss before he spoke. "It's possible we might not have expressed her role in those terms."

BLOOD BETWEEN LOVERS

"You lied to her. Vampires can detect—"

"I'm an accomplished liar, and I've certainly dealt with enough vampires. I mixed in enough truth so that she won't recognize the lies. I told her Mr. Eyre had no idea he'd created a vampire, so she holds him blameless. I told her he's moved on with his life; however, another vampire, Dr. West, is trying to manipulate his behavior, and we—the government—don't want to see him manipulated. So we've asked Ms. Monroe to disrupt their relationship. She's mastered femininity. I'm sure she can confound his thoughts. That's all."

"She honestly believes she's helping Bobby."

"And you're honestly going to release her if she performs for you?"

Jake tilted his head with an exaggerated motion.

"Even for you, Jake, this is a first. I can't believe I allowed you to talk me into this. How many vampires are alive by your grace?"

"No one talks you into anything. You weigh the risks, calculate the odds, and decide on a course of action. You give me too much credit. No one has that kind of influence on Dog."

The old woman laughed at Jake's dyslexic jibe. "Except a really good liar? It's a wonder you're not a politician. Why don't you have my job?"

Jake snorted. "If I had your job, I'd miss all the fun."

"Didn't enough people use Marilyn Monroe when she was alive?"

"Good thing she's not alive anymore."

Dog stirred her tea. "Time frame?"

"Won't take long for Marilyn to stir blood between lovers."

CHAPTER 22

Lara paced the bedroom, dodging Bobby's grasp. She spun to face him, index finger pointing toward the door. "How could that be Marilyn Monroe?"

Bobby's gaze fixed on hers. "I didn't know this would happen."

"What're you talking about?"

"I thought Marilyn died in 1962. We had a relationship, but I didn't change her. A bounty hunter chased me away, and before I returned, Marilyn committed suicide. I thought it was depression, a withdrawal symptom of Vampirical Harmony. Other than Marilyn, I'd always wiped the memories of the women with whom I shared all five stages."

"Five stages? You've only taken me through two stages." Lara glared. She cocked her head. "Have you wiped my memory?"

Bobby's hands shot up, palms out, and he shook his head. "Never."

"You haven't shared the other three stages with me, then."

Bobby blushed a shade Lara had never seen before.

"That doesn't explain how this . . . *thing* downstairs is Marilyn Monroe."

"I didn't realize that after five stages of V-Harmony, if there's no memory wipe, the person turns."

"You're a vampire. You don't know how to make another vampire?"

"You're a vampire, and you don't know."

"But you've been a vampire for more than seven hundred years. You've had plenty of time to learn."

"Sorry, they don't teach Vampire 101 in night school."

Lara shook her head. She gyrated away from Bobby and glared out the window. His story sounded unrealistic, but then, how plausible were vampires? Regardless of who this woman was, she certainly looked like and sounded like Marilyn Monroe. Lara didn't want her in their house, and she didn't want her in Bobby's life. The unexpected arrival drew a veil between Lara and her lover. His attention amassed on Marilyn, a beautiful, sexy angel and a self-sufficient vampire. She'd existed for fifty years without Bobby's knowledge.

Was it effortless to her? Bobby obviously preferred this autonomous, oversexed movie star.

BLOOD BETWEEN LOVERS

What demands could Lara make on Bobby?

They'd never spoken about the nature of their relationship. This was Bobby's house, and Lara was a guest. Before she'd met Bobby, she'd never bothered to make time for a relationship, so jealousy was a new emotion. Exaggerated by vampire awareness?

"Bobby," a sultry voice called.

"Are you coming back downstairs?" Bobby asked Lara.

Lara wheeled. "One word and you run into her arms?"

Bobby shook his head. "This is not an attractive trait." His bow seemed patronizing.

"Don't go down there."

Bobby stopped and spoke over his shoulder. "She's our guest."

"Not mine." Lara stepped closer, and her voice softened. "Don't go. I need you."

Bobby hesitated. "What do you need?" His tone reflected hers.

"Bobby." The single word reverberated, wafting on the air like the song of a siren.

The bedroom door drifted open. Marilyn's dress clung to her hips, tighter than Lara's jeans. The material had an unusual sheen and exuded a trace of a chemical odor. High heels accentuated the arch of her back, thrusting her breasts across the doorway threshold.

"I didn't realize I was . . . interrupting."

Marilyn glided closer, the words conflicting with her seductive tone. Her gaze trained on Bobby, yet Lara shivered, vulnerable before a self-sufficient vampire-goddess-icon.

Marilyn wheedled her way inside Bobby's personal space, so close her breasts must've grazed his chest, her head tilted back to peer into his eyes.

"I need blood," Marilyn said. "Is there somewhere nearby we can feed without harming anyone?"

Great. Marilyn Monroe's sensitivity just adds to the equation.

"The hospital." Bobby glanced over his shoulder. "Coming?"

A third wheel on a date. Lara's inadequacies magnified by a voluptuous vampire? Marilyn also glanced at Lara, and a silent message passed between them.

Unhappiness.

Bobby and Marilyn paraded out the doors. Lara froze in the bedroom. Human Marilyn Monroe was a larger-than-life tragic figure who never recognized the sphere of her power over men. Abused from her stepfather to—what, the president of the United States? Lara gnashed her teeth. Empathy for the vampire who was invading her domain, fraternizing with her lover, conflicted with the overriding emotion. Her face flushed hot. After decades, did Bobby still have feelings for an ex-lover? How could Lara compete with Marilyn Monroe?

Inadequacy fed insecurity far beyond that caused by Bobby's early-evening disappearances.

What if he chooses her?

Marilyn's image materialized in her mind. Lara hissed. "This woman doesn't belong here. She's a—" *A what? A woman who needs sympathy for what she's suffered? Why would the sympathy she needs have to come from me?* Lara rolled her eyes and moaned.

I am such a freak.

Lara stormed into the night. Agent Jake Plummer leaned against a vehicle, ankles crossed, smugger than when she'd last seen him a week ago in DC. Lara pounded the hood of his SUV, denting the polished surface.

"Tense, are we?"

Lara scowled. "What gave it away?"

Jake studied her. "Fed recently?" He answered himself. "I didn't think so." He rubbed his chin. "Not so easy, huh?"

Lara remained silent. Jake unbuttoned his cuff, rolled up the sleeve, and offered his wrist. "I still have to drive home tonight, so stop before I pass out."

Nocturnal vision targeted a pounding vein. A drop of perspiration glistened on Jake's forehead.

Fear? Curiosity, more likely.

Lara hesitated. Jake did nothing without benefit. What would this cost her?

A knife flashed in Jake's hand. With the precision of a surgeon, he opened a vein in the exposed wrist. Jake's blood gurgled; the aroma drifted on the autumn breeze, and Lara's fangs erupted. She rushed forward. Rational thought swept away. She clutched his arm, glowered, and sucked the blood from the open wound.

The warm liquid spurted into her throat, intensifying the effect already raging inside her. The ground spun and reared up to infringe on the night sky. The more she drank, the more she wanted. A distinct component of consciousness warred for control: ugly, insensitive. Lara fought to maintain restraint. Blood invigorated her, but gave rein to the unwanted persona of her beast.

BLOOD BETWEEN LOVERS

Jake moaned and struggled to pull away. Lara groaned, and reality pushed into perception. She shoved Jake. He wobbled against the SUV and would've collapsed if Lara hadn't caught him.

Tears filled Jake's eyes. Pain? He raised his head, and a smirk creased his lips.

"Holy freakin' cow." His voice emerged hoarse. "What a rush. Was it good for you, too?"

Power poured through her limbs. Night vision sharpened. Her nose twitched with assaulting odors of lingering gas fumes and overpowering cheap cologne. She raked her tongue across her fangs and sucked in the few remaining drops of blood. "Shut up."

She pinched his throat between thumb and index finger. Jake stretched up on his toes to relieve the pressure, but he didn't struggle. Reality shook Lara, and she warred with her beast. She released Jake.

"Sorry. I guess I'm not in a mood for joking."

He sucked in a deep breath. "Don't worry about it," Jake said. "I can imagine how difficult it's been for you to adjust."

An empathetic Jake didn't improve her mood any more than an insightful Marilyn Monroe. A subtle tone in his voice fired a tingling alarm.

"You need more blood than I can offer," Jake said. "Why don't you try the shopping center?"

"The what?"

Even this pittance of warm blood made her hyperactive. Senses reeled, magnified beneath a half-moon in Bucks County. *Blood*, called an inner voice. This small taste didn't sate. Lara needed more. Her body craved more. Hunger burned in her soul.

Do vampires have souls distinguishable from their human soul? I should ask Bobby. Or maybe I should ask Marilyn.

Craving—or jealousy?—urged her to action. She couldn't attack Jake again, though. His words didn't make sense.

"The shopping center?"

"Lots of restaurants there. Go feed."

"I don't need food." *Doesn't he understand?*

Jake waved her silent. "I know. I meant, restaurants are open late. There'll be people at the shopping center. Find a woman alone. You can feed and wipe her memory. If you take a little too much blood, she can sleep it off in her car. Come on, Lara, suck it up. You can do this."

Jake tugged open the SUV door, climbed behind the wheel, and started the engine. He leaned out the window.

"Go ahead. Take a stroll to Summit Square. Remember what I told you before, though. Stay away from the shoe store." He gunned the engine and sped off into the night, no lights.

Hunger clawed at Lara, for blood and more. Her breasts ached and her thighs twitched. She wanted Bobby. He'd tried in vain on numerous occasions to encourage her to suck his blood while they made love. Now, in this moment, for the first time, she felt capable of puncturing his skin without being incited by thirst or anger, and taking the blood of a vampire—embrace beyond human capacity.

Did the jealous animal propel her along this path?

If Bobby chose her over Marilyn, would confidence in feeding be bolstered? She hadn't succeeded yet. Nursing on Jake didn't count. He'd volunteered, puncturing the skin for her. The violence of attacking still revolted her, but a different persona inhabited her body in the moment of feeding. Could her beast be controlled?

Bobby had explained his struggles to control Roberre over the centuries, and how he'd lost the battle and Roberre had killed indiscriminately until Bobby had met Freud. Freud taught Bobby that the key to mastering the beast was fulfilling bloodlust with blood and sex. That must've been what had happened between Bobby and Marilyn. Bobby had harnessed Roberre because Bobby had made love with Marilyn and she'd allowed him to drink her blood. Lara still refused to share her blood. Who would Bobby prefer now?

Stinging electrified her from the inside out. Bloodlust jumped to a new level, insisting on a side order of sex. She'd released Jake before she'd harmed him, and she wasn't about to have sex with Jake. Too weird. She didn't want sex with anyone besides Bobby.

She'd fed without harming the donor—she could do it again.

Jake had suggested she feed at the shopping center. He wanted her there. She laughed. He was so obvious. If he wanted her at the shopping center, she'd stay away. She'd feed at the hospital but avoid Bobby and Marilyn. Easy—she knew where they'd be.

CHAPTER 23

Tony showered, then dressed in all black. He tossed hospital scrubs and a lab coat on the backseat of the Toy and headed to Langhorne. The sun creased low in the sky; the half-moon had already risen. He parked far enough away to be off-property, close enough to see the church door with his new equipment and a clear view. He refused to think of the building as a house. He pulled on a mask and gloves so no skin showed. He kept the car doors and windows closed, so no scent escaped. Besides, he sat downwind. It was unlikely a vampire would notice him behind tinted glass at this distance.

He donned the goggles. There was no car in the driveway. No car meant a vampire would either walk or fly to the hospital. Tony needed to be sure where Bobby was headed to feed. Failure on the first night of his first assignment would not bode well for his relationship with Eyve.

Tony waited. Less than four hours. He peed five times behind a tree. Someone entered the church during his last pee, and Tony didn't see who it was.

"Shit."

Bobby and a curvy blonde emerged from the church before Tony climbed back into the car. Definitely not Dr. West. Lara had curves, but not like this. Tony guffawed behind the tree. The blonde was a Marilyn Monroe look-alike, only more so. Too much so to be a look-alike. With vampire speed, they disappeared around the side of the church.

"Holy shit." *Marilyn Monroe is a vampire.*

Tony would need a break to beat them to the back of the hospital. Hungry vampires would enter through the parking garage and wouldn't want to be seen. If the bloodsucker and his new girlfriend arrived first, he'd have a difficult time finding them inside. Where was the bitch Dr. West? In Langhorne or DC?

Tony scrambled into the Toy, but headlights on the church driveway caught his attention. If he paused to discover the visitor's identity, he'd lose track of the two he was chasing. He settled behind the wheel. Then someone else emerged from the church. Instincts stopped Tony from leaving. He adjusted the goggles. Lara West approached the tiny man who hopped from the vehicle.

Confirmation of her presence was important information.

The doc suddenly attacked the small guy. She used vampire speed and sucked blood from his wrist. A minute later, the man drove away, and Dr. West disappeared in the night.

"Double shit." *Lara West is a vampire, too.*

Robert had tortured the doctor, biting her, draining her blood, but he'd never turned her. Tony knew vampires rarely made new vampires. Like a prohibition. Robert had expected the doomed doctor to beg for death, but he was destroyed before his plan was fulfilled. What if Bobby Eyre brought Dr. West across that night? Death or darkness might've been her only choice.

His discovery that Lara West survived as a vampire would impress Eyve. Theories, though. He'd have to be certain of the circumstances.

Tony yanked off goggles, mask, and gloves and gunned the engine. He put on his flashers and passed a car across a double yellow line. Not much chance he'd beat the bloodsuckers to St. Mary's, but he'd try.

The traffic light in front of the hospital cycled red before Tony arrived at the intersection. He cursed, then ran the light, but slowed enough to keep his tires from squealing as he cornered the building and approached the garage from the unfrequented side. Hopefully, Bobby Eyre and Marilyn Monroe—he still couldn't believe it was her—hadn't arrived yet. He wheeled into the garage, climbed to the roof, and parked as close to the back railing as possible. Gloves, mask, and goggles in place.

From this vantage point, he couldn't see straight down, close to the building. If they waited just five yards out, he wouldn't notice them. "Shit, shit, shit." He slid across the seat and exited the passenger door.

The interior vehicle lights faded before he crept to the edge, peeked over the wall, and scanned in all directions, adjusting and readjusting the goggles. No one. He cursed again. Either they were already here or they were feeding elsewhere. Tony sighed. Before he devised a new scheme, he spied two strolling vampires—less anxious to feed than Tony had thought.

Tony exchanged spy clothes for scrubs and the lab coat. He peered across the back of the hospital. No windows were open, and vampires would avoid ground-floor crowds.

Voices of a man and a woman carried through the night air, and the garage elevator stopped only on the fourth floor.

Tony rode down, and read the signs in the fourth-floor hallway. None of the departments jumped out as a likely vampire destination. Blah, blah, blah, and maternity. Tony stopped at an unoccupied nurses' station. He examined documents taped above the desk. On a floor map, an asterisk had been added next to maternity. *Temporary housing for psychiatric patients.* Bingo.

Thanks to his lab coat, no one questioned Tony's presence, though few people wandered maternity at this hour. *Not a single woman in labor. Not a married one, either.* Tony chuckled at his joke. He captured movement in his peripheral vision: a door closing.

Vampires—hunting blood. He saw no one, and only a vampire moved that fast. Tony rambled past, noted the room number, and kept going. He didn't want to draw attention. He'd follow up tomorrow, return as Dr. Tony and investigate who was in room—he checked his pad—431.

Tony headed for the roof. If Bobby Eyre hunted with Marilyn, where was the bitch headed?

He tried to imagine the situation. Dr. West didn't seem the type to share her boyfriend with another woman, especially not a looker like Marilyn, and especially not another vampire. Tony hustled back to the church to see who returned before sunrise.

CHAPTER 24

L ara loped across the field and entered the hospital through the parking garage, onto the second floor. The internal elevator presented too great a risk of being seen. Stairwell doors were still locked, and security monitored them. She'd never checked on Marty. Had she altered his memory? She'd seen Bobby use mind control often enough, as it was an important aspect of a successful feeding. She needed a test subject. Before she could dine, she had to prove her memory-altering ability.

Few people wandered hospital halls after visiting hours. Another employee might recognize her as Marty had, which would be a greater problem if memory adjustment failed. A patient—a stranger—would be safer. She needed someone with no heart issues, no internal bleeding or major organ damage. She could read charts at the main desk.

She waited out of sight in an alcove. The head of the night shift, Nurse Cron, manned the station haranguing Philippe. For fifteen minutes, no one approached and no one called them away. Lara didn't want to wait for scheduled rounds. Besides, Philippe's life choices weren't Nurse Cron's business. Lara could rescue him at least for a few minutes.

She hurried to the far end of the nurses' jurisdiction and stole into a double room. One woman slept on her side; the other, larger, slept on her back, snoring. Lara pushed the call button, then dumped a pitcher of ice water on the blanket, soaking the feet of the snorer. Didn't wake her or stop the snoring. Lara flipped on the light switch, left the pitcher upside down on the bed, and hurried out of the room before a rescuer arrived.

One nurse occupied, one to go. She needed another patient in distress. She circled the floor the long way and peeked around the corner. Philippe headed down the corridor to deal with waterlogged sheets.

Lara's nose wrinkled. Nurse Cron deserved something less delicate to deal with.

She sniffed outside of doors and chose one by the odor and the sounds of sleep, closer to the nurses' station than she hoped.

"Sorry," she said to the sleeping patient, then dumped a bedpan on the blanket and pressed the call button. A mess on the floor could be mopped too quickly. She shook the patient's foot to wake her, and whisked out of the room.

"What is it now?" Nurse Cron splayed her book on the desk.

"Come and see," Lara whispered.

She hid inside the doorway across the hall. Nurse Cron shuffled into the bedpan room. Lara raced to the unoccupied station and skimmed charts.

Howie Long. Single room. Admitted as a precaution for an extensive early-morning proctologic exam. Developed a priapism in-house. Because of the upcoming procedure, no pseudoephedrine or any other amphetamine was administered. *Perfect.*

She hurried along the corridor to Howie's room. Half a floor apart, Philippe and Nurse Cron squeezed mops and shook sheets. A dim light shone over Howie's headboard. Lara closed his door quietly. Hunger tugged at her throat. She'd have to be sure she could adjust his memory before she attemp–

"Are you the new doc?"

Lara jumped. *Sheesh, aren't there rules about scaring vampires?* "I'm Dr. West. I–"

"It's about time." Howie struggled to sit up. "I asked for another urologist hours ago."

"Why aren't you asleep, Mr. Long?"

"Could you sleep like this?" He pointed to the tented sheet below his waist.

She'd assumed he'd been aspirated, since the staff couldn't treat him with drugs. Lara glanced, then gazed at Howie's face. Ancient eyes stared back at her. She hadn't noted his age on the chart, assuming it irrelevant.

"Why did you request a new urologist?"

"The first one is in emergency surgery. The other doctor said I had to wait. Ridiculous. He said if I was a younger man, well . . ." His face reddened. "He'd have a nurse deal with it. I couldn't tell if he was joking. He said at my age, it was best for a specialist to take care of my condition, so he ordered me to sleep until the urologist was out of surgery. I can't sleep this way. This is what she did to her third husband, too. Killed him. Told people it was too much sex, but it was too much Viagra. She brought the pills to the hospital tonight and put a couple extra in my dinner. She must do it for the kicks, because at my age you can't order life insurance."

He wasn't making sense. "Who must do it?" Lara asked.

"Antonia. My wife. Antonia Kellogg. She's not out in the hall again, is she?

The nurse said she had to go home. Antonia wanted to play. Hell, if I knew the doctor was going to be in surgery so long, I would've let her. This is too painful to leave like this. Can you give an old guy a hand, Doc?"

"How old are you, Mr. Long?"

"Ninety-one. Antonia's ninety-two. A year and two days older than me. Except in leap year. Then she's a year and three days older. Funny how that works, huh?"

"Hilarious."

"So, Doc, you just gonna stand there lookin' pretty? I can't stay like this"—he gestured again—"and I can't fall asleep. You gotta give me a hand. One urologist is as good as another. The other doc said I'm too old for him to drain blood. He wants the specialist to do it. Says he's worried about my heart. Look at my vitals." He jerked his thumb over his shoulder at the monitor. "Does that look like the heart rate of an old man?"

Lara scrutinized the monitors. Clearheaded and strong as a fifty-year-old. Discretion suggested she escape from Howie's room. Leave this floor. Leave the hospital. Bobby had taught her vampires were only safe if they lived in anonymity. But Dr. West couldn't abandon a patient in discomfort when she could assist.

No priapism syringe. No indication cold pressure had been applied to reduce swelling. What was Nurse Cron thinking? Ice in the water pitcher would offer an old geezer OD'd on Viagra a little relief until his urologist showed up and aspirated him. The situation offered the perfect opportunity to test memory alteration.

She glanced at Howie's tent. She'd need a rubber glove or a plastic bag, something to mold into a compress. Nothing other than a glass rested on the nightstand. The bathroom yielded a trash liner and Crest. Unused, inside out, the trash bag would suffice for sanitary reasons against Howie's skin. Crest would provide a lubricant to prevent the plastic from sticking to his flesh.

"You're going to drain me?" Howie sighed.

Lara switched off the headboard light. "Don't worry, Mr. Long, you'll have relief in no time."

The monitor wouldn't cast enough light for Howie's antique eyes to see what she was doing. She pulled back the sheet. Pulsing veins made her stomach gurgle. Thirst for blood leeched on. Her skin itched everywhere. Her stomach twisted, and her brain throbbed. *Blood*, urged an inner voice, and her fangs erupted. Hunger gripped Lara and shook reason aside.

BLOOD BETWEEN LOVERS

Howie expected blood to be drained, not for ice to be applied. Lights dimmed, he'd assume she'd used a needle. She could practice feeding and altering memory with one patient. What if memory alteration didn't work? If Howie believed he was drained medically, it wouldn't make any difference. Besides, he was old enough, he might just forget.

She peered into Howie's face.

"Is that a syringe in your pocket, or are you just happy to see me?" Howie sunk into his pillow.

Lara grinned and pressed her lips together to conceal treatment. No longer part of the plan, she wiped the toothpaste on his belly. "What do you think?" she whispered.

She leaned to block his view, just in case, and realized she'd need a firm grip. Her hand, still sticky from Crest, slid up and down.

Howie sighed—Lara attacked and sucked with the same speed she'd used on Jake—Howie screamed.

Lara dropped the sheet and covered his mouth. "Shh. You'll wake the neighbors."

Howie wiggled free. "Holy freakin' cow. What'd you do to me?"

Howie sounded like Jake's grandfather. Lara leaned closer to Howie's ear. She cleaned blood from her fangs and retracted. Hunger still pounded head and stomach. She recalled Bobby's words, like the airlines explaining oxygen masks. *See to your needs first, then...*

"You will not remember Dr. West." Lara repeated the mantra several times, removed her hand from Howie's mouth, and flipped on the headboard light.

Howie cocked his head. "Are you the urologist?"

"Why do you need an urologist?" Lara asked.

Howie's eyes widened, his expression stating the obvious. He pointed at his collapsed tent before he realized it had collapsed. "What the hell happened?" He dove under the sheets to investigate, and came out with goop dripping in his hand.

"Let me find you a towel, Mr. Long."

"Did you do this?" Howie called to her back.

Lara emerged from the bathroom dangling a towel and managed a straight face.

The room door popped open. "Howie?" an elderly voice demanded a response. A woman hobbled into the room in orthopedic shoes. "Are you okay, sweetheart? I had to sneak in to help. Surgery is taking forever. I know you can't sleep—" She spied Lara. "Who're you?"

"Antonia," Howie said, "that's no way to talk to my new doctor. Look what she did for me." He raised the goop-filled hand.

Antonia frowned. "I was going to do that for you. How'd she do it?"

Howie shrugged. "I have no idea."

Antonia wobbled closer to the bed. She sniffed. "Did you just brush your dentures?"

Lara handed Antonia the towel. "Young lady, please make sure Mr. Long is clean and dry."

"Excuse me?" Antonia said.

"Mr. Long, I advise you to rest. Priapism can drain your energy." Lara ducked out of the room before either could ask more questions.

Despite feeding twice tonight, hunger raged. How did Bobby survive feeding this way? She glanced down the hall. Nurse Cron headed into the bedpan room, towing janitor Blissockiss behind her. How'd he escape hospital reprimand or criminal charges?

Lara scampered around a corner before Nurse Cron reemerged. Confidence filled her thoughts. She'd fed herself and altered the memory of her prey.

"Clean the bed frame as well as the floor," Nurse Cron commanded the disgusting janitor. "And make it snappy. These patients have to get back to sleep. I'm going to send another nurse in here to change the sheets. I'll be at my station."

So much for feeding in the hospital tonight.

Lara exited through the garage and headed across the field. Bobby would find her more attractive as a self-reliant vampire. The image of an hourglass blonde laughed at her feeble feeding but offered sympathy for the attempt. Hunger wrapped tentacles around Lara. Her fangs ached for blood. The half-moon glared, daring her to take the next step, the full transition into the self-sustaining vampire of her demon.

No.

She couldn't drain a victim of his blood as her beast demanded, but she could feed again tonight. She glanced over her shoulder at the hospital fading in the distance. What alternatives did that leave? A sincere Jake? He'd offered his blood. He wouldn't want her to be discovered. He must truly believe shopping for blood at Summit Square would be the safest place for her to feed.

Bobby was sincere when he said she could feed anywhere. She needed to be careful not to take so much blood as to be noticed.

BLOOD BETWEEN LOVERS

An owl peered at her from an upper bough a hundred yards away. She snarled. The owl hooted and flew away; his eyesight almost matched hers. She trotted the half mile to Summit Square Center without exertion. The parking lot lights cast a dim glow over the buildings. Jake always had ulterior motives. What did he really want?

At one end of the lot, a few cars huddled in front of the grocery store. At the near end, restaurants attracted a crowd, as Jake had suggested. Safe feeding required a plan.

What if she saw someone walking alone to his car? Follow? Then what? She'd need to be subtle, encourage a conversation, and seduce her prey into acquiescence.

A man and a woman loitered in front of the pub, smoking. Lara drifted in the shadows. The couple inhaled together, ignored the giant ashtray, and flicked cigarette butts on the sidewalk. They hugged, he groped, she groped, and they laughed and careened toward a car.

Lara waited. Her skin prickled in anticipation. Her tongue glided over the points of her fangs and ripped the flesh. She swallowed the spurt as the wounds healed. Dr. West found self-healing the most amazing aspect of her transformation, and oddly—after several excruciating attempts—the piercing of her tongue nearly painless.

An edgy laugh trilled from Lara the vampire. Hunger propelled her actions. A true creature of the night, Lara West hunted blood.

The pub door opened, and a plump man stumbled out. Alone. Intoxicated.

CHAPTER 25

If Lara waited, resolve might falter. She emerged from the shadows, stepped onto the sidewalk, and approached the drunk. He swaggered and leaned against a post supporting the overhang. She'd have to direct him someplace private to feed. Her townhouse? Okay, if she was sure of the memory wipe. It'd worked on Howie. Would it work with everyone? Bobby said Philippe remained resistant to mind control. No idea why.

"Beautiful night, isn't it?" Lara said. Too late to worry now.

The man twisted in slow motion, not to see who spoke to him but to study the night and determine if it was, in fact, beautiful. He belched. His gaze swept full circle and settled on Lara.

"Beautiful." He belched louder.

Lara sidled into his space. Her arm encircled his. "Walk with me," she suggested.

The man hitched up his pants with one hand. He beamed and smirked as though he'd done something to warrant the attention of a woman.

Lara's nose twitched. He reeked of alcohol and body odor. Drunk enough. Perhaps she could feed under the trees behind the shopping center and not have to bring this disgusting man into her home. She pulled his arm closer to her hip as they strolled down the sidewalk, away from the pub and the other restaurants. His hand grazed her thigh, causing a noticeable reaction behind his zipper.

Hunger propelled her along this path. She gripped his arm with her other hand. Her meal would not escape.

The drunk's neck veins popped, outlined by starlight. His body gurgled. The size of this man combined with his revolting presence and the voice in her head and tempted her to drain all of his blood.

Sate your hunger.

She swallowed temptation. "No." Lara refused to acknowledge the voice as an aspect of self. That couldn't be her. She had to drink blood to survive, but her human persona had to remain in control at all times. Her prey would live and never know he'd been the vessel of a vampire's meal.

BLOOD BETWEEN LOVERS

The man hiccupped, stretched, and patted Lara's hand. "Don't worry, sweetie, I'm all yours." He spoke with a Midwestern twang. "Did you know I'm a powerful man?"

Liar. This man isn't what he seems, and he's not drunk. He sounds more like a vote-shucking politician than a horny stumbling bastard.

"Bill. Where do you think you're going?" a female voice behind them demanded. A short-haired woman postured on the sidewalk in front of the pub, dressed in a power suit, feet spread, hands on hips. "You pig. We're heading back to the farm. Now."

Bill the pig tugged his arm from Lara's grip and spun to face his farmer. Lara glided backward, into the shadow of the building.

"Nowhere, darlin'. I was just window-shoppin' with my new friend." Bill spoke, and his new friend whisked away.

From the opposite end of the shopping center, Lara observed her flabby meal shrivel. The woman glared in Lara's direction—as if she too had vampire sight—before ducking into the car. Lara gritted her teeth and hissed. She stretched her toes and clenched and unclenched her fingers. Her skin crawled with desire. *Blood.* Lara swallowed the word only and rocked back on her heels.

She closed her eyes and imagined feeding from Bill, not as she'd fed from Jake or Howie, but attacking Bill's neck with reckless abandon and sucking until Bill's blood was drained, as her demon desired. Her eyes popped open. Lara was filled with a sanguine passion and the overwhelming urge of her human side to be sick.

She waited an hour. Two hours. The restaurants closed. The pub kicked out the last of the power drinkers and locked the door. Cars drove away. Opportunity dissolved. Lara strode along the sidewalk. Tonight encouraged hope. Jake's blood energized her. His pep talk, combined with her jealousy for Marilyn, had driven her to feed from Howie. A small amount of blood, but it was the first blood neither volunteered nor provided for her.

Lara laughed. Blood from a ninety-one-year-old priapism.

She slowed to window-shop. The jewelry store pulled all the merchandise from their nighttime display window. The clothing store didn't match her taste. The shoe store displayed an interesting mix of footwear, however. The In-Step. She'd browsed here with Philippe. Jake insisted she stay away. Why? Go to the shopping center, but stay away from the shoe store. Were stockroom shadows related to Jake's warning?

"Beautiful evening, isn't it?"

Lara jumped. Tingling arced through her limbs, and she spun around. She'd used the same line on intended prey hours ago. Her fangs erupted, and she fought to control the urge to lash out. A tall man scrutinized her, though he backed up half a step at her aggressive stance.

"I'm sorry." His handsome face wrinkled. "I didn't mean to startle you."

The dulcet tone soothed, the trace of an indeterminate accent. Continental? Lara's fangs dissolved, and she regained control. "I wasn't expecting anyone," she said.

"I don't know why not. Lots of people shop for shoes at two thirty in the morning." The man forced a smile. Perfect teeth peeked from between his lips. He pointed at the display. "I like the one with the shiny toe."

His voice cracked, as though she'd scared him more than he'd scared her. She'd never seen such a gorgeous man. Chiseled lines on his face and neck lent an authoritative air, contrary to his fear. His ears were small for a man his size, and close to his head. Muscles rippling beneath his shirt suggested an athlete. Though he presented a calm demeanor, Lara sensed he might run away at any moment.

"Typical male choice. Put a woman in high heels." The corners of Lara's lips curled up, but the man blushed.

"I . . . I didn't mean . . ."

He seemed horrified he might have insulted her. She didn't want him to feel bad. "No, no, please, I'm teasing," she said. "Is this when you usually shop for shoes? I prefer shopping alone."

The man glanced at the sidewalk, his lips pursed. When he peeked up, his amber eyes reflected moonlight. "I'm sorry to bother you, then. I'll go." He whirled.

"No, wait," Lara said.

The man paused, but no hope of reprieve graced his façade.

"I didn't mean I want to be alone now." How did he study her without invading her privacy? "When I shop, I'm used to being on my own." She flashed an encouraging grin. The man scrunched nose and eyes.

"Maybe we can start again?" Lara suggested. She glanced at the sky, then back at the arcane face. "Beautiful night, isn't it?"

The man's posture flattered his features. His hair was black and swept back. His sideburns were long and blended into that scruffy look that complemented certain men. He inhaled a deep breath. "Once your eyes adjust, it's surprising how many stars you can see despite the shopping center lights."

Lara sniffed. Something familiar in his scent, but no trace of alcohol. He hadn't been a pub customer. No cars remained in the parking lot. Where'd he come from? "Kind of late for stargazing, isn't it?"

"You mean, later than it is for shoe shopping?" He beamed. "The Perseids." His eyes lit up like a child at the circus. "Meteor showers. This is the second-best time of year to see them." He pointed. On cue, a meteorite streaked across a patch of sky and disintegrated in the atmosphere.

"Wow. I thought only gods commanded celestial bodies." Lara's voice teased.

The man waved. "Parlor trick."

"Or a portent?" Lara asked.

"Of more parlor tricks? Consider yourself warned."

"I'll be on guard. But against whom, Mr. . . . ?"

"Nalbandian."

"Mr. Nalbandian."

The man curled his lips, tighter than before. "No, just Nalbandian."

"Nalbandian, then. Surname? First name?"

"Neither. Just Nalbandian, Ms. . . . ?"

Lara was about to say "Dr. West," but she resided in Bucks County, and people who knew her here knew her as a nurse. "Meridian Jones." Lara extended her hand, something she wouldn't do in an empty parking lot with a strange man if she didn't have the superiority of a vampire. Hell, if she weren't a vampire, she wouldn't be in a deserted shopping center at two thirty in the morning, Perseids or not.

Nalbandian clasped her hand with a firm grip, and a quiver frolicked up her arm and across her shoulders. Warmth spread outward from the pit of her stomach. His eyes danced beneath brooding eyebrows and curled her toes. Heat rose in her face. She was aroused by a handsome stranger. Not the reaction she'd expected.

They maintained the handshake longer than decorum demanded. His respiration increased, and his heart rate spiked.

I'm turning him on, too.

"This is an unexpected pleasure," Nalbandian said. "I didn't anticipate company stargazing tonight."

"I seem to be interfering with your plans."

"On the contrary. If one of these establishments remained open, I'd offer to buy you a cup of coffee. Sit and talk."

"I'd be happier talking under the stars."

"Perfect. Allow me to direct you, then, to our open-air planetarium."

Warmth expanded. Their grips disengaged. Lara leaned back to enjoy the moonlight splashing across the most beautiful face imaginable. An aquiline nose, high cheekbones, and almond-shaped eyes lent the man a regal air. For the first time in months, someone other than Bobby sent butterflies flitting across her stomach.

Bobby.

He'd left her tonight.

He'd chosen Marilyn, hadn't he?

Lara had choices to make, too. Tonight's successes had boosted her confidence.

Blood, an inner voice demanded. A second urge surged forward, sexual, sensual, enhanced by bloodlust and the blood she'd already drunk and the anticipation of more, and a gorgeous, shy gentleman posing just beyond arm's reach. Urges collided. Drinking blood heightened her desire for more blood. Desire extended beyond longing, beyond want or need. Bloodlust exploded into passion, and the passion consumed her soul, overriding humanity.

Blood.

Feelings froze. No concern for the well-being of this man. Stripped away was the Hippocratic oath of Dr. Lara West. She'd introduced herself as Meridian Jones, her persona in the moment, a vampire. Epiphany. Meridian was to Lara as Roberre to Bobby. Meridian the beast. She growled.

"Excuse me?" Nalbandian said.

Lara insisted on control over her beast. She stretched up on her toes. "Sometimes I talk to myself. I'm sorry. Are you a professional stargazer, or is this a hobby?"

"I've studied the night sky from the Artic to the Gobi Desert to the Himalayan peaks. It's not my business, but it's certainly more than a hobby. I'm fascinated by the finite immortality of stars."

"Finite immortality? I don't understand."

"Human life is brief by comparison. We mistakenly think of celestial bodies as immortal, yet even stars die. They go nova. It's rare that a human would ever witness such an event, but over the span of enough lifetimes . . ."

"I thought you were looking for a meteor shower tonight. Isn't that the opposite of what you're talking about?"

"The meteorite is a microcosm of the star's life. Time compressed: birth, existence, fire and passion, then death."

Odd this man related passion to the life of an inanimate object. But was it any odder she'd related passion to bloodlust? "You've traveled the world on business?"

"I've traveled the world on life."

"Life takes you from majestic world peaks to Bucks County, Pennsylvania?"

Nalbandian shrugged.

"Do you have family here?"

"No."

"What's the connecting thread between the Gobi Desert, the Himalayas, and Pennsylvania? I don't see—sorry, I'm being too personal."

"I don't mind. We all have choices to make; urges drive us along one path or another. Urges in my life have delivered me to Langhorne. Whatever the universal force, it's steered us to cross paths tonight."

"Fate?"

"I don't believe in fate. What happens next is up to us. Universal forces have swirled our paths so they may intersect, not by necessity but not randomly, either."

Lara didn't respond. Whom had she stumbled upon? Gorgeous and a philosopher? Eloquent. Humming electricity in the parking lot lights disturbed the air and interrupted her thoughts. The occasional passing car on the highway, a freight train rumbling in the distance, a cacophony of cicadas and crickets and frogs—all played in the background.

Hearing, like her other senses, magnified, and a police radio intruded. No patrol car was visible, but one approached. Better not to be seen. She needed privacy for feeding. They could hardly make love in the open. She could—

Nalbandian cleared his throat. "There's a farm nearby. Less interference from the lights. Can I entice you to take a walk?"

Coincidence? They'd pass her townhouse to reach the field. She could invite him in, or suggest a pretense to stop. This handsome, enigmatic thinker would be a joy to seduce.

She imagined her fangs puncturing his flesh and the sweet taste of blood squirting into her mouth. She'd tease him first, and he'd grip her shoulder, part in pain, part in delight, unaware until too late that she drank his blood. Then she'd wipe his memory and scoot him outside to watch his meteorites.

Lara glanced over her shoulder. A patrol car glided into the parking lot. Lara and Nalbandian escaped unseen.

"Do you believe in fate?" Nalbandian asked.

"I believe events happen randomly, and we make our own choices."

"Coincidence then we met tonight, but we choose to travel this path together now?"

"Being together now is our choice, and no force delivered us to this moment. Wherever we were, whatever we were doing the moment before we met and the moment before that were also conscious choices."

"Are we defined then by our choices or our actions?"

"Choices."

"A fortunate decision for me to cross the parking lot instead of following the road to the field. Perhaps I should also choose lottery numbers tonight?"

Lara eyed him, uncertain if he joked or flirted. "We'd have to split the winnings."

They followed the road behind the shopping center, around a curve, and into a neighborhood of townhouses.

"I live here." Lara pointed. "Can I convince you to choose to stop at my house for a minute?"

"Master of my fate, lead on." Nalbandian swept his arm in a grand gesture.

Sinew and bone molded hard behind his shirt. The even set of his jaw and moonlight grazing off a neck vein ramped up her desire. Lara fought to keep her fangs from erupting. The inner voice warred for control. More than blood, the voice demanded passion, a sensual mixture of blood and sex. What would it hurt? She'd experienced Stage One of Vampirical Harmony often enough with Bobby. VH heightened his feeding experience, despite the bottled blood she insisted he drink instead of hers. Fresh blood in the moment after climax could expand her orgasm as well. Come sunrise, she could sleep here, cravings in body and mind satisfied.

"Have you lived here long?" Nalbandian asked.

Jake and Bobby had taught her to avoid revealing personal information. They answered questions with questions. "I didn't notice a car in the parking lot. Do you live nearby too?"

"In Newtown. I found an old house for sale, and I'm fixing it up. I'm doing as much of the work myself as I can. Construction prices are astronomical, and I enjoy working with my hands."

Nalbandian didn't ask about the empty driveway. Lara propped the screen door open with her hip and inserted the key. Nalbandian followed her into the kitchen, closing the door behind him. Lara tossed the key on the counter. She sniffed an attractive male muskiness. Her enhanced senses exposed a goofy but uncertain grin plastered on her guest, shrouded in the dark. Lara sidled closer. She'd kiss his neck, taste the salt on his skin, feel his pulse throb. He'd moan when her hand slid across his trousers.

"Would you mind . . ." Nalbandian said. "I mean, since we're here anyway, may I use your bathroom?"

Lara struggled not to laugh. She summoned memory. The downstairs bathroom was closer. "Top of the stairs, through the doorway, turn right." Sending him upstairs enhanced the eroticism of the moment.

"I, ah, sorry, I can't see the stairs."

Lara brushed against his chest and tapped the wall light. A dimmer switch created a soft glow on the staircase. Nalbandian climbed with the fluid ease of an athlete.

How to seduce him? Wait upstairs in the bedroom. Naked? Enter the bathroom while he washed his hands? Simply overpower him?

Philippe and Jake had volunteered. They realized she would drink their blood. Howie hadn't known, but he couldn't see what occurred under the sheet, and he got what he expected—a prick. Her other victims were all either sedated, dead, or tied down. She didn't have anything with which to sedate Nalbandian, and she preferred him alive.

Decision made, she kicked off her shoes and dashed up the stairs. The toilet flushed. She searched the bedroom closet, pulled the terry cloth sash off her robe, and waited in the shadows by the bed. A wall of windows spread behind her, and a vaulted ceiling stretched the darkness into a comfortable space.

Nalbandian washed and dried his hands; then awareness dawned that Lara observed from the depths of the bedroom. He ambled toward her, leaving the bathroom light on behind him, his expression perplexed.

"Did I do something bad? Use the wrong towel? I put the seat back down." He crossed his heart and sidled inside Lara's personal space.

Lara's free hand splayed on his chest. "You startled me at the shopping center, but you've impressed me with your knowledge and self-awareness. I'm aroused." She held his gaze and stroked his jaw.

Nalbandian frowned. "You're not, you know . . . a nightwalker, are you?"

"Excuse me?"

"Maybe that's the wrong word. Um, a streetwalker?" His weight shifted from hip to hip. He shuffled in place, and blushed. He glanced at the carpet. "This is all kind of fast. You're not expecting me to . . . pay you, right?"

Lara laughed. Her fingers drifted into his hair. "You can pay me, but not in money."

"I don't understand."

Lara raised the robe sash. "If I tie your hands behind your back, push you onto the bed, and take advantage of you, will you be mad?"

"How would a little thing like you get my hands behind my back, let alone tied?"

"If you'll remove your shoe, I'll show you." Lara pointed.

Nalbandian glanced to see which foot she meant. Lara yanked his wrists behind his back, slid a slip knot over them, and tightened it.

"That's not exactly loose." Nalbandian peeked at her. "How'd you do that?"

Lara spun him around, his back to the bed. Her breath quickened, and heat rose from her neck into her face. She undid his belt and the hook on his trousers and let them fall around his ankles. She gripped the expanding bulge in his boxers. "You seem as excited as I am."

"What're you doing?"

She released him and pushed his chest. He fell on the bed, and Lara tugged off his shoes and socks.

"Hey!"

He wriggled, but that just made it easier for her to pull off his boxers too. Bathroom light stretched to the bed and cast an impressive shadow. She paused to admire; he was twice the size of Howie. Lara backed up. The advantage would be hers in the dark.

"Where're you going?" Nalbandian asked.

Lara pirouetted and tapped off the bathroom light. Her prey lay trussed and primed on the bed. After his eyes adjusted, the skylights would allow enough light for Nalbandian to see her outline but not her fangs. She peeled off her clothes and climbed on top of him, wet with anticipation.

Unable to control her lust, she settled over him, and he bucked. She guided him into her, and they moaned in unison. He thrust upward, lifting her knees off the bed. She squeezed her thighs around his hips to keep from being thrown. Wave after wave of intense pleasure filled her core. Tension mounted. She leaned back, her shoulders touching his knees, the oblique angle reflecting exquisite pain in Nalbandian's expression and expanding her smile.

She glided back and forth. His breathing grew ragged before hers. She detected his increased pulse and the precursor flush to his orgasm. The smell of sex filled the bedroom.

Not enough time to savor the experience.

She hopped off and pinched him between thumb and forefinger, preventing the imminent explosion.

"Meridian."

"You know what it means when a man is naked in your bed, gasping and calling your name?"

"You stopped a second too soon?"

"It means you didn't hold down the pillow long enough."

Nalbandian laughed. "That's not funny, considering the position I'm in."

"That's funny regardless of the position you're in."

He raised his head. "How about untying me?"

Lara pushed his shoulders. "Not until I'm finished."

"You know you can't leave me like this."

"I can for a while."

Lara spun around and knelt over his chest, back to face. She leaned forward and stroked from hips to ankles and up again. Her breasts brushed his thighs, and his excitement greeted her.

She fluttered over his knee and nibbled on his flesh, careful not to puncture. Yet.

Tension remounted, and his toes stretched up and in.

Nalbandian's femoral artery pulsated, high on his inner thigh. A sensation struck her, more obvious now than with any feeding with Bobby—bloodlust filled her being, inseparable from her sexual thirst. Her fangs erupted. A low rumble emerged from deep in her throat. Greater satisfaction would arise in the simultaneous explosion of orgasm and blood. She needed to feed at the moment she came. Longings for blood and sex intertwined in such a way Lara couldn't disconnect them.

Even with vampire agility, she couldn't ride him and bite high on the femoral artery at the same moment. Untying and allowing him to use his hands presented an unacceptable risk. She'd have to orgasm a different way, and she couldn't wait.

Blood. Her flesh smoldered in anticipation of sexual fulfillment. The idea of concurrent gratification delivered her to a frenzy, unable to control her actions. She needed to feed now.

She pulled his legs up in the air and hooked them under her arms. She luxuriated in an erotic moment, and slid backward toward Nalbandian's face. His tongue trailed high on her inner thigh, teasing her flesh. He wanted to play. She no longer had the time. She needed satisfaction now.

A corner of her brain urged caution, not to hurt this man, allow him the pleasure of Stage One in exchange for a morsel of blood.

The frenzy allowed no time to think. She shoved her hips down, forcing his tongue where she wanted it to go, and she gasped as it found its mark. Eroticism overrode all other sensations. She massaged him, her fangs bared. He engorged further. How could that be? But his excitement fed hers. Nalbandian rocked, and his legs trembled. His tongue darted in and out of her. Eroticism expanded consciousness. She sensed his climax imminent.

She focused on the blood flooding his groin, inches from her mouth.

Seconds away from orgasm, this was her conquest, this erected her triumph in her primary persona. A solitary existence was possible; satisfaction of sexual urges and blood thirst spread eternity like a giant banquet, and her victims survived unharmed. This was the balance she sought between humanity and vampire.

The orgasmic explosion rocketed through her, emanating in all directions, beginning somewhere near Nalbandian's mouth and surging toward her extremities. In the same instant, she felt his explosion race through him. This time she didn't stop it. Mutual satisfaction included the blood of her partner. She eyed a pulsing artery and attacked.

The instant before her fangs pierced his flesh, inexplicable simultaneous sensations ripped through her. He seized her hips. Somehow, he'd managed to free his hands, and he locked her over his face. She screamed as fangs bored into her buttocks.

CHAPTER 26

P ain intensified, and Lara struggled in vain. Nalbandian slipped his ankles behind her neck and pressed down. His fangs ripped her flesh. Blood poured from the wound into his mouth. A childhood nightmare of falling filled her psyche, and weakness seeped into her limbs. Helplessness overwhelmed, and her body surrendered to the shadows.

Lara fought to maintain consciousness. A face loomed close to hers, fathomless eyes much like Bobby's but not Bobby. Disenfranchised feelings intersected her mind. She tried to utilize Bobby's teachings, to protect herself from a vampire, but nothing she did prevented Nalbandian from invading her thoughts. He forced his will upon her in a way she didn't understand and couldn't defy.

She lay on the bed, unable to summon the strength to resist or to run or even to cover herself. Nalbandian posed nearby, also naked, and admiring her. His eyes glistened crimson, transformed from the shy stargazer to the feral hunter. No escape. No hope remained.

Blood dripped from his fangs and smeared his lips. He bathed in it, relishing the act and flaunting control. Fear arced through consciousness. Life as she knew it ended. She belonged to Nalbandian's will.

"You're not being forced," Nalbandian said. "A moment ago, you made a conscious choice. You're about to make another, and our paths will be forever linked."

To emphasize her thoughts, Nalbandian raised her feet, braced them against his thighs, and rubbed her ankles. Lara did not resist, unable to resist. His act was pedestrian in its innocence, subtle in its sensuousness.

"Hundreds every hour," Nalbandian said.

Lara didn't understand.

"The Perseids. Hundreds of meteorites every hour, though human eyes miss most of them. You and I will see them all."

Lara didn't want to see anything with this vampire. She wanted to escape, but she remained unable to veer from his beautiful face.

"In a few minutes, you'll beg me." Nalbandian's softened tone was replaced by confident command, equally as sensual.

What if he dragged her outside? What if he forced her eyes open? Tilted her head to watch the sky? Why would she beg him?

"The urge for sexual gratification will be as powerful as your bloodlust. Forever entwined, you can no more avoid one than the other. You've tasted the power that arises from drinking blood. Sexual passion is equally demanding."

Lara shook her head. His words were disjointed. Nalbandian didn't expect her to beg for shooting stars. He expected her to beg for–

"I sense you're newly turned, resisting the bloodlust. You've never killed, have you?" He didn't wait for an answer. "Time evaporates human frailties and overrides the remaining morality. We're creatures of this world, with every right to exist that mankind maintains. Our existence may require the occasional human sacrifice. So what? If desire wells, take life from the bottom-sucking scum. No one will miss the drug dealers or the shoe salesmen."

Nalbandian lowered her left leg to the bed, but stepped closer and raised the other to rest against his shoulder. He nuzzled her calf and tilted her leg to kiss her ankle.

"You've crossed another barrier. Only human blood can satisfy your one need, but no human can satisfy the other. Even as we speak, you're losing control to your urges."

Lara blinked and clutched her shrinking human will, surrounded and squeezed by bloodlust. She'd drunk Howie's blood, and she'd pursued Nalbandian.

"I sensed the frenzy when you attacked me," Nalbandian said. "You lost control then, and you're about to lose it again."

"There's no frenzy in me now. Only fear."

Nalbandian's attention never altered, and Lara couldn't look away. His fangs glistened, licked clean. He pricked the tip of his index finger, and a scarlet bead shimmered in the dark.

"Smell it," he commanded.

Lara could do nothing else. A single drop of blood intoxicated her, but the aroma entwined with the smell of sex lingering on the bed and in the air. Blood and sex combined in a new sensation, unique in this plane of existence. Bobby had hinted at the connection, but never delivered this dimension.

BLOOD BETWEEN LOVERS

Desire for blood boiled under her flesh. Her fingers ached, but her hands couldn't move. The throbbing in her fangs demanded fulfillment. Her toes arched when Nalbandian's teeth grazed her foot. A shiver raced across her shoulders. He fondled her leg. The smell of sex expanded in her consciousness, and she gasped. Desire laced her senses with a dual design: the taste of blood and the simultaneous taste of sex.

Nalbandian's other hand graced the dark, palm open, and the drop of sanguine fluid glided toward Lara's mouth. She yearned for the satisfaction of blood and sex, a synchronized experience. She wanted to raise her head, grab his finger, and suck. She fought the urge to arch her hips and invite Nalbandian to enter.

He draped her leg over his shoulder and edged onto the bed. He raised her other leg—nothing she could do to prevent him from taking what he wanted, but she wouldn't beg for it. She braced for the violation sure to come. Nalbandian didn't move. He held his hand just beyond reach, food tantalizingly close. Her stomach gurgled in confession.

"I know you want this." Nalbandian opened his palm wider. "And I know you want this." He glanced below his waist. "Your desire is building. You think it's wrong to suck blood from your victims. You'll find a surprising number of volunteers. Here." He raised the finger. "This will be yours when you ask for it."

He expected her to beg for blood.

He angled his hips forward. "This will be yours too, when you ask."

He expected her to beg for sex.

The scent of trepidation filled her nostrils. She'd drunk fresh blood tonight, but she needed more. She'd stolen blood tonight, and she'd been so close to draining more, to attacking the flesh of this man at the same instant he'd given her an orgasm. She'd thought him human. Feelings and tastes coalesced into new sensations. Desire flowed, twisted on like a spigot whose threads are stripped, unable to be shut off.

The taste of blood lingered in her throat.

The taste of sex lingered in the pit of her stomach. Neither could be exorcised. Both could be quenched. Both could be satisfied now.

No.

Nalbandian's finger glided under her nose. The bouquet enticed her. On his knees, he inched closer. The desire to be filled spread from her hips to the tips of her toes.

Nalbandian waited. Epiphany allowed a glimmer of understanding: force wasn't necessary. Craving for blood and sex reared up inside her. Lara fought for control of urges she didn't want in this moment. She had no idea how to rule them or to disengage.

"How do you stop a vampire from wanting blood?" Nalbandian asked.

The idea of drinking blood had nauseated her id, ego, and superego not long ago. "I'm still human."

"Once you succumb to your nature, your actions will define your existence." Lara shivered, denying comprehension.

"You can't deny who you are," Nalbandian said. He leaned close to Lara's face and licked the drop of blood from his finger. "This is who I am. This is what I am." He closed his fist. "I can choose to torture this being by hating myself, or I can accept the reality of the situation."

He opened his hand again, and another drop oozed on his fingertip.

"Yours when you ask."

"I'm still human."

Did the words hold less conviction? Was she not defined by her thoughts? Her thoughts were her choices.

I choose to be a doctor.

"You've experienced the frenzy tonight. Not something you thought about, not something you chose, but nothing would have prevented it. It's your nature. It's my nature. It is what defines us. We're vampires."

She admitted to those urges. No, *admitted* didn't accurately describe reality. She was loath to concede Nalbandian was right and nothing she could've done would have prevented the frenzy. His jaw glided along her ankle, and he nibbled there. A deep sigh escaped her, the world clarified with that exhalation.

What had happened to her fidelity to the Hippocratic oath?

Nalbandian knew she wanted blood. She needed it. Bobby had taught himself to endure a month between feedings. Couldn't she control the urge in this moment?

Her attention narrowed on Nalbandian's finger. How could one drop of blood exude such a powerful scent? Her skin crawled. The sun tattoo flamed on the small of her back. Moments before, she'd climbed on top of this man, unable to restrain desire. She needed blood and sex to survive. Nalbandian had touched nothing more than her ankle in the last half hour, but the overpowering scent of her sex wafted around them as though they'd made love for hours.

BLOOD BETWEEN LOVERS

"Let go of your inhibitions," Nalbandian said. "It is false hope of a people you can no longer cling to."

If Lara surrendered all her human inhibitions, she'd be lost in a world of darkness. "No."

"I'm speaking to the vampire in you, not the human. It's your vampire inhibitions you need to release. Your human side has already been walled off and will disappear completely soon enough."

"I can maintain humanity indefinitely." Bobby did, but the emptiness behind these words filled her with melancholy. "The loss of humanity would be sad, but sadness at least is a human emotion."

"You're confusing emotions with a state of being. You'll still have emotions, and like your senses, your feelings will be magnified. Where humans are servants of their feelings, the will of a vampire is strong enough to override any sensation. You'll cut the strings of human attachments and function as a truly autonomous being, except of course when you're in the influence of another, more powerful vampire."

"You mean, forced against my will."

"No. Influence means you'll agree with my will. Voluntarily."

She'd been captured by a vampire before. Robert Helstrom. He had forced her to perform scientific experiments, but she had never been under his influence. He'd coerced her cooperation by threatening her friends with his servant, Tony. Tony, the pyromaniac. She knew Tony was capable of harming her friends.

Nalbandian laughed as if he read her mind. "Coercion isn't necessary. You're about to beg me to feed." He raised his hand a few inches. "Not out of fear, but out of desire. Passion will dominate your emotions, but it's passion you can no longer compartmentalize or contain. Yours is now the true obsession of a vampire: blood *and* sex." He lowered his head and mapped a thin line between her thigh and her pelvis with his tongue.

Lara couldn't stop the jolt rocketing through her, or the goose bumps Nalbandian's mouth raised on her skin. She didn't want to have this reaction. She didn't want him to touch her that way—and she did—and she didn't. Confusion reigned.

"Don't worry. Your mind will sort it out in a moment. Odd as it sounds, you'll reason you need to concede to your passion. Abandon your vampire inhibitions. Humankind is ruled by logic and reason. Vampires utilize logic and reason, but ours is governed by our passion for blood and sex."

Lara couldn't think clearly.

"The onset of frenzy clouds the mind. Don't fight it. Allow the feelings to wash over you. Allow passion to rule. It will anyhow. Your desire will overwhelm all aspects of being. Your existence will be defined by your frenzy. You're a vampire. There's no avoiding it."

Lara's thoughts swirled, rationalization impossible. She couldn't succumb to the frenzy. Fear she'd be lost to her beast restricted breathing—breathing that no longer mattered. "I'm Dr. Lara West." She clung to the mantra. With logic and reason?

"Logic demands you ask, who was Dr. West? What has she become in this moment?"

Moonlight swept into her room through the skylight. Her thoughts were unable to walk a straight line, drunk on the smell of blood, but staggering toward discovery. Her body craved an explosion beyond a human orgasm. Her flesh demanded the sensations of blood and sex combined, a new plane of existence.

The tip of Nalbandian's finger touched Lara's lips, the blood within easy reach of her tongue. "You thought you were lying to me when you made your introduction, but you spoke a truth you were not ready to admit," he said, and pulled his palm back a few inches. "Care to try again? Who are you?"

Feelings rushed her, feelings she couldn't control and that defied comprehension. Human reality slipped away. Blood and sex, sex and blood, nothing distinguished them from each other. No longer two thoughts, but one.

"Who am I?" she whispered.

She was about to respond "Dr. Lara West," but passion intervened. "I am Meridian Jones," she whispered again.

"Ah. The truth at last." His gaze locked with hers. "And?"

Meridian's nostrils flared. Blood scent laced the air already riddled with sex. She glanced at his body, hovering inches above her, ready, waiting.

"You will be defined by your actions," Nalbandian's voice mimicked her whisper.

"Fuck me," Meridian said. She captured his finger in her mouth, then corralled his hips and eased him into her.

CHAPTER 27

"I had no idea you'd been turned."

Marilyn coddled the back of Bobby's head. "Sweetie, don't worry about it. It's not an issue, but I've missed you."

Bobby laid his hand in the palm lock, and the first door opened. Lara had left the house. For tonight or forever?

"Why didn't you contact me? Where've you been all this time?"

"Tied up." Marilyn winked at him. "I'm here now." She squeezed his biceps. "Your house looks comfortable, though I imagine you move frequently?"

"Every five years. This is my favorite home in the last two centuries, and I'd like to stay longer."

"You seem familiar with hospital routines."

"Until recently, I worked as a nurse in that hospital."

Marilyn nodded. "I can imagine you as a nurse, but I see you as the man you are." She drifted her fingers through his hair, just above his ear, and her fingernails tantalized his scalp. "You always saw me for the woman I am, more than an actress."

The line of her cheek, the curve of her hip, endured as he'd remembered them. Marilyn Monroe. "You were a perfect example of a woman greater than the sum of her parts," Bobby said.

Marilyn studied the manuscript of *Romeo and Juliet* and spoke without looking up. "You took a job to feed there. Always like tonight? From psychiatric patients?"

"I've been trying to teach Meridian to do the same. She hasn't adjusted to the darkness yet."

Bobby salivated with the sway of Marilyn's hips, her bearing unchanged across decades. What male wasn't attracted to the visceral Marilyn? But he'd fallen in love with the complex creature—unpredictable, perceptive, impatient and a little insecure.

Marilyn wove through the sanctuary, stroking statues and artifacts, as if enticing the inanimate objects with—what had Freud called it?— vampirification. Everything she touched came alive in his imagination, accentuated by her caress. The sensuousness that had endured in the human Marilyn had followed her across the boundary into life as a vampire. When her fangs had erupted and grazed the flesh of Bobby's victim tonight, when she'd punctured the skin and sucked the blood, that's when realization had sunk in.

"Difficult to believe I'm here?" she asked.

"The world thought you committed suicide. So did I."

"Touch me." She slipped inside his personal space. "Caress my cheek." She cocked her head. "I hear your heartbeat. Much slower than a vampire's. Why do you do that?" She didn't wait for an answer. "To fit into their world, of course." Her lips quivered. "I can slow my heartbeat, too."

A pulse appeared in her neck. The flutter of flesh on her breast enticed human and vampire—he hadn't noticed what she wore until now, a camisole exposing rounded mounds of soft skin.

She captured his hand. "Feel my heartbeat." She guided his fingers over her chest.

Excitement coursed through him and hardened just left of his right pants pocket. Warmth emanated from Marilyn, her human heartbeat steady beneath his palm. The last time he'd touched her breast, her heart had raced, her breath came in gasps, and her pupils—those delicious eyes—had dilated with rapture. Her pupils now blended into irises, the fathomless eyes of a night creature, exquisite beauty of a different nature.

She inched away, allowing his fingers a tickling departure. "The windows are covered by shutters. To lock you in, or to keep others out?"

Bobby struck the keypad, opening the shutters and illuminating the backlit stained glass. Marilyn gasped.

"I've spent hours enjoying the lights," Bobby said.

He tapped more keys. A fan hummed, and mist swirled around the ceiling, four stories above, and drifted lower. Outside lights rotated in random patterns, creating rainbow streaks across the sanctuary, like the myriad colors of a nebula.

"The window maker imbedded giant prisms in the stained glass. When intense light strikes a prism and bends through the vapor, the cloud is striated by colors."

"It's beauty that's on display just for you." She studied him. "I've missed the expression on your face when you experience something as simple as these lights or Shakespeare's manuscript."

Marilyn slipped inside his personal space again, her breasts pressed against his chest, her fingers massaging his shoulder. She danced around him, never

BLOOD BETWEEN LOVERS

breaking contact, never allowing his excitement to wane.

His thoughts narrowed, though he didn't understand why, nor did he care. How many years had he longed for the touch of human Marilyn? To feel her breath against his cheek or her tongue tickle his? Odd that with human Marilyn he could've made love across decades, but as a vampire, immortality demanded they make love in the moment only.

"Bobby." Her weight shifted ever so deliciously. The allure of her voice trilling his name, the enticing shimmy of her hips, as if she was reading his mind. Could he extend this moment? For Marilyn. Immortality—

"Show me the lights." Marilyn unbuttoned his shirt and dug her nails into his chest.

The artificial cloud floated above his head, brilliant colors dancing around him, mimicking the actress.

She brushed the shirt off his shoulders and nipped at the base of his neck, exposed to the night, exposed to Marilyn Monroe's imagination. Anticipation oozed from his flesh like blood from a fresh wound. Pressure expanded exponentially behind his zipper. Marilyn inched the sleeves down his arms, and when the shirt came free, she draped the garment across a statue.

She scurried behind him, brushed against his ribs, then disappeared before he reacted. She approached again, unhooked his belt, and pulled it through the loops. He pivoted to face her, but she'd already backed into the shadows of darkness and smoke.

Vampire speed ignited an unrelenting attack against his clothing. She appeared out of the fog and shoved him backward onto the sofa. He fell, and she tugged off his trousers, shoes, and socks.

She darted close, grabbed the fly of his boxers, and ripped them through the seams in both directions, and Bobby lay exposed in mind and flesh to Marilyn's whims.

* * *

Tony assumed Lara hadn't already returned to the church, or there would've been a catfight when Marilyn arrived, and one of them would have left again. Tony needed more information.

After a gourmet brunch and three chapters, Tony headed to Westover to shower and change clothes. Somehow, Eyve had discovered Lara had worked at St. Mary's, but not as a doctor. She'd disguised herself, probably hiding from Robert, and worked as nurse Meridian Jones.

Hospital administration would have an address for a former employee, not that they'd part with the information easily. Investigating Lara's former residence would prove to Eyve he was thorough and perhaps suggest a theory for the vampire triangle he'd discovered.

He had seven hours before sunset to read, plan, and gather information.

Tony skirted the St. Mary's parking lot twice. Crowded. He chuckled. "I can't believe no one saved me a spot." He yanked a royal-blue-and-white handicapped hangtag from the glove box, draped it on the rearview mirror, and parked in a no-parking zone. He'd stopped at a florist on the way here and purchased a one-hundred-dollar oversized arrangement, written *Meridian Jones* on the small envelope, and pocketed the card.

He strode through the main entrance and pulled up at the information desk. "Do you have a floor-by-floor map of the hospital? Please?"

The woman tried to study him, but Tony remained hidden behind the flowers. She opened a drawer and pulled out a sheaf of pages stapled together. "We give this out to deliveries. Be sure to return it before you leave. I've never seen you before."

"Temporary," Tony said. "Substitute for today. Can you direct me to the administration office?"

This floor, down the hall, through the doors . . . Tony recalled chasing Dr. West in this hall one night a couple of months ago. He pocketed the four pages of maps and followed directions. He'd waited until lunchtime, when most of the staff would be gone and likely someone less familiar with procedures would be on duty. He entered the administration office, flowers in front of his face.

Bingo. An old man with a bald head and trousers hiked up on his round belly was the lone office occupant.

"Excuse me." Tony pitched his voice higher, more jovial. "Can you help me? I'm going to be in a lot of trouble if I can't deliver these flowers, and I can't find this person anywhere."

The old man grinned well-polished dentures. "I'll do what I can. Who're you looking for?"

Sounded like a New England accent. Tony twisted the arrangement to read the card, as if he didn't remember the name. "Um, Meridian Jones. She's supposed to work here, but I can't find her."

"No, no, she's gone. Moved to Washington. DC. More than a month ago."

BLOOD BETWEEN LOVERS

"Do you have a new address for her? We'll have to ship the flowers."

"I'm sorry. We don't have an address, but even if we did, I couldn't give it out. I'd get in trouble."

Tony sighed. "Oh, I understand trouble, all right. That's where I'm headed now. These flowers have to be delivered today—special occasion, I guess. If I can't deliver them and I tell my boss she moved, no address, he's not gonna believe me. My head's gonna roll."

He set the flowers on a desk, pulled a hankie, and mopped his brow. "I don't mean to dump my troubles on you, pal. I'm sorry. I've only had this job a few months. If I get the boot, my wife isn't going to be happy. She's sick, you know. My wife. In and out of doctors' offices. Can't figure out what's wrong. It's tough paying all the bills on one salary. I just can't lose this job."

"I wish I could help."

"If I found where she used to live, maybe someone there would have a current address for her. I just want to keep my job. Oh, well." He mopped his forehead again. "You know, maybe since she doesn't live there anymore, you could give me the old address? You're not giving out personal information that way—I mean, since she isn't there."

The bald man scratched his ear, as if pondering the logic. "I don't suppose anyone would mind. She's not there. It isn't private anymore. She was a friend of mine. Nice girl." He sat at his desk and typed on the computer, waited, then typed something else. "Four thirty-two Blackrow Court. Langhorne."

Tony tapped his forehead and saluted. "Thanks, man, I appreciate this."

He hoisted the arrangement and headed toward the main entrance. Women in black-and-white habits crisscrossed the huge lobby. Tony approached two nuns engrossed in conversation. He handed the shorter one the vase, yanked the envelope off, and, in the same motion, filched the hospital ID security badge that dangled on a ribbon looped around Shorty's neck. Neither nun noticed.

"I'm sorry to interrupt, sisters, I was hoping you could complete a charitable act for me. You see"—he swiped at his eye as though to wipe a tear—"the person these were intended for . . ." He choked. "Won't be needing them. Could you see that a patient without family gets these?"

"What a gracious man you are," Shorty said. "You'll be rewarded, surely."

Tony forced a smile. "Oh, I expect a reward all right." He backed away, then spun and pocketed the security badge. "And don't call me Shirley. Shorty."

RAZ STEEL

The GPS located Blackrow Court behind the Summit Square Center. Tony parked a block away. No need to pull into the driveway and attract neighborly attention.

No car in the driveway of 432 either, no mail in the box, shades pulled on the front windows. No real estate signs. The townhouse couldn't have transferred ownership that fast. Tony rang the bell twice, just in case. No answer. He studied the lock, American classic. He pulled a zippered bag from his pocket, chose a tool, and soon found himself in the kitchen.

He closed the door and left the blinds down. Sunshine poured through the foyer skylight.

The search wasn't for anything specific, just signs of Dr. West. The refrigerator seemed a good place to start.

Not a single bottle of blood.

If her boyfriend lived in Bucks County, they would stay at this house or his place. No blood here was a strong indication they had settled at Bobby's house. Tony left the refrigerator door open. He smirked. If vampires returned to this house, they'd suspect a bounty hunter had been here. Leaving the refrigerator open reflected his contempt.

Tony climbed the stairs. One large bedroom with a skylight, shades pulled on the windows, no bureaus. He opened the closet door, surprised to find the closet stocked with clothes, including hospital scrubs. A full closet contradicted an empty refrigerator.

The rumpled bed implied someone had slept on top of the covers. A crimson spot caught Tony's attention. Someone bled here last night. Maybe Bobby had fed from Lara and drooled? Nah, Bobby returned from St. Mary's with Marilyn Monroe and didn't go out again.

Not-yet-dried blood on the bed but nothing in the refrigerator: what did that suggest?

All three vampires had left the church to feed, but Bobby returned with Marilyn, which implied Lara spent the night at Blackrow Court. Blood at Blackrow didn't belong to Dr. West and Bobby, but to an angry Dr. West and someone else. A victim? Another vampire?

Lara's townhouse was near Summit Square. Did another vampire claim territory in the shopping center? Tony had driven through the center but never stopped. He'd return tonight and investigate, though. He glanced at the bureau clock. The digital numbers glowed crimson. Time to spy on vampires.

* * *

~ 158 ~

BLOOD BETWEEN LOVERS

The sun draped low in the early-evening sky. Jake parked the SUV in a field, off-property, upwind from Bobby's house. Marilyn would find him.

The WPA–VU spent decades experimenting with Marilyn, an opportunity they'd never previously experienced with a vampire. Like humans, vampires trained circadian rhythms. The VU trained Marilyn to waken a few minutes before sunset. Time now to report to Jake and return before Bobby woke.

The chemical the VU had developed to treat her clothing didn't work but afforded a modicum of protection from the late-day sun, enough for the few minutes Jake required.

The heat of the day hadn't dissipated, and Jake had driven here with the windows closed, no air conditioning. Streams of perspiration stained his clothes. He frowned and hopped out of the SUV. He needed to create the impression that when they were alone, Marilyn made him nervous. Jake leaned against his vehicle, arms folded, ankles crossed.

His degree in psychology notwithstanding, it didn't take Jake long to figure out what carrot to offer his prisoner with immortality. Autonomy. And freedom from being hunted. The top edge of the sun dipped below the tree line, obscuring the fiery ball. Jake's inner ear droned. He'd spent years honing his senses to detect the presence of a vampire. He breathed faster and his gaze darted around, pretending nervousness.

Marilyn whisked in front of him. "Would you mind if we get into your car?" She glanced down and gestured at wisps of smoke. "These magical clothes don't perform as advertised. I need protection from the sun."

Jake opened the passenger door. Marilyn climbed in, and her dress pulled tighter across her hips, providing a view worthy of another Trojan War. Jake sighed and trotted to the other side. He used the steering wheel to haul himself in.

Marilyn didn't wait. "The woman left shortly after I arrived last night and hasn't returned."

Jake nodded. "We know." He flipped his hand. "Look, would you mind?"

"Mind what?"

"If I secured you?"

Marilyn's lips curled in a seductive smile. "You seem tense."

"I'm in the middle of a deserted field with a vampire." Jake stated the obvious, but Marilyn's limited human contact in the past fifty years limited her understanding of psychology.

She shrugged.

Jake pressed a button on the steering wheel. Metallic restraints snapped out and whipped around Marilyn's breasts and waist, pinning her arms to the sides. Jake mopped his brow in pretend relief.

"Would you mind?" Marilyn asked.

"Mind what?"

"Hurrying along. This isn't exactly comfortable."

Jake's head bobbed. "Was Bobby contacted by Dr. West since she left last night?"

"Not a peep."

"Were you and Mr. Eyre able to feed in the hospital?"

"I don't know how he sustains himself one sip at a time."

"Is he worried about Dr. West's disappearance? Is he ready to find her?"

Marilyn twisted sinuously. "He was too preoccupied last night to find a grain of sand on a beach, but as soon as he wakes I'll remind him she's gone and needs his help."

"Good. You remember the plan." Marilyn was a great actress, but everything in Jake's perception screamed, *Liar*.

"It's not exactly complicated. Did you think I was a dumb blonde?"

Jake chuckled. "Hardly, Ms. Monroe." He tapped the dashboard clock and pointed at the glowing globe nearly gone from sight. "You'd better get back. I'll see you here tomorrow." Was Marilyn orchestrating an escape plan? Eternity with mercs hunting her couldn't be what she wanted.

He leaned across and opened Marilyn's door, then pushed the release button on the steering wheel. The restraints unwound into the seat.

Marilyn howled and throttled Jake's neck, pinning his throat to the headrest.

"Would you mind if I cut off your breath?" she asked in a guttural voice. "I'm alone with a government agent, and the air in here stinks." Her mouth was close enough to kiss his—her eyes unfathomable in the intoxicating blend of irises and pupils. "I just hope you remember your end of the plan," she said. "It's not exactly complicated." She squeezed tighter, expunging Jake's thoughts of duplicity.

Jake forced himself not to struggle. She released him abruptly and disappeared. Jake took a deep breath and exhaled through his mouth.

"Perfect," he said.

CHAPTER 28

H e woke in a fog bank, hard, nestled in sofa cushions. He sensed Marilyn's presence, surprised she wasn't snuggled against him after their first sleep together in fifty years. A crackling fire entwined with the low hum of a song, broken by an occasional sob. His present experience of Marilyn surpassed his memory of her. Marilyn had crossed into darkness alone, but managed to maintain more than a sliver of humanness. No monster had surfaced in her.

She'd had fifty years to learn how to sing, much as he'd mastered many human tasks. Sadness filled the sanctuary, eerie in the echoes behind clouds, subtle in its effect. Loneliness surfaced in her perfect pitch, the grace in her voice desperate for a companion, the tear rolling across her cheek a sentinel of existence.

Bobby had blamed himself for her suicide; perhaps this was worse. How had she survived without a teacher?

The five stages of Vampirical Harmony without a memory wipe must've turned her. Freud had never suggested the possibility. Bobby had never anticipated he'd turn anyone. He'd transformed someone else. Who?

A siren's song called to him. Sweet sounds clouded his mind, slowing thoughts and blocking memories. *Submit*, demanded the siren. Easy to acquiesce. No reason not to. He'd found Marilyn. She wanted to stay with him. She wanted to touch and be touched. *Surrender.*

Before he relaxed, before he accepted, another word arose, lodged into consciousness by his beast . . . *Meridian.* Where was she? Not in the house.

Didn't matter. He shunted Roberre aside. Bobby had sired Marilyn. Instincts failed to override emotions, but it was his duty to be sure his progeny survived to enjoy immortality.

The song deepened. Sadness spread. Marilyn's need, her desire, expressed so clearly in actions yesterday, filled her voice now and pulled him back into the moment. *Marilyn.*

He pressed the remote. Fans whirled, lights winked out, and the smoke evaporated. Marilyn lounged on the carpet in front of the massive fireplace.

She hugged one knee, the other leg tucked beneath her. A fire raged, more wood piled on than necessary. She wore his shirt, nothing else.

Bobby hopped the sofa. Flames warmed his flesh. Damp wood ricocheted sparks in every direction, smoldered by the stone hearth.

"You weren't next to me. I thought you'd gone," Bobby said.

The crackling fire blurred Marilyn's words, her shoulders bowing beneath the weight of melancholy. "I'm afraid to stay, and more afraid to leave." She sobbed, her forehead resting on her wrist.

Bobby rushed to her side, sat, legs splayed, and wrapped Marilyn in his arms. "Fear is a human foible. It tells you two things. You haven't surrendered your immortality to the frenzy, and *Marilyn* is still in control."

She appeared smaller tonight. Vulnerable.

"I need your help," she whispered. Her hand grasped his and squeezed.

After a half century of loneliness, he'd found the woman he'd mourned. Another woman had also rescued him from solitude. The other woman— Marilyn sobbed, refocusing his attention.

"I'm afraid to ask. I'm afraid you'll say *no*, and I'll be lost forever," Marilyn said.

"I'd never abandon—" He choked on the words, realizing the lie.

"I'm starving," Marilyn said.

Hadn't he abandoned Marilyn for decades, leaving her to fend for herself? A vampire could be heartless, but vampirical instinct would never abandon progeny. At times, he embraced the animality of Roberre, and Roberre always defined their instincts. "What?"

"I'm starving."

"I have blood in the refrigerator." He rose, and just as fast, Marilyn seized his wrist.

"I need fresh blood. Like last night, only more. That little taste . . . how do you exist? I need to feed now." Marilyn wrung her hands.

"Put on hospital scrubs. We'll find another patient."

"I need more." Tears blurred her eyes.

Bobby held her shoulders. "Don't worry. We'll find more blood."

Marilyn's chin drooped. "I'm sure we will. I don't want to kill, but I can't control myself." Marilyn closed her eyes.

Bobby recognized frenzy from the moments Roberre had wrested control before they'd met Freud. What if his understanding was wrong? Marilyn's beast defied detection. He'd spent centuries recognizing his beast and learning to control it, reining in his desire for daily feeding. He could teach Marilyn. He taught someone else. An image formed of—

"Help me."

Marilyn Monroe—Bobby could think of nothing else.

Dressed in scrubs, they dashed across the field to St. Mary's and entered, unseen, through the parking garage. They risked the elevator to the fourth floor and searched rooms near maternity for a sleeping psych patient. Bobby wasn't feeding, and Marilyn wasn't practicing Vampirical Harmony, so any psych patient would do. They found three.

"You can't feed from them all."

"I need the blood."

"It's not safe."

"You'll be there to stop me if I lose control."

"I mean, it's not safe for us to stay in one place that long. I don't work here anymore. We'll have to be careful. Pick one."

They entered room 433 in darkness, silently closed the door behind them, and approached the bed. Bobby sensed Marilyn's mind cradling the sleeping patient, keeping her asleep. She fed from the underside of the woman's breast, nonsexual, strictly a matter of practicality. The large artery allowed quick access to blood, and the wound would not be visible to staff unless they performed an examination. When Bobby tugged on her shoulder, Marilyn stopped, licked the wound, then traced her lips with her tongue.

"More." Her eyes narrowed, her tone petulant.

"We'll risk the third floor, ICU. If we can find a stable patient receiving a transfusion, we can sneak blood, and they'll feed the patient an extra unit."

"I don't understand."

Understanding didn't matter. No ICU patients were hooked up. Marilyn squeezed Bobby's biceps. Her face blanched.

"I can't control myself much longer."

"We'll gamble with a non-psych patient. Someone elderly whose mind will be easier to confuse, but healthy enough he can afford to be a little low on blood."

Bobby led her to the unoccupied nurses' station. He scanned the charts, tapped the seventh one. "Howie Long. An in-house priapism delayed a routine proctologic exam by a day, otherwise, the picture of health."

"Excuse me," an indignant voice sounded. "Excuse me. What do you think you're doing?" Nurse Cron stomped down the hall.

Bobby dropped the charts, grabbed Marilyn's hand, and angled away from the desk. Nurse Cron quickened her pace, giving chase.

"Just a minute," she called. "Do I know you?"

Bobby and Marilyn rounded a corner, out of sight. Speed delivered them silently to Howie Long, before Nurse Cron reached the corner and saw which room they entered. Bobby listened for footsteps, in case Nurse Cron decided on a room-by-room search. No one approached. The patient monitors beeped erratically, and labored breathing proclaimed a presence, not of someone struggling for breath but of two people in the throes of ecstasy.

Bobby yanked back the curtain guarding the room's lone bed. An elderly couple lay clinched in each other's arms, deed done, regaining respiration and pulse. Two sets of ancient eyes peered at the interlopers.

"Doc, can't we get a little privacy here?" the old man said. "Antonia and I were quiet."

Bobby cleared his throat. "Mr. Long, after priapism, you need to give it a rest."

"Sorry." Howie shrugged. "Antonia couldn't wait." He noticed Marilyn for the first time. "You know how it is, don't you, young lady?" He frowned. "Why're you here anyway? I thought all you doctors would be asleep at this hour."

Bobby didn't expect Mr. Long to be awake at this hour either, and he certainly didn't anticipate company. Marilyn couldn't feed here. They needed to exit without a fuss. "Mr. Long, you have a procedure scheduled in the morning, and you need to rest. If everything goes well, you'll be discharged by tomorrow afternoon. Ma'am, go home. This can wait until then."

Antonia humphed. "Young man, if there's one thing I've learned from all my marriages, when the sexual urge strikes a couple in love, it shouldn't be delayed."

She squeezed Howie's nipple. Antonia and Howie giggled. Marilyn tittered, feeding adjourned.

Bobby guided her into the vacant hall. He raced away from the nurses' station, Marilyn in tow. Bobby pulled her inside a windowless room the size of a one-car garage and locked the door. The back of his legs pressed against one of three gurneys. Pillows, linens, and lab coats lined the shelves; laundry detergent and cleaning fluids were the overwhelming scents.

"We'll be safe here for a while. If we wait until morning, they'll begin operations, and we'll find someone receiving a transfusion," Bobby said.

"We won't be able to get home once the sun comes up."

"You'll be okay."

"No I won't."

"Keep your voice down," Bobby hissed. "There's a way to get home during the day."

"You don't understand. I have to hide where no one can find me."

"No one can find you here."

"They can."

"Who?"

"I'm being manipulated by the government. They held me hostage and threatened my existence if I don't . . . perform for them." She sniffled. "It's just a matter of time." She clung to Bobby's shoulders, burying her face in his chest. "I've put you at risk. I'm sorry. I had no right. I have to leave." She pushed away, catching him off-balance.

Bobby seized her arms and tugged. "Why didn't you say so when you arrived? You risk us both." He held her tight. Her shoulders convulsed. "Don't worry. I can take precautions now."

Marilyn glanced into his face, her lips parted, borrowed scrubs too tight on her chest and hips. "I'm sorry. I want to stay with you. The government doesn't want that other woman to stay with you. But I don't want anything to happen to her on my account." Words and actions collided. Marilyn wasn't telling him everything, but Bobby rejected the scent of a lie.

She stretched up on her toes and found his lips. Her tongue glided into his mouth, warm, tickling, the way it used to be long ago. What other woman? Whatever Marilyn was trying to tell him could wait.

The door handle rattled. A man cursed.

A key slid into the tumbler. The lock clicked, and the door sprung open. A square room with shelves, no place to hide. A tiny man paused in silhouette until he flipped on the light. A smirk smeared across his face.

"I've caught all kinds of couples in storage. This is a first for me, though. A fag and . . ." Davey Blissockiss screwed up his face and crossed the threshold. "What're you? A lesbo?"

Marilyn tensed. Bobby stepped in front of her, blocking the janitor's view.

"Not a patient, but perfect for what we discussed," Bobby said. Marilyn peeked past his shoulder.

"We weren't talking about anything." Blissockiss craned his neck to see around Bobby. "What're you lookin' at, butch?"

Bobby answered for her. "I suspect she's never seen such a little man with such a big mouth."

Before Blissockiss could answer, Bobby raced behind him and closed the door, sealing the three of them in. He pushed Blissockiss's shoulder, forcing him into the middle of the storage room. Blissockiss blinked repeatedly, unable to comprehend what he saw, though he spit at the result.

"What the fuck do you think you're doin'?"

"Giving my friend, Marilyn Monroe, a better view of her next meal."

Blissockiss twisted around to glance at the hourglass blonde, then pivoted back to face Bobby, his muscles rippled, on edge. He jerked his thumb over his shoulder. "That ain't Mari-fuckilyn Monroe." He chuckled as though he'd said something clever.

"I assure you," Bobby said, "she is Marilyn Monroe."

"What if we can't adjust his memory?" Marilyn asked.

"That's why he's perfect," Bobby said. "No need to modify this degenerate's memory. Here's someone who deserves the experience he's about to participate in, and he deserves to remember every agonizing moment." Bobby nodded. "No one will ever believe this asshole. Besides, you can take a double shot. I have a plan."

"A double shot of what?" Blissockiss demanded. "What the fuck're you talkin' about?"

Bobby winked at Marilyn. "Where do you think will be most painful?"

Marilyn arched an eyebrow. "His balls, of course. Feeding will be slower for me, and excruciating for him."

"Excruciating it'll be." Bobby circled back to the janitor. "Remove your clothes."

"For a faggot? You've gotta be joking." Blissockiss chuckled. "I might bop your girlfriend there"—he squeezed a fist and pointed his thumb—"but I ain't doin' nothin' for you."

Bobby rushed at him, shredding his clothing and ripping it from his body. Blissockiss flailed but couldn't make contact. He stood naked except for his boots. Bobby pushed him backward and, together with Marilyn, flung him onto a gurney on his back, legs pulled over his head. Blissockiss opened his mouth to object, and Bobby stuffed in a pillowcase to stifle him.

BLOOD BETWEEN LOVERS

Blissockiss squirmed, but the two vampires locked him in place. Bobby gestured, open palm. "Go ahead, double shot—make it memorable."

The janitor's eyes bugged out when Marilyn maneuvered between his legs and her fangs erupted. He struggled to spit out the gag.

"How's it feel to be helpless?" Bobby asked. He yanked the cloth out of the janitor's mouth.

Blissockiss spit. "Let me go. What the fuck do you think you're doin'?"

Marilyn shook her head. "What a potty mouth. I can't believe you have people like this working in a hospital. What I'm doing is taking a blood donation." She pushed on the back of his legs. "Wow. I've seen men with bigger mouths, but I've never seen anyone with a smaller dick."

Blissockiss opened his mouth to yell, and Bobby stuffed the pillowcase back in. "Sorry, we don't want to disturb Nurse Cron."

Marilyn roared and attacked. Blissockiss screamed through the linen. He struggled and wriggled and eventually passed out.

Marilyn backed away and slurped the blood from her lips. "I've never fed through a man's balls before. I can only imagine the pain."

"In case he'd enjoy a little more pain . . ." Bobby smeared iodine on the janitor's wound, then applied more tape than necessary to seal a bandage to his pubic hair. "Help me gown him."

They donned lab coats and wheeled the unconscious man into the corridor, toward Howie's room. Bobby ducked in, not surprised to find Antonia still lying with Howie. Bobby plucked the clipboard from the end of the bed. "We just need to borrow Mr. Long's chart. You two should rest."

Bobby peeked down the corridor, noticed an unfamiliar nurse manning the station, Nurse Cron nowhere in sight. They stopped in front of the desk, and Bobby snatched a pen. He wrote *emergency* on the chart in front of the proctologic exam and added *plus 2 units*, signed an illegible signature, and tossed the clipboard on Blissockiss's belly.

"Nurse, the procedure can't wait. Wheel this man to the ER."

The nurse gaped.

"Haul him to the ER now," Bobby's voice, low and guttural, wove an intricate pattern in the air. "Be sure they retype his blood. You will not remember us."

Bobby guided Marilyn's arm. "No more chances. We're going out through a window. We can't allow a government agent to track us."

~ 167 ~

Marilyn surveyed beyond the shutters of Bobby's bedroom. Moonlight graced the back windows of the hospital they just left. "I want to control the urge. I want to feed once a month, around the full moon, like you."

"You can teach yourself to—"

"I may harm someone. I need you, Bobby." She rushed into his space, curled her arms around his neck, and pulled his mouth toward hers. Her tongue traced across his lips. "Teach me," she whispered.

Not what he would have expected from a vampire who'd survived from day one for fifty years on her own.

Humans excelled vampires in vulnerabilities. Physically weaker, emotionally more unstable, but the most enchanting of the vulnerabilities was unpredictability. "You surprise me," Bobby said.

"Am I a contradiction in existence? Charming humanness, but weak in the vampire world?"

Bobby sighed. Marilyn was sensual, still impatient, attractive beyond imagination, and emotionally appealing in an impulsive way. And vulnerable. Didn't her vulnerability outweigh a vampire's need for solitude? She could feed herself, but she didn't want to harm anyone; Marilyn's moral conflict resolved in Bobby's mind: Marilyn clung to humanity as he did. What if bloodlust overwhelmed her morality?

To confess the government manipulated her revealed the deepest vulnerabilities. Hadn't the government manipulated him as well? To do what? He thought of nothing other than existence and Marilyn. Bounty hunters had tracked Bobby across decades. Marilyn would face the same unconscionable perils. If she could've escaped the government alone, she would have. She asked for his help. He'd sired her without realizing. Did that count? Instinct didn't overwhelm him, yet her success as a vampire was his responsibility.

* * *

Tony steered into the center and drove the length of the parking lot to be sure the police weren't here guzzling coffee. He slid the Toy into a spot near the pub, at the end of the line of cars to be inconspicuous. A man in khakis and a T-shirt and a woman in short-shorts loitered in front of the pub, smoking. A bicycle rested upside down on the sidewalk, and music and laughter filtered out the door.

He didn't expect to discover anything significant, but after the hospital,

BLOOD BETWEEN LOVERS

Summit Square Center was the closest vampire feeding ground, and Tony wanted to be thorough in his first report to Eyve. The more information he gathered, the more impressed she'd be.

Tony glanced in the beauty salon window as he approached the sidewalk. One night-light, no movement inside, just what he'd expect this late. The pub was packed; the shoe store and deli were closed. Each burned a single night-light. He strolled and peeked in each store as he passed; no bells, gongs, or alarms all the way to the supermarket anchor store. Across the parking lot, a few outbuildings, same result. Tony opened his car door, but a strange sensation danced up his spine.

Robert had taught him that while his brain might not register vampire movement on a conscious level, an impression was still made subliminally, and he could train his mind to react to a subconscious message.

A subliminal impression flashed from the shoe store door. Curiosity and the desire to please propelled Tony forward. He strolled past the parked cars toward the pub to not be obvious. He hooded his eyes to inspect beyond the reflections, window-shopping in the pub then the neighboring shoe store.

He studied the presentation. Odd, they used all left shoes in their display. The window was the width of the store, about twenty feet wide. Edges allowed the best view. Nothing nudged him from the door side, but on the other end, he peeked past the counter and a second subliminal image triggered alarms in his brain. He forced his gaze back to the display, pretended he was torn between styles, tapped the glass, and headed for his vehicle.

He climbed in and read the green-crimson-and-blue sign on the building: *The In-Step Family Shoe Store.*

Eyve purred when Tony conveyed all he'd learned, curious about his subliminal impressions, though he hadn't described them with that language.

"You didn't see anyone in the shoe store?"

"Nope."

"You sensed someone, though?"

"More or less." Tony didn't want to divulge secrets Robert had revealed. It didn't feel right. "This was a creepy sensation, and not much creeps me out. You know what I mean?"

"Perhaps an unfamiliar vampire in the shoe store?"

"Might've been another—" He was about to say *bloodsucker*.

Eyve paced away, lost in thought. "You believe Mr. Eyre may've brought across Dr. West, yet last night another vampire accompanied him. And this other vampire is *the* Marilyn Monroe, not just someone who looks like her?"

"I'm sure. I've seen plenty of Elvis look-alikes. They *look* like him, but they don't look like *him*. You see the difference? This vampire didn't look like Marilyn. She looked like *Marilyn*. I mean, I watch a lot of movies."

"I'll go to the shopping center and see what I can discover. Perhaps there's a connection between the shoe store and Dr. West. I'll be back before sunrise." She glanced over her shoulder. "I have a reward for you."

Tony followed her into the back bedroom. Eyve flipped on a small lamp angled into the corner to produce indirect light and shadows. An attractive woman, thirty-something, lay on the bed, shackled to the headboard, eyes wide. Her clothing was unrumpled, her hair frizzy but neat. Moaning emerged from her throat, like the noise made by someone trying to talk or scream from behind a gag, only this woman wasn't gagged. Tony peered closer.

The woman's lips had been sewn together.

"Yours," Eyve said, "until I return. You may do anything you like, but I want her alive." Eyve backed away. "Try not to spill any blood."

CHAPTER 29

"Time's up. Destroy Nalbandian now."

"You know there's an innocent life involved."

"Collateral damage. Oh, well," Dog said. "We're talking vampires. We're not just going to let this one run a shoe store."

"I need more time."

"No."

"Too bad. Could be worth millions of dollars in savings to the government in health-care costs, not to mention preventing downtime."

Dog eyed him, glanced at Agent Katie Ingbritsen, expressionless near the door. Dog sat behind her desk in a swivel rocking chair and sipped tea. "I'm listening with half an ear."

"Jason Storm fits shoes differently; that's what made his store famous. He's cured or prevented plantar fasciitis, knee pain, and lower-back pain in hundreds of instances. If we save his life, we could hire him to size thousands of government employees, cutting or reducing doctors' bills for preventable injuries." Jake shrugged. "But I understand. Collateral damage."

"Millions of dollars?"

"Hundreds of millions of dollars. He's told me four out of five adults walking into his store are wearing the wrong size, and many of them have these pains. I know because I was one of them. He made me change sizes, and instead of the doctor and the chiropractor bills, I have a surround-sound, sixty-inch flat screen. What if he measured everyone in the armed forces? How much could the government save on doctoring? But, collateral. I get it, I get it. I'll shoot Nalbandian with a magic bullet." He spun and headed for the door.

"You've had plenty of time. You released Marilyn two days ago. Why hasn't your plan worked?" Dog asked.

Jake stopped. "It did. Love's blood lost. Dr. West is now under the influence of Nalbandian."

Dog offered an expectant look.

"Mr. Eyre has been so confounded by Marilyn he's ignored Dr. West's predicament."

"The solution seems obvious, then."

"I'm afraid if we lock Marilyn away, Mr. Eyre will chase her instead of Lara."

"As I said, the solution seems obvious."

Jake nodded and headed for the door. Dog's voice stopped him again. "You have forty-eight hours to force the issue. After that, Nalbandian's finished, collateral damage be damned. The government doctors will have to slug on."

Katie followed Jake into the hall. She opened her mouth, but Jake silenced her with a gesture. Katie acquiesced. Jake didn't want their conversation to be overheard.

They hopped into his SUV.

"When did you ever go to a chiropractor?" Katie asked.

"Who said I went to a chiropractor?"

Jake strummed on the steering wheel and mumbled the words to a song for a few minutes, then slapped the side of his head.

"Assemble the team in Bucks County," Jake ordered.

"We've kept Marilyn alive all this time, now we're going to kill her?"

"She's been dead all this time, now we're going to destroy her."

"Jake, don't you have feelings? This isn't just any vampire. This is Marilyn Monroe. The world thought she was gone. She's not."

"She is. Get over it, Katie. She's been gone since you were knee-high to a grasshopper. It's our job to make sure her destruction is beneficial to the United States government."

"I take it you're not going to shoot her with one of your magic bullets and bury her with Jimmy Hoffa?"

"Won't help the situation or motivate Mr. Eyre. I think the shoe store vampire needs to destroy Ms. Monroe."

"How're you going to arrange that?"

"Doesn't matter, as long as Mr. Eyre believes Nalbandian is responsible."

CHAPTER 30

"I'm in, boss," Katie said. "What am I looking for?"

"You have your CSI light?"

Jake ignored Katie's laugh.

"We know Dr. West brought Nalbandian there night before last. Blood between lovers would be nice, preferably on a moveable object."

"Not much point checking the kitchen counter, then. The refrigerator is open and empty. I'll try the living room sofa. Maybe the cushions."

"Make it fast. An operation like this, you have to be in and out."

"There's something here, boss. On the arms of the sofa . . . wait, too old."

"I don't want a history lesson, Katie. Find me something from two nights ago."

"I'm going upstairs to the bedroom."

"I don't need a geography lesson either."

"You're in a snitty mood, aren't you?"

Jake didn't answer.

"You don't like doing this, do you?" Katie asked. "I don't mean searching Lara's townhouse. I know what you're planning. Dog is forcing your hand. Your friend—"

"Shut up, Katie. Do your job."

"I'm in the bedroom. Bingo. Sanguine fluid on the coverlet. And semen."

"Perfect. Blood and sex."

"I'm coming home. I'll bag the blanket."

"Bring your team in fast. You'll have to set this up personally. My scent might be recognized at Summit Square."

Jake flipped the cell phone shut. "Sorry, Katie. Didn't mean to snap at you."

Jake angled the SUV onto a grassy knoll fifteen hundred miles from the book depository, assassination at the hands of a government agent a quarter mile from where he parked yesterday. He wouldn't display any behavioral patterns, confident Marilyn could find him two days in a row.

Katie and Owen had volunteered to ride along. He'd refused both. His plan, his responsibility. A pinprick of empathy welled for Marilyn, and he quashed it. His performances yesterday would explain his nervousness today; she'd understand in advance why he wanted her secured.

He checked his gun, loaded with reengineered bullets lethal to vampires. A bullet like this, though less potent, had first pulled Lara West into the WPA. One new slug into Marilyn's body would destroy her. Katie's team would pull her fangs and stake her head on top of the shopping center, at the far end from the shoe store—less obvious. They'd drape Lara's bedspread over the cross. Bobby would smell blood and sex. He'd realize Marilyn was lost forever, and he'd need to save Lara from the same fate.

When he rescued Lara, Bobby would also be releasing Jason from Nalbandian's influence—Jake hoped. Bobby remained Jason's only chance, and Jake had fought Dog for this opportunity. Jake clung to one tenet: before any of this began, human-Marilyn was already dead—Jason wasn't.

Jake hopped out and paced clockwise around the vehicle. The sun scratched the treetops on the horizon. She'd be here soon. He patted the weapon beneath his jacket, unsure which made him sweat more.

"Rookie nerves," he mumbled. "It's not like this is your first destruction."

He wheeled and paced in the opposite direction. "You never acknowledged the vampire as a movie-star icon before, that's all."

He twirled and circled clockwise again. "She's not Marilyn Monroe. Ms. Monroe died before JFK died. This is a bloodsucking monster. It's okay to use her to save Jason."

Jake spun 360 degrees. "Who're we trying to convince? Me?" He caught his reflection in the tinted glass. "Or me? I sound like a schizophrenic."

Too late to change his mind or change the plan. Jake needed Bobby to save Jason now. Marilyn played her role. Overplayed it. Bobby was too distracted. The surest way to refocus Bobby's attention was to remove the distraction. Permanently.

His cell phone vibrated. He pulled it out and checked caller ID. Dog, verifying he'd pull the trigger. Jake stuffed the cell into his pocket. Message received. He raised his foot to the bumper and untied his shoe, then leaned against the SUV, folded his arms, and crossed his ankles. Eyes closed. Deep breath.

When he opened his eyes, Marilyn froze in front of him, inside his

BLOOD BETWEEN LOVERS

personal space. The SUV prevented Jake from backing up. Marilyn would sense his nervousness. She'd play on it. He had to be careful.

He forced down the lump in his throat. Marilyn cocked her head. She enjoyed the game. Her stance was seductive.

How could Marilyn Monroe be anything but seductive?

This isn't Marilyn Monroe.

Marilyn leaned close. "I was going to say, 'Your dog has arrived,' but I remember you call your boss Dog. Makes me what? A puppy?"

Jake frowned. Peculiar analogy, child of Dog. Wisps of smoke rose from her exposed flesh. "Come on, let's get in the truck," Jake said.

"No. I like it out here today."

She had to be uncomfortable, and Jake needed her secured. He'd never trigger a shot otherwise, not this close. He stretched and brushed by her. "Whatever." He yawned.

This mound wasn't a random parking choice. A break in the distant trees put the knoll in a sunset spotlight. In those trees, three hundred yards away and downwind, Owen perched with a high-powered rifle and a telescopic sight, Jake's backup plan. Stretching meant *ready*. Yawning meant *aim*.

Marilyn would never sense the assassin with the sun directly behind him. She'd never see the bullet streaking toward her. Kneeling to tie his shoe meant the signal to *fire*. The easy way out. Assassination from a distance by someone else's hand.

Jason was Jake's friend. Moral acts remained Jake's responsibility. He yawned again, but halted between target and shooter, forcing Marilyn to face the sun and shield her eyes.

"You know how uncomfortable I feel alone with you unsecured," Jake said, "so if we have to meet this way, best we do it in the sun so you can be equally uncomfortable." Jake stepped aside to let the full force of the light bathe her and provide Owen a clean shot, just in case.

Marilyn studied him, then shifted her weight across her hips in an alluring sway. She angled away from him. "Get in the car," she said, "but I'll sit behind the steering wheel, and we'll secure you."

Jake imitated the sway of her hips, though he imagined himself less alluring. "I changed my mind. Let's stay in the sun," he said.

Marilyn bared her fangs, opened the passenger door, and stepped up. "Get in."

Jake loped to the driver's side. He used both hands to grab the wheel and

~ 175 ~

hoist up, but one finger slid over the activation button, securing Marilyn before he was seated.

Marilyn squawked. "I'm doing everything you want." She struggled against the steel bonds. "This isn't necessary."

"Today it is." Jake pulled his weapon.

Marilyn's gaze darted from the gun to Jake's face. Her eyes flashed crimson. "I urged Bobby to find the girl. He got angry, and we fought." Faced with destruction, a vampire would say anything, do anything.

"Doesn't matter. Whatever the reason, you couldn't motivate him last night. We're out of time." He raised the weapon, about to shoot Marilyn Monroe.

This isn't Marilyn Monroe!

"I can give you what you want," Marilyn said. The words floated in the air. Her voice charmed. Even secured, her body played a seductive chord.

Jake's cell vibrated. No point checking caller ID. He pulled the cell but steadied on Marilyn. Fathomless irises blended into pupils.

Not human.

He flipped the cell open. "There has to be another way," he said.

"Shoot her now," Dog commanded.

"We can't take her from the world again."

"Pull the trigger."

Marilyn wiggled her hips, inviting Jake to . . . what?

"We owe her," Jake said.

Marilyn spread her legs in a sinuous motion. She raised her foot to the dash, shoeless. Beautiful feet. Of course, her feet would be gorgeous.

"Shoot now."

Jake studied Marilyn's foot, mesmerized. Her leg twisted impossibly and kicked Jake in the face. His head reeled.

* * *

"Shoot now," Dog commanded.

"I can't see her behind the tinted glass," Owen said.

"Shoot out the windows."

"I might hit Jake."

"Damn Jake. Destroy her before it's too late."

* * *

BLOOD BETWEEN LOVERS

Jake compelled his mind to reconnect in the moment. Marilyn contorted, the metal binders tearing her flesh, but one long leg crossed the console, and her foot pinned his neck against the door frame, choking the air from his lungs. Her thigh pinned his weapon against the seat, and her other foot searched the steering wheel for the release button.

Jake forced his muscles to relax.

The rear window shattered. Glass cut Jake's flesh. The horn honked, the wiper blades streaked across the sun-dried windshield, and Marilyn's toe pinched the steering wheel release mechanism. She roared, and her binders slid back into the seat. Owen fired. Jake fired. Again. Once more. Marilyn Monroe collapsed on top of him.

* * *

"What the fuck. Wait until Eyve hears about this." Tony yanked off the goggles and grabbed the cell. "He was the government agent at Robert's house. The bastard who shot Robert with a magic bullet just shot Marilyn Monroe." Tony massaged both chins. "He's like Abraham Lincoln, a damn vampire slayer."

CHAPTER 31

"Allow me to introduce the former owner, Jason Storm. He's now my assistant."

Nalbandian escorted Meridian to the counter of the In-Step Shoe Store, just two nights after she'd met him on the sidewalk. A handsome man, not as tall as Nalbandian, glared from behind the cash register.

"What's his problem?" Meridian asked.

"Mr. Storm is not as accepting as you are of circumstances. He didn't appreciate the demotion. I've made changes in the way we run the business; it's infinitely more profitable now."

"Is that important?"

"Living a comfortable life in anonymity is expensive. We have to pay for it somehow. Mr. Storm's clientele includes numerous trained athletes. Influencing them, I've been able to manipulate the outcome of several professional contests. We place large wagers and earn huge profits."

"No one has noticed?"

"Well, Mr. Storm has." Nalbandian chuckled. "He's not one hundred percent in favor of our new corporate policy. However, he does what he's told. Interesting—he's been able to partially resist my influence. I've never run into that circumstance before, though I'm happy to say I've still been able to avoid coercion in securing his cooperation."

Jason counted money from the cash register without looking up.

"You haven't threatened his life?"

"Nor the life of his enchanting girlfriend. Fascinating woman. Plant psychologist. Never heard of such a thing until I met Mr. Storm."

"Dr. Kerry Rand?"

Jason's attention jumped to Meridian.

"You've met her?" Nalbandian asked.

"No. Her name came up in conversation. You didn't—"

The door opened, bells jingled, and two young men entered.

"Excuse me," the wider man said. "We were sent from the Philadelphia football team. We're supposed to see Mr. Storm to be sized."

BLOOD BETWEEN LOVERS

Nalbandian stepped forward. "Gentlemen, one of you can have a seat here, the other can sit there." He pointed to blue plastic chairs fifteen feet apart. "Mr. Storm will start with you, young man, and Ms. Jones will start with you." He nodded to Meridian.

Jason darted into the stockroom to retrieve a Brannock device and then engaged the wider man in conversation, drawing his attention from staring at Meridian.

The second man wore a hunter-green-and-white jersey with a large number 7. His hair was cropped, and his grin exposed a gold tooth. Meridian sidled close.

"Does game pressure cause you to change decisions?" Meridian asked him.

The man failed to hold her gaze, and his focus drifted below her chin. "Sorry?" he said.

"Playing in front of fifty thousand screaming fans, playing on national television before millions of viewers, the rush must bowl you over. Do you find the excitement heightens your senses? Do you see the field more clearly? When the linemen dig in, do you hear cleats grind? Can you taste the energy in the air?"

The man leaned back and tilted his head. "Are you from the press?"

"Has your trust ever been violated by a dog like me?"

"What?"

"Does the pressure to win make you anxious?"

Number 7 shrugged. "You play in Philly, you expect that."

"You have a game tomorrow afternoon. You can play without the pressure." Meridian's voice dropped a decibel, but the words drifted in the air. "Your anxiety will lessen if you help players on the visiting team relax. They'll relax if you throw them the ball."

"I throw the ball to my players."

"Help the visiting players relax. Throw them the ball." Meridian's voice grew guttural. "You'll feel better if they feel better." She leaned closer. "You won't remember me."

Nalbandian and Jason approached Number 7. Meridian backed away. She glanced at the wider player sitting across two plastic chairs. Nalbandian and Jason blocked Number 7's view and occupied his attention.

"You have an easier time relaxing than your friend," Meridian said, sitting on a stool in front of the man wearing number 69.

The wide man grinned, missing a few teeth. "I'm invisible. We walk down the street, people know his name, not mine."

"He puts pressure on you. He expects you to perform."

"Yeah."

"He gets tense during the game."

"He's uptight."

"He's your quarterback. Help him relax during the game. He's worried because he doesn't know when the other team is going to hit him. That puts pressure on you."

"He puts pressure on me."

"Relieve the pressure. Step aside. Let the visiting team hit him on pass plays. Then he'll relax because he'll know when he's going to be hit."

"He needs to relax."

Meridian's voice grew hoarse. "You'll feel better if he relaxes." She leaned forward. "You won't remember me."

* * *

Bobby bolted upright.

Danger.

Marilyn.

Every nerve end spiked. Bobby rushed through the house. Marilyn was not home, nor did he perceive any other presence. Marilyn must've been hungry. Twilight deepened. Dangerous to feed while so many humans were awake.

She'd be drawn to the hospital. Bobby had to stop her before she exposed the existence of vampires in the community. The sun set minutes ago. She couldn't have been gone long. Bobby dashed toward St. Mary's, dragging a nagging sense of foreboding.

He didn't bother to change into scrubs. This early in the evening he blended with hospital visitors, a curious juxtaposition—easier to penetrate, harder to feed.

Bobby entered through the parking garage, more by habit than necessity. He'd rushed across the field to get here, but inside the hospital, he had to search for Marilyn at a human pace. He began where they'd fed before, on the maternity ward.

He sniffed the corridor outside room 431. No trace of Marilyn's sweet perfume or the overriding scent of her sex. He circled the fourth floor, then rode the elevator to three. No trace of Marilyn here either. Desperation filled his thoughts. The sense of urgency to find Marilyn, to save her—from what?

Bobby paced the roof of the parking garage. He'd searched the remaining floors. He retraced and searched maternity again, in case he'd somehow arrived before Marilyn, but she wasn't in the hospital and hadn't been here since their visit last night.

Bobby froze, hoping to jar his thoughts. She'd pleaded to stay, to be with him. She needed help, and she'd expressed desperate hunger. She must be feeding. Where else?

Summit Square?

Bobby never fed there. Open and dangerous. In despair, Marilyn might ignore the dangers. Bobby didn't know her as a vampire. What if she killed someone? What if she killed someone and failed to dispose of the body?

He approached the shopping center, and foreboding magnified. His fangs erupted, and his skin pricked. Three hundred yards away, scent acquired: the air, foul.

Anxiety pitched to the forefront of his mind. Anguish expanded. He wanted to scream her name and warn her.

Too late, Roberre said.

"No, it can't be." Bobby rushed forward.

Caution, Roberre urged.

Bobby fought his desire to fly, slowed instead. He needed to remain unobtrusive. Danger lurked here. He approached from the back of the shopping center and angled around the building. Past the pub, he peered into the shoe store Philippe mentioned once, the In-Step. Jake had mentioned that, too, hadn't he? A lean man, glasses, too young for the traces of grey, worked behind the counter.

Tingling pushed Bobby to pause. Hopelessness spun him in the opposite direction, and he retraced his steps. No need to stroll the sidewalk.

Marilyn's scent dragged along a trail of dumpsters and back doors. Her perfume delivered him to the far end of the center. The odor overwhelmed him. He glanced up and cringed, Marilyn's fate exposed.

How could he have not sensed another vampire this close to home?

He had to be wrong.

He scaled the building and sprinted over the roof of the supermarket. The cross faced the other way, and he raced around it. His jaw slackened.

Marilyn's mouth dangled open, her fangs pulled. She'd tried to feed here, invading the territory of another, more powerful vampire.

Revenge, screamed Roberre.

"I have to find him first."

Destroy him.

Grief drove Bobby to one knee. How could this happen? After fifty years of his feeling responsible for a human suicide, Marilyn returned to him as a vampire, absolving decades of guilt. She was scared, uncertain, seeking the guidance of her maker.

Anger would follow grief—Freud taught him that—but for now, sadness maintained a stranglehold on his dwindling humanity.

Minutes, hours passed. Bobby summoned memories of fifty years ago and the last two nights. He rose to go, but he couldn't leave her here. Her head deserved whatever honor he could bestow, a burial at least.

Removing her head would warn the vampire responsible. Bobby didn't care. He thought nothing of the cloth draped over the cross until he touched it. He sensed the blood was Marilyn's beneath the head, but on the left arm, a small, dried stain seized his attention, and his mind reeled. He smelled man, a vampire, the one responsible for this atrocity. He raised the blanket to his nose and inhaled deeper than necessary.

Another memorable scent filled his nostrils.

Meridian.

* * *

Tony used night-vision binoculars, careful to note the spot where Bobby dug.

* * *

Nalbandian flipped the cell phone shut. "The last of the bets, one in Mr. Storm's name and two in your name. Philly is heavily favored. You've influenced two important players. Along with the defensive players, I'm confident they'll lose. We'll clean up."

Nalbandian mounted the wooden steps to his historic Newtown home. Meridian admired the splay of muscles beneath his clothing, broad shoulders and a small waist for a man. His dark hair was swept back and he carried a continental aristocratic look. His powerful arms could've pinned her down when they had sex. No need. His muskiness drifted on the air. Meridian tilted her head back and sniffed. Desire swelled. Nalbandian had fulfilled her wishes for two nights.

Nalbandian whirled around her. "You're hungry," he said. "I can sense your craving for sex and blood. Human blood this time, not mine. Do you smell the woman walking the dog?" He flicked his chin without looking.

Meridian glanced up the street. A block away, a woman paused, her dog on a leash taking care of business.

"Too close to home," Nalbandian said. "The smell of humans arouses desire. Feed when you need to, but don't put yourself at risk. You have two choices. Take so little blood from each victim he lives but you're never satisfied, or drain your victim. If you're going to kill, stalk your prey. Be sure of two things: no one will miss him, and you can dispose of the body."

"How often do you feed?"

"Doesn't matter. Whenever the urge strikes."

Nalbandian's nostrils flared. He jumped from the porch to the sidewalk next to Meridian. "Do you feel the urge to feed?" he asked.

Meridian nodded.

"You're controlling it. Release your feelings. Control your actions, not the urge." Nalbandian rushed around Meridian. "Let go your feelings. Trust vampire instincts."

Meridian's fangs ached. Her skin strummed, most incessantly across her hips. Her mind screamed, *Blood*, her flesh burned with desire, the physical aching to touch and be touched. She allowed the sensations to flow through her, observing as a Roman spectator, cheering at the weakness of the innocent, howling with blood thirst, eager for the inevitable spectacle.

Somewhere deep inside, an inner voice formed a single word: *No*.

Meridian laughed at her reflection in a car window, dispelling a common belief vampires lacked a mirror image. Unearthly strength and the glowing eyes of a feral hunter; hubris, not love, tied vampires to humanity.

Nalbandian dashed into her space—his reflection dwarfed hers. He kneaded her spine. His lips skimmed her neck, and his tongue bathed her skin.

She tilted her head, exposing vulnerability. Nalbandian wrapped an arm around her breasts. His fangs drew thin blood lines from ear to collarbone, and he lapped the blood as it rose. Meridian moaned in ecstasy. Submerged in consciousness, Lara couldn't even cry at the violation of her essence. The wounds healed, and Nalbandian sneered.

"I've done the legwork. Tonight, you'll feed from William Nike. He lives in Wrightstown, the neighboring community. Always feed more than three miles from where you sleep. Suburban authorities target missing persons and murder investigations in a three-mile radius around the crime."

He pulled her head back, kissed her lips, then spun her around. "You're a beautiful woman." His hand slipped lower, teasing. "Because we'll have a body to dispose of, we'll travel by car."

He pointed to a luxury vehicle with a large trunk and tinted windows, double-clicked, and opened the passenger door before the vehicle beeped a second time. He pulled an onyx evening gown from a bag and tossed it to her.

"When you hunt, dress for sex and blood and, if necessary, for distraction. Being a woman"—he gestured toward her curves—"provides advantages over male prey."

They drove out of Newtown, late enough for the traffic lights to be blinking. "Who's William Nike?" Meridian asked.

"Scum. A man who fits the profile of feeding victims: he lives alone, and no one will miss him." Nalbandian accelerated far beyond the speed limit, as if no police lurked in the small town. "He's been arrested several times on DUI, his license revoked, though he continues to drive. A week ago, drunk, he ran a stop sign, plowed into two kids on their way home from a Halloween party. He killed the girl. The boy is lingering."

Nalbandian drifted around a corner.

"Mr. Nike has been released on his own recognizance. He has friends. No charges will be filed."

Nalbandian directed the vehicle along Route 413, past the Newtown police building, slowing to the speed limit until the building disappeared behind them. He drifted another steep curve into townless Wrightstown. Nalbandian switched off the headlights and wove onto one secluded road after another. No streetlights in farmland. Fields, trees, grazing deer—the transition from suburban to rural in a few short blocks. A possum streaked across the pavement. The moon remained hidden behind a cloud bank.

He stopped the car in front of a darkened colonial, set back from the road. No neighbor to the left. A tree grove blocked the view of the house to the right. A house across the street sat one hundred yards away, situated sideways, so no windows faced Mr. Nike.

Nalbandian pulled into the driveway and parked close to William's house.

BLOOD BETWEEN LOVERS

"His car is in the shop, being repaired."

"How do you know all this?" Meridian asked.

"Stalking research. Night court. It's as though the humans designed the system with us in mind." He chuckled. "They present candidates, names, addresses, stories. They tell us about their crimes and whether they'll be punished or slapped on the wrist. The government can't promote vigilantes, but it's as if they're hoping a secret group exists to rid society of the otherwise untouchable elements."

They approached the back door of the house. A night creature flitted in the bough of a nearby tree, and the branches creaked. A skunk fouled the air.

"Doesn't matter who's protecting Mr. Nike in court. Nothing can save him from our urges tonight. He's crossed our paths, demanding attention, not by necessity but by circumstance of our choice."

Nalbandian jiggled the doorknob, tested the windows and back slider. All locked.

"Easy enough to break in, but never leave physical evidence. Nothing for authorities to investigate." He stepped back from the house and pointed to an open second-floor window. "The entrance to the diner."

They scaled the siding. Nalbandian gestured for Meridian to enter first.

"Take him and don't drip. No evidence."

Meridian hopped through the open window and landed silently on a tattered Persian rug next to a double bed. She blocked out the stale odor of a man in need of bathing, reeking of alcohol with every breath he exhaled, flung across the bed as he'd collapsed, fully clothed.

He clutched an empty bottle in his left hand and snuggled it against his chest like a child's teddy bear. A wallet and keys rested on top of a five-drawer wooden bureau that supported a mirror. Mr. Nike had draped the mirror with a sheet, as if he couldn't bear the image.

A nightstand stood sentry next to the bed, a digital clock glowed scarlet numbers, and a small chain lamp attested to life. The room contained no other furniture. A closet on the wall opposite the bureau exposed the drab clothing of an unpunished murderer.

Mr. Nike lay on his back, head cocked to the side, legs dangling: one straight, one crooked.

Meridian sensed Nalbandian close behind her. No need to hide the bite, no desire for sex with this victim—though the sexual urge still filled her psyche, certain Nalbandian would fulfill her later. Throbbing expanded from her temples, dull but incessant.

Blood, screamed every aspect of being, overriding all other thoughts and stomping on the inner voice that squeaked, *No*. Nalbandian's demon obviously controlled his consciousness: he'd killed to sate thirst, he'd learned how to stalk, and now he taught her to do the same.

Mr. Nike's carotid artery pulsed in slow rhythm with his breathing. His stomach rose and fell, the corner of his mouth twitched, and he snorted. His neck bulged.

Pounding expanded in Meridian's skull; she wasn't sure whether this blocked all other sounds or if there were no other sounds. Tingling rushed into her extremities. Her head neared the edge of explosion. Her fangs erupted.

"Yes." Nalbandian encouraged her with his chin.

Meridian's muscles tensed. She hopped onto the bed, trapped her victim's head, and pinned his shoulders. Her fangs tore into his throat.

Blood surged into her mouth. She paused to savor the taste.

Mr. Nike's consciousness broke through his stupor, his eyes wide with terror, pain etched across his features, but unable to utter a sound. Warm human blood of limitless supply invigorated Meridian. She attacked again and sucked harder.

The more she extracted from Mr. Nike, the limper he grew. Meridian's senses exploded in a world of darkness such as she'd never before experienced. Nalbandian grabbed her waist. He hiked up her dress and pulled down her underwear as she drained the blood from her victim. Nalbandian moaned with a single thrust, and he entered her from behind, engorged in her excitement, feeding vicariously through her will, her desire.

She regripped Mr. Nike as Nalbandian regripped her hips, and with the speed only a vampire is capable of, thrust himself in and out of her until she exploded, saturated in blood and sex.

Her orgasm precipitated his, and she collapsed, her victim drained, her face screwed, Nalbandian riding her back.

"Where're we taking him?"

"Whenever you purchase a new home, be sure that somewhere close, but more than three miles away, is a place to dispose of bodies that will be untraceable."

Nalbandian drove to Route 413 before switching on the car lights.

BLOOD BETWEEN LOVERS

"Across the county, outside of Bristol, is a battery factory. Before it's cut, folic acid is stored there in a twenty-two-hundred-gallon vat. Undiluted, folic acid dissolves flesh and bone. Mr. Nike's remains will never be discovered."

They'd closed the upstairs window, straightened the bed, and stuffed the wallet and keys in Mr. Nike's pockets, then Meridian wrapped her victim in the bloodstained bedspread, carried him downstairs and out the back door. They stuffed him in a plastic bag in the trunk, switched off the house lights, and locked the doors, leaving no evidence of foul play. Mr. Nike appeared to have slinked away and disappeared. No one would care.

CHAPTER 32

B obby sealed the door and paced his vault, the inner sanctum of his home. He'd buried Marilyn's head, wrapped in the blanket, deep in the field between the church and the hospital. Too deep to ever be unearthed. Marilyn's sudden appearance had jolted his senses. Perhaps she'd bewitched him as well, blocking thoughts of Meridian from consciousness.

With Marilyn's death, his subsequent grief, and the shock of the blanket—the scent of Meridian's blood and sex had assailed him, unmistakable—emotions flooded back. He had been mesmerized. The vampire who'd destroyed Marilyn also bound Meridian under his sway. The arrogant bastard had signed his name in her blood: Nalbandian.

Bobby had failed Marilyn, again. He'd loved her passionately once. When he thought he lost her, he submerged that obsession, much as he submerged Roberre. Fear his demon would ravage human blood kept emotions in check with Meridian, and he'd never expressed his passion. He never shared his most intimate thoughts. What was the point of teasing her or himself?

Marilyn—his creation—had asked him for help. He failed her. His fingernails pierced his palms. The scent of blood made him growl. He would not fail Meridian too. Meridian existed as his creation by intention. His progeny. And he'd loved the human. She had to be saved. Tonight. Now. He needed to express his true feelings, and he couldn't. How could he tell Meridian he loved her, then push her away forever? Vampire existence demanded he shunt her aside—immortality was too great a prize to risk over any woman.

Protective instincts of the sire and what remained of his human emotions demanded he rescue Meridian, then deal with the demon who stole her.

The demon must be destroyed. Anything less, and the leech would hunt Bobby and stake his head, then stalk Meridian until he dominated her again. Neither of them would feel safe if Nalbandian survived tonight.

Nalbandian had staked Marilyn at the shopping center to proclaim his territory.

"No." Bobby's voice emerged low and guttural. "This is my territory."

BLOOD BETWEEN LOVERS

* * *

Jake watched from the roof of the office building across the parking lot. Downwind and four stories up, with the aid of night-vision binoculars, he felt confident his role hadn't been detected, and now, Bobby would save Lara. Jake gazed at the stars. The Big Dipper, the Belt of Orion. A meteorite glowed bright for half a second. An omen?

Jake flipped open his cell. "Katie, is your team set?"

"Ralph is inside a house across the street. Owners are out of town. He has the best vantage point. We're filming in high-def and watching the replay in slow-mo so we don't miss anyone coming or going."

"Perfect." Jake snapped the cell shut and slipped it in his pocket.

He shook his head and yanked the phone out again. "Owen?"

"Bobby just arrived at his home. Alone. I'll let you know as soon as he leaves again."

Jake jerked open the rooftop door and descended the emergency stairs. Had he neglected details? A stroll in the night air would clear his head.

A rescue squad siren screeched down the bypass and careened onto the Newtown-Langhorne Road, headed for St. Mary's, performing an *L* around Jake.

Jake ambled across the macadam. Cars huddled in the near corner. Only the pub remained open this late. Jake closed his eyes for a moment and inhaled the autumn air. Logic dictated his thoughts. Bobby would rescue Lara when Nalbandian left to feed. He'd probably secure her in a secret vault. Didn't every vampire have one these days? Then he'd return to destroy Nalbandian.

Jake stationed teams at both houses. Jason's life depended on Bobby's next move.

A couple in conflict in front of the pub captured Jake's attention. The man groped, the woman pushed. Jake raised the binoculars. An attractive woman, narrow hips, tight dress, skinny legs, and an unhappy expression, involved in a heated discussion with a potbellied man. She didn't seem to be drunk. He might be.

Muscles relaxed. Jake stuffed the binoculars in a pocket and continued at the same pace toward the couple. One of them might need assistance. He wasn't sure which until the woman leaned forward as if whispering to the man, then he seized the woman's biceps and slapped her face.

The woman didn't cry out but glared, her eyes partially hidden behind jet-black hair falling across her forehead, draping longer on one side than the other.

"Hey, hey." Jake trotted up onto the sidewalk. He flashed his badge. Late at night, in the eyes of a drunk, a badge is a badge. "Let her go. Now."

The man staggered. Jake pointed to the pub. "Back inside. Stay there till you calm down."

Jake guided the woman's elbow and angled her away from the pub, past Jason's store. They passed the end of the overhang before the woman addressed him.

"Thank you. I don't know what would've happened if you hadn't intervened on my behalf."

She spoke with a foreign accent Jake couldn't place, French but not French. The side wall of the Italian restaurant cornered in front of the camera shop, creating an alcove. The woman guided Jake to the right, as if she wanted to look in the camera shop window, but twirled to face him instead. She latched on to his shoulders and slammed him against the concrete, knocking the wind from his lungs. The back of his head throbbed where it banged the wall.

The woman growled and bared fangs. Jake gaped into fathomless eyes, pupils and irises blended together.

"I need your help, Agent Plummer."

Jake struggled in vain. Her grip tightened.

"Who're you?" he managed.

"My name is of no importance. I'm a woman in distress."

"All evidence to the contrary."

"Nonetheless, I need your assistance."

Jake needed to keep her talking till his thoughts stopped spinning. "What's your name?"

"Persistent, aren't you?" She tilted her head, studying him. "Eyve L'Veigne. Now you'll acquiesce?"

"I might if you put me down."

"This conversation will be easier on us both if your feet aren't touching the ground."

Jake's mind cleared. The scene with the drunken man had been feigned. Somehow, she'd known Jake lingered nearby with backup. She'd maneuvered him out of sight, then attacked. Her eyes weren't glowing. She wanted something other than his blood. He'd listen and fake resistance. She'd use a compulsion, and he'd pretend to succumb. Fortunately, he was immune to vampire mind control.

BLOOD BETWEEN LOVERS

Eyve laughed. "My dear man, I doubt you'll be immune to me."

* * *

Bobby rushed to the center of the parking lot. Businesses were closed this late in Summit Square. Beer and whiskey scents escaped every time the pub door opened. Bobby scanned the row of stores. The shoe store jumped out as memories poured back, and he cursed himself.

He had known of another vampire. Jake had told him a bloodsucker had assumed control of the In-Step, and Jake's cheap cologne was attached to everything; he'd probably been here within the last hour.

Bobby strolled like a shopper, window gazing. Shoe shopping at one in the morning. Ha. He sensed another vampire, not present in the moment but here recently, and someone else . . .

Meridian.

He followed the scents into Newtown, curved at the corner of the clock shop into an older, residential neighborhood, the trail undisguised. It ended at a distinguished colonial, three stories, with a wraparound porch, and two vampires tucked inside.

He'd have to wait for Nalbandian to leave the house. He could sneak Meridian to his vault, lock her in for her protection, then return to deal with Marilyn's executioner.

Other vampires Bobby had encountered craved blood nightly, dominated by their demons. If Nalbandian had already hunted tonight, Bobby would return at sunset tomorrow to await his opportunity. He couldn't allow Meridian to endure this fate, nor could he endanger her with a frontal assault.

She must be desperate, wondering if Bobby bothered to look for her. If he touched her with telepathy he could soothe her mind: *Help is coming.*

Bobby steered his thoughts. He grazed around Nalbandian, careful not to disclose his presence. Hypersensitivity located Meridian. As he was about to project his feelings into her mind, an ugly sensation wrenched his stomach. Thoughts of blood and sex emanated from Meridian, more violent than anything he'd ever felt from her before.

Bobby staggered. This wasn't the woman he loved. This vampire stalked her prey. This vampire had killed. She swayed under the influence of a dominant bloodsucker.

Another persona, softer, more familiar, snagged his attention. Fear, confusion, the desperation he expected to find in Meridian he found instead in the inner voice.

The Meridian he knew had been submerged. Meridian the demon assumed control of their personality.

The demon wouldn't want to be rescued.

Nalbandian had attacked Meridian, weakened her body and mind, then influenced her to relinquish consciousness. Her demon would be bound to the beast who released her. He would've used a compulsion. Overwhelmed and terrified, human-Meridian had no chance.

Bobby fought the urge to break into the house, rush this animal with a stake, and destroy him.

If Nalbandian's compulsion was too strong and he was destroyed, Bobby might never be able to release Meridian from her demon. Nalbandian's control must be broken before this monster was ended. Too many unknowns to risk destruction before rescue.

The process might work in reverse. Meridian's one chance. Bobby needed to be willing to destroy Meridian, if necessary, to prevent her demon from existing. Only a genuine threat would convince her beast to relinquish control.

He remained hidden in the shadows, cloaking his thoughts. How had he allowed Meridian to fall prey to another vampire? Guilt stung. Marilyn had been eliminated forever. He couldn't lose Meridian too.

The distinct outline of a man, a vampire, taller than Bobby, framed an open third-floor window. The man studied the night. A smaller, familiar silhouette rushed into the man's embrace. A dress of ashen fabric clung to her hips and breasts.

It's not Meridian, Bobby repeated to himself. *It's her demon.*

The man kissed her. He bit her neck. Bobby sniffed blood.

"Ahh, Nalbandian," the demon moaned. Bobby ground his heel.

Nalbandian released her and disappeared into the night.

Bobby restrained himself from rushing forward. Nalbandian had to be too far away to sense his home being invaded. Bobby would have to sneak up on Meridian—her demon would attack him.

Bobby paced around the property. An idea formed, and he composed his thoughts. If he projected Nalbandian's image around himself . . . the aura wouldn't fool the demon for more than a second, but he only needed an instant of hesitation.

The demon paraded back and forth to the exit window. Bobby timed his attack as she angled away. He rose to the third floor, adding to the illusion of the last moment she'd seen Nalbandian.

He landed in a bedroom, tensed, incisors bared. The demon spun around. Before her smile evaporated, Bobby rushed her. Her eyes flared lavender red, unmasking.

Bobby bellowed and sunk his fangs into her neck. The demon snarled and fought to escape. Bobby pinned her arms and sucked her blood. Her gyrations lessened.

A man clutching a stake charged Bobby from the doorway. The guy from the shoe store. Jake's friend.

Bobby released Meridian's arm to protect himself, and the demon clawed him. Jason thrust the stake. Bobby caught Jason's arm and twisted. Jason winced, hollered when Bobby's fangs pierced his flesh, then buckled to the floor.

Blood oozed from wounds the demon had inflicted on Bobby's chest. He recaptured Meridian's arms. The demon wouldn't surrender until he posed a true threat of destruction. Bobby growled. He'd have to deliver her to the edge.

He attacked her again. She howled, but Bobby twisted both arms behind her back and held them with one hand. He retrieved the discarded stake, and gripped it like a weapon.

The demon's eyes widened. "You wouldn't," the demon said.

"Nothing will stop me."

He gulped more blood from her neck. Her muscles slackened, the tension eased from her face.

"Bobby, it's me," she gasped.

Bobby glanced into her eyes. Lavender red. Demon's trick. He sucked harder and raised the stake.

"Bobby, please . . . I love you," she whispered.

Words spoken with deceit.

Bobby leaned back and bellowed. "I'm doing this because I once loved you too." He'd taken most of her blood; now he poised the stake.

The demon groaned, her fangs retracted, and the lavender-red glow faded from her eyes, leaving them steel blue with golden flecks, eyes Bobby had grown accustomed to.

Meridian collapsed. Bobby caught her, cradled her head, and lowered her to the floor. He bit his wrist and allowed blood to drip into her mouth.

"You're Meridian J—"

An epiphany struck him. Meridian coexisted with her demon, at least in her world.

"You're Lara West. Dr. Lara West. You're a surgeon and a woman of her own mind."

Lara pulled his wrist to her mouth, drawing the blood necessary for existence. He would forever think of her as Meridian, but that wasn't how she thought of herself.

The unconscious man next to them stirred. Bobby's attention pivoted to Jake's friend. Jason's eyes opened, and something other than human glared at Bobby. Bobby pinned Jason and raised the stake over his head, aimed at Jason's chest. Jason struggled.

"You dared to attack me. Your life is over, you insignificant little man." Bobby snarled.

"You're not as powerful as him. He'll destroy you."

"Too bad you won't be around to see that."

"What're you going to do, kill me?" Jason sneered, like the idea was preposterous.

Bobby jerked back on the stake, about to strike. Bobby roared, and his fangs whipped into place. Jason's eyes widened, pupils dilated, human only.

"Who are you?" Bobby demanded.

"I'm Jason Storm. I-I work in a shoe store for—"

"You work for no one. Who are you?" Bobby screamed at him.

"I-I'm Jason Storm. I'm an author."

One corner of Bobby's mouth curled up. "Really? What do you write?"

"Romance. Vampire romance."

Bobby chuckled once before his smile vanished. He maneuvered eye-to-eye with the man beneath him. "You're Jason Storm, shoe store owner . . . and romance writer. Your life is your own. You can be whatever you want," Bobby said.

"I want to be a bestseller," Jason whispered. He blinked repeatedly and rubbed his forehead. "Where am I?" He focused on Bobby's blood-smeared face, then his fangs, and he fainted.

Meridian tugged Bobby's arm, demanding more blood. He re-punctured his wrist and she fed until strength returned to her limbs. The color of her eyes held steady. Bobby pulled his wrist from her grasp. Another moment passed before circumstances sunk in, and Meridian dove into his embrace.

BLOOD BETWEEN LOVERS

"I was afraid I'd lost you," Bobby said.

"No matter what happens, I'll always be with you."

"Are you ready to travel? We have to get you out of here before Nalbandian returns."

"Nalbandian. He's—"

"I'll deal with him, but I need to know you're safe first."

Jason groaned and raised his head off the floor. Bobby tore Jason's shirt and wrapped a swath around the man's bleeding wrist.

"Too tempting otherwise." He grunted. "Don't faint," he added. "You have to get out of here, too. Go home. Or better, leave town for a few days. Go to a hotel." Bobby bit his lower lip as though restraining an impulse. He gestured toward Jason's wound. "That'll heal quickly."

"Who're you?" Jason asked.

"Lone Ranger. Forgot my mask. I don't have any silver bullets either, so don't ask, but take this." He handed Jason the stake. "A memento of our time together."

Jason struggled to his feet and staggered to the door. "Is Jake involved?"

"Jake's always involved."

Bobby lifted Meridian and glided to the window.

Jason glanced over his shoulder. "Aren't you coming?"

"We have our own escape route. Get out of here. Take the stake."

CHAPTER 33

Nalbandian had taught her how to control eyes and voice, a simple thing for her to pretend being Lara West. She'd tricked this simpleton, the man who betrayed her for another vampire.

She'd restricted the flow of blood when attacked, and hadn't been nearly as close to destruction as the fool believed. He thought the woman who replaced her was an actress?

Nalbandian would find her. She'd help him overpower Bobby, and Nalbandian could exert his will: destroy Bobby or influence his voluntary cooperation.

She wrapped her arms tighter around Bobby's neck and snuggled against his chest. Bobby cuddled her. Protector. Hero. Ha. Nalbandian would come as soon as he returned from feeding.

Bobby sealed them into his home, falsely secure behind the palm-lock doors and the metal shutters. She'd unlock the doors and allow Nalbandian to enter. Not yet, but when he called to her.

"Do you need to feed again?" Bobby asked. He settled her in the sanctuary and studied her eyes. The fool.

She remained demure, weak.

"We can't risk going out for human blood," Bobby said. "I have a bottle in the refrigerator."

"Could I . . . take more from you?" Would he be stupid enough to weaken himself further?

Bobby slipped behind her and draped his arm over her shoulder. Meridian's fangs erupted, but she restrained the urge to attack.

"I-I can't pierce the skin," she stammered, in character.

Bobby bit his wrist and offered it again. She'd drink whatever he allowed, making Nalbandian's job easier.

Bobby pulled away quickly this time, perhaps surprised by her voracious appetite. She licked drooling remnants from her lips.

"Wait in the basement vault," Bobby said. "You'll be safe there. I can feed, then deal with Nalbandian."

"I'm frightened." Meridian clung to him, buried her face in his neck. "Please don't leave me yet."

"I can't wait long. For your safety, I have to deal with this tonight."

"I was afraid you wouldn't come for me," Meridian said.

"I'll never make you feel insecure again."

"He attacked me." She sobbed.

Bobby hugged her tighter.

"He surprised me at the shopping center and forced me to go with him."

Bobby stroked her hair.

"I didn't know what to do. I didn't have a will of my own. Do you know what that's like?" she asked. Nalbandian would arrive in minutes.

"I've never been subjugated to another vampire, but I can imagine."

"I want you, Bobby. I need you." She fondled his trousers.

"Not now," Bobby said.

"I'm still frightened." She leaned into him. "Don't go."

Her lips searched for his. He couldn't refuse her kiss. She teased, allowed the passion to build. She pushed lightly. He backed up half a step to the sofa and sat. She straddled his hips. Her mouth found his again, and as he kissed her, she moaned in the throes of ecstasy, knowing the effect on his psyche. She wiggled sinuously in his lap, a dance of passion, a dance of betrayal.

"I want you forever, Bobby."

Bobby grasped her wrists. "No, you have to understand, I rescued you because I'm the one who sired you. It was my responsibility to teach you the meaning of being a vampire, but no matter how you've learned, we can't stay together. This is your final lesson. Vampires live alone because our immortality is more important than any relationship."

I'm here, Meridian. Open the door, Nalbandian's will laced through her brain and assumed tacit agreement.

"I-I think I understand," she said to Bobby. Her lips swept over his mouth and chin and found his neck, the quickest source of blood. "I'm defenseless though. I need more blood."

She sunk her fangs into his neck and sucked hard, the way Nalbandian had taught her to drain a victim.

Bobby pushed feebly, then harder as she didn't relent. "Too much, Lara. I need the blood. Stop."

Meridian leaned back and slavered the thick liquid around her lips. "Too late."

She hopped off, rushed to the doors, and opened them. Bobby chased and met her halfway across the sanctuary, on her way back to him.

"Lara. What're you doing?"

"Returning the favor. You introduced me to your friend, so I'm introducing you to mine. I love you."

She wrapped around him, pinning his arms. Even weakened, she couldn't hold him for long, but Nalbandian only needed a fraction of a second.

"Lara. No!"

Nalbandian rushed at Bobby and attacked his neck from behind. Bobby broke Meridian's hold, but Nalbandian re-pinned his arms and sucked his blood at will until Bobby crumpled.

"I'm proud of you." Nalbandian kissed her neck.

"I knew you'd come for me."

"We're bound together." Nalbandian's fangs grazed her flesh like a double-edged razor and drew two thin lines of blood. He licked the wounds, and Meridian moaned. "Blood and sex entwined," Nalbandian said.

"I need to feed," Meridian said.

"Later tonight. What's his name?" Nalbandian toed the body slumped at his feet.

"Bobby Eyre."

"This is where you lived." It wasn't a question. Nalbandian glanced around the massive room. "Pretentious."

"His home, not mine."

"I'll take Mr. Eyre to Newtown. Bring anything you want to keep. We're going to ensure no vampire lives here again."

"Holy water?"

"Fire. Fueled by an accelerant in the middle of the night, volunteers will never put it out in time." Nalbandian scooped up Bobby. "He'll work for us. I sense his demon."

"Roberre."

"You've met him? Easier for us to release Roberre and control him. You'll assist me, and I'll teach you."

Nalbandian rushed from the sanctuary, clenching Bobby.

Meridian rejoiced, spread her arms, and twirled 360 degrees.

She rose in the air to the fourth-floor bedroom landing. Nothing she wanted to take, but she strolled around their bedroom nonetheless and sucked in a familiar stench, like salt on a sea breeze.

She glowered at the opened black bag, her ophthalmoscope poking out the top. A souvenir from the last time she'd studied Bobby's eyes? She turned her back. Another world, unimportant now.

CHAPTER 33½

Lara struggled for consciousness. Bobby had arrived, at last, to rescue her. She sensed the demon weaken when he drank her blood, and she understood his plan. Her persona would resurface. She was as surprised as Bobby the plan didn't work. Sublimated, she was unable to warn him.

Nalbandian would enslave Bobby's mind too and release Roberre, not controlled the way Bobby occasionally shared consciousness. With Nalbandian's help, Roberre would shunt Bobby aside, and Bobby would be forever lost. Nalbandian taught her demon about being a vampire, but Lara shared the experience, and she processed the information differently.

The demon wandered Bobby's home, sneering at possessions and memories of his and Lara's existence, but realization dawned on Lara. Bobby's rescue attempt didn't fail. She failed to act.

The demon's departing consciousness wouldn't create a vacuum into which Lara could float. Lara's persona would only reassert itself when it seized control and submerged the demon. Too late to help Bobby now, but she'd be prepared for a second chance.

She needed a foothold. She needed to drive a metaphorical stake into the demon's psyche. The trick, she realized, was to keep the demon oblivious to penetration. Lara needed to exert her will without the demon's awareness. A small victory, but proof of her theory, proof hope remained to win back consciousness. If she forced the demon's behavior, a task the demon would otherwise never fulfill . . .

* * *

Meridian hopped over the balcony and drifted to the sanctuary floor. She smirked; Bobby had failed to teach her such a simple conquest for a vampire.

She strolled around the artifacts Bobby had amassed over centuries. Drawings of female anatomy signed by Freud. The spear of Genghis Kahn. Meaningless, easy to abandon.

She rushed toward the still-open doors and didn't understand why she hesitated in the foyer. Her feet skidded on the rough slate. A spotlight framed the marble stand. She caressed the parchment of the hand-scribed copy of *Romeo and Juliet*, about to become a victim in the impending fire.

"Too bad," she murmured.

She circled to leave, but stopped again and gazed at the letters that flourished across the title page, a different scrawl.

Meridian snapped the bound manuscript shut, scooped it up, and rushed from the house with the single memento. A whim. Nalbandian wouldn't care.

CHAPTER 34

"The doors are open," Katie said.

"They're all gone?" Jake asked. His plan had worked, and it hadn't.

"Do you have your friend?" Katie asked.

Jake glanced at Jason stretched out, a doctor attending. "Got him." That was the part that worked. "Nalbandian carried Bobby out of the house? You're sure it's not the other way around?"

"They emerged as a blur, but Owen filmed it in high-def. I'll replay the image . . . Bobby is unconscious in Nalbandian's arms."

Damn. "Lara. What about Dr. West?"

"Bobby carried her in. She departed of her own accord. Alone, after Nalbandian. Confirmed on film."

"Which way?"

"They both headed toward Newtown. If she's going to Nalbandian's, Ralph should be able to verify momentarily."

Jake sniffed antiseptic and fresh bandages. "Take your team into the sanctuary. Use caution. I need a clue. What's going on, Katie?"

"We're already in place. I'll signal you when we're inside. Won't be long."

Jake peered over the doctor's shoulder, jumped back when the doctor rose suddenly.

"He'll be fine in a few days. Bruises, abrasions, a nasty wound on the left wrist. Lost a surprising amount of blood, but I've given him two units. Rest is essential," the doctor said.

"No more missions today." She frowned, gathered equipment, and left.

Jason pushed up on his elbows. "I couldn't help myself."

"I know," Jake said. "It's not your fault."

"This whole operation was set up to rescue me?"

"We're inside," Katie's voice snapped in Jake's earpiece.

"Close the door behind you." Jake pivoted away from Jason.

"There's no one here. We're—"

"Close the door, Katie. If Nalbandian returns, the door won't stop him, but it'll give you a fraction more reaction time. You need every advantage."

BLOOD BETWEEN LOVERS

"Done."

"Good. Now, tell me a story."

"There's fresh blood in the middle of the sanctuary, on the floor and splattered around. Footprints indicate a struggle. Everything else seems intact. This looks like a home, or a museum."

Jake nodded. "Our plan has gone awry. Jason was freed, then Nalbandian should've been destroyed. Instead, Nalbandian is both alive and dead, Dr. West is still under his influence, and we might've lost Mr. Eyre too."

"Ralph just confirmed—Dr. West entered Nalbandian's house on Chancellor Street. Three vampires in one location, Jake. We can destroy them all."

"No."

"I don't think I heard you."

"I'm not sure I owe Mr. Eyre anything, but I do owe Dr. West. We're going to save her, and if Mr. Eyre is also rescued, so be it."

"Wow, you're treading a thin line, boss. You sound almost human."

"Can it, Katie. Reposition your team at Chancellor Street, but maintain distance. I'll meet you there. Have a plan ready."

Jake pulled the earpiece.

"Are you talking about the man who rescued me?" Jason asked. "And Dr. West? Do you mean Meridian?"

"Yes and yes."

Jason sat up. "I'm going with you."

"We just secured you, and the doctor said no missions."

"If it wasn't for that man, I'd still be there. If you're going to save him from Nalbandian, I'm going to help."

"Can you stand?"

"Drag me if you have to."

Jake laughed and hauled Jason to his feet. "You sound too much like me."

"You knew vampires existed, and you never told me? What kind of friend are you?"

"You sold me the wrong size sneakers. What kind of friend are you? I tripped running around the gym."

"Natural clumsiness."

"I'll give you natural." He helped Jason down the steps, to the SUV. "You faint at the sight of blood," Jake said.

"That happened to be my own."

Jake squeezed Jason's shoulder. "Truth is, my friend, you engaged your first vampire several years ago. Remember when we met? Searching for the Black Stone of Calcutta? You were introduced then to the paranormal world. Vampires, witches . . . Remember Amy? As I recall, you enjoyed a grand old time."

"I think I'd remember if I ever met a vampire."

Jake shook his head. "Memory wipe."

Jason opened his mouth, but Jake cut him off. "Wasn't my idea."

Katie frowned. "I thought he was the reason we did all this? Why'd you bring him here?" Katie pointed at Jason.

"He wants love, Katie. Love. Without blood, this time," Jake said.

"Seriously."

"Seriously, he owes a debt to Mr. Eyre, and he wants to help. He'll stay in Owen's van, coordinate communications, and watch the cameras for us. That'll free up Owen. What have you come up with?"

"Nalbandian has fed late every night for the last week. When he leaves the house tonight, we go in. The only way you're going to convince the demon to relinquish its grip on Dr. West is to be prepared to destroy it. Given the true choice, destruction or submission, we should retrieve Dr. West."

"Destroying the demon means we destroy Dr. West too. I truly want Lara back."

"It's covered. I've reissued the old bullets."

"Why?"

"We have Dr. West's formula for the antidote she synthesized for Robert Helstrom. We can shoot her if necessary, then save her before she succumbs. We can also shoot Mr. Eyre if that's the only way to separate him from Nalbandian."

Jake patted her arm. "You're gonna have my job soon, doll."

Katie snickered. "Everyone's in place."

Jake snagged Jason's arm and headed for Owen's van. He glanced at his watch. "It's three thirty. If Nalbandian doesn't leave soon, we'll either have to wait for tomorrow night or go to plan B."

"What's plan B?" Katie asked.

"Back on the other side of the humanity line."

BLOOD BETWEEN LOVERS

Jake escorted Jason along the dark street at the best possible speed given Jason's condition. Owen provided a quick run-through on the equipment, then disappeared to join Katie.

"Keep the doors locked," Jake said to Jason. "I'll be in touch. Watch these screens." He pointed to the top row of monitors. "They'll beep if there's movement outside Nalbandian's house. This button is rewind, this one slow-mo. Let me know the instant you confirm he leaves."

Jake planted his feet in the street. A dog barked. A freight train rumbled in the distance. Sticky autumn air preceded a storm and wrapped around him, altering his mood. "Hang on, Lara. We're coming."

"He left." Jason's excited tone conveyed the message Jake awaited.

"Signal your team, Katie. I'm going in the front door," Jake said.

Jake drew his weapon. He dashed across the street and hopped onto the porch. No telling when Nalbandian would return. Soon. Jake decelerated. His senses heightened in a microcosm of WPA–VU slush. He snagged the door handle. Unlocked. What did that mean?

He slung open the door. Lights out. He donned night-vision goggles. Classic center-hall colonial: living room left, dining room right, steps straight ahead, hallway leading past the steps, presumably to the kitchen.

A grand piano, opened, dominated the living room. Handwritten compositions spread across the music desk. Antique chairs; a grandma sofa straddling a Persian rug; a chess set, game in motion, hugging a marble stand. Jake spun around to inspect the dining room. Oak table with heavy legs, armoire loaded with books instead of dishes, and a wall of shelves, more books. Jake read a few titles. An astronomer's library.

Katie's team entered behind him. A dozen agents, left, right, and center, equipped as he was. More at the back door and side windows. They swarmed the house. Katie signaled.

"What?"

"We've found Mr. Eyre. Unconscious. Chained. Third floor. We–"

"Leave him for now. Find Dr. West. Shoot her. Hurry."

Didn't feel right. Jake lowered his weapon. Tension poured into his shoulders. That shouldn't happen. His muscles always relaxed under stress. *If there's a vampire ready to attack . . .*

His mind froze. *Something's wrong.* What?

The music and the books? They suggested a man of refined sensibilities, not a bloodsucking brute.

Jake tried a window. Locked.

The front door. Unlocked. Why?

He was expected. A trap.

Jake paused before signaling Katie. Nalbandian wouldn't concede his prizes easily. He'd want Bobby, a more powerful vampire than Lara, whom he could still dominate.

But he let us invade his house.

What was the trap then? Nalbandian knew his bounty would be raised astronomically if he hunted Jake or the team.

What did Nalbandian want?

What do we all want?

What's taken from us.

Jason.

Jake streaked out the door and jumped off the porch.

"Katie. She's not in the house."

He angled up the street. How could he be so dense to leave Jason alone? "Katie! Get out here."

How could he be so stupid to bring Jason back after rescuing him?

Half a block away, metal ripped. Lara tore the door off the van. Jake aimed his weapon.

Katie's voice crackled in his earpiece, "No, Jake."

"What?"

"I forgot to switch your bullets. You can't shoot her," Katie said.

"Shit." Jake holstered the weapon.

Lara hopped into the van. Jason screamed.

"Don't faint on me, you bugger," Jake shouted.

Lara attacked. She swirled with unearthly speed that still amazed Jake and a ferocity he'd never witnessed in her before. Her demon. Nalbandian would want her to bite Jason again.

She pinned Jason, but Jason produced a stake. Where the hell did he get a weapon? No time to analyze. Jake dove into the van and crashed into demon Lara West. They tumbled on the floor. The demon growled—or was that Jason?

Not sure how it happened, but Jake arose next to his kneeling friend. The demon glared, eyes glowing lavender red, fangs bared. She charged. Jake grabbed the stake and thrust, but Jason didn't let go. Their force combined, and low-angle trajectory pierced Lara's stomach.

She howled, dropped to her knees, then collapsed onto her back, the stake protruding from her belly. Jason released his grip, but Jake leaned over her writhing body.

"What're you doing?" Jason asked.

"We missed her heart."

Jake regripped the weapon and tugged, but the stake stayed deeply embedded. Lara raged. Jason grabbed Jake's biceps.

"You can't."

Jake shook off Jason. "We have to destroy her."

"She's a person."

"She's a monster." Jake wriggled the stake in her stomach.

The demon blustered and struggled, her face contorted in pain. Jake drove his knee into her shoulder and yanked on the stake. She howled. The stake cleared her flesh, dripping blood. Jake raised the weapon over his head, poised to strike.

"Jake, you can't do this," Lara rasped.

Jake rammed the stake toward her chest. Lara captured Jake's wrists, counterbalancing his force and holding fate in abeyance.

Jake leaned into the thrust, grimacing, teeth bared. "Jason, help me shove this into her heart."

"I can't."

"Do it."

The weapon inched closer. Lara's strength seemed sapped.

Katie hopped into the back of the van. She pushed Jason aside, hesitated for a fraction of a second, then snagged Jake's arms. "It's Dr. West, Jake, Lara West."

"How do you know?"

"Look at her eyes."

The glow in her eyes receded to Lara's human steel blue.

"You're going to stake me? Again?" Lara said.

Jake shrugged and eased back. Lara sighed and released his wrists. Jake pivoted suddenly, driving the stake toward her chest, his full weight on top of it. Lara screamed and caught the stake inches from penetration.

"Jake, no, it's me, it's me." Her voice gurgled.

Katie pinned his arms, and Jason latched on to his calf.

RAZ STEEL

"It's Lara," Katie insisted.

Jake kept his focus on Lara's eyes. They never flipped back from steel blue to crimson, not even a glimmer of red. Jake relaxed.

"Okay," he said, and plopped onto the floor of the van, still grasping the stake.

Lara glowered, wary of another attack. "Going to impale my heart when I'm not looking?" Lara gasped, unable to catch breath she didn't need in the moment and apparently unable to understand why she didn't need it.

"Of course not." Jake shrugged and tossed the stake aside. "That was then."

Lara grimaced and hugged her hips, rocking from side to side. "This really hurts."

"Don't be such a baby. It's only a wooden stake in your stomach. You'll heal."

Jason slumped backward. "I think I'm going to be sick."

"Not in my van," Owen shouted from the street.

Lara recoiled from Jake. "Would you have really . . .?"

"If the demon in you didn't relinquish consciousness . . ." Jake said.

"Where's Bobby?" Lara coughed.

"Katie?"

"Still in the house. Our people are out. Ralph reported Nalbandian returned. We can't reach Bobby now."

"We have to help him," Lara said. She pushed up on her elbows, but fell back to the van floor. "I need blood." Pain arced across her face.

"I don't think you'll find any walking, talking volunteers, but Katie packed a snack." Jake pointed at a cooler tucked under surveillance equipment.

Katie opened the lid and retrieved two packets of blood and shrugged. "Great taste. Less satisfying."

"You sound like a beer commercial," Jake said. "Let her drink. We need a new plan, Katie. Quick, if we're going to save Mr. Eyre."

"I thought—"

"You thought my first plan shoulda worked. All right, so one failed plan in five years, that's not so bad, is it? Bobby's unconscious, chained, and down a quart of blood. What're we gonna do?" He glanced around the van. "Katie? More blood in cold storage?"

"One more packet."

"Dr. West?" She punctured and drained the second bag. "The hole in your stomach seems smaller," Jake said.

"That's not funny. It hurts like hell."

"Your finite immortality stirs little sympathy."

"My what?"

"Finite immortality. You're vulnerable to a wooden stake in the heart, otherwise, you'll live forever. Finite immortality."

"He said the same thing."

"Who?" Katie asked.

"Nalbandian." Jake understood.

"I don't understand," Jason said.

"It means Nalbandian recognizes his vulnerability. Eternal existence is too precious to risk."

"How does that help us?"

"Nalbandian will fight for what he wants, but only to the point where rewards still outweigh risks. It's why he commanded Lara to retrieve Jason. With our agents around, the threat to himself was too great. To save Bobby, we need to convince Nalbandian the danger supersedes the prize. Finite immortality suggests a strategy."

* * *

Tony parked on State Street, two blocks over, parallel to Chancellor Street.

"You understand what to watch for?" Eyve asked.

Tony nodded.

"The house behind this one is where the government agents are gathered. I'll disrupt their video. No one will see me. Lara West and Bobby Eyre are going to suffer."

"This fool vampire, Nalbandian, is making their lives easy," Tony said. "He's interfering with your plans."

Eyve grinned. "You've done well unearthing information so quickly. You'll be rewarded." She handed him a cell phone and inserted her earpiece. "Contact me as soon as they take the shoe man away. I'll only let them drive a block or two down the street before I stop them. I want to be sure the other agents hear the gunshot."

"If you let the shoe guy live, won't he recognize you?"

Eyve's lips spread. "I can cast an aura, the persona of another. To him, I'll be that fool vampire."

"You'll look like someone else?"

Eyve cast the persona of Nalbandian and assumed his features.

Tony's eyes widened. "Robert never did that."

"An old Jedi mind trick." Eyve laughed. "A compulsion will convince the shoe man Nalbandian's been shot and Nalbandian is responsible for the death of the agent. I'll take the agent's blood, but I'll also have his gun with the government's bullets. The ones they don't have an antidote for."

"How do you know about the bullets and the antidote?"

"Agent Plummer is under my influence, he just doesn't know it. He's shared some of his thoughts."

"What if Nalbandian escapes with Bobby or Lara?"

"I won't allow the interfering bloodsucker to run away. The government agents will think he's been shot. I will shoot him with a new bullet. He will be destroyed, then we can go about our business of torture. I want Lara West and Bobby Eyre to endure exquisite pain before I destroy them too."

* * *

"We have to act fast," Katie said, "before Nalbandian escapes with Mr. Eyre."

"First step, we have to make sure Mr. Eyre stays put." Jake swiveled to Lara. "Your job. He's on the third floor. You'll have to enter the house there. Wake him, feed him, and unchain him if you can—keep Nalbandian from taking him."

"How can I stop Nalbandian? His plan was to release Bobby's demon. He might've already done that."

Katie tossed her a weapon. "Magic bullets. You only need one shot. He won't be expecting you, at least not Dr. West. It'll give you a moment before he realizes his mistake. Use your speed. Shoot them both if you have to."

Jake winked at Katie. "My girl."

Lara pinched the gun between thumb and index finger. "Where do I keep it in this dress?"

"Yeah, your change of attire." Jake nodded. "That will go over big in the ER."

"Shut up, Jake."

Jake shoved his weapon into his waistband, slipped off his holster, and handed it to Lara.

"Strap it high on your thigh, where it won't be seen. Katie, organize your team into squads of three. We need a united front at all times. We'll enter the house from as many directions as possible. Lara, you're gonna have to go in just before we do. You know your goal. Katie will direct two squads to the third floor for backup. If Nalbandian flees to the third floor before we do, deal with it."

"What do I do?" Jason asked.

"You, buddy, are going home. I made the mistake of bringing you back here, I won't repeat it."

"But—"

"Argue all you want. We'll put you in cuffs if we need to. You did your part. We appreciate it. I'm sure Dr. West appreciates it. Look." Jake pointed. "Her stomach's almost healed." Jake made a fist and aimed his thumb over his shoulder. "You're outta here. Katie, have one of your people escort Jason home, and stay with him. Everyone's in place in two minutes." Jake glanced at his watch.

Katie hopped out of the van barking orders, organizing squads. "Owen, you get Jake's friend out of here. Stay with him," she said.

"No way," Owen said. "I'm not going to miss all the fun. Send Ralph."

"Ralph's busy watching monitors. You go."

"Someone in his squad can watch the monitors. Nalbandian isn't going anyplace in the next two minutes."

Katie whined. "You never obey orders."

"Neither do you."

Jake shook his head. "You two remind me of my kids. Stop bickering."

"You don't have kids," Owen said.

"And you two are the reason why not," Jake replied.

"You owe me big time," Katie muttered to Owen.

Jake rolled his eyes, but she was already speaking with Ralph.

Jake tossed Lara an earpiece. "Get into position. I'll signal you in a minute." Lara disappeared with inhuman speed.

Jake shook his head. "I won't ever get used to that."

Ralph arrived in a VU SUV, lights out. Katie signaled. Ralph pulled his weapon, ejected the clip, and tossed it to her. She snagged it with one hand, frowned, and returned it to Ralph with a second clip.

"You're out of here with old and new bullets. Use your discretion."

Jake opened the passenger door as Jason opened his mouth. "Not a chance," Jake said. "Just go. I need you safe." He tilted his head toward the vehicle.

Jason climbed in. Jake squeezed the door shut and tapped the roof. Ralph guided the car past a few driveways before switching on the lights.

Katie tossed Jake a skinny box.

"What's this?" Jake asked.

"Clips of the old bullets in case you need to shoot Mr. Eyre."

Jake tossed it back. "That was then. I'm on my side of humanity now." He headed down the street and spoke to his Bluetooth. "Thirty seconds to showtime, everyone."

Katie trotted after him, issuing orders. They approached the front of the house. The porch door was still open. Why hadn't Nalbandian closed it?

A single gunshot echoed in the distance. Behind them. Jake crouched, weapon drawn. Katie crouched, back-to-back.

"He's dead." Jason's voice sprayed Jake's ear. "The driver—Ralph. Jake. Jake. Are you there? He's dead. Ralph is dead."

Jake cursed. "What happened? Are you okay, Jason?"

"Ralph shot Nalbandian, then Nalbandian killed Ralph. Bit his neck. Jake, I was so scared. I couldn't do anything. I thought he'd take me again. Ralph's dead. He's dead, Jake."

"Deep breath, Jason. Are you okay?"

"I'm—yes. Nalbandian left. He didn't touch me, but he was shot."

"Stay put. I'll send someone."

Jake studied the house and rubbed his chin. No one saw Nalbandian leave. "Katie, order a squad to deal with Ralph and Jason. I want my friend safe. Understand? I'm going in. Send in all squads. You've got my back."

Adrenaline charged through his system. Jake sprinted across the street and hopped the steps onto the porch. His senses prickled. An indistinguishable person raced past him into the house. Nalbandian—who else?

Jake whirled. A wounded vampire would be desperate. Shot with an old bullet, he might survive for hours. Struck by a new bullet, he'd be on a shorter leash. Ralph possessed both. Jake crept into the living room. He'd been in this exact spot not long ago. Foreboding raised his hackles. A flush rushed across his face.

Another trap.

CHAPTER 35

A scuffle on the second floor.

Jake spun around. Trained senses insisted a vampire streaked past him. Again. Daring him to step forward? Testing his resolve? Time ticked in his skull. Jake needed to understand the dynamic.

Nalbandian had attempted to recapture Jason a second time. Or had he? Was Jason the real goal? Jason would be integral to Nalbandian's short-term plan to control the shoe store.

Nalbandian wouldn't know Lara had overcome her demon. But he'd realize she'd been staked as soon as he saw the hole in her dress. What would Nalbandian want then? Who would be more important to him, Jason or Bobby?

Bobby. Definitely more important to survival. Jake glanced at his watch. Nalbandian must be figuring out he wasn't shot with a normal bullet. If he wasn't healing, his priorities would change. Unsure how long his strength would hold out, he'd need Bobby's demon to protect him and Lara's medical knowledge to save him.

He's counting on them both.

Running around is a diversion. He wants us to zero in on the first floor. Lara and Bobby will be on the third floor. Once Nalbandian reaches the third floor, they won't need long to escape.

Jake paused at the foot of the stairs. What if he was wrong? What if Nalbandian had moved Bobby, and they were all on this floor?

Katie, deploy teams, he texted. Nalbandian would hear their plans if he spoke aloud. *Going to 3rd floor*

Coming with u

Stay. Coordinate 1st floor search

I have your back

Stay

Jake mounted the stairs. On the second-floor landing, he shuffled over the three bodies of the first squad, two with weapons in hand, unconscious or dead—no time to determine their fate now. He needed to find Lara and Bobby. A muffled cry emanating from the floor above drew his attention.

The steps going up squeaked. Of course. No hiding his approach. Instincts screamed vampires were on the third floor.

"Katie. Now I need you."

"Can't. I have Nalbandian trapped in the kitchen."

Jake blinked. What? Had to be a trick.

"Shit. Nalbandian just disappeared," Katie said.

Someone rushed past Jake and crashed through the window at the end of the hall. Jake kicked open the door to the lone third-floor bedroom.

Lara posed in the middle of the room, flanked by Nalbandian and Bobby, each pinning one of her arms. Their eyes glowed crimson. Nalbandian must've circled outside the house and reentered through the bedroom window. Didn't make sense. Neither did any other explanation.

Jake cursed. Nalbandian knew Lara had overcome her demon—his trap, though, was devious. Lara attacked Jason in the van. If she succeeded, Nalbandian would have them both under his influence again. If she failed—as she did—Nalbandian knew she'd attempt to rescue Bobby, so Nalbandian hurried to release Bobby's demon. When Lara made the rescue attempt, Bobby's demon recaptured her. Nalbandian risked nothing in the attempt to retake Jason.

"Agent Plummer?" Nalbandian snorted.

Nalbandian towered over Jake, gazes locked.

"Under different circumstances, I'd stay and drink your blood. You'll have to forgive my lack of propriety."

"Can it. You have something I want." Jake shifted his attention to Lara.

Nalbandian leaned forward. "I counted on that." He raised a weapon.

Jake realized why only two of the three agents he'd stepped over had been armed.

"Interesting piece of hardware. Not the gun, of course, but the bullets," Nalbandian said. He pressed the gun to Lara's ribs and fired.

She screamed and slumped. Nalbandian scooped her up and tossed her.

Jake caught Lara, but the force knocked the weapon from his hand, and he stumbled backward.

Nalbandian and Bobby crashed through a window, into the night. Jake cursed. Most of his people were inside the house. Shots echoed in quick succession. Three from the depository, one from the grassy knoll? No chance one agent could bring down two flying vampires simultaneously. Footsteps pounded on the stairs behind him, and voices sounded outside.

BLOOD BETWEEN LOVERS

"Jake." Katie's voice rang in his earpiece. "Do you have Dr. West? Are you okay? We've got them both. Nalbandian and Bobby. Jake."

"I'm okay, Katie. I'm okay."

He forced himself to concentrate. Thoughts muddled. Scenes replayed in his head, out of sequence. What just happened? If Nalbandian planned on surviving, he needed Lara's medical attention. Fast. He'd sacrificed her, though, and taken Bobby.

Why?

And if Nalbandian had been on the third floor all along, who did Katie trap in the kitchen? Who in fact had pushed past Jake on the landing? He needed to hear Katie's report.

Agents were stationed on roofs on opposite sides of the house, watching windows, but to down both escaping vampires at the same time was prodigious shooting by one agent. Maybe Lee Harvey could've succeeded. Maybe if they'd been moving at presidential procession speed–but they bolted out the window with vampire speed. As with JFK, there had to be information to which neither he nor the world was privy.

"Katie, I need Dr. West's antidote. She's been shot."

"I'll send it up. We're convincing Bobby's demon to relinquish control now."

CHAPTER 36

E yve savored a trace of blood from her lips. Tony paced the sidewalk at Summit Square, reading Janet Evanovich's book six of the Stephanie Plum series. Eyve had reeled through the series in a day. Tony reminded her of Lula. She studied his gait—peculiar for such a big man.

The sky lightened, heralding the sun. Or was that light from the flames? She'd torched Bobby's home. They'd all assume Nalbandian was responsible. One task remained to complete the night's work.

Lara West and Bobby Eyre resided in the sphere of her influence. Pain defined their futures. Eyve sniggered. Fresh blood invigorated her veins—the WPA–VU agent assigned to protect the shoe man. She'd drained him and left the body. "Ralph," the shoe man had screamed. He would swear Nalbandian was responsible. She'd destroyed Nalbandian. As Agent Plummer said, *All evidence to the contrary.*

In the guise of Nalbandian, she'd streaked through the house, confounding the agents, allowing herself to be trapped momentarily in the kitchen. With Ralph's gun, she'd shot Nalbandian twice when he fled the third floor, new bullets, *fait accompli.* The agents would assume one of the shots was Ralph's.

She shot Bobby with an old bullet, so the agents could save him. They'd find the timer she used to start the fire. So what? They'd never suspect her involvement.

A dark SUV pulled into the center and parked in front of the shoe store. A small man in the rumpled clothes of a dime-store detective hopped out. He headed toward the sidewalk. Close-cropped hair, pointy teeth—stereotypical government agent.

Eyve dashed past the display windows and timed her appearance in front of the shoe store with his.

"Agent Plummer, lacking in fashion but punctual," she said.

The man nodded.

"I want a report on Dr. West. Did you stake her?"

"Skewered her stomach as you suggested."

"Describe her reactions."

"She writhed on the floor and howled. I pinned her down and threatened to re-stake her through the heart."

"You submerged her demon, then?"

"Yes. The demon believed the threat real, and Lara West has control of consciousness." He laughed. "She complained how much it hurt."

"Good. What have you done with Nalbandian's body?"

"He's being shipped to Washington. Tonight."

"How?"

"Sealed container in a private truck."

"Guards?"

"Driver and shotgun."

A tingle crept up Eyve's spine. A cock crowed.

"Reschedule shipment for tomorrow night," she said.

She flipped open a cell and pushed the call button. A phone vibrated in Tony's pocket. She watched him glide a finger across the screen to unlock. "Go," she said. He'd fetch the body of a vampire she'd destroyed in Trenton to switch with Nalbandian's body, and she'd bottle a few drops of Nalbandian's blood.

Eyve stalked behind Agent Plummer. "Waste no time," she said. "Tomorrow night, you must coerce Mr. Eyre to assist with another mission. Use the same threat—you'll expose Dr. West as a vampire if he doesn't cooperate."

"What mission?"

"Doesn't matter." Eyve circled and whispered in his other ear. "Tell Mr. Eyre you'll send Marilyn Monroe to work with him on this mission."

"I destroyed Marilyn Monroe."

Eyve bared her fangs and hissed. She yanked Agent Plummer's shirt up and clawed his back. He winced but didn't move. Blood welled under her fingernails.

"I know what you did. Tell Mr. Eyre Marilyn Monroe will need to live with him while they work on this mission."

"Will Dr. West work with him as well?"

Eyve laughed and disappeared in the creeping dawn.

CHAPTER 37

Bobby's home burned. Lara sagged. Spectacular flames shot high into the night and danced across the roof. Fire engines, police cars, two rescue squads circled the property. The firemen had already surrendered the structure; their job now was containment, easy enough without a breeze to disturb the chilled dawn.

"Nalbandian's plan," Lara said. Tears and smoke stung her eyes. "I didn't realize he gained time to do this. I should've warned Jake. He could've stopped—"

"The fire is not your fault," Bobby said.

A scowl hung across his features, and Lara imagined his pain. Centuries of memories destroyed.

"Jake couldn't save you from your demon and save my house at the same time." Bobby studied the sky. "We need a place to stay. It's too risky to enter the vault while the fire is burning, and there're so many people around. A hotel won't be ideal, but we're out of time."

"I have another idea," Lara said. "A bed-and-breakfast. Pineapple Hill Inn. Secluded. It's a few miles away in New Hope. I've stayed there before. We'll need to hurry."

She asked Bobby how he had found her. The hunt had begun when he'd discovered Marilyn's head staked on the cross. Anger was quick to resurface. Even in death, Bobby had chosen Marilyn over her. She didn't want to be sealed in a small space with Bobby right now, but there weren't many options.

The Pineapple Hill Inn Bed and Breakfast was set back from River Road on a wooded tract. Nearby, the Delaware River lapped its banks, and pre-dawn creatures foreshadowed the sunrise. Ruins and ancient stone walls graced the grounds. A single light burned in the lower level of the restored colonial manor house. A portico, reminiscent of an era long past, protected the front door.

The sun crested the horizon by the time Bobby knocked. He apologized, and Lara flashed a credit card.

"Two weeks. Charge it in advance, but we need our room right away." She clung to Bobby's arm like an anxious lover.

Settled in the Sandpiper Room, Bobby draped a blanket over the curtains, ensuring darkness. A king-size four-poster bed dominated the room.

"We need to sleep," he said. "And I need blood. Soon."

Lara held out her arm, no compassion in the action. "Take what you want. We can feed at the hospital tonight."

She knew why Bobby hesitated. She had *never* offered her blood before. Her eyes narrowed and crease lines furrowed her brow. Lara bit her wrist. The smell would incite him. Hunger defined his actions. Self-betrayal defined hers.

Bobby rushed at her, fangs bared, but he stopped when she spun around and withdrew the offer. She lapped blood till the wound healed. Her demon would never have made such an overture. Nor would Lara West. Who had she become? Bobby snarled but resisted.

"Enough." She fronted him. "The bed or the bathtub. Your choice."

"Meridian—"

"Don't call me that. I'm Lara West. Dr. Lara West." She repeated it, affirming her identity.

"I'm sorry." Bobby squeezed her shoulders.

Lara rushed away, the bed a buffer. "I don't want an apology. Since you turned me two months ago, I tried to learn what it means to be a vampire. I wanted to be self-sufficient. I was afraid I'd be alone for eternity. All I wanted was for you to be proud of me. My failure to learn how to feed led to your incisor dysfunction. I was distraught I'd done that to you."

Lara studied his tight-lipped reaction. "Then you brought that thing, that woman, that vampire, into our house. She sauntered into our bedroom, and you left with her instead of staying with me. I felt betrayed. I was so angry."

"Meridian. Lara. I—"

"I don't want to hear excuses. I want you to listen to me." Lara dragged her tongue across her fangs. Blood would wash down the lump that rose in her throat.

"I was determined to prove worthy of your love, and my worthiness was meaningful only if I didn't lose the battle for conscious control. I found a victim. A man. You preferred your old lover. I needed to feed, and I was angry with you, so I seduced him with Stage One.

"But I didn't realize he was a vampire. He attacked me. I was weakened.

Vulnerable. He held my consciousness on the tip of his finger and offered it to my demon. I didn't have the strength to resist. My demon, Meridian, submerged me.

"You were lost to that damned likeable sexpot blonde. Helplessness dragged me down, smothered by my demon and controlled by a vampire's will more powerful than anything I'd ever felt."

Bobby kept his lips pressed together, and his weight shifted. *He must be uncomfortable with the conversation.*

Too bad.

"Nalbandian tolerated no compassion for humans, and he taught me the true meaning of bloodlust."

Lara dropped to her knees, pounded the mattress, and hid her eyes. Finally, she steadied her head and held Bobby's gaze.

"I killed a man. Meridian drained him of blood. I—I couldn't stop her. It doesn't matter he was scum, an unpunished criminal."

Tears flowed freely. "Who am I to choose life or death for anyone else?" She struggled to her feet and twisted away from Bobby. "I drank his blood and disposed of his body. I hate myself for doing it, but do you know why I hate myself even more?"

She whirled around and growled, fangs bared. "In the moment, I enjoyed it. The thrill, the rush of sensations from feeding on warm human blood invigorated every nerve in my system, a total body orgasm."

She rushed to the bathroom window, yanked off the blanket, and parted the curtain. She screamed, unsure which hurt more: the pain derived from the sun searing her flesh, or the guilt searing her mind.

"I betrayed you to Nalbandian. I opened the doors. I pinned your arms. And I may as well have tossed the match on your home."

Bobby dragged her out of the sun. She struggled, but he shoved her toward the bed and, with vampire speed, re-hung the blanket over the window.

Lara slid to the floor, her head buried against the mattress. Tears streamed down her face, blurring her vision. Bobby cradled her shoulders. He'd made it clear though—she was self-sufficient, and their relationship was all but over.

"Get away."

She shrugged, but words and actions lacked conviction, and Bobby hugged her tighter.

She sobbed into his chest and clung to his back. Tension eased in his muscles.

"I'm sorry, Lara. I betrayed you. Our goals for the relationship were different. I can't say, 'I'm not a mind reader.' I am, but I failed to interpret your human emotions. I don't feel worthy of you, but I'll do whatever it takes to prove my sincerity."

Lara sagged. She wanted him to prove his trustworthiness, but that wasn't what he was offering.

* * *

Bobby slept standing in front of the door. He told himself it was for security. The inn stood secluded, but without a safe room, vampires were vulnerable. Meridian—Lara—didn't want to sleep with him.

Anger. Human emotion flashed in her eyes and pervaded her thoughts. Betrayal deserved whatever punishment she doled out. Had his role as teacher been fulfilled by another vampire? If she had learned everything she needed to survive, then for the sake of their immortality, it was time to push her away anyhow. But he didn't want to leave with hatred in her heart.

He woke, fully clothed. Neither had bothered to undress. No need. Lara woke minutes after him. A scowl flickered on her face, mood unaltered.

Bobby guarded the door. "We need to feed tonight. The hospital—"

"Can wait. We won't go until later anyhow. I want to be alone. Here. Now."

Acquiescence in silence. The dead bolt slid into place behind him. Time alone with his thoughts—not what every vampire craves.

He headed toward St. Mary's. Scouting. He trundled along, scuffing the ground. No need to rush, eyes downcast, not paying attention to his surroundings. Life hadn't been this complicated since . . . he'd been in love with Marilyn fifty years ago, competing for her attention with more than one member of the administration.

Shocked to discover Marilyn survived as a vampire, he'd been overwhelmed by emotion, a human frailty, but that at least grounded him on an earthly plane of existence. Still.

A sequence of images flashed through his mind and wove a pattern he'd not seen before: Dr. Byra compelled not to retire, the shoe store guy subverted by a vampire, Lara overwhelmed by the same vampire, and Marilyn's staggering reappearance. All these images contained one common element: Agent Jake

Plummer of the WPA–VU.

Jake's friend owned the shoe store. Bobby had refused to help. Jake had warned he held another card, though his connection to Marilyn had yet to unravel.

Bobby's pace quickened. What did Jake have to do with Marilyn Monroe? Marilyn said she was being coerced by the government. She had to mean Jake.

The sudden urge to see his home filled his mind. Was Jake involved with the fire? Lara said arson was Nalbandian's plan.

Bobby stopped at the edge of the field overlooking the charred remains of framework. The roof had collapsed. A single wall stood, a sentinel in the ashes, the other walls caved in. Scorched. Muddied. Tire marks from rescue vehicles, footprints from firemen and the curious. No one knew the man who dwelt here.

Oddly, the metallic shutters still closed, fireproof as advertised, and seven of the eight stained-glass windows were miraculously intact. He'd surrounded himself here with his past. Works of art, possessions of people he'd encountered, the spear of his sire—each described a moment in his life. A few of these prizes had been shipped to Washington, displayed in their brownstone, but most had been destroyed.

A shiny object at the base of a window caught his attention. Lara's ophthalmoscope dangling from her medical bag, the bag sooted, but otherwise unharmed by the inferno. He could deposit it in her townhouse. A surprise.

Bobby wove through the rubble, checking to be sure the basement remained hidden. To ensure his privacy, the basement lock activated a staircase seal flush to the ground, undetectable—at least, until debris was cleared or excavated. He'd contact his agent tonight and have reconstruction started immediately, before the basement could be discovered by the VU.

A group of preadolescent boys arrived on bicycles. They dropped their rides and circled halfway around the structure. The tallest boy plucked a stone from the field and hurled it at the house. It thudded off the metal, true to his aim.

"Let's break the windows," the boy said.

"Are you nuts, Drew? The cops'll grab us all."

Drew laughed. "You're scared. There're no cops around here. No one's living in the house. There're no neighbors. No witnesses. The cops'll never know unless you tell 'em."

"I'm no snitch."

"Good." Drew scooped another stone and tossed it to the other boy. "Just to make sure, you break the first window."

BLOOD BETWEEN LOVERS

Bobby rushed toward the bicycles. He twisted handlebars and seats. Crunching metal attracted the boys' attention.

"Someone's messin' with our bikes."

A true coward, Drew trailed the gang. Bobby picked him off, knocked him to the ground, and dragged him behind a stained-glass window. The metal shutters blocked the view of the other boys racing to protect their property.

Bobby bared his fangs and drooled. "No witnesses," he said. "The cops'll never know." He sneered, close to the boy's face. "I know who you are, Drew. You're responsible for the safety of these windows. If anything ever happens to them, I'll find you." He sniffed. "You should go home and change your underwear before your friends notice."

Bobby snatched Lara's medical bag and rushed away. Unease chased him, nothing to do with the boys.

* * *

"You don't just look like her," Tony said, "you look like *her*."

Eyve offered a sultry smile. Her ruby lips puckered.

Tony's head bobbed. "Robert never did this."

"He didn't live long enough to learn how to create alternate personas." Eyve thought of little else these days. Robert, the favorite of her three creations, had been stolen from her. Staked.

Hatred arced through her, the lone human emotion to which she clung. Dr. Lara West and Bobby Eyre would be the catalyst of her humanity for a long time. The government agent unwittingly helped when he brought Marilyn Monroe back into Mr. Eyre's life and then destroyed Marilyn, suggesting a strategy.

The pain of that loss would be excruciating—if it were magnified a hundred times, Bobby might understand what the loss of Robert meant to her. Bobby's behavior proved he bore stronger feelings for Marilyn than for Lara. How better to magnify his pain than to re-present Marilyn Monroe to Mr. Eyre? *Not to mention Lara's pain when Bobby betrays her with Marilyn again.*

* * *

Bobby approached St. Mary's and entered through the parking garage. Maternity hosted a plethora of new mothers tonight, but administration always reserved a couple of rooms for psych patients. It would be easy to avoid detection amongst the horde of visitors.

He paused long enough outside room 431 to detect a young woman behind the door. Beyond the usual hospital antiseptic, a trace of perfume wafted from her skin—a new patient. A peculiar tingling danced across Bobby's neck, heightening his senses, signaling imminent danger.

His fangs erupted. Peril. Didn't make sense. What danger lurked in the hospital? He sniffed again. Fresh blood from a birthing room reignited pangs of hunger. He needed to feed. He'd return with Lara late tonight, and fought the urge to feed now. Too dangerous. A single patient wouldn't be enough to satisfy both their needs. Another patient in the next room? A hospital employee? His path ahead was unclear.

How long would Lara continue to hold him at arm's length? Would feeding together help? She said her demon murdered for blood. Draining a man portrayed a tremendous leap for a vampire unable to scratch flesh for a sip. What had Nalbandian done to her? Bobby raked his tongue across his fangs.

Blood fed his hunger. A voracious desire for satisfaction hurled him along an unfamiliar path. For the first time in decades, hunger compelled him to feed despite the imminent risk. Bobby hesitated. The psych patient in room 431 would be the least likely to have visitors or doctors at this hour.

Still in the corridor, he aligned his breathing with his prey's. She rested, drifting in a dream state. Bobby could deepen her sleep and avoid discovery. There wouldn't be time for all five stages of Vampirical Harmony. He glanced in both directions, then entered the room undetected and closed the door behind him.

The woman slept and dreamed of an erotic encounter, guided by Bobby's thoughts. Hunger for blood and sex drove him to frenzy. Bobby slid the sheet off her body and watched the rise and fall of the hospital gown across her stomach and perfectly shaped breasts. Skinnier than he preferred, but he was saturated too deep in the moment to care. Roberre surfaced and massaged the woman's feet and ankles. His hands glided up her calves and across her thighs. The scent of her sex exuded through the room. Bobby stiffened with excitement, yanked off his pants, and mounted her. He'd suck blood from the underside of her breast as they both orgasmed.

The woman moaned in her sleep. Bobby increased the pace of thrusting. Her vagina throbbed, the verge of her explosion about to coincide with his. One more thrust.

BLOOD BETWEEN LOVERS

In the instant of their explosions, the woman's eyes flashed open, her teeth bared—fangs—and she attacked. He should've paid more attention to his damned instincts, *imminent danger*, but there was no reason for him to suspect a vampire patient in the hospital. Still, to have masked herself as a human so effectively revealed true dominance.

Her legs wrapped around his waist, pinning him inside her, tighter than a virgin. She grasped his shoulders with unfathomable strength, and she sucked blood from his neck.

Bobby struggled. He wanted to scream. Venom—or loathing?—seeped into his system and seared flesh and bone. Pain was unbearable. Escape was impossible. Low on blood and weakened before he entered the hospital, he was no match for this vampire. His thoughts swirled, no longer his, then consciousness faded.

Bobby glanced across the corridor. Hunger welled, but he repressed the urge. His fangs dissolved. An inexplicable tingling arced up his spine and settled in his shoulders. Time, finite immortality, and apprehension swirled together in non-cohesive thoughts, as if there existed a ten-minute gap in his life.

Memory delivered him to St. Mary's, maternity, room 431, where he paused now, outside the door. He shifted his weight from hip to hip.

Moments ago he'd craved blood to the verge of frenzy. Too dangerous to feed in the hospital mid-evening, so what caused his uneasiness? Jake? Bobby frowned. Were his last few minutes truly unaccountable? His skin itched everywhere, especially his neck. His fingers grazed the flesh—unblemished. He needed to leave the hospital. Find Lara. They would feed together on this psych patient. He'd do anything to regain Lara's trust.

He avoided eye contact and escaped the way he entered, through the parking garage. He raced beyond the pavement before his thoughts coalesced, and he jumped to alert, his space invaded. Another vampire followed him from the hospital.

CHAPTER 38

L ara paced the room, antsy to wander under the night sky. And watch the meteorites? Meridian had reveled in that with Nalbandian. Were Meridian's feelings resurfacing? Lara wouldn't allow it. Lara had to remain in control. Her face flushed. She refused Bobby the chance to talk. She meant what she said. Excuses rankled. She didn't feel the need to understand his behavior. She needed to understand how his behavior affected her.

Could she forgive his betrayal?

She'd never forgiven anyone for anything. She wasn't even sure what forgiveness meant.

Worse—what if Bobby didn't want her?

Her betrayal had been equally as devastating. First, it was essential to deal with her anger. Chasing him away had been a good idea. She needed time alone with her thoughts. Didn't all vampires?

Lara headed into the night, wandering, chased by hunger, thirst for blood. Alone, she could satisfy that need. She'd crossed a boundary with Nalbandian from which there was no return. A threshold Bobby had failed to help her break.

Lara strolled along the tow path of the Delaware Canal. Night creatures played an accompanying symphony. She integrated into the moment. Trees swayed in a gentle breeze, bare of leaves, and brackish canal water rippled with an occasional frog or something much less pleasant.

Hunger gnawed. She'd forever prefer sex with her blood, but right now, any warm human blood would suffice. Car tires traversing the metal grid of the Washington Crossing Bridge a half mile away whined. An owl hooted, and night vision found the bird on the bough of a forest tree. She could drink blood without harming a human. She finally grasped what being a vampire meant to Lara West.

Would her understanding exist in a world with or without Bobby?

Wasn't trust the basis of all human relationships?

She didn't trust him, and he didn't trust her. Who would jump first, or had they reached an impasse? Trust wouldn't develop from words. Bobby had fed

BLOOD BETWEEN LOVERS

with Marilyn instead of attending Lara's needs.

If Bobby wants to be with me, he'll have to show it. If he trusts me, he'll have to show it. Our relationship will be defined by his actions.

A flood of images assaulted her mind, dictated by a pattern she'd not recognized before: Dr. Byra's inexplicable decision, a warning about the shoe store, Marilyn insinuating her way into Bobby's psyche, Lara subjugated by the same vampire who subjugated Jason—and she'd been staked. The physical pain expanded beyond any known experience, and the memory retrieved vicarious feelings she didn't want to repeat.

She rubbed her stomach. A final image tied the pattern together, involved or present in each moment: Jake.

* * *

Bobby's fangs erupted. A vampire flashed across his vision so fast his heightened senses could not clarify the image.

Female.

Blond.

He rotated sideways to present a smaller target. She streaked past—her hand swept across his chest. No malice, but he couldn't follow. Again, and she brushed his ear with her tongue.

An impossible image formed in his mind, then materialized into a woman standing inside his personal space. She grazed his trousers, and tension expanded from his groin to his throat. Words, like the vision, skirted reality.

Marilyn Monroe shook her head. "A terrible hoax. I had nothing to do with it. That dreadful man, Agent Plummer, and his friends, they took my blood so you'd think it was really me. But it wasn't. I'm here. I'm . . . alive, so to speak. Touch me."

Her eyes pleaded beyond comprehension. Surrender became Bobby's only option—surrender to the moment. Surrender to her will. He gathered her into his arms, tentative, disbelieving her existence, despite physical evidence.

She melted, muscles relaxed, tension dissolved, and she cried on his shoulder. Small sobs at first, then full-blown tear-jerks.

"Please forgive me, Bobby. It wasn't my fault. He forced me. He's an awful man." She pushed back but gripped Bobby's biceps. "The government has held me hostage since you turned me. They've ensured cooperation through intimidation.

"Decades ago, they threatened to investigate my father. Incarceration. I know what it's like to be locked up. I couldn't allow anyone to suffer that on my behalf. Now, they coerce me with descendants whom I've never met, and Agent Plummer threatens . . ."

She averted her gaze and stepped back farther. "He wants more. He's not done using me. I'm afraid when he is done, he'll destroy me. I can't survive alone yet. I need your help, Bobby. Please. I have to go back now. Find me. Soon."

His mouth gaped open at the speed with which she disappeared. He could never move that fast. What else had Jake done to her? Bobby couldn't follow, and he couldn't contact her. Few options remained. A wave of nostalgia washed in her wake, overtaken by a stronger force. A chill raced up his spine, and the unease from earlier tightened its grip.

Time to find Lara.

No, a long-silent, guttural voice said. *The clock shop. He's waiting.*

"Nalbandian's not destroyed either? Another hoax?"

It's not Nalbandian.

Bobby landed near the clock shop mid-evening.

The door opened. Agent Jake Plummer emerged, coffee cup in hand. Jake acted more empowered with successive meetings and brought less backup to each.

Bobby glanced up the sidewalk in both directions and across the street. The female agent with the military haircut lounged in front of Starbucks.

"I want to thank you on behalf of my friend Jason. Without your assistance, we would've never freed him."

Sincere, straightforward—not what Bobby'd expected, and that set him on edge. All of his uneasiness massed on the small man three concrete steps above him. Distrust, subterfuge, deception contradicted his words.

"Other than the sour taste, what will stop me from ripping out your throat?"

Jake sipped coffee. "You're a violent man. You need to control your temper. People will like you better."

Bobby glowered and leapt to a step below Jake, to stand eye-to-eye.

Jake held up his hand. "Just kidding. No one will like you better." He sipped again. "Let's get right to business. I called you here—"

"You didn't call me."

BLOOD BETWEEN LOVERS

"Of course I did. You just happen to wander here this evening?" Jake brushed by him, descended to the sidewalk, and pivoted, positions reversed. "Ready for the next mission? You'll have another opportunity to work with Ms. Monroe. Sorry about the deception, but we needed you motivated. Worked, didn't it?"

Jake stopped him with a hand gesture and shook his head. "Don't bother to say it. Can't we skip the part where you refuse and I persuade you again? Seems so repetitive."

"You can't coerce me."

"Blackmail 101." Jake shrugged. "My favorite class in government school. First axiom: if the threat of physical danger to a loved one worked once, it'll work again. Threatening two loved ones doubles the incentive for cooperation. But let's focus on one, shall we?"

Jake cocked his head. "How would Dr. West deal with bounty hunters chasing her daily? It's not like fifty years ago. With today's technology, once we've identified a vampire, we're relentless."

Jake broke eye contact. "Please don't feed me that lame line about having played this card before. We're the United States government. We reshuffle the deck, and sometimes you're dealt the same card." He rubbed his nose. "Lara West is in danger, or she will be if you don't cooperate. I'll be in touch soon about your assignment. By the way, Marilyn is going to stay with you."

Jake sauntered toward his SUV. Bobby rushed after him and pinned his chest against the vehicle, his mouth inches from Jake's face. Bobby's fangs erupted.

"I missed the part that stops me from ripping out your throat. Now."

"You are dense, aren't you? The agency knows where I am and what I'm doing. Our head honcho has a policy. How does it go?" Jake tapped his teeth. "Tooth for a tooth? That can't be it. We can't call it *a death for a death* either because you're already dead, but you get the picture? Kill me. Which of your girlfriends do you think will be destroyed in the next two minutes? Even with the speed of a vampire, you can't save both of them."

For the first time in Bobby's memory, Jake's constant smile evaporated with a sneer.

"Now back off before one of my people gets antsy and skewers someone in the stomach again. Did Dr. West mention how we staked her? Did she explain the excruciating pain of a pole piercing her gut?"

Bobby released Jake suddenly but banged Jake's head against the SUV window, then disappeared in the night.

"Ouch." Jake chuckled.

Bobby couldn't outrace the phone if Jake intended harm to prove his point. His thoughts swirled with recent events. Either way, he had to help *her*.

* * *

Eyve peeked over her shoulder. "I like this persona. Bottom heavy, but it has appeal."

Tony shook his head, and his jowls sloshed back and forth. "You look so much like Marilyn Monroe, it's scary."

"When a vampire assumes a persona, we don't just look like the person. We capture their essence."

"Can you teach me how to do that? I don't mean look like someone. I mean, capturing their essence. Could be helpful."

Eyve acknowledged with half a head-tilt.

Tony bounced from foot to foot, like he had to pee. "How'd it go in the hospital?" he asked.

"I pretended to be a psych patient. So easy to fool Mr. Eyre. I weakened him by drinking his blood, then I planted a suggestion he do whatever he deemed necessary to regain Dr. West's trust."

"I thought you'd want them apart?"

"The more she trusts him, the more painful it'll be when Mr. Eyre betrays her again."

"I appreciate your idea of love relationships," Tony said. He held up one finger. Eyve acknowledged with a flick of her chin, and Tony backed into the bathroom.

"I appreciate your gift of understatement." Eyve spoke to the empty room and chuckled.

Tony returned in a moment and cleared his throat. "The feds left mid-morning. I searched Nalbandian's home as you ordered. I don't know why you care what he's reading, but I scanned his books. Astronomy and chess. This is the most dog-eared volume."

Tony handed her *The Ancient Night Sky*. He pointed to a bag. "Some of his clothing."

"Go to St. Mary's," Eyve said.

"You want room numbers of psych patients?"

Eyve turned her nose up. "She's tasted male blood. If Lara West is going to feed, she'll want a man young enough, strong enough to fulfill her need for blood and her desire for . . . a male psych patient maybe, but that's not her either. She'll want someone safe, preferably immobile, with a clear mind."

"Should I meet you here?" Tony asked.

"The shopping center. I'm expecting Mr. Eyre to come looking for Marilyn any time now."

Tony's eyes glistened, and he snorted.

"If you see him, stay away," Eyve said. "If you see us both, we'll need video for Dr. West. If we're both gone, be here before sunrise. He chose Marilyn over Lara before. He'll do it again."

"If he doesn't?"

"That's why you're still gathering information. We have contingency plans. Did you get the acid?"

"Small drums, four. I can maneuver them easily."

CHAPTER 39

L ara returned to the inn, surprised not to find Bobby waiting for her. She paced, human speed, and in a few minutes sensed him approach the door. He wouldn't enter unless invited. Head clear, Lara was ready to talk—and listen. She opened the door and backed up.

Bobby's nostrils flared. "You've fed."

"A disagreeable hiker along the tow path. He thought he could hit on me, a woman, alone in the night, vulnerable."

Bobby's eyebrows arched.

"I didn't harm him. Scared the shit out of him, though, and I drank a gulp more than a standard donation. He won't remember anything when he wakes up tomorrow. Without his clothes."

"You have a mean streak."

"Don't cross me."

"I've missed you, Lara."

She bit off a response. *Let him talk.*

"A month ago in Washington, Jake threatened to expose your existence if I didn't persuade Dr. Byra to continue working. I refused to risk exposing you to bounty hunters and chose what I believed the lesser of two evils— betraying your trust."

Nothing could've been more painful.

Lara pressed her lips together to enforce silence.

"Like the rest of the world, I believed Marilyn Monroe committed suicide in 1962. I had no idea she'd been turned or that the government kept her prisoner. Jake forced her to interfere in our relationship, then directed you toward the shoe store, foreseeing Nalbandian's influence. Jake assumed I'd rescue you, which would coincidentally save his friend Jason—Jake's plan all along."

"You knew what happened and didn't come for me?"

"Marilyn manipulated me more than Jake anticipated, so Jake faked her destruction and set it up to appear as though Nalbandian was responsible. Jake used my feelings—"

BLOOD BETWEEN LOVERS

"Marilyn Monroe wasn't destroyed? She's still dead?"

"The story gets worse."

"You've seen her."

"She asked for aid."

Blood rushed to Lara's face. "You've agreed."

"Jake threatened to compromise your safety if I don't work with Marilyn on another mission."

"And I imagine she's going to stay here with us?" Lara circled away and closed her eyes. "Don't you get it? What she's done to us? What she'll continue to do if—"

"It doesn't matter, Lara."

Her eyes winked open. "I don't believe you. You can't just—"

"I can't ignore Marilyn."

He sounded so earnest. She empathized with his desire to intercede on Marilyn's behalf in terms of a physician helping a criminal patient, like she had saved Robert Helstrom once. She wanted to have faith in him. But Bobby wasn't a doctor, and she didn't trust him any more than he trusted her.

Bobby's decision forced her to reexamine her feelings. Was she in love? Love couldn't exist without mutual trust. What did it matter? He was going to force them apart anyhow.

Any chance to regain each other's trust would materialize before Marilyn arrived.

"You have feelings for Marilyn still."

"I'm not in love with her."

"But you were?"

"Yes."

"Why did you turn me?"

"It was the only way to save your life."

It wasn't the answer she wanted, and it was. She wanted him to say, *Because I love you*, but she didn't want to orchestrate the words. Bobby had been a vampire for so many centuries; did he remain capable of such emotion?

Bobby answered every question she asked with a sincerity difficult to doubt. She wanted to believe him. She wanted to trust him. They talked until sunrise, then slept, nothing settled, nothing decided, except Lara chose to continue along this path. She wanted to regain trust in this man/vampire, and she wanted him to trust her. Lara used his chest as a pillow, unable to snuggle closer.

She woke before him, before sunset, her desire for blood and sex overwhelming and independent of trust. Why wait? He stiffened with her touch but remained asleep. She mounted him, backward, and guided him inside, then growled and ground her teeth, reasserting an act of anger, not love.

* * *

"Agent Plummer will force Mr. Eyre into action tonight. Construction is scheduled to start tomorrow at the ruins. Go there now," Eyve said.

Tony grinned. Eyve cherished revenge. He mounted a ladder on the roof of his vehicle, brought a hard hat, a large funnel, and asbestos gloves. If anyone noticed him, he'd look like part of a construction crew.

He arrived in twilight. The sun dangled above the horizon and glared off the metallic shutters, three stories tall, daring anyone to violate their treasure. Tony whistled while he worked. He leaned the ladder against the farthest shutter, adjusted the angle, glanced up, and adjusted again.

He donned goggles, pulled on the protective gloves, pried the lid off the first drum, and climbed. At the top, he paused to admire the visible edge of the stained glass. Magnificent. He propped the funnel so the spout angled toward the panes.

He decanted half the drum into the funnel, savoring the effect as acid burned into the glass and dribbled down a twenty-foot arc. Tony performed the same ritual on each window.

He backed off the ladder for the last time, and closed his eyes. Sizzling, popping lead melted in the sunlight. A peculiar odor burned his nostrils.

Tony waved to a couple of boys riding by on their bicycles. The bigger boy paled, as if Tony scared the shit out of him. Tony chuckled.

* * *

She rocked back and forth, and the tension escalated. She snorted. How long since she'd made love to Bobby? Seemed a lifetime ago. She laughed out loud because she didn't need him awake for this, but this satisfied flesh only. She craved an emotional orgasm. She wanted Bobby to make love to her, to caress her with words as well as his tongue. She wanted the true pleasure of a partner concerned as much about her feelings as she was about his.

She wanted a man in love with her, willing to show his love, willing to prove his affection genuine. Absent trust, would Bobby ever become that man again?

She quickened her pace, and pleasure raced through her body. She screamed with the release, then screamed louder when he woke up and bucked forward, sending her sprawling on the bed as he rode on top of her. She'd taken her physical pleasure; she had to allow him his. She insisted they talk afterwards, share emotions, thoughts, dreams, though it seemed like they were having independent conversations.

"I want to wake up every night alongside a man I love," Lara said.

"Excavation on the house will begin tomorrow. Working double shifts, it'll still take three months," Bobby said.

"I wanted you to hold me while we slept yesterday."

"The architect will incorporate the stained glass into the new design."

"I've never been this intimate with anyone."

Bobby hopped out of bed and paced around the room. "Of course we're intimate. I sired you. Your success as a vampire is my responsibility."

Lara glanced away. She didn't want to hear that their intimacy was grounded in obligation.

"We can't stay in the same inn for three months. It's not safe for us," Bobby said.

"I want you to be my best friend." *I need to trust you.*

"There's lots of B and Bs in Bucks County. We'll have to move around."

"I want us to share our dreams and our goals." *You need to trust me.*

The darkened room smelled of perspiration and sex. Bobby's eyes glowed, like a feral hunter's. "My home will be built with steel and glass. Our relationship will be built with trust."

Lara squeezed his hands. "We've betrayed each other. That'll take time to heal."

"'There are many events in the womb of time which will be delivered.' *Othello.* Act one, scene three. We have time. It's most important our actions show we trust each other."

Was he reading her mind, feeding her lines he knew she wanted to hear? Lara gazed into his face, trying to discern sincerity. *Read this: I don't want you in my mind.* "Nalbandian released my demon, but Jake guided me onto Nalbandian's path."

Muscles tightened in Bobby's jaw. "Jake released Marilyn and put her in my path."

"Jake sent us to Bucks County. He said Dog threatened to reveal—"

"Who?"

"Dog. Jake's boss. He's dyslexic."

"Jake manipulates everyone."

Lara's cell phone vibrated. "Speaking of manipulators . . ."

Bobby glanced at her.

"He's the only one with this number."

"You should give me the number in case I need to reach you in a hurry."

Lara found the cell in her rumpled clothes, glided her finger across the screen to unlock, but didn't speak.

"Catch you with a mouthful of blood again?" Jake asked. "Sorry. Let me talk with your boyfriend."

Lara tossed the cell to Bobby.

"No matter which you choose, I can harm the other. The clock shop. Now," Jake said.

The cell went dead, and Bobby tossed it on the bed.

"Not much as phone conversationalists, are we?" Lara snickered.

Bobby paced across the room and peeked into the night beyond the curtains.

"I need to feed again," Lara said. "Soon."

"Control the hunger. Don't allow it to dominate you. Jake is threatening you and Marilyn if I don't meet him. Now. In Newtown."

"He'll continue to threaten us both as long as we acquiesce."

"He needs to understand I won't be bullied, but I can't allow him to harm either of you. I'll meet with him once more, convince him I'm done performing, and persuade him to leave us all alone."

"It's Jake. I doubt it, but go ahead and try."

Bobby caressed her cheek.

"What?" Lara asked.

"I need to know that if I meet Jake, you'll be safe."

"I'll be fine."

"The cell was a gift from Agent Plummer? I'm sure a GPS signal is attached to it. He knows where we are."

"I'll toss the phone in the canal. Do you want me to come with you?"

"Not to the meeting. Let's get out of here in case Jake's people are watching. We can feed later tonight. There's one place I know for sure you'll be safe."

BLOOD BETWEEN LOVERS

* * *

"It's disconcerting seeing you as a man," Tony said.

They entered the hospital through the parking garage.

"I'm still a woman," Eyve replied. "This is just one persona, another façade."

"You're sure Dr. West is going to show?"

"After being staked and losing so much blood, she'll feed again soon. I was close enough to Nalbandian to absorb his thoughts. He taught Dr. West to combine blood and sex. She won't feed on female psych patients anymore. She'll want a man."

"There're no longer any male patients in the hospital who meet the qualifications you laid out."

"That's why I've created this persona." She handed him a clipboard. "I convinced an employee to enter this profile into the hospital computer. Dr. West will find me, Timothy Sproul, thirty years old, head injury, long-term coma. Mr. Sproul will function with no chance of waking up."

"What if Bobby Eyre is with her?"

"Not tonight. After they discover the stained glass you just destroyed, Mr. Eyre will be otherwise occupied by Agent Plummer. Did you check the third floor?"

"The room is still empty."

"You have your cell?"

Tony tapped his pants pocket.

"I'll meet you upstairs. Bring my chart. Watch the hall until I'm hooked into the monitors."

Eyve composed herself, setting bodily functions to match her understanding of a young man in a coma. The monitors read correctly. She inserted the catheter, lay back, and pretended sleep. No need to block her thoughts. Dr. West would not search the mind of a comatose patient.

Lara would arrive soon, and torture would follow.

CHAPTER 40

Lara and Bobby arrived at the rubble that used to be their home, eerie in the moonlight. The eight steel shutters standing like pillars protecting seven stained-glass windows struck a pose in the shadows. An unfamiliar stench overwhelmed them. Bobby twirled in a 360-degree sweep of the horizon, then wove his way into the center of the miasma.

"I'm afraid to ask what the odor is," Lara said.

Bobby knew before he inspected the stained glass, blistered and scarred. He snarled. Acid was not the prank of twelve-year-olds.

Tears glistened in Lara's eyes. "I know how much you enjoyed the inherent beauty of those windows. Your home would've been rebuilt around them."

"Someone went to a lot of trouble to destroy a source of such pleasure."

"Even Jake appreciates art," Lara said.

"Who else, then?"

Bobby glided around the ruins, but neither sight nor smell revealed clues. Time pressed. He had to secure Lara in the vault. He toed rubble in a three-foot square.

"What light through yonder window breaks?" he said.

An opening appeared in the ground, revealing familiar stairs.

"The basement is intact?" Lara asked.

Bobby exaggerated a shrug.

"It opened on a verbal command."

"Specific words plus voice recognition."

"You invoked Shakespeare."

"Those words opened doors for Romeo."

"It's fiction."

"It's romance. A tragedy, but romance nonetheless. Both tragedy and words are more fitting now."

He led her down the steps and repeated the command. The door closed, sealing them in darkness before a low glow eased across the room like a sunrise over Verona.

BLOOD BETWEEN LOVERS

"It's amazing this wasn't damaged in the inferno," Lara said.

"The basement is lined with Kevlar and titanium, protected from fire and explosions. A contingency plan in case I needed a place to sleep after a disaster."

"Your vault?"

"It's sealed against intrusion. Even if Jake's people found the basement, you'd be safe inside the vault."

Bobby uttered another command, and a round metal door swung inward. Red laser lines crisscrossed a foot and a half off the floor, blocking the opening.

"Step over," Bobby said. "Keeps the undesirables out."

Lara didn't mention she'd met his rodent friends down here before.

She stepped over the threshold. Indirect lights softened the harsh reality of underground existence. Plush carpet cushioned her feet. Contemporary furniture, a glass desk with a flat-screen computer, a high-backed swivel rocking chair cozied up to the desk, and cantilevered shelves lined the walls with hundreds of manuscripts. A Van Gogh she'd seen once before hung amidst the volumes. The Rembrandt tapestry that used to hang in their DC brownstone draped across the wall to the left of the massive stone fireplace. Had Bobby shipped other treasures?

"Entertain yourself. I'll be back as soon as possible."

"Before dawn?"

"Long before."

Lara rushed into his arms but stopped herself from further embrace. "Jake is dangerous, but he wasn't responsible for your windows. I'm sure of it."

Bobby's lips covered hers. He sucked her tongue into his mouth, and she withdrew it before he pierced the flesh, but it didn't inhibit her from sealing the vampire's kiss and drinking a glimmer of his blood. Bobby hugged her tighter, but she still refused to share her essence, identity recaptured.

"I want you to stay here until I return," Bobby said.

"What if there's no time to feed later?" Lara asked.

"You can feed from me tonight. I'll be fine."

"I'm becoming more sensitive to it—frenzy isn't far away. What if you're not back soon enough?"

"Promise you're not going to follow me out of the vault."

"Promise me you won't harm Jake."

Mutual assurances sounded hollow.

Bobby grabbed her hands. "If we're ever separated, I swear, Lara, I'll come find you, no matter what, Jake be damned."

* * *

Bobby sealed the vault, then the basement door. He kicked rubble over the frame, leaving no evidence of the hidden room beneath. Bobby didn't want her sneaking to the hospital without him, so he didn't mention the tunnel. She didn't understand the imminent danger to herself Jake and his people represented. No time to argue with her now, either.

Lara would only be trapped in the vault for a few minutes, not hours. Jake wouldn't delay him.

He landed a block away from the Newtown clock shop.

Caution.

Jake had arranged surprises before, but Bobby sensed no other agents in the vicinity. Jake felt empowered and lounged on the steps.

"What fascinates me about the clock shop is not the clocks." Jake spoke without pivoting, as though he boasted a sixth sense detecting Bobby's approach. "It's the concept of a store peddling time."

Bobby paused in front of the display window.

Jake twisted around. "Time is an idea, not a physical construct. It's not something that needs to be purchased." He regarded Bobby's wrist. "I'm sure you don't own a watch."

"Do you need the time, Agent Plummer? Seventeen of the twenty-four clocks in this presentation are reasonably accurate."

"It's amazing we can discuss such an abstract concept with such simple terms as hour of the day. We don't even use twenty-four hours; we use twelve and repeat. Simplicity. Odd then, isn't it, another simple concept in itself, such as immortality, becomes so intricately woven into the concept of time, and therefore, difficult to comprehend."

"Immortality is as straightforward as time," Bobby said.

Jake shook his head. "Time is infinite. If it's not, any meaningful discussion of time falls apart. However, we can have a meaningful discussion of finite immortality. Yours, for instance. Time is not dependent on the hands of a clock or the rotation of the planet or the orbit of the moon. Time is an independent universal truth. Your immortality, however, is dependent on several things. You have to drink blood."

Jake pulled a crimson packet from his jacket pocket and tossed it to

Bobby. "You didn't appreciate my offer of coffee last time. I assure you, this is untainted."

Bobby unfastened the seal, raised the container, and sniffed. "Another volunteer?" he asked.

"Hell, yes. That's the only blood you're entitled to, that of volunteers, but not your only dependency. You see, Mr. Eyre, we can smash all the clocks, blow up the moon, and our sun can go nova, but time will continue.

"On the other hand, your immortality is finite—it ceases to exist if we cut off your blood supply, or shoot you with a magic bullet, or sever your head."

"Which are you planning for me?"

* * *

Lara paced the vault. Concentration proved difficult. She'd have to sit still to use the computer. She couldn't. Her skin crawled. A wave of hunger overwhelmed her, propelled by the blood kiss. The tang incited thirst, and Meridian urged her to find blood.

Lara fought the outburst, but cramps twisted her stomach, she retched, and her brain fired every pain receptor in her body, screaming for blood—the onset of frenzy. She needed to feed. Now.

One wine bottle of cold blood stored in the vault refrigerator did nothing to slake thirst or dampen frenzy. What if Jake's people delayed Bobby for hours, or all night? Lara couldn't wait that long. St. Mary's was close by. She could feed and return to wait for Bobby. If he returned before her, he promised he'd come find her.

And she'd promised not to leave the vault.

No, I didn't. I promised not to follow him out of the basement.

She was breaking the spirit of her promise, but at least not the letter.

Lara's memory surged forward. The Rembrandt tapestry hid another exit that opened onto a foul-smelling tunnel she'd discovered on her last visit to Langhorne. She never asked Bobby where it led in either direction, but what would be the point of accessing a tunnel to nowhere? He probably didn't realize she knew about the tunnel.

She removed the tapestry. This mechanism also operated on voice command. "What light through yonder window breaks?"

The words bounced back, lacking voice recognition. The lock was keyed to Bobby's vocal chords. She was trapped in the vault. Bobby had implied she could escape, though, if she needed to feed. Her voice should be recognized, too. She punched the door.

"It's not optional," she said. "I need blood."

Maybe Bobby changed the command for the tunnel. Another Shakespeare quote? One that would make sense, at least to Bobby. The next line?

"It is the east, and Juliet is the sun."

No opening, but she grasped it now, Bobby's vampirical sense of irony.

"Arise, fair sun, and kill the envious moon."

The mechanism clicked and tumbled. The handle spun, and she jumped back. The door swung open, revealing a dark tunnel.

"Ahh." Cramps tightened.

Blood, urged Meridian.

"Which way?" She hoped to exit the sewer somewhere close to the hospital.

Lara sniffed and winced. Equally foul in both directions. She paused. Something else Nalbandian had taught her while searching the night sky: vampire senses could determine direction without points of reference.

Could she do that? She closed her eyes and imagined standing in the ruins in front of the hidden door. St. Mary's was to her left. In her mind's eye, she descended the steps, curved into the basement, entered the vault, and pictured the wall with the tapestry. She'd spun around. St. Mary's wasn't just to her right—the sewer pointed directly toward the hospital.

The sewer was Bobby's private pipeline to blood.

* * *

Jake leaned back on his elbows. "Mr. Eyre, seriously, it's not you we're threatening."

* * *

Lara carried her shoes, just in case. Nalbandian had taught her to fly. She didn't have much practice, though, and didn't want to end up shin-deep in muck. She didn't want to peer at it either, as vampire senses would illuminate every detail.

Several hundred yards, she estimated, same as crossing the farmer's field to the hospital parking garage. Lara arrived at a skinny door. The hospital. No handle, no hinges, no visible lock. Voice controlled. The next line?

"Who is already sick and pale with grief?"

BLOOD BETWEEN LOVERS

Nope. Couldn't be that simple. Not with Bobby.

"Strange" best described his sense of humor. What would Bobby say when he arrived at a hospital to drink blood from a sleeping patient?

"It is my lady, oh, it is my love."

The door slid open. Pipes, clanging machinery, the subbasement, boiler room, *Maintenance only*. Lara stepped onto the cement slab, and the door sealed behind her on command, camouflaged with safety posters.

She climbed a staircase, emerged in the morgue, and realized then she still carried her shoes and an awful stench. She'd rolled her pants, but they'd been splashed. She stripped them off and stretched one leg at a time into the morgue sink and cleaned mystery gunk off her flesh. She scrubbed her skin with Dr. Raymond's stainless-steel brush and rinsed again, eager to dissolve the slimy feeling. She soaked her trousers and left them to dry.

She couldn't roam the halls in a shirt and underwear. Dr. Raymond's lab coat dangled on a hook. That would do. The lab coat draped to her knees. Anyone would assume she wore a skirt underneath.

Hunger renewed its call. Lara wanted blood. And sex. Despite their relationship, Bobby still used Vampirical Harmony. They'd agreed that each could use it with a human partner—but only to feed. She could use VH too; she just needed a willing male patient or, easier to manipulate, an immobile male patient, someone whose condition could afford a pint a blood, and who was still physically capable of sex.

After midnight, the administrative office was shut down but unlocked, the computers sleeping—no warm chairs. Security was lax. She woke Marty's computer, typed his password, *ILOVESUE*, and waited while the requested files booted.

A quick search yielded what she needed: thirty-year-old male admitted three weeks ago with head injuries, comatose, but the trend line progressed optimistically. All other functions normal. If he rested in a light enough coma, sexual stimulation might be possible. Lara chuckled. She was about to conduct the first-ever study to test the coma-sex theory. She noted the room number, signed off, and headed for a sleeping Timothy Sproul.

* * *

Jake shrugged his shoulders. "It's the way the world works, Mr. Eyre."

"I'm not performing for you anymore."

"What do you think you're doing here now?"

"Let's call it a courtesy. You pose no threat to control my behavior. That's what this is about, isn't it, threats? You threaten me, I threaten you?"

Jake's grin broadened. "I'm the government. You threaten me with what? Not paying your taxes?"

"I'll mirror your threat. Ultimately, you're threatening the existence of Lara and Marilyn."

"You're threatening my life?" Jake shook his head. "Sorry. I don't believe you. You forget. I've seen you destroy another vampire, but as despicable as my actions may be at times, you've had the opportunity to kill me, and the most you've been able to do is squeeze my throat. You're a nice guy. You'd have to be, or Dr. West wouldn't've fallen in love with you. Threatening me carries no weight."

"Lara and I are ready to run."

"You've decided to sacrifice Marilyn?"

"You forget. I've seen you destroy another vampire, but you faked destroying Marilyn. You're not a nice guy, but threatening Marilyn again carries no weight."

Jake's cell phone vibrated. Once. He didn't bother to look at it. He smiled, like a hungry boy clutching a cookie jar. "You can't protect Dr. West, either."

"You can't touch her."

"In your basement? Please. If we needed to . . . but as it turns out, we don't, since she isn't in your basement. She's at St. Mary's even as we speak."

* * *

Long-term comatose patients with a positive trend line didn't require constant, in-person monitoring. The room was remote. Timothy subsisted on intravenous nutrition, his body rotated at the beginning and middle of each shift, so no one would disturb them for hours. Lara's senses heightened. In the bowels of the hospital, the aroma of blood swirled, pushing hunger to the edge. She imagined lying in Bobby's arms, and her desire to make love expanded into all aspects of being. Lara wanted to feed, to taste the sanguine fluid as it exploded into her mouth at the same instant her orgasm exploded in her mind. And her victim deserved something in exchange for a blood donation.

She rushed along the deserted hall, careful no one watched as she entered

BLOOD BETWEEN LOVERS

Timothy's room and closed the door behind her. Monitors over the headboard generated the only light. Timothy inhaled the slow, easy breath expected of a comatose patient.

Blood pressure was elevated, but heart rate synched with his condition. Responsiveness to painful stimulus would indicate the state of his coma. Lara squeezed his finger, and Timothy withdrew, consistent with positive trending. Sexual stimulus seemed possible.

Lara peeled back the sheet, pushed up the hospital gown, and removed the catheter. She could straddle him and bite beside his nipple the moment her orgasm hit. She stuffed her underwear in the lab coat pocket. No need to remove the lab coat.

She stroked him, and he stiffened. Lara smirked. If she fed from enough comatose patients, maybe she could publish an article. Ha.

She climbed onto the bed and swung a leg across, never releasing her grip. Timothy's hard flesh pulsed against her palm. This was what Bobby did, wasn't it? He made love to sleeping victims. They got off, he got off, and he gulped a mouthful of blood. Same thing she planned. She hiked up the lab coat and inched forward. Her juices flowed with the excitement of pre-penetration. Hunger ravaged her stomach.

Why, then, did she hesitate?

She understood what it meant to be hungry, overwhelmed by frenzy. She appreciated what it meant to be horny, but this went beyond. Lara wanted to make love with the man she loved, not have sex with a stranger. She needed to feed, and feeding would taste sweeter coupled with an orgasmic explosion, but she could hold her orgasm for a few more hours, couldn't she?

* * *

In a predictable situation, Eyve anticipated all of Lara's movements. Lara shed the covers, and Eyve probed her mind, careful not to disturb Lara's consciousness. An unexpected attack now would be successful, but not satisfying. Eyve wanted Lara to experience pain. She wanted to torture her, over and over again. Delving into the girl's mind gained information. Eyve could create a scenario much more delectable, something to torment Dr. West.

Dr. West's hands were warm—a vampire unwilling—or unable—to suppress human aspects. Eyve had assumed male personas before. She'd experienced sex from the male perspective, so different from a woman's expectations. Easy, really. Relax, and the male orgasm would wash over her without contemplation.

Surprised Lara stopped, Eyve fought to maintain comatose composure, already so close to an explosion. She extended further, empathizing, and respecting Lara's hesitation. Guilt.

Perfect. The rest of the night would go even better.

She wheeled through Lara's thoughts, picking up snatches of information about Bobby Eyre, their relationship—Vampirical Harmony?

Ah, an interesting idea.

In a corner of Lara's mind, she found the terror she hoped for: Lara's beast.

Lara's hand movements accelerated, bringing Timothy close again, and Eyve recognized Lara was about to feed. Vampire blood exhibited a distinct taste. She had to mask hers, careful not to awaken Lara's suspicions.

Remain rooted. The build-up of a climax. The ripping explosion. Fangs sinking deep in her ribs, just above her hip. Blood drained, little more than a mouthful, and Lara backed away, reinserted the catheter, pulled up the sheets, and disappeared into the bowls of the hospital. Eyve laughed.

* * *

Bobby rushed into the night. He'd never mentioned the tunnel. He'd changed the voice command so it was different than the one for the basement steps or the vault entrance. Even so, why would she leave the safety of the vault or break her promise? Either Jake's people had discovered the basement or frenzy had overwhelmed Lara. She said she sensed the imminent approach of frenzy. Bobby lacked experience. He'd only ever turned two people, and one was a mistake.

What if Jake had lied again and Lara stayed in the vault? What would Jake gain if Bobby searched the hospital?

Time. For what? To break into the vault? Seize Lara?

If Bobby chose wrong, Lara's safety would be compromised. She'd promised not to leave the basement. Jake was the liar. Bobby headed toward the vault.

CHAPTER 41

Lara rushed to the end of the corridor and waited in a shadow for the elevator door to open. Certain the elevator was empty, she slipped on board and used the call-override button to deliver her to the basement without further risk of being seen.

Voices from the morgue's inner sanctum froze her outside the swinging doors. Dr. Raymond and two men. She didn't know any way to reach the boiler room except through the morgue. She listened to the grisly sound of an autopsy. They'd just begun—could take two hours, especially if Dr. Raymond found something interesting. Lara might be able to modify Dr. Raymond's memory, but she had no idea how to modify the memories of three people at the same time. Maybe she could rush past without them noticing? Maybe not.

Lara couldn't wait or risk being seen. What if Bobby returned before her? If she couldn't travel through the tunnel, she couldn't reenter the vault. She'd have to hide nearby. Not what Bobby wanted, but she had no choice. In a field, the woods, she'd be safe for an hour or two.

She exited the hospital through the parking garage. Wispy clouds scudded across the night sky. An owl, a dog, a freight train rumbling in the distance, cicadas, and crickets, her senses heightened with the feeding. Grass crumpled beneath her feet, then sprang back into shape as she treaded along. A bat flitted between trees and alighted upside down on a branch.

Cramps subsided to a dull throb, her hunger satisfied for the moment. Her skin twitched, and she licked her lips. Blood held a unique taste, indescribable in human terms. It invigorated her and charged every nerve ending. She hurried without rushing, but tingling morphed into itching. Everywhere. The sun tattoo flared on the small of her back, and a voice in her head warned of danger.

She was being followed.

* * *

Eyve followed Lara through the hospital. She anticipated the elevator rush to the basement. Easy to arrange Dr. Raymond's unexpected appearance—Eyve dismembered a body and ordered Tony to call the morgue doctor, pretending to be from administration, an unusual emergency to be examined as soon as possible, with witnesses. Predictably, Dr. Raymond dropped whatever she was doing and hurried to work. Nine minutes. That's how long Tony reported it would take her, including time to park and reach the basement, effectively blocking Lara's retreat.

Eyve tracked Lara across the field, masking their scents. The torture of Dr. West would continue full-throttle.

* * *

Bobby arrived at the ruins. Didn't matter if Jake's people were watching.

"What light through yonder window breaks?"

The basement door slid open, then closed behind him on command. Lights on, the vault was sealed as he'd left it, but the tapestry lay draped across the desk.

Jake told the truth.

Bobby had guessed wrong. He bolted through the tunnel. A faint trace of lavender overrode the stench. He climbed the stairs to the morgue. Voices stopped Bobby—Dr. Raymond and two men.

Lara must've scurried through here before they began the autopsy. No time to waste, he'd have to risk exposure. Speed and shadows, Dr. Raymond and friends were so preoccupied, they could note the swinging doors and only guess they'd had a visitor.

Bobby sniffed Lara's scent, fresh on the elevator. What floor? He didn't know. Her expanded tastes suggested she wouldn't seek a female patient. He needed to search floor by floor, hoping to stay out of sight and pick up her trail.

The first floor, admittance and emergency, would have the most late-night activity. Hopefully she'd avoid that. He rushed through the second-floor corridors, tracing a huge square, returning to the elevator. Search renewed on the third floor. At the end of the far corridor, he reacquired her scent, unmasked in the stillness.

Room 353. Empty. Monitors switched on, but leads disconnected, not the way a nurse would leave the room, unless the patient was rushed to emergency surgery. Bobby sniffed spilled blood. What had Lara done? If her aggression had injured a patient, she would have rushed toward the vault, only to discover Dr. Raymond and friends blocking her retreat. She'd feel forced to escape outside, in the open.

Bobby tracked her through the garage. He trailed only moments behind her. He crossed the blacktop to the field, but Lara's scent dissipated, masked somehow in the autumn breeze. He assumed her path now and headed for the rubble that had been their haven.

* * *

Tracked? Jake's people? How would they have found her at the hospital? No one could've seen her arrive or leave.

She rushed toward the ruins and sensed footsteps racing behind her. Another vampire.

She sprinted, but the vampire gained. A lump rose in her throat. Adrenaline hyped her system.

Don't panic.

Bobby had met Jake in Newtown, just beyond the shopping center. She headed in that direction, past the ashes and the bizarre steel shutters posing like pillars holding the sky.

The vampire chased her, near her townhouse, behind the shopping center; he drew up with a sudden burst of speed.

"Lara, wait," the vampire commanded.

Lara stopped, compelled by the familiar voice. "Bobby, it's you." Lara sighed. "I was scared."

Bobby rushed into her arms. "So was I. Jake said you'd gone to the hospital. I caught your scent leaving just as I arrived."

Lara snuggled against his chest. "I didn't intend to leave the basement, but the frenzy overwhelmed me again. I was afraid if I stayed there alone, without blood, I wouldn't be able to control myself if you were delayed." She hugged tighter. "How did Jake know I left?"

"Maybe a signal." Bobby shrugged and sniffed. "You've fed."

"Kind of."

"How do you 'kind of' drink blood?"

Lara leaned back in his embrace. "I drank, but I wasn't satisfied." Her hands slipped across his trousers, toying with the tension that rippled through his muscles. "I want you, Bobby. I want to make love and drink your blood." A cry pulled from her throat surprised her as much as it did him.

"I want to take you now," Bobby said.

"You said we shouldn't go back to the inn."

"I can't wait."

"The vault?"

"Jake's people will be watching."

Lara giggled. "My townhouse. It's around the corner."

Bobby grinned like a kid invited to a day at Disney. No one in sight, they raced hand-in-hand up to Lara's porch. She propped the storm door open with her hip and inserted the key, and Bobby chased her inside. He glided the dead bolt behind them. Stars hugged Bobby's shoulders through the foyer skylight, every detail of flesh and clothing discernable with vampire vision, clearer than she'd grown used to, enhanced with fresh blood. Her medical bag rested on the kitchen table. How'd it get here?

Lara sidled into Bobby's arms. "You rescued my bag."

He stroked her cheek and rubbed behind her ear. "Why would your bag need rescuing?"

He must be teasing me. She didn't want to worry about it now. Their lips met, and he sucked her tongue into his mouth. She knew what he wanted, and she still refused her blood, but she could take his, but like her, he pulled back before she could puncture flesh. Was he refusing to share his blood? He unbuttoned the lab coat and slipped it off her shoulders, along with her blouse.

"What happened to your trousers?"

"New fashion at the hospital." Lara twirled in her underwear. "Like it?"

Bobby knelt. His hands traced from her ankles to her hips. He nuzzled the flesh above her knee, enflaming desire. "You know how I like to tease you."

Lara moaned and swayed and steadied herself against the counter. Bobby's tongue followed the line of his hands, across her belly, lingered on her breast, as he unfastened her bra and slipped it off her shoulders. He scooped her into his arms, and she encircled his neck.

Lara blazed with anticipation of her lover, unsure if his feet touched the steps or if they floated up the stairs. He laid her on the bed, hooked her underwear and peeled it off her legs, then backed away, admiring. He pulled his shirt over his head and skinnied out of his pants. His naked body gleamed in the pale light.

Lara stretched out a leg and pressed her foot against his thigh. He fondled the foot and raised it to his mouth. His tongue trailed her instep. She tried to escape. He twisted around, his back to her, but held her foot securely.

"What're you doing?" Her voice trilled in a laugh.

"This." Bobby tried to sink his fangs into her arch and suck, but Lara jerked hard and her foot escaped. Sex—making love—didn't and never would involve sharing her blood, her essence. Bobby had to understand that by now.

He continued to caress, and an orgasmic wave rose quickly. She pushed up on an elbow and plunged between Bobby's legs. His fangs retracted, and he stepped out of her grasp.

"We can't have that," he said. "Not yet."

"We can't?"

"I'm going to take you first."

"What did you have in mind?"

Bobby's grin expanded, somewhere between sensuous and mischievous.

He whirled and opened the closet door.

"What're you looking for?"

He rummaged and emerged with a pair of panty hose.

"Dressing in a new fashion?" Lara asked.

Bobby approached the bed. "Roll over."

Lara's first instinct was to resist, but curiosity won. She could resist in the next moment.

Bobby straddled her, sitting on her ass. He kneaded her spine. Tension dissolved, and she moaned. He massaged her arms, to her fingertips. Her muscles relaxed.

Bobby pinched her wrists, twisted her arms behind her back, and tied her with the panty hose. Tight. He rose up and flipped her over, her arms pinned against the mattress.

"Hey."

Bobby kissed her mouth, smothering further complaints. "I want to take you without interference. You'll have to lie there and accept whatever it is I'm doing to you."

No, she didn't. She possessed vampire strength. Lara wiggled, but the nylon held. Wrapped multiple times around her wrists, it was surprisingly strong. She could break free. Eventually.

Bobby's lips caressed hers. He slid lower. His breath cooled, and his tongue burned. Excitement expanded. His excitement pressed against her thigh, then a rush of sensations. He cupped her breast, his other hand glided over her belly and settled between her legs. He sucked her nipples, then his fangs traced a line across her skin, on the verge of piercing.

His eyes morphed feral red, the blood hunter. She knew what he wanted.

"No, Bobby. I said no. I'm not sharing my blood. We can do anything else you want, but not that." Cramps tightened in her stomach again. Frenzy. She'd have to feed. She could drink Bobby's blood. He'd promised her—soon. Pain now coupled with sexual tension.

She absorbed this pain. He wanted to take her by force. Wrestling excited him, and she wanted to please her lover, but how would she wrestle unless he untied her, or she broke free? He sucked on her breast without piercing skin, he pinched her other nipple to the edge of discomfort, and increased the pressure between her legs. A scream rose in her throat, and he suddenly backed off.

"Bastard." She gasped. "Take me over the edge."

Bobby grinned and slid lower. "I'm going to take you someplace you've never been before."

"Stage Three?" Lara guessed.

Bobby had continued to refuse her knowledge beyond Stage Two of VH, for her protection, he'd said. Protection from what?

"Stage Three?" Bobby chuckled. He hopped off and reentered the closet.

"What're you looking for now?" Lara asked.

He emerged, dangling another pair of panty hose.

"Oh, no."

Lara squirmed, but Bobby had already wrapped the nylon leg around her ankle. He tied the other end to the bed frame, pinning her leg to the bed, knee crooked over the edge of the mattress. She kicked with her free leg and pushed against his torso.

"That'll never do," he said.

He rushed to the closet and back, cradling two more pairs of panty hose.

Jake had arranged her Bucks County wardrobe when he'd assigned her here months ago. What had Jake thought she'd need all that for anyway? She didn't dress up, and he couldn't have anticipated Bobby's pleasure.

Bobby secured her other leg, leaving her spread-eagled, then hopped behind her and lifted her shoulders. At least he would untie her hands so she could grab him. She'd slip out of the ankle bonds then, too. The nylon loosened, but her arms were jerked up until her wrists touched her shoulder blades, and the nylon retightened. Panty hose wrapped multiple times around her wrists, tighter than before.

He stretched the nylon taut and tied it to the bed frame behind her, forcing her arms higher behind her back.

"Ouch."

"Don't worry," Bobby said. "I want you to survive."

Survive? What did that mean? She was pinned, vulnerable to whatever Bobby devised. He wanted her blood, but he wouldn't violate her trust like that.

Bobby towered over her. "Time to bring you close again."

Merciless sexual torture. "You have to let me come." She played his game—Roberre's game.

Bobby stiffened with her words and advanced. "I don't think so."

Penetration proved exquisite. Even tied, she arched her hips to suck him in farther. He accommodated, cupped her breasts, and increased the speed and power of his thrusts, way beyond human.

Tension enveloped her. She stifled her moans and tried to mask the approaching orgasm, but Bobby studied her face and pulled out before she could climax.

"You can't leave me unsatisfied." She moaned and wriggled in a sensuous twining, enticing him to continue.

Playing turned him on. He'd release her soon.

"I don't think there's anything you can do to stop me, Lara."

Twice more he brought her to an increasingly frustrating edge. He stroked her cheek. Cramps engaged every muscle.

"Please," she whispered. "I want to come with you. I need blood. Now."

Bobby leaned back and nodded. "Time for you to drink."

Lara sighed. At last. They always exploded together. They would orgasm, and she would have sex and blood.

Bobby knelt beside her. His hands drifted up and down, still teasing, but fulfillment would finally be hers. Chin up, head back, she closed her eyes. He gripped her leg, in position. Time, she realized, to share her true feelings.

"I love you so much," she said.

She sensed him shudder. His weight shifted. He barked, deep and guttural, then mumbled, the words slurred, unintelligible.

"What?" she asked.

Her eyes popped open. His dulcet voice struck a chord of recognition.

"I love you too, Mer—"

She screamed.

CHAPTER 42

N albandian grinned, his head between Lara's legs. He'd deceived her, pretending to be Bobby. She'd allowed him to bind her in this vulnerable position. How had he survived? She'd identified the body, and Jake had reported him destroyed.

"How easy it is to fool your authorities," Nalbandian said.

Didn't matter how. She needed to resist him. Bobby would search for her when he realized she was no longer in the vault. He could follow her scent. Surely, he was already tracking her. She had to resist until Bobby found her. She steeled her mind.

I need to protect myself from someone like you.

Nalbandian would command her demon. Lara had to keep the demon submerged.

"You're quite beautiful." Nalbandian patted her legs. "It's time to drain your blood." He leered, and his fangs ripped high on her femoral artery, her essence hijacked.

She arched in pain until his fingers penetrated her lips, teasing, making her reaction unavoidable. But as he had in the persona of Bobby, Nalbandian stopped before her orgasm materialized. He hissed and sucked the blood from her, extinguishing her will to resist the beast. Blood had gushed from her foot, her breast, and now her leg. Cramps renewed. She understood why he'd refused to share the sanguine kiss. She couldn't see through his persona, but she would've recognized the taste.

"Please don't release my demon," Lara said.

The words wouldn't affect Nalbandian, but maybe the idea would. Nalbandian exhibited pleasure in pain and sex. If she played along, she might hold out until Bobby saved her.

"Surprisingly easy to trick you, too," Nalbandian said. "You surrendered so easily into my arms." He laughed.

"I don't want to become a beast," Lara said.

"The choice is not yours."

Cramps tightened another notch.

BLOOD BETWEEN LOVERS

"There are many places more painful than your thigh to bite. Your foot, as you've already experienced. The blood doesn't flow as freely, but the trade-off is worth it. I want your beast. I want Meridian."

"No."

Nalbandian hissed, and his fangs pierced the arch of her other foot, and he sucked. Lara howled with the viciousness of the attack. She needed blood. Blood and sex. Sex and blood. Not with Nalbandian. She couldn't. She wouldn't last much longer without nourishment. He drew blood at a horrendous pace, then released her abruptly, leaving her beast in abeyance.

What did he really want? She couldn't outlast the pain. Why stop short of forcing her surrender?

He clawed her ribs and assaulted her breast again. Stinging rifled through every nerve. Her arms ached from the awkward position. Her throat tightened. Goose bumps rippled over her flesh, and Nalbandian postponed any chance to reunite with Bobby.

* * *

Bobby searched the ruins. No trace of Lara, or that she'd passed this way. She wouldn't be silly enough to return to the inn. Bobby sniffed. Instincts told him to head into Newtown. The clock shop.

Despite his instincts, Bobby's eyes widened when he discovered Jake still there.

"Can I interest you in a watch?" Jake asked.

Bobby rushed at him, pinning him against the display window, stretched up on his toes.

"What's going on?" Bobby roared.

"Sorry, the clock shop is closed."

Bobby pinched his neck, and Jake gurgled.

"I guess you mean in the vampire community? I assure you, I don't know."

Bobby tightened his grip and raised Jake off the cement. "Where's Lara? I assure you, I am capable of the violence you're so certain you're safe from."

"Maybe you are, but how would I know where Dr. West is?"

"What kind of game are you playing?"

"I'm being straightforward."

Vampire senses agreed. Jake had fooled him before, though, and could be doing it again.

"How'd you know she headed for St. Mary's?"

"I didn't know that. Why don't you look for her there?"

Bobby rumbled and tossed Jake on the sidewalk. Jake scowled, gathered himself into a sitting position, dusted his pants, and hugged his knees.

"What can I do for you, Mr. Eyre?"

"Half an hour ago, you told me Lara was headed for the hospital."

"You must have me confused with your travel agent. Or a fortune-teller. How would I know where Dr. West was headed?"

Jake seemed dumbfounded by this conversation.

"You received a phone call," Bobby said.

"Not in the last half hour. I'll show you." Jake pulled the cell from his pocket, flipped it open, and pushed buttons. He cocked his head, studying the screen in disbelief. "Seems I did receive a call." He pushed another button and waited. "I need a trace. 215-555-2421." He listened for a moment, closed his phone, and slipped it into his pocket.

"Burner cell, purchased with cash. I would know if someone called me, though. In any case, I haven't spoken with you in the last half hour either, so how would you know I'd received that call?"

"Doesn't make sense," Bobby said.

"The American political system? Our tax structure? Jason's first novel?"

"You're acting as if you're under a compulsion to forget, but you're not susceptible to vampire mind control. You threatened Lara and Marilyn if I didn't meet you here half an hour ago."

"How could I threaten Marilyn? She was destroyed."

"I met Marilyn outside the hospital just before I met you earlier tonight."

"Maybe you're the one under a compulsion. Not one of my proudest moments, but I know Marilyn was destroyed. I did it. Four days ago. We staked her head on top of the shopping center so you'd think Nalbandian destroyed her. We needed you motivated to save Dr. West and my friend, the romance writer."

"I'm telling you, I met Marilyn tonight."

Jake shrugged. "I know you can regenerate a wound, but I've never heard of a vampire regrowing a head. Besides, as you noted, I'm not susceptible to mind control. Why would I want to meet with you again?"

"Another mission."

"Not yet, anyhow."

"The most likely explanation for lack of memory would be you are susceptible to mind control, at least from a vampire more powerful than me."

"You're suggesting someone's pulling my strings."

"How's it feel to be manipulated? Not many choices. Marilyn's not a powerful enough vampire."

"Not to mention she doesn't exist anymore."

"That leaves Nalbandian."

"Already crossed off our list."

"Your list needs updating."

"We shipped Nalbandian's body to DC on ice."

Bobby arched an eyebrow.

Jake flipped open the cell and scrolled through his contact list. "Owen, I need confirmation on Nalbandian's remains."

"We did the research. He's been incinerated as per Dog's orders," Owen said.

"Pull up the report."

"File's loading."

"Read the description."

"Male, vampire, age unknown. Appearance: late thirties. Fangs: removed. Eyes: irises and pupils blended. Blood: fifteen quarts, typical vampire range. Incinerated two days ago."

Jake faced Bobby, palms open. "That closes the book on Nalbandian."

"How tall was he?" Bobby asked.

Jake shrugged. "Height?" he said into the cell.

"Five feet eleven inches," Owen said.

Jake opened his mouth, but Bobby cut him off. "I heard. Nalbandian was at least six three. We can't regrow heads, and we can't shrink our frames after we're destroyed."

"Damn." Jake scrutinized Bobby. "Dr. West identified him. We had Nalbandian. Bodies must've been switched. He remained under guard from the time we shot him." Jake spoke into the cell again. "Have the driver and shotgun scanned for memory alteration. Call me with results." He stuffed the cell back into his pocket.

Bobby paced the sidewalk. "While I met with you, Lara must've gone to St. Mary's to feed. She disappeared from the hospital, and I couldn't track her."

"Losing your abilities?"

"The scent was masked. The phone call you received had to be a subliminal signal. We're both being manipulated. If Nalbandian wasn't destroyed, he'd want Lara again. He'll release her beast." *In her frenzy-weakened state, she'll be easy to subjugate.*

"What can I do to help? I don't want to lose Dr. West. She's too valuable of an asset."

"Has Nalbandian's home been rendered unusable to vampires?"

"The sleeping cell."

"You only located one sleeping cell?"

"If there was more than one, we would've found it. My people are thorough."

"As thorough as you are transporting bodies?"

"Nalbandian may be at his house again with Dr. West?"

"You didn't expect him to be anywhere, but if you did, that would be the last place you'd look."

Jake opened the SUV door. "Can I give you a lift?"

Bobby frowned. "Catch up with me." He disappeared into the dark.

CHAPTER 43

"Lara West will be submerged so far this time, she'll never resurface. You'll forever be Meridian." Nalbandian slavered blood, twisted Lara's head, and held her cheek pinned against the mattress, neck exposed. His breath, cold against her flesh, ignited sensations fueled by memory.

Nalbandian had given rein to her beast and taught the beast to feed, unconcerned about the death of a victim. Lara refused to surrender to that life, the life of true darkness. She fought to maintain sanity. Bobby would save her. He had to.

No one arrived. No one rushed up the stairs to her rescue. Nalbandian touched her in the most intimate places. He held no right. Lara held no options. He drew out the minutes of agony into what? Hours? Lara lost track of time.

Nalbandian clawed and consumed her. He pinched, she screamed, and his fangs ripped her flesh, sucking out what little blood remained. His fingers glossed over her throat, but he inched his fangs into her carotid artery. She shuddered in pain. He withdrew his fangs, and the torture continued, surrender foisted upon her. Why hadn't Bobby come to rescue her?

"Is your lover as much a coward as you?" Nalbandian asked. "With Meridian's knowledge of his secrets, we can release his beast too, forever submerging the vampire you've known. You won't miss him, will you?"

Lara squeezed her eyes shut and struggled to remain conscious, her physical pain amplified by emotional threats. How could she protect Bobby? She couldn't protect herself. She was as helpless now as she'd been when he'd enticed her with blood on his fingertip.

Nalbandian must've read her mind. He punctured his finger and dangled it under her nose. The sweet scent, reminiscent of the blood she'd taken in the hospital, invigorated her and weakened her simultaneously. If he bit her again, if he drained any more of her blood, she'd surrender consciousness to her beast. If Meridian controlled consciousness, Lara's only recourse would be to watch for an opening into which she could reassert herself. Any small clue she could leave for Bobby to let him know her persona was submerged but ready to regain control would give them both hope.

"Your lover won't save you."

Lara's grip on consciousness slipped a notch. She gritted her teeth. Bobby didn't love her.

Nalbandian nodded. His fingers delved between the lips of her vagina, tickling, teasing, and enticing her to orgasm. Her body stiffened as the wave of pleasure rushed through her. Nalbandian's head disappeared between her legs, and his fangs bored into her thigh. Meridian screamed in pleasure—Lara screamed in pain but craned her neck and captured Nalbandian's bleeding finger in her mouth.

* * *

The cell vibrated, and Jake pulled it off his hip as he drove. "Talk to me, Owen."

"Hypothalamus activity suggests memories were altered in both agents within the past three days. We can't be any more precise than that."

"Keep them in isolation observation. No chances. Contact Katie. Tell her to have the team ready. Now."

Jake tossed the phone on the passenger seat. He'd reach Nalbandian's house in a moment.

Bobby would already be there.

He needed to sort out the events. Didn't make sense Nalbandian would bring Dr. West here. Didn't make sense Nalbandian would be walking around, either. Jake didn't doubt bodies had been switched, his agents subverted. But he'd seen Nalbandian's body. He'd debriefed the agents who shot Nalbandian. *Right?*

Who had raced past him on the third-floor landing the night they rescued Jason? Who else but Nalbandian?

Bobby wanted to protect Dr. West. He had nothing to gain by lying about her disappearing tonight or meeting him, except Jake hadn't met Bobby earlier. *N'est-ce pas?*

Bobby insisted he'd witnessed Jake receive a phone call. Jake's phone confirmed one missed call at the time Bobby suggested, but Jake had no memory of an earlier meeting or the call. What if he was under the influence of a vampire? He wasn't susceptible to Bobby's mind control, but he'd never experienced mind control with other vampires.

Bobby also insisted he'd met Marilyn tonight. Impossible. Bobby would gain nothing by lying about that, either. If Marilyn had been that powerful, she would've escaped the government long ago.

So if the other two suspect vampires had been destroyed, who did that leave?

No answers sprang to mind, but the conclusion wasn't pleasant. Another formidable vampire orchestrated their drama.

Jake arrived at Chancellor Street, slammed on the brakes, and hopped out of the SUV. His senses registered one vampire in the vicinity: Bobby. Nonetheless, he pulled his weapon. He popped the magazine with new bullets and replaced it with bullets from the older formula. If he had to shoot Lara, her antidote would save her.

He dashed across the street and mounted the steps to the wooden porch. The front door tipped open, lights out inside. Jake hated the night-vision goggles, but tapped his pocket. There if necessary. Weapon pointed up, he crossed the threshold into the foyer. Wooden floorboards squeaked.

No surprising a vampire.

He angled through the living room toward the back of the house and the kitchen. No sense of foreboding.

"No one's here."

Bobby appeared behind Jake's shoulder.

Jake patted his heart. "I know we've had this discussion before, and I'm sure you promised to stop sneaking up on me."

"I found the other two sleeping cells. Both empty."

"The other two?"

"The ones not part of the thorough search."

"Has anyone been here?"

"Not since your people left."

Jake holstered his weapon. "Let's assume my memory has been tampered with. I know it can't be you, Dr. West, Marilyn, or Nalbandian. The only conclusion is a more powerful vampire has taken an interest in our affairs and wants us to think Nalbandian and Marilyn are still alive. Dead. You know what I mean."

"Vampires were beheaded in Trenton less than a week ago, the bodies unaccounted for."

"Could be one of the bodies swapped for Nalbandian."

"Why would another vampire want us to think Nalbandian still exists? Makes less sense than your god-playing-vampire theory. It's most likely Nalbandian wasn't destroyed and he fooled everyone."

"I don't believe it, but let's assume that's correct and he altered my memory and manipulated my behavior. Why?"

"He wants Lara. He controlled her for a while by releasing her beast, magnifying his power. Power is an aphrodisiac for a vampire."

"You're sure Lara was at St. Mary's tonight?"

Bobby scowled.

"If Nalbandian recaptured her, he'd need time and space to release her demon. If not here, where are they?" Jake asked.

"Her townhouse."

Bobby disappeared. Jake hopped into the SUV and gunned the engine. Halfway to Lara's, the cell vibrated on the seat next to him: his friend, the man who once saved his life, Jason Storm.

* * *

"I'm so pleased you've rejoined me," Nalbandian said.

Meridian muttered. "I'm hungry."

"I know just the place to feed. If we can't control the shoe empire, no reason for Mr. Storm to control it either."

"Do you know where he is?"

"I know where he'll be if we set off the shoe store security alarm."

"Won't the alarm bring the police?"

"They won't stay long if nothing's wrong."

Meridian closed the door, hesitated, and didn't bother to lock it. Nor did she bother to ask why Nalbandian had unstoppered a flask of his own blood and sprinkled a few drops on their bed.

They strolled to Summit Square. Nalbandian gazed at the stars and pointed out constellations. He chuckled as though struck by a sudden amusement.

"By the way," he said, "you won't remember I ever cast the aura of Bobby Eyre. You were caught in the field by Nalbandian. I dragged you into your townhouse, and I resurrected your demon."

Meridian acknowledged him in silence.

No vehicles were parked in the lane behind the shopping center. The stench of trash exuded from open dumpsters, and Meridian sniffed fish where a restaurant employee had spilled grease on the blacktop.

Nalbandian located the wire in the back of the shoe store, pulled one, tapped a lead, and set off the alarm. Doors weren't forced, windows weren't broken, motion detectors didn't register, and the police weren't summoned, but Jason Storm arrived within ten minutes.

Meridian and Nalbandian watched from across the deserted parking lot as Jason parked his car.

Nalbandian grabbed her arm. "Wait. Let him unlock the door."

"Don't we want to guide him somewhere secluded to feed?"

"No one else is here. Death of a salesman in the shoe store. I'm sure everyone involved will appreciate the irony."

"I'm not sure I do."

"Darling, Mr. Storm is seeking a career in another field. He fancies himself a writer of paranormal romance."

Hunger gnawed at Meridian. The cramps that subsided when Nalbandian fed her returned. His blood tasted different than she remembered, like the blood of the comatose man in the hospital.

Jason inserted the key and opened the door to the store. Bells jingled.

"Now." Nalbandian shoved the small of her back.

Meridian raced across the parking lot and caught Jason at the threshold. She kicked off her shoes on the sidewalk, pinched Jason's throat from behind, and pushed him into the dark store. He stumbled and dropped his cell phone.

"Not a word," she said. She shoved him forward and forced him onto a customer's chair beneath the night-light.

Jason coughed, rubbed his throat, and twisted around. "Dr. West? What's—" His eyes widened when a man loomed behind her. "Nalbandian. Jake said you were destroyed."

"Agent Plummer seems prone to mistakes. People shouldn't be so quick to trust his judgment."

Jason's gaze darted around.

"No way out, Mr. Storm," Meridian said.

"I'm sure Mr. Storm knows that, my dear," Nalbandian said. "I suspect he's looking for this." Nalbandian held up Jason's cell phone. "Who would you call? Your ill-informed friend, Agent Plummer? Good idea."

Nalbandian pressed the contacts button and scrolled. He guffawed, then pushed another button and waited for an answer.

"Agent Plummer, there's someone here who'd like a word with you." Nalbandian dangled the cell in Jason's direction. "Don't be shy, man. You're in a lot of trouble. You've been confronted by two hungry vampires."

Jason remained flabbergasted.

Nalbandian pulled the phone back to his ear. "Sorry. Your friend seems ill-disposed to chat. Too bad you can't join us in time. I don't think Mr. Storm even believes I'm talking to you." Nalbandian tapped on the speaker phone.

"Jason? Jason."

Nalbandian dropped the phone and smashed it under his heel. "Timing seemed off for a conversation tonight." He rubbed his hands together. "Now, where were we?"

Meridian hissed.

Jason pulled a stake from his waistband.

"Doesn't that give you splinters?" Nalbandian backed up, palm open. "He's all yours, my dear, but do be quick. I'm sure Agent Plummer has a GPS fix on that call. After all, we want him to be first on the scene of the pending blood loss."

CHAPTER 44

Bobby rushed to Lara's townhouse. A trace of lavender lingered on the porch. She'd been here recently, but wasn't here now. His shoulders slumped. The front door opened without a key. Not like Lara. A message?

Instincts delivered him upstairs. The aroma of familiar blood and that of another vampire swirled in the dark and stained the rumpled bed. Bobby sniffed. He couldn't place the scent nor understand the dynamic of another vampire in their drama. Panty hose, the legs tied in slipknots, ends attached to the bed frame, littered the floor and attested to Lara's torture.

Blood droplets on the bed caught his attention, still wet. He dabbed his finger and tasted. Lara's blood and a second, dissimilar tang—distinctly Nalbandian—rocketed through his system.

Horrific images flashed in Bobby's mind of Lara, bound, forced to submit to Nalbandian's will, drained of her blood until she succumbed to her beast. Lara would fight, but couldn't hold out for long. Bobby taught her that even submerged, she should never relent. Somewhere, she'd find a chink in her demon. The unlocked front door must be a signal she was waiting for his help.

* * *

Jake headed for Summit Square before Owen confirmed the origin of the GPS phone signal. Seconds away, he'd arrive sooner than expected, hopefully soon enough to help his friend.

He entered the center the back way and parked on the road behind the building, unseen, and perhaps unheard. He unholstered his weapon. Not many places to hide in the shoe store, a simple twenty-by-one-hundred rectangle with a counter in the front and a four-foot-wide stock aisle that angled down the right wall and dumped into a back office.

Jake cut in front of the display window and ducked. Bells attached to the top of the door ensured he couldn't sneak in, but at least arriving early would be a surprise. He yanked open the door, rushed two steps inside, and crouched, weapon ready.

Lara pinned Jason against the mirror outside the stockroom, beneath the night-light. Jason threatened her with a wooden stake. Jake tensed—another vampire lurked in the surrounding darkness.

A tall man flickered in his view, then dodged out of sight. The rear delivery entrance would be dead-bolted at this hour. Jake blocked the only escape path.

Lara growled, ignoring Jake, fixed on her prey. She snared the pointed end of the stake and wrestled with Jason for control. She had to be toying with him—Jason couldn't hold out against the strength of a vampire.

Another shadow zipped across Jake's vision. He pivoted, gun aimed in the nebulous dark.

"Agent Plummer, we've met, though never formally introduced." A dulcet, mid-pitched voice spoke over sounds of struggle.

Jake dialed in, aimed to sound, and fired. The bullet whipped through the store and crashed into the back wall. A vampire would never stop long enough for Jake to target. Next time he spoke, Jake would guess right or left of the sound.

"A conundrum, my dear man?" The voice drifted.

Jake followed with his weapon and fired, left. The bullet streaked through the dark and shattered the window of Jason's office. The vampire had read his thoughts. He'd have to guess without thinking.

"You realize your friend won't last much longer against Meridian? If you move to his aid, you know I'll escape . . ." Lara growled again on cue. "You are familiar with Dr. West's alter ego, right?"

"I'm more interested in your ego. I missed the introduction," Jake said.

"Tsk, tsk, all the time you spent at my house, and you still don't know my name."

Jake realigned weapon with voice, guessed right, and fired. Sparks suggested he hit the electrical box.

"Jake. Is that you?" Jason asked. "I could use a little help." His voice tremored, high-pitched.

"Your friend needs you now," the vampire in the dark said.

The words lingered in consciousness, squeezing Jake's soul, forcing him to action. *Your friend needs you now.*

"Jake."

Lara leaned, her mouth buried in Jason's shoulder, as they jostled for control of the stake.

Your friend needs you now.

BLOOD BETWEEN LOVERS

"Jake!"

Jake wheeled and fired. A bullet thunked into Lara's shoulder. She sagged. Jason rammed the stake into her gut as she collapsed. Behind Jake, the bells jingled on the door, and the vampire–Nalbandian?–escaped.

* * *

Guns fired in the distance.

Jake should be here by now.

Bobby's senses jumped to a unique level of awareness. He rushed to the end of the short driveway and sniffed, catching Lara's familiar scent laced with that of the second vampire. He followed the aromas toward Summit Square, past an SUV he recognized as Jake's. Traces of cheap cologne. He tracked the telltale odors around the corner and spotted Lara's shoes on the sidewalk in front of the In-Step. Lara, Jake, the other vampire–all paths led to the shoe store.

The door burst open, and a vampire streaked across the parking lot. Bobby followed, then stopped. Lara was inside the shoe store. Hopefully Jake hadn't shot her. Bobby streaked to the door and jerked it open. Bells jingled overhead. Jake spun around, crouched, aiming his gun, but didn't fire.

Lara writhed on the carpet. Jason froze against the mirror, blood pouring from his shoulder, gripped by whatever had transpired, and perhaps his role in those events.

Bobby raced to Lara and recognized Meridian snarling up at him, her eyes fiery. He lingered over her, waiting. Jake holstered his weapon, stooped, and snatched the end of the stake protruding from Lara's stomach.

"No," Bobby said. He dragged Jake back. "It's the demon. We have to let her reach the brink of destruction to convince Meridian to relinquish consciousness. I want Lara back."

"So do I," Jake said.

He glanced at Jason. The severity of his wound sunk in. Jake snagged socks off a rack and pressed them against Jason's shoulder, flipped his cell open, and pressed buttons with his thumb. "Katie. I need you now at the shoe store, and we need medical assistance."

"Are you–"

"For Jason. I'm fine. Make it fast. And we need–" He paused and texted the rest... *the antidote for the original bullet.* He slid the cell back into his pocket. Jason slumped. Jake propped him up. "Jason? Stay with me, buddy. Help will be here soon." Jake peered over his shoulder. "Lara?"

"Still Meridian," Bobby said.

"I could use a doctor," Jake said.

"We all could." Bobby knelt at her side. Meridian glared at him. Bobby stretched across. "Sorry," he said, and he screwed the stake into her gut.

Meridian howled. Her eyes smoldered.

"I won't be fooled again." Bobby grimaced and twisted the stake.

Meridian thrashed, eyes shut, fangs bared and bloody. Bobby tortured her and wrenched the stake until her eyelids shot open, and Lara's steel-blue eyes flashed. She flailed until she recognized him.

"Bobby," she managed.

He studied her for a moment before he yanked the stake out of her. "I know," Bobby said. "It hurts. You need blood." He bit his wrist, then held it over her mouth.

Lara clutched his arm and sucked.

"Enough." Bobby pulled back, and lifted Lara.

"Where're you taking her?" Jake asked. "We need the doctor."

"The doctor still needs blood, and the patient is wasting his." Bobby carried her to the mirror and let her lean next to Jason. "Don't suck," he said. "Drink what's coming out of him."

"She can't—"

Bobby shoved Jake's arm aside. "She can. If we invigorate her with enough blood, *Dr.* West can help Jason."

The door jerked open, and the bells rattled.

"'Bout time you got here, Katie," Jake called before he turned. "I could've used—"

"Sorry, Jake. I borrowed this weapon from your agent in the parking lot. I assumed she wouldn't need it anymore. Anyway, thought I'd return the bullet. I can't have you continuing to interfere with my plans."

Nalbandian aimed and fired.

Bobby rushed in front of Jake and Lara. The bullet thudded into his chest. Jake drew his weapon. Half a dozen vehicles roared into the parking lot. Bobby sunk to his knees.

"*Merde*," Nalbandian said.

Jake fired left on instinct, but Nalbandian escaped again.

"Bobby." Lara took one step and collapsed, too weak to move.

CHAPTER 45

E yve crashed into the vehicle and wrenched open the door. She fell inside, hands jumpy, eyes wild. Tony tossed his book over the seat. "You're injured."

"Shot." Eyve gasped, teeth clenched. "I don't remember it being so painful. Something's wrong. The wound isn't healing."

"Who shot you?"

"*Merde*. What difference does it make?"

"Who shot you?"

"Government man. Agent Plummer."

Tony gunned the engine and peeled onto the highway. "He's the one who shot Robert. Probably used the same bullets. They're special. Designed to destroy vampires."

"I told you, I know about the bullets. They shouldn't affect me. Robert survived the shooting."

"Dr. West removed his bullet. Then Robert forced her to formulate an antidote."

"Not available in the local pharmacy?"

"We need to get you to a doctor. A surgeon."

"I can't go to a hospit—"

"I know. And I don't know any surgeons around here. I did the research for Robert in DC. Dr. West was the top surgeon."

"Who's next on the list?"

"I don't remember." Tony swerved onto I-95 North.

"Where're we headed?"

"We have to get you to DC. Fast. Don't worry. I'll remember the name before we get there."

"Washington is south."

"Trust me. Speeding, it'll still take us two hours. You're going to need blood. One mile north of the Newtown exit, southbound side, is a rest stop. Candy machines and a toilet. Truck drivers park and sleep overnight. You'll suck a trucker before we head south."

Eyve nodded. "For a human, you're rather shrewd."

* * *

"Jason? Jason. You hangin' in there?" Jake tapped Jason's cheek. "Help is here. They're coming in now."

The shoe store door flew open. Agents poured in, weapons drawn.

"Jake," Owen shouted.

"Fine," Jake called. "Medical help over here. Lara needs the antidote."

The emergency team rushed past the agents.

Jason opened his eyes. "Jake." He struggled to speak.

Jake leaned closer. "Right here, buddy."

"Do me a favor."

"Anything."

"Next time I ask about vampires, lie to me."

The medics supported Jason by his arms and shoulders and lowered him to the floor. They pulled back blood-drenched socks.

"Nasty bite," the older man said, "but all he'll need is stitches and a transfusion. We can take care of both."

Owen holstered his weapon. "Jake—"

"Give Lara the antidote."

Owen hesitated. "Katie—"

The second medic pointed at Bobby. "I'll take a look at him."

"Covered." Lara winced as she waved the medic away and wriggled next to Bobby. She was still a physician. Anger and blood between lovers would have to wait.

"Stay with Jason," Jake ordered the medics. He glanced at Owen, eyebrow arched.

Owen frowned, retrieved a vial from his pocket, and tossed it to Lara. She uncorked it and chugged the contents. Jake hunkered next to her. Owen peered over Jake's shoulder.

"What do you need?" Jake asked Lara.

"My medical bag. This is the next bullet? Your guys are using the new bullet, right? We'll have to remove it right away."

"No, no," Jake said. "We all switched to the old bullets, in case you caught one by mistake. The antidote will work on both of you."

"Jake," Owen said.

Jake didn't turn. "Owen, we need more antidote. Now."

"Jake," Owen said. "It wasn't—"

"Now."

"It won't help, Jake. We found Katie's gun in the parking lot. It's the new bullet. Her gun's loaded with new bullets."

"Damn," Jake said. "We need Dr. West's medical bag, Owen." He peered at Bobby's slumped figure. "Lara. Where's your bag?"

Owen grabbed Jake's shoulder. "Katie's dead."

"Owen, Dr. West needs the instruments in her bag."

"Jake, did you hear me?"

Jake angled toward the medics. "Dr. Abir, do you have surgical instruments? Scalpel? Forceps? I don't know, what else do you need, Lara?"

"My bag, at the townhouse."

"Sorry, we're not surgeons," Dr. Abir said.

"Owen, we need the bag as quick as possible."

"Katie . . ."

"I know. I know. We'll deal with that later. Let's help the ones we can now." Owen darted out of the store.

Dr. Abir hurried to Lara and pointed back at Jason. "His wound is deeper than it appeared. Would you . . . ?"

Lara nodded. "Jake, keep the compress tight."

She crawled to Jason and probed his shoulder. "There's excessive internal bleeding. The worst is close to his arm."

"Get him to the hospital then," Jake said.

"Better not to move him yet. I can stitch him."

Dr. Abir shook his head. "The smallest needle we have is a number three-oh. Besides, you can't see to stitch that fine in this light. You'll need a magnifier."

"I've got a seven-oh needle in my bag, as soon as Owen returns."

Dr. Abir shrugged. "We need to stanch the bleeding."

"Ice," Lara said. "Any of the restaurants. Break in."

Jake signaled, and two agents scurried out the door, returning in moments with a loaded bucket.

"Stuff the ice into socks and we'll use that as a compress, chest and back," Lara said to Dr. Abir. "Prepare the transfusion. Start a saline drip."

Owen returned before Jason froze. Lara dug into her medical bag and produced scalpel and needle, then intensified her examination of Jason's wound.

"How's Bobby doing?" she asked Jake.

"No breath, no pulse—still dead, so okay, I guess."

"Bobby, talk to me." Lara stole a glance in his direction. Blood poured out of him and drenched his clothes.

"I've been better." He gasped. "This is worse than last time."

Lara refocused on Jason.

"The new bullets work faster," Jake said. He crouched near Lara. "You'll run out of time soon. If it's a choice"—he cocked his head toward Bobby—"I have to go with our asset."

Lara opened Jason's wound wider to irrigate and explore. "Jason's going to bleed out if I don't stitch him now. He can't be transported safely. This isn't up to you or Dog. I'm making the medical decisions."

"I'm not going anywhere," Bobby said.

Jake tapped his watch. "Fifteen minutes. Max. I told you, these aren't the same bullets."

"Now what?" Lara asked.

"This bullet disintegrates into a dozen tiny shards. Each shard contains enough poison to destroy him. You'll never get them all."

"Impossible to stitch this patient before the bullet fragments," Dr. Abir whispered to the other medic.

Lara probed Jason's wound. She gestured to the medics. "Hold him still and keep the ice pressed to his back and shoulder."

"More light," Dr. Abir ordered one of the agents.

"Don't need it," Lara said.

Jason moaned. "You're operating in the dark?"

"Don't be such a baby," Jake said. "Dr. West saved three of the last seven patients she stitched in the dark."

"Four," Lara said.

"Three." Bobby coughed. "The last guy died from tetanus. I told you to stop using rusty needles."

Jake chuckled. "It's no wonder I like you two."

Jason shuddered.

"Pain management?" Dr. Abir asked.

"Ice will have to do for now," Lara said. "We increase the risk of shock with anything else. Besides, there's no time. He'll have to deal with the pain."

Jason groaned. "You've been hanging around Jake too long."

Vampire vision allowed Lara a unique view of Jason's brachial bleeders as she stitched.

"Twelve minutes," Jake said.

The intoxicating scent of fresh blood combined with sight and texture to cramp her stomach, unwanted distractions. She didn't want to stop the bleeding; she wanted to drink it.

I'm Dr. Lara West. This man is my patient, not my dinner.

She repeated the mantra as she worked.

"Nine minutes."

Unlike any other surgical experience with human eyes and human dexterity, Lara manipulated needle and thread faster and more accurately.

"Lara." Jake fidgeted. "Lara, Bobby's fading. His eyes have closed, and it looks like he's having a seizure."

Lara concentrated on Jason.

"Dr. West."

"I can't stop now. Bobby will have to hold on."

One after another, she stitched ruptured vessels until the bleeding ceased. "Start a morphine drip. I want five milligrams per hour. Once his vitals stabilize, he'll be ready for transport to St. Mary's."

She removed a cloth bundle from her bag, unrolled it on the floor, and chose a different scalpel. She irrigated Bobby's wound and cut into his flesh.

"Two minutes," Jake said.

The bullet embedded against an interior wall. Experience told her she'd have to cut the tissue around the wound and extract a chunk; otherwise, the bullet would reattach. Lara checked from habit: no respiration, no pulse, pupils and irises impossibly blended, no dilation detectable.

Bobby squirmed beneath her digging.

"Hold still." Forceps in one hand, scalpel in the other, Lara maneuvered around the wound.

"Less than a minute," Jake said.

Bobby's eyes rolled back in his head.

"Got it."

Lara sunk back on her haunches and examined the slug. The bullet disintegrated and splintered to the floor. She focused on her patient, expecting Bobby's complexion to darken from ashen to pale. It didn't. She called over her shoulder to the medics.

"Do you have a unit you don't need for your patient?"

Dr. Abir cradled a packet of blood. Lara broke the seal, squeezed the contents into Bobby's mouth, and waited. The medics gawked at one another, then at Lara.

"That's different from the transfusion procedures we learned in med school," the second medic said.

Lara studied Bobby. No change in presentation.

"He's going to need more blood. A lot more. Do you think we can find volunteers from your group, Jake?"

Bobby trembled, wrapped in Lara's embrace. She held him tight until his legs steadied beneath him.

"Can you walk?"

"Faking for Jake. I can race when we need to. You?"

Lara nodded. She gazed at Jake and his people near the front of the store. The medics rolled Jason away on a stretcher.

"You need to rest someplace safe," Lara said to Bobby, "but I can't have Jake take you. We don't want him to know where you are. You'll need more blood."

"The hospital," Bobby said.

"Jake will follow."

"Your townhouse first. We can sneak to St. Mary's. If Jake's people see us at the hospital, it won't matter."

"What—"

"Jake doesn't know we can enter my vault from the morgue. They may be watching the ruins, but they won't know we're inside. If they break into the basement, they still can't enter the vault or detect us. Neither can Nalbandian. It'll be safe."

"For you."

"You need to rest too."

"I'm going to Washington. I want to attend Katie's funeral, whenever it is." And she needed time away from Bobby. A risk with Nalbandian at large, but he'd never know she'd gone to DC.

"Katie?"

"One of Jake's people. Nalbandian killed her tonight to get to us. I've known her from the start."

"You'll be careful?"

"I've recently learned how to take care of myself."

"I mean, Nalbandian will still want you."

"Yeah, Marilyn still wants you," Lara mumbled. She twisted her head away from Bobby. Her eyes narrowed and the corners of her mouth twitched down.

Frenzy was inescapable and had driven her from the basement. Why hadn't Bobby followed her as he promised and rescued her before Nalbandian released her demon? *Probably distracted by Marilyn again.*

They sidestepped the two agents at the front door.

"Where're you going?" Jake asked.

"Bobby needs rest. I'm taking him to my townhouse. There's no time to reach anywhere else before sunrise. Can your people guard outside? Keep Nalbandian away? But leave us alone for a few days?"

Jake saluted, bowed, and backed away.

Lara and Bobby hobbled around the side of the shopping center.

"Jake's people are trailing us," Bobby said, then winked.

They pretended to struggle toward the townhouse. They'd escape through the back slider before Jake's agents set up a perimeter. Jake wouldn't know they'd left until too late.

They entered the vault undetected. Lara wanted private space the small room wouldn't afford. She'd head to Washington in a few hours, as much to give her time to think as to attend Katie's funeral. Would Bobby stay in the vault, or would he chase Marilyn? Lara bit her tongue, and blood surged into her throat. She scowled and twisted away to hide her feelings from Bobby. If he wanted Marilyn, there was nothing she could do about it.

Nalbandian had taught her something Bobby couldn't: the essence of being a vampire.

I can take the blood I need to survive.

Bobby cleared his throat, as if he'd swallowed blood too, and spoke to her back. "I fell in love with Marilyn Monroe fifty years ago. Marilyn who showed up here isn't the woman I knew. She's not the woman I fell in love with. She's a vampire." He said the word as though it was distasteful.

"I'm a vampire," Lara said to the wall.

"I turned you."

"You turned Marilyn."

"Not deliberately."

"Doesn't matter. She's a child of your creation. She's your progeny." Lara faced him with the accusation.

"I may have given her death, but Jake has molded her life. She's a weapon of the WPA."

"You invited her into our home. You chose her over me." The words choked in Lara's throat.

"Jake needed an alluring agent. I was in shock when Marilyn arrived on our doorstep. I had no idea she existed, let alone that Jake coerced her to drive a wedge between us."

"She just waltzed in and wiggled her hips."

"Jake threatened your existence tonight if I didn't work with Marilyn again. A half hour later, he denied doing that."

"Toying with you? Not like Jake." She couldn't avoid the sarcasm.

"Marilyn found me at the hospital tonight too. She pleaded for me to rescue her from the WPA."

"Marilyn Monroe is drop-dead gorgeous. And she needs your help. How could you not want her?"

"Marilyn was always seductive. Now she's a manipulative spawn of the government. She'll have to deal with her problems herself."

"Are you trying to convince me, or you?"

"I don't need convincing. I'm not chasing Marilyn." Bobby's voice emerged low and guttural. "I'm not helping Jake. I know what I want. You are more important to me than anything in the world, including my immortality. I won't compromise our relationship, and I won't betray you again, no matter what. If that means Jake unleashes the forces of hell, we'll face hell together. For eternity.

"I turned you because I love you."

Tears welled, and Lara rushed into Bobby's arms.

EPILOGUE

Tony wriggled into the Toy behind the steering wheel. He tapped his cell phone. "Sunrise is an hour away."

Eyve grimaced, her eyes lidded. "You found a way inside? He's alone?"

"Better. Dr. Quincy Summerfield is sleeping with a woman."

Eyve sucked in her cheeks. Sunrise be damned. "*Merde*. No time for your diversions. Wake him. Kill her."

Tony risked touching Eyve's arm. "We need her. You need her. After the doc removes the bullet, you'll need to feed. Her blood will be more effective if it's warm."

Pain rifled through Eyve. In all her centuries, she'd never experienced anything like this. The WPA had developed a dangerous weapon. Lucky she wasn't shot with a second-generation bullet.

"Smart man." She patted his hand. "You're sure Summerfield was second only to Dr. West on your list of DC surgeons?"

Tony nodded. "Higher risk-reward ratio, and his success rate is a cut above number three." He raised his cell phone. "But I remembered that name too, and Googled his address, just in case. We can stay here for the day, then I'll torch the house tomorrow night, along with the doctor and his girlfriend. You can drain them both. After the fire, autopsies will disclose nothing. We can visit number three tomorrow night if Dr. Summerfield is negligent."

Eyve hunched forward and hugged her hips, trying to squeeze the pain from her mind. "No fire," she said. "You'll dispose of the woman's body if I decide to drain her. Once he saves my life, I have other plans for Dr. Summerfield, but keeping his girlfriend around for a while may be useful leverage." She coughed blood.

"Let's go inside," Tony said. "I'll wake the doctor."

Eyve struggled out of the vehicle. "I'll wake the doctor. You secure the house."

Tony directed Eyve to a back door.

"The lock was easy. I disabled the alarm." He scratched his belly. "Once he removes the bullet, don't you want him dead?"

"Oh, he'll be dead. Eventually. We're going to entice Dr. West back to DC sooner than she thinks, and Quincy Summerfield can head the welcoming committee."

"That won't make Bobby Eyre happy."

"I'm counting on it. But we're going to find an unpleasant distraction for Mr. Eyre too."

* * *

His fangs pierced Dr. Surinder Byra's sole at the same moment the orgasmic wave barreled into her.

She screamed.

Bobby Eyre tightened his grip on her hips. He languished in the sanguine fluid as he rode her over the edge. Another contraction wrapped around him. Careful not to take too much blood, he withdrew his fangs. Betrayal rankled.

Surinder screamed again, her breath ragged, heart racing. Veins in her neck throbbed as the sexual flush cascaded from her face across her chest. Multiple orgasms induced by Stage Five of Vampirical Harmony left her vulnerable. In this moment, Bobby's suggestions would be most effective. Usually a memory wipe sufficed; feed and leave the victim alive and wondering about the wound-healing itch and the aftershocks of compound delights.

Tonight was different. He needed more from Surinder. This wasn't about feeding; therein lay the betrayal. And he rode Surinder to a sexual peak he'd never driven Lara to. Surinder had passed out twice.

"You will retire from your position as chief of emergency medicine," Bobby whispered. "Soon." The words floated on the air and wound around the doctor.

Ironic. A few days ago he rescued the woman he loved; tonight he betrayed her trust, making love to another woman when he didn't need her blood, only her cooperation. A scowl draped across Bobby's face before he escaped into the night.

Darkness enveloped him much the same way as Dr. Byra's orgasmic contractions had, and he surrendered to life without sunlight. His beast's thoughts slammed into consciousness, and his fangs erupted. His eyes narrowed. Head tilted back, nostrils flared, he acquired a scent of cut-rate cologne. The human male he sought lingered in the vicinity: Witness Protection Agent Jake Plummer, of the Vampire Unit, drinking coffee.

Bobby snarled—manipulation left a dirty taste that even blood couldn't wash away.

He landed inches behind Jake and growled. "We have unfinished business," Bobby announced.

Jake spilled espresso on his shirt. "You're going to work for the WPA?" Jake pirouetted, backing up, cup to the side.

"You're going to find Nalbandian and destroy him," Bobby said.

"We're looking, but so far, no trace. It's as if he vanished from society."

"Lara is having day-mares. We need to reassure her."

"We? You sound like a team player."

"Do your job. And lock up Marilyn."

Jake chuckled. "I told you before. Marilyn was destroyed. I don't know who you think you saw, but it couldn't be her."

Jake the manipulator. Bobby frowned. He hadn't just seen Marilyn; she'd touched him. She was real, all right. And Jake pulled her strings. Jake was resistant to Bobby's compulsions—Bobby couldn't read his mind—but Bobby summoned all the menace of his demon, Roberre. He snarled, low and guttural. Jake had been nonplussed by Roberre's threats before. An epiphany struck.

Jake stopped him like a traffic cop. "Difficult to believe you came all the way from Bucks County to DC just to threaten me. Dr. West is here, too, though you didn't come together." Jake's lips curled up at Bobby's reaction. "You still think you're dealing with amateur vampire hunters. You and Lara entered her townhouse, then sneaked out the back door ten seconds later."

Jake studied him. "Lara doesn't know you're here. Hmm." He tapped an eyetooth with his index finger. "What could you possibly be doing in Washington that you wouldn't want Lara to know?"

RAZ STEEL was born in a chalet in Frisco, Colorado. His alter-ego was born farther east—or farther west if you go the long way. A storyteller his entire life, Raz finally decided to put stories to paper. He's a pilot, a teacher, a recycler, and a dad. He holds a degree in Philosophy from Lafayette College and currently resides in Pennsylvania.

Raz's writing career began after he became a pilot. Being terrified of heights (anything over the third rung of a ladder) the choice didn't seem difficult: fly or write.

He tortured himself to get his pilot's license to cure his fear, and now feels qualified to offer advice to other acrophobiacs – "Let me assure you, if there's anything more terrifying than flying a single engine airplane 2000 feet above the ground with your flight instructor, it's flying a single engine airplane 2000 feet above the ground—alone." You have to fly solo to get your license. What could he have possibly been thinking?

Raz studies anything he finds of interest: tennis, ballroom dancing, psychology... vampires. He finds humor in all aspects of life and indeed includes it in all of his books. Raz is currently working on several new projects. The father of two, Raz states that although his kids are grown-up, they'll always be "kids," and that he'll always be "Dad."

To learn more about Raz Steel visit his website at
RazSteel.com
Interact with Raz on his Facebook Fan page at
RAZSTEELAuthor

www.ingramcontent.com/pod-product-compliance
Lightning Source LLC
Chambersburg PA
CBHW071850220626
47052CB00002B/51